HERLAND
AND RELATED WRITINGS

broadview editions
series editor: L.W. Conolly

Charlotte Perkins Gilman, ca. 1910.
Photo by Lena Connell. Courtesy of the Schlesinger Library, Radcliffe Institute for Advanced Studies, Harvard University.

HERLAND
AND RELATED WRITINGS

Charlotte Perkins Gilman

edited by Beth Sutton-Ramspeck

broadview editions

Library and Archives Canada Cataloguing in Publication

Gilman, Charlotte Perkins, 1860-1935
    Herland and related writings / Charlotte Perkins Gilman; edited by Beth Sutton-Ramspeck.

(Broadview editions)
Includes bibliographical references.
ISBN 978-1-55111-987-8

    I. Sutton-Ramspeck, Beth, 1954- II. Title. III. Series:
Broadview editions

PS1744.G57A6 2012   818'.409   C2012-905648-0

Broadview Editions

The Broadview Editions series represents the ever-changing canon of literature in English by bringing together texts long regarded as classics with valuable lesser-known works.

Advisory editor for this volume: Juliet Sutcliffe

Broadview Press is an independent, international publishing house, incorporated in 1985.

We welcome comments and suggestions regarding any aspect of our publications—please feel free to contact us at the addresses below or at broadview@broadviewpress.com.

North America
PO Box 1243, Peterborough, Ontario, Canada K9J 7H5
2215 Kenmore Ave., Buffalo, New York, USA 14207
Tel: (705) 743-8990; Fax: (705) 743-8353
email: customerservice@broadviewpress.com

UK, Europe, Central Asia, Middle East, Africa, India, and Southeast Asia
Eurospan Group, 3 Henrietta St., London WC2E 8LU, United Kingdom
Tel: 44 (0) 1767 604972; Fax: 44 (0) 1767 601640
email: eurospan@turpin-distribution.com

Australia and New Zealand
NewSouth Books
c/o TL Distribution, 15-23 Helles Ave., Moorebank, NSW, Australia 2170
Tel: (02) 8778 9999; Fax: (02) 8778 9944
email: orders@tldistribution.com.au

www.broadviewpress.com

This book is printed on paper containing 100% postconsumer fibre.

Contents

Acknowledgements

The portrait of Charlotte Perkins Gilman is reprinted with permission of the Schlesinger Library, Radcliffe Institute for Advanced Study, Harvard University.

I would like to thank Nelle Smith and Lynsey Kamine, who helped me compare editions of *Herland*, and with their sharp eyes helped me locate passages missing from other modern editions. Alexis Alberts helped me proofread the manuscript, and Todd Moenter corrected its formatting.

Thank you to the anonymous readers of my proposal and to Susan Gubar for their excellent suggestions regarding the contents of the Related Writings and Appendices. Many thanks to the helpful staff at Broadview Press, including Marjorie Mather, Leonard Conolly, Tara Lowes, Eileen Eckert, Lisa Brawn, Anne Hodgetts, and especially copy-editor Juliet Sutcliffe.

Thanks to Doug Sutton-Ramspeck, who gave me advice about the introduction, along with constant and much-needed moral support. A special thank you to Mildred Sutton, my own model of motherhood, and to Lee Sutton-Ramspeck from whom I learn daily the joys of being a mother myself.

Introduction

In August 1935, weakened from inoperable breast cancer, Charlotte Perkins Gilman typed a note that was reprinted in newspapers throughout the country and included in the last chapter of her autobiography. The note summarized ideas that had shaped her life and her writing, including her novel *Herland*:

A Last Duty
Human life consists in mutual service. No grief, pain, misfortune or "broken heart" is excuse for cutting off one's life while any power of service remains. But when all usefulness is over, when one is assured of unavoidable and imminent death, it is the simplest of human rights to choose a quick and easy death in place of a slow and horrible one.

Public opinion is changing on this subject. The time is approaching when we shall consider it abhorrent to our civilization to allow a human being to die in prolonged agony which we should mercifully end in any other creature. Believing this open choice to be of social service in promoting wiser views on this question, I have preferred chloroform to cancer. (Qtd. in Davis 397)

From her youth until she wrote this suicide note, Charlotte Perkins Gilman placed "mutual service" among human beings as her most important value. The primacy Gilman gave to changing public opinion and "promoting wiser views" is key to understanding her life and writings, including *Herland*.

Charlotte Perkins Gilman was intensely proud to come from a family of "world servers" (*Living* 3). Charlotte Anna Perkins was born in 1860 into the Beecher family, one of New England's most distinguished intellectual families. Her great grandfather (her father's grandfather) was Lyman Beecher, the most eminent minister of the early nineteenth century. Lyman Beecher's even more famous offspring—Charlotte's great uncle and aunts—included Henry Ward Beecher, an influential clergyman, reformer, and abolitionist; Harriet Beecher Stowe, the author of *Uncle Tom's Cabin*; Isabella Beecher Hooker, an author and suffragist; and Catherine Beecher, pioneer in women's education and the author of *A Treatise on Domestic Economy*. Charlotte would adopt many of the family intellectual and reformist interests, including women's rights, religious reform, physical fitness, home design, and of course writing.

Gilman's most recent biographer, Cynthia J. Davis, has speculated that another reason Gilman put such emphasis on service to others is that her youth was full of privation. Although the details remain sketchy, Charlotte's father, Frederic Beecher Perkins, a librarian and writer, was living apart from the family much of the time by the mid-1860s and had separated permanently from Charlotte's mother, Mary Westcott Perkins, by 1869, when Charlotte was nine years old and her brother Thomas was eleven. Charlotte would later write "my childhood had no father" (*Living* 5). Her mother withheld affection from her children in the belief it would make them independent. After Frederic Perkins left, the chronically cash-strapped Mary Perkins and her children lived with a series of relatives, in rooming houses, and for a time in a "cooperative" household, in New York, Connecticut, Massachusetts, and Rhode Island—nineteen moves in eighteen years. Charlotte's formal schooling ended when she was sixteen, though she read avidly on her own: at seventeen, she had determined that she "wished to help humanity" and wrote to her father for advice on what she should read (*Living* 36). It was during this period that she became interested in the social Darwinist theories that are so important in *Herland*. At eighteen, having sold a few watercolors of flowers, she enrolled in the newly opened Rhode Island School of Design. She continued to make money with her art, developed an abiding devotion to physical fitness, and had a passionate friendship with a young woman named Martha Luther. She was devastated when, in 1881, Martha became engaged to be married.

Then, early in 1882, when Charlotte was twenty-one, she met the handsome painter Charles Walter Stetson, who proposed to her less than three weeks later. She declined, but he continued to pursue her. Intensely attracted to Stetson, Charlotte vacillated, concerned that marriage would interfere with her ambitions to be a "world-server" like her ancestors. Nevertheless, the couple married on 2 May 1884, and their daughter Katharine was born in March 1885. Charlotte quickly slipped into a profound depression, which lifted that fall when she and the baby left to visit her friend Grace Channing in Pasadena, California, for several months. She returned to Providence, but by the winter of 1887 she was spending days crying. Perceiving she was "Getting back to the edge of insanity again," she traveled to Philadelphia for Silas Weir Mitchell's rest cure, which is fictionalized in "The Yellow Wall-Paper" (*Diaries*, 20 March 1887). Mitchell's prescription that she confine herself to domesticity and "never touch pen, brush or pencil as long as you live" had devastating results: she came "perilously close to losing [her] mind" (*Living* 96). Recovery began when she resolved to end her marriage and return permanently to California. Although she struggled with depression for the rest of her life, she never descended to the levels of suffering she experienced during her first marriage.

With the move to California, Charlotte Stetson's public career took off, along with her opportunities for "world-service," influenced by Edward Bellamy's *Looking Backward: 2000–1887*, which she read shortly after its publication in 1888. In this best-selling utopian novel, the protagonist, an upper-class man from 1887, awakens from a trance in the year 2000, and discovers that America has been radically transformed during his 113-year sleep. Capitalism has been abolished, and all industry is done in the "service of the nation," animated by the workers' sense of duty both to the nation and to humanity in general (Bellamy 100). This culture based on nationalized industry and distribution was what Bellamy—and Charlotte Stetson—meant by the term "Nationalism." Bellamy called Nationalism "nothing more than Christianity applied to industrial organization (qtd. in Davis 122), but it also incorporated social Darwinist ideas about the gradual evolution of society. Much like *Herland*, the society described in *Looking Backward* rejects individualism in favor of cooperation and mutual service, with the important difference that although Bellamy's utopia has abolished housework and made women economically independent, their situation reflects the same presuppositions about women's inherent weakness that the male travelers bring to Herland. Nevertheless, Charlotte Stetson was immediately taken by Bellamy's philosophy, and in California she soon became active in the Nationalist movement, supporting herself in part by lecturing on Nationalism to various groups. Lecturing on a shifting range of topics would continue to be a primary source of income for most of Gilman's life. In California she also began publishing stories and poems, including, in 1892, "The Yellow Wall-Paper," and, in 1893, a book of poems, *In This Our World*, which attracted considerable notice. In the mid-1890s she was elected president of Pacific Coast Womens' Press Association and became the managing editor of its bulletin, *The Impress*, to which she also contributed stories, verse, and news stories. Her most successful work of nonfiction, *Women and Economics*, was published in 1898. This internationally successful study of the negative consequences of women's economic dependence on men was translated into seven languages.

When her divorce from Walter Stetson was finalized in 1894, she sent their daughter to live with him and Grace Channing, whom he had married, a decision that she contended was in her daughter's best interest, but which led to her widespread condemnation in the California newspapers as an "unnatural mother." For several years beginning in the mid 1890s, Charlotte Stetson traveled the country and the world, lecturing on Nationalism, women's rights and duties, dress reform, public ethics, "physical culture," and economics, among other topics. In 1900, after a courtship of several years, she married George Houghton Gilman, a Wall Street attorney and her first cousin (also descended from Lyman Beecher), and the couple were joined in New York by her daughter a few months later. This marriage proved a very happy one. In the decade that followed her marriage, she continued to lecture in a range of forums, worked for a time as an editor and contributor to the feminist *Woman's Journal*, and published a few poems, stories, and articles, as well as two books, *Concerning Children* (1900) and *The Home: Its Work and Influence* (1903).

In November 1909, Gilman embarked on her most ambitious project, the journal she called *The Forerunner*. She ventured into self-publication, she would later explain in her autobiography, because "as time passed there was less and less market for what I had to say, more and more of my stuff was declined.... [F]inally I announced: 'If the editors and publishers will not bring out my work, I will!'" (*Living* 304).[1] Not only did Gilman write every word of every issue, but she also served as editor, publisher, and marketer. Some of the poems and short stories that appeared in *The Forerunner* had been published before, but most of the material was freshly written. The journal featured poems, stories, criticism, commentary on current events, and two books serialized each of the seven years, one fiction and the other nonfiction, except in 1911, when two novels were serialized. *Herland* first appeared in 1915 in *The Forerunner*.

The Forerunner was never self-supporting; Gilman financed it by lecturing, and she continued to lecture after discontinuing the journal at the end of 1916, but demand for her lectures flagged, as did sales of her writings. The last of her books to be published in her lifetime, *His Religion and Hers*, appeared in 1923; during the 1920s she began her autobiography, *The Living of Charlotte Perkins Gilman*, and completed a murder mystery, *Unpunished*, in 1929,

---

1 This quotation also appears in the extract from this book reprinted in this volume. See p. 212.

but could not find a publisher for either. By 1930 all her books were out of print. Early in 1932 Gilman was diagnosed with breast cancer; little more than two years later, Houghton Gilman died suddenly of a massive stroke. In June 1935, at age seventy-five, and after completing her autobiography and finding a publisher for that and an article entitled "The Right to Die," Gilman committed suicide. Although she was at that time largely forgotten, she left behind an astonishing body of writing—more than 2,000 items listed in the bibliography of her work (Scharnhorst *Bibliography*). These include nearly 500 poems and songs, more than 170 stories, ten novellas, half a dozen short plays, thirteen nonfiction books, and hundreds of articles.

Gilman's Social Darwinism and Eugenics

In her lifelong commitment to promoting human progress, Gilman embraced a feminist social Darwinism that was a cornerstone of both her nonfiction and her fiction. By Gilman's time, few intellectuals questioned evolution itself; rather, the debates concerned how the fact of evolution should be applied to social policies. The most prominent strand of social Darwinism, associated with the philosopher Herbert Spencer, resembles that initially espoused by *Herland*'s male explorers—especially Terry—and roundly rejected by Gilman. In this view, the principle of "survival of the fittest" provides evidence that unfettered competition among individuals is necessary for the human race to improve. For the conservative Spencer, that principle meant that charitable or governmental support for the poor and infirm or efforts to improve their conditions or to regulate the wealthy and powerful runs counter to the best interests of society because such actions would contribute to the degeneration of the human species (see Appendix C1). Conservative social Darwinists believed that women are inferior to men and that their inferiority is the result of evolution, which means it is both inevitable and good. Moreover, even though women are intrinsically incapable of the same achievements as men, they should not attempt them; to do so would be counter-evolutionary—dangerous to human progress. Therefore, according to the conservative social Darwinists, feminism's challenge to traditional gender roles exemplified "degeneration" and could even lead to "race suicide," because women's education and employment supposedly diminished their reproductive fitness, thereby undermining their offspring's health and evolutionary fitness.

There was, however, another school of social Darwinism, reform Darwinism, which held that humans can and should consciously intervene in the evolutionary process. Among the leading adherents of reform Darwinism was Lester Ward, whose 1888 article, "Our Better Halves" (reprinted in part in Appendix C3) Gilman called "the greatest single contribution to the world's thought since Evolution" (*Living* 187). In stark contrast to the misogynist conclusions Spencer drew from evolution, Ward posited a "Gynæcocentric theory of life," that the female is the origin of the species. Life on the cellular level began with parthenogenesis—asexual reproduction like that in *Herland*; thus, the first life forms were female, and the male was secondary, important only for reproduction. Among higher animals, Ward argued, the female is consistently superior to the male: "Woman *is* the race, and the race can be raised up only as she is raised up."

Like Lester Ward, Gilman argued that women "inherently" possess traits superior to men's. She says, for example, that "The constructive tendency is essentially feminine; the destructive masculine. Male energy tends to scatter and destroy, female to gather and construct" (*The Home* 127). It is therefore racially disadvantageous that men have developed government, industry, art, religion, and science, according to her. Because these are areas of women's "inherent" strength, they have not evolved as quickly nor as well as they might have with more of women's contributions.

Elsewhere, Gilman insists that the sexes are fundamentally—and naturally—equal. In *With Her in Ourland*, the Herland visitor to Ourland concludes, "They are born equal, your boys and girls; they have to be. It is the tremendous difference in cultural conditions that divides them ..." (185). Gilman delighted in analogies with other species: the equal strength of migrating birds, grazing herds, or breeding salmon, and hunters' fear of the greater ferocity of protective mothers (See "Females" and the excerpt from *Women and Economics* in this edition, pp. 197-98 and p. 200).

Nevertheless, while assuming that the sexes inherit shared traits, Gilman also assumes "inherent" gender differences. Some of the differences are dysgenic—harmful to human evolution. Gilman, who, like Lester Ward, accepted the theories of French naturalist Jean-Baptiste Lamarck (1744–1829) that acquired traits are inherited, argues in *Women and Economics* that human courtship and marriage customs are the primary causes of differences between the sexes. Humans, she says, are "the only animal species in which the female depends on the male for food, the only animal species in which the sex-relation is also an economic relation" (5).

Because the human female's survival depends on her attracting a mate to support her, humans' "secondary sex-characteristics," differences whose sole function is to attract a mate (analogous to a peacock's plumage), have become exaggerated. Due to the human "sexuo-economic relation," because human males have preferred small women, women have indeed evolved into "the weaker sex," and behavioral traits such as dependence and "meek surrender" have become hereditary. Gilman identifies the "feebleness and clumsiness common to women, the comparative inability to stand, walk, run, jump, climb, and perform other race-functions common to both sexes" as "an excessive sex-distinction" that harms both women and their offspring of both sexes, and "the ensuing transmission of this relative feebleness ... retards human development" (*Women and Economics* 46). Although they have been considered "natural" for women, these traits are counter-evolutionary for humanity in general. In order to explore what might happen if women alone—rather than men alone—had responsibility for major cultural institutions, Gilman created her all-woman utopia in *Herland*.

Reform Darwinism provided Gilman with a way to explain who we are and how we got this way, but it also offered both insight into and control over our future. One of the primary means of intervening in evolution, she believed, was eugenics, a movement founded by Francis Galton in 1883 (see Appendix C2). Although eugenics has acquired a well-deserved bad name in the subsequent century, at the turn into the twentieth century its pedigree was generally progressive rather than conservative, with such enthusiastic, reform-minded adherents as H.G. Wells, George Bernard Shaw, John Maynard Keynes, Margaret Sanger, and W.E.B. DuBois. Both progressive and conservative eugenists believed that human progress depended on encouraging reproduction by "fit" members of the population ("positive eugenics") and discouraging—in more extreme views, preventing—reproduction by the unfit or degenerate ("negative eugenics").

Gilman believed that wise marriage could advance human evolution—and prevent degeneration of the human race. Adopting the animal model where males compete for the attentions of a female who then selects her mate, Gilman asserts, "woman's beautiful work is to improve the race by right marriage" (*Women and Economics* 92). A significant aspect of that "work" is knowing how to avoid "wrong marriage." For humanity in general to attain Herland's perfection, women must consider reproductive fitness and avoid diseased mates. These moderate methods represent a far milder form of negative eugenics than that described in Gilman's earlier utopia, *Moving the Mountain*, in which radical social transformations are engineered in thirty years using radical methods, including a negative eugenics: at first, "We killed many hopeless degenerates, insane, idiots, and real perverts, after trying our best powers of cure" (136). Births to those with "infectious diseases"—sexually-transmitted diseases—were prevented by passing laws "requiring a clean bill of health with every marriage license. Diseased men had to die bachelors—that's all.... A man who has one of those diseases is so reported—just like small-pox" to the "Department of Eugenics" (77–78).

Because Gilman's Herland has had no men for centuries, its focus is on positive eugenics. In Herland, every growing thing is bred by selecting for maximum utility and beauty, including, of course, the Herlanders themselves: strong, daring, and athletic, but graceful and "womanly": in short, admirably built to bear healthy daughters. To avoid overcrowding and to ensure continuing racial progress, most Herlanders give birth to only one child; a few superior "Over Mothers" are encouraged to have more than one, a "positive eugenic" practice that reproduces the most valuable traits. On the other hand, "atavistic" women "forgo motherhood" for the good of the country. As a result, the Herland race has been "steadily developing in mental capacity, in will power, in social devotion ..." (pp. 115, 95, 98).

Despite the progress attributed to Herland's eugenic methods, even Herlanders consider what they call "bisexual reproduction" superior to parthenogenesis, the evidence deriving, naturally, from evolution: "two sexes, working together, must be better than one.... It *must* be best or it would not have been evolved in all the higher animals" (*Ourland* 88). The arrival of three eligible males in Herland affords an opportunity to, as we would say today, strengthen the Herland gene pool. Herlanders see their visitors as potential fathers, and of course not just any man will do for that function. Accordingly, Gilman shows us the kind of man approved by citizens in a highly evolved female culture that places eugenic motherhood above all other values. The three visitors to Herland, Jeff, Terry, and Van, represent a range of male types: Jeff is the chivalrous idealist who wants to worship and protect women; Terry is an athletic ladies' man who likes to master women; and Van, the narrator, is a sociologist who wants to understand and befriend the women he meets in Herland.

According to standard social Darwinism, Terry, the most aggressive, would most likely win a battle of survival of the fittest, but

Gilman pointedly rejects that way of judging. Van, as a sociologist, at first attempts to explain to his hostesses that "the laws of nature require a struggle for existence, and ... in the struggle the fittest survive, and the unfit perish," (p. 88) but Herland's history eventually teaches Van that when the country faced "the pressure of population," (p. 94) they resisted the kinds of responses that Darwinians might have predicted. Here Gilman alludes to Thomas Malthus (1766–1834), a political economist whose *An Essay on the Principle of Population*, an important influence on Darwin, had argued that inevitable population growth—"the pressure of population"—would always outpace the growth of the food supply, leading to famine, disease and warfare, a "struggle for existence." But Herlanders did not engage in "a 'struggle for existence' which would result in an everlasting writhing mass of underbred people trying to get ahead of one another" (p. 94). Instead, Herlanders, cooperatively, as mothers, analyzed the best interests of future generations—the children of the future—as a basis for selecting parthenogenetic mothers. When the time comes to involve men, Herlanders have no concept of choosing a lover, but instead select fathers in "the highest social service" (p. 112) to their nation.

For Gilman, mere biological evolution represents too slow a form of progress, and controlling human evolution through eugenic reproduction is a small and inefficient aspect of the evolutionary project. While humanity evolves slowly through biological processes such as sexual selection, it can evolve far more quickly through "social evolution," augmented, as Gilman believed, by the inheritance of acquired characteristics. In an 1892 essay, "The Labor Movement," Gilman cites Spencer's theory that evolution is "progress from indefinite, incoherent, homogeneity, to definite, coherent, heterogeneity, by a series of differentiations" (62). That is, just as the evolution of organisms has entailed increasing specialization of each cell and organ, so, as society evolves, individuals have become more specialized, each contributing something different to the "social body" and each depending on the others for existence. Gilman argues that "The more perfectly this specialization is carried out, the more powerful is our collective existence" (64). For this reason, women's lack of specialization in the home—in which each woman is an amateur cook, cleaner, decorator, childcare worker, teacher, and so on—retards human progress, whereas the professionalization of household tasks—including childcare—would represent evolutionary progress. With specialization comes greater interdependence, greater social cohesion, and greater altruism—a more highly evolved society.

According to Gilman, motherhood was the original source of altruism, for the mother's unselfish love for her baby is the first social bond, but it is only the first step in social evolution: "Love began with the mother; but it should not stop with her" (*Home* 165). In a "Gynaeocentric" culture, the "private" world of mother and child would not separate from the public world but define it: maternal values shape public values. In *Herland*, Gilman describes an entire culture with a vision of motherhood that is the complete opposite of our own: "A motherliness which dominated society, which influenced every art and industry, which absolutely protected all childhood, and gave to it the most perfect care and training ..." (p. 99). Such a value system is more than the simple role reversal on which Gilman bases much of the humor and commentary of the novel; it is a complete paradigm shift, a revolution—or evolution—in thinking.

Gilman, Literature, and Utopia

Charlotte Perkins Gilman liked to deny that she wrote "literature." She even asserted that her most respected literary production, "The Yellow Wall-Paper," "was no more 'literature' than my other stuff, being definitely written 'with a purpose'" (*Living* 121). By distancing her own work from so-called "literature," Gilman was not so much rejecting literature itself as distancing herself from the avowedly apolitical quality of the literary fashions of "art for art's sake" or "self-expression" that were prominent in the early twentieth century. In her "Summary of Purpose" in the penultimate issue of *The Forerunner*, she declares "The subject matter, for the most part, is not to be regarded as 'literature,' but as an attempt to set forth certain views of life which seemed to the author of real importance to human welfare" (286). Gilman believed that genuine literary value is inseparable from "social" value. For Gilman, creating art is (like all human productions) a "social process," so "The value of an artist to the world is that he shall do as good work as he can for as many people as he can reach" (*Human Work* 352). Specifically, literature at its best can "build up and tenderly develop" the human capacity for "higher perception and emotion." A work of nonfiction, Gilman says, may "stir a nation to think more wisely," but "conduct is modified not only by what we know, but by how we feel." A book of fiction—and here Gilman cites her great aunt's *Uncle Tom's Cabin*—can "rouse the nation to act" (see "Effect of Literature," p. 206).

Furthermore, in Gilman's view, literature can also contribute to human evolution. Books from the past distill our past evolution—"the thought and feeling of all time stand bottled on our shelves" (*Human Work* 192)—so "Those who make books make the race mind" (*Our Brains* 135). The creative expression of the "race mind" has unfortunately been limited in the past, in Gilman's view, by the conventions of fiction, which have reflected men's disproportionate influence on human culture. In *The Man-Made World*, Gilman optimistically anticipates that as women writers begin to contribute more to the "race mind," literature will emerge from these limitations. A literature written by women will focus on growth, Gilman argues, and not only as a topic but as a goal of the writing; that is, it will have a "purpose": to foster social growth. With the progress of the woman's movement, "we are beginning to look at [the world] as also woman's world, to be nursed and cared for, fed, protected, educated and improved, according to the cult of feminine productiveness" ("Coming Changes in Literature" 230).

Gilman proudly wrote fiction with the purpose of fostering social growth, and much of it might be compared to the "exemplum" of a sermon or classical rhetoric—not surprising, perhaps, from the great granddaughter of Lyman Beecher, a woman who was beginning her career as a lecturer at the same time she was honing her craft as a fiction writer. The exemplum provides "a concrete example from which a general conclusion (the 'moral of the story') can be drawn" (Suleiman 27). Traditionally, an exemplum includes a narrative, an interpretation, and a "pragmatic discourse" that "derives from that meaning a rule of action" (Suleiman 35). This pattern is typical of much of Gilman's fiction. Carol Farley Kessler has described Gilman's exemplary stories as "pragmatopias," "realizable" scenarios, stories that subversively adapt the techniques of realism to describe how her "readers might go about realizing her utopian visions" through everyday changes (131). Stories such as "Five Girls" and "Bee Wise" in the present collection, as well as the novel *What Diantha Did*, exemplify this pattern. Thus, while *Herland* differs profoundly from Gilman's best-known work, the short story "The Yellow Wall-Paper," it is actually quite typical of her stories, which are frequently parables, allegorical sermons, "pragmatopias," and utopias.

Herland, though generally considered Gilman's most successful foray into utopian fiction, is one of several utopias she wrote. Following some utopian short stories, her first sustained attempt in the genre was *A Woman's Utopia*, the first chapters of which appeared in 1907. *A Woman's Utopia* begins with an "Introductory" (reprinted in this edition) in which Gilman places her work in the context of other such books: Plato's *Republic*, Thomas More's *Utopia*, Edward Bellamy's *Looking Backward*, and H.G. Wells's *A Modern Utopia*. In the opening chapter of *A Woman's Utopia*, the wealthy, conservative narrator makes a proposition to the idealistic young woman he loves: he will go away and travel for twenty years, leaving her and her equally idealistic friends twenty million dollars; he wagers that even with that much money they cannot realize their reformist ambitions. Chapter 2 and those following describe the smokeless, orderly America he finds on his return, transformed by a "new religion"[1] that focuses on "perfecting our social relation,"[2] a religion that was widely adopted by women, who set about cleaning the social house along motherly lines. Unfortunately, the journal in which *A Woman's Utopia* appeared, *The Times Magazine*, went out of business and Gilman's story was left uncompleted.[3]

Gilman returned to the genre in *Moving the Mountain*, serialized in *The Forerunner* in 1911. In this story the narrator, John Robertson, is an explorer who returns from Tibet in 1940, after a thirty-year bout of amnesia, to discover a vastly improved America, which was transformed because "The women woke up" and awakened the rest of society. The improvements permeate every segment of society, but especially those in which Gilman thought women naturally excel: education and child-rearing, food preparation, cleaning up the environment, and so on; Gilman calls *Moving the Mountain* a "baby utopia, a little one that can grow." She says the story "indicates what people might do, real people, now living, in thirty years—if they would" (37).

Herland represents a natural progression from utopias spurred by women to a utopia where the convenient absence of men has facilitated even greater improvements. In *Herland*, Gilman once again follows the narrative conventions of Utopia—a traveler encounters a strange new culture and gradually embraces its superior values. One might suppose that the appropriate traveler to a woman's land would be a woman, but Gilman cleverly takes

---

1   "A Woman's Utopia," 148.
2   "A Woman's Utopia," 150.
3   Only the first four chapters were published; the page proofs for Chapter 5 are in the archives of the Arthur and Elizabeth Schlesinger Library, Radcliffe Institute for Advanced Study, Harvard University; all five existing chapters appear in Kessler's anthology *Daring to Dream*.

advantage of the conventions by having Vandyck Jennings, her seemingly open-minded narrator, share the same sexist expectations as his companions (and most of her readers): a land in which only women live is, of course, impossible, "the stuff that savage dreams are made of" (p. 34); but if there were such a place, one "mustn't look for inventions and progress; it'll be awfully primitive" (p. 40). The men expect that women will "fight among themselves" and are sure that "We mustn't look to find any sort of order and organization" (p. 39). When the men first encounter Herland, they view the Herland landscape as a female body that they penetrate and that the phallic mountains overshadow, a humorous echo of the metaphors of male conquest identified by Annette Kolodny in her classic study of American exploration narratives: for example, "When we reached that [lake] and slid out on its broad glistening bosom, with that high gray promontory running out toward us, and the straight white fall clearly visible, it began to be really exciting" (p. 41; compare the exploration narrative in Appendix A1).

The men's reconnaissance is from a biplane, technology that at the time of *Herland*'s serialization was being deployed for the first time in warfare, in the war that today we call World War I, a conflict Gilman wrote about in an essay called "Masculism at its Worst" and attributed to women's absence from government. In *Herland*'s second chapter, whose title, "Rash Advances," punningly combines military and sexual metaphors, the men's "ardor" takes them in quest of the imagined "national harem," and their first "objects of pursuit" are three young women in a tree, who are compared to "peaches" and to "so many big bright birds on their precarious perches" (pp. 43, 45). Although Terry, in his "ardor," attempts to snare this prey, they outsmart him and escape, at which Van dryly observes, "Inhabitants evidently arboreal" (p. 47). The men's anthropological impulse is thus firmly associated with warfare, sexual predation, exploitation of natural and human resources—and mild incompetence. Thus begins the education of the narrator and his companions—and of the readers who accompany them through their discovery of the Herland utopia.

The Reception and Heritage of *Herland*

After its serialization in *The Forerunner*, *Herland* was not reprinted as a separate book during Gilman's lifetime, and there is no record of its earliest readers' response to it beyond Gilman's brief 1916 *Forerunner* article "As to Parthenogenesis" (reprinted in this edition), which she identifies as an answer to questions from "several subscribers" about the biological reality of *Herland*'s asexual reproduction. The novel slipped into obscurity until Ann J. Lane revived it in her 1979 edition, which quickly landed the book in classrooms and active scholarly discussion. Studies of the book in the 1980s initially focused on its feminist and utopian elements; these issues continue to interest scholars and have been joined by discussions of the literary techniques of the novel and such matters as its environmentalism, its responses to Nationalism and socialism, and its ideas about education and religion. In the past decade or so, critics have focused a good deal of attention on Gilman's attitudes towards eugenics and race, calling attention to the racism and xenophobia that undermine much that otherwise puts Gilman far ahead of her time.

Charlotte Perkins Gilman would probably be amused or puzzled, perhaps even annoyed, by the studies of her novel's literary technique, but she would welcome debate on the many controversies her utopia addresses, particularly if the debate contributes to the "social service in promoting wiser views" (p. 9) of the issues raised by her work. No doubt what she would prefer, however, would be for her utopian writings to "rouse the nation to act" ("Effect of Literature" p. 206). Polly Wynn Allen has traced the influence of Gilman's ideas on a few model neighborhoods and communities that were built early in the twentieth century, and a case could be made that Gilman would approve of some recent developments such as frozen microwavable dinners and other convenience foods (but presumably not their general quality) and shared accommodation such as college dormitories and independent living facilities for senior citizens, which provide professional cooking and cleaning. She would be pleased to see more women in the public sphere in the twenty-first century, but would no doubt question whether their presence had contributed to a more altruistic, "motherly" world. She would surely hope most of all that future readers of *Herland* would take from it a greater awareness of the "power of service" and would set about to create a better future for their daughters and sons.

Works Cited

Allen, Polly Wynn. *Building Domestic Liberty: Charlotte Perkins Gilman's Architectural Feminism*. Amherst: U of Massachusetts P, 1988.

Bellamy, Edward. *Looking Backward: 2000–1887*. Ed. Alex Mac-Donald. Peterborough, ON: Broadview P, 2003.

Davis, Cynthia J. *Charlotte Perkins Gilman: A Biography*. Stanford: Stanford UP, 2010.

Gilman, Charlotte Perkins. "Coming Changes in Literature." *The Forerunner* 6.9 (September 1915): 230-36.

———. *The Diaries of Charlotte Perkins Gilman*. Ed. Denise D. Knight. 2 vols. Charlottesville: UP of Virginia, 1994.

———. *The Home: Its Work and Influence*. 1903. Rpt. New York: Charlton, 1910.

———. *Human Work*. New York: McClure, 1904.

———. "The Labor Movement, a prize essay read before the trades and labor unions of Alameda County, Sept. 5, 1892." Oakland, CA: Alameda County Federation of Trades, [1893]. Rpt. in *Charlotte Perkins Gilman: A Nonfiction Reader*. Ed. Larry Ceplair. New York: Columbia UP, 1991. 62–74.

———. *The Living of Charlotte Perkins Gilman: An Autobiography*. New York: Appleton, 1935. Rpt. Madison: U of Wisconsin P, 1990.

———. *The Man-Made World: or, Our Androcentric Culture*. New York: Charlton, 1911. Originally serialized in *The Forerunner* 1 (1910–11).

———. "Masculism at Its Worst." *The Forerunner* 5.10 (Oct. 1914): 257–58.

———. *Moving the Mountain*. In *Charlotte Perkins Gilman's Utopian Novels: Moving the Mountain, Herland, and With Her in Ourland*. Ed. Minna Doskow. Madison: Fairleigh Dickinson UP, 1999. 37–149.

———. *Our Brains and What Ails Them*. Serialized in *The Forerunner* 3 (1913).

———. "Summary of Purpose." *The Forerunner* 7 (1916): 286–90.

———. "A Woman's Utopia." *Daring to Dream: Utopian Fiction by United States Women before 1950*. 2nd ed. Ed. Carol Farley Kessler. Syracuse, NY: Syracuse UP, 1995. 131–74.

———. *Women and Economics: A Study of the Economic Relation between Men and Women as a Factor in Social Evolution*. Ed. Carl N. Degler. New York: Harper, 1966.

———. *With Her in Ourland*. Westport, CT: Praeger, 1997. Originally serialized in *The Forerunner* 7 (1916).

Kessler, Carol Farley. "Consider Her Ways: The Cultural Work of Charlotte Perkins Gilman's Pragmatopian Stories, 1908–1913." *Utopian and Science Fiction for Women, Worlds of Difference*.

Ed. Jane L. Donawerth and Carol A. Kolmerten. Syracuse, NY: Syracuse UP, 1994. 126–36.

Kolodny, Annette. *The Lay of the Land: Metaphor As Experience and History in American Life and Letters*. Chapel Hill: U of North Carolina P, 1975.

Scharnhorst, Gary. *Charlotte Perkins Gilman*. Boston: Twayne, 1985.

——. *Charlotte Perkins Gilman: A Bibliography*. Metuchen, NJ: Scarecrow, 1985.

Suleiman, Susan Rubin. *Authoritarian Fictions: The Ideological Novel as a Literary Genre*. New York: Columbia UP, 1983.

Charlotte Perkins Gilman: A Brief Chronology

1860   Born Charlotte Anna Perkins in Hartford, Connecticut, 3 July, to Frederic and Mary Perkins. The family moves repeatedly, frequently to stay with relatives, and Frederic is absent for long periods.

1869   Parents separate permanently.

1873   Moves with her mother and brother to Providence, RI.

1878–79   Attends Rhode Island School of Design.

1880–84   Supports herself in Providence as a governess, art teacher, and greeting card designer.

1884   Reluctantly marries Charles Stetson with concerns that she will not be able to continue "work in the world" and be a full-time wife and mother.

1885   Daughter, Katharine, is born. After the birth, enters a deep depression.

1887   Undergoes the popular rest cure administered by Dr. S. Weir Mitchell.

1888   Moves with Katharine to Pasadena, California, fearing that her marriage is threatening her sanity. Publishes *Art Gems for the Home and Fireside*, a collection of classic art works, with commentary.

1890   "Similar Cases," her most famous poem, is published in *Nationalist*.

1891   Moves with her daughter and ailing mother to Oakland, where she writes, lectures, and manages a rooming-house with nine boarders.

1892   Writes "The Yellow Wall-Paper," a commentary on her rest cure; it is published in *New England Magazine*. Lectures on "The Labor Movement" at Alameda County, California, Labor Union Meetings. December: Walter Stetson sues for divorce on the grounds of desertion. The story is covered by newspapers nationwide.

1893   First edition of *In This Our World*, a collection of verse, is published (revised and expanded editions appear in 1895 and 1898). Charlotte's mother dies of cancer. Elected president of Pacific Coast Women's Press Association and becomes managing editor of its bulletin, which she renames *The Impress*.

1894	Divorce from Walter Stetson finalized (April); daughter Katharine sent to live with Walter and wife-to-be Grace Channing (May), instigating more newspaper scandal. Shares a house with Helen Campbell and Paul Tyner, her collaborators on *The Impress*, which begins weekly publication in October.
1895	*The Impress* fails after twenty weeks, partly because of its editor's scandalous reputation. "An Unnatural Mother" appears in its final issue.
1895–1900	Lives "at large," with no permanent address, lecturing throughout the United States.
1895	Stays three months at Jane Addams's settlement Hull House in Chicago, then moves briefly into Unity Settlement in Chicago with Helen Campbell.
1896	Participates in National American Woman Suffrage (NAWSA) convention in Washington, DC, at the invitation of Susan B. Anthony; testifies in support of women's suffrage before House Judiciary Committee. Attends International Socialist Workers' and Trade Union Congress in London.
1897	Renews contact after twenty years with cousin (and future husband) George Houghton Gilman ("Ho"). Writes *Women and Economics*.
1897–98	Helps edit journal *The American Fabian*, in which she publishes some of her poems and essays.
1898	*Women and Economics* is published to international acclaim.
1899	"The Yellow Wall-Paper" is published in book form.
1900	Marries Houghton Gilman. The couple settles in New York City, along with Charlotte's daughter Katharine. *Concerning Children* is published.
1903	*The Home: Its Work and Influence* is published.
1904	Serves as associate editor for the weekly, *The Woman's Journal*, to which she also contributes a weekly column, as well as articles and poetry. Invited featured speaker at International Congress of Women Quinquennial in Berlin. *Human Work* is published.
1905	"Charlton" Publishing Company founded, its name derived from the first syllable of "Charlotte" and the last of "Houghton." Lecture tour of Europe.
1907	Appointed executive officer of Equality League of Self-Supporting Women (later called The Women's Political Union—WPU). First installments of "A

	Woman's Utopia" serialized in *The Times Magazine*, which ceases publication before the novella is completed.
1909	Begins publishing *The Forerunner*, a literary magazine. Seven volumes are published between 1909 and 1916. *What Diantha Did* and *Our Androcentric Culture, or The Man-Made World* are serialized in *The Forerunner* through 1910.
1910	*What Diantha Did* is published in book form.
1911	Novels *The Crux* and *Moving the Mountain* and plays "Three Women" and "Something to Vote For" are serialized in *The Forerunner*. *The Man-Made World; or, Our Androcentric Culture, Moving the Mountain,* and *The Crux* are published by Charlton Co. *Suffrage Songs and Verses,* Gilman's second collection of verse, is published by Charlton Co.
1912	*Mag-Marjorie* and *Our Brains and What Ails Them* are serialized in *The Forerunner*.
1913	*Won Over* and *Humanness* are serialized in *The Forerunner*. Lecture tours of Europe; International Congress of Women in Budapest.
1914	*Benigna Machiavelli* and *Social Ethics* are serialized in *The Forerunner*.
1915	*Herland* and *The Dress of Women* are serialized in *The Forerunner*.
1916	*With Her in Ourland: Sequel to Herland* and *Growth and Combat* are serialized in *The Forerunner*, which ceases publication after the December issue.
1919	Writes daily column for *New York Tribune* syndicate from March 1919 to April 1920.
1922	The Gilmans move to Norwich, Connecticut, after Houghton and his brother Francis inherit a house from their aunt, sharing the house with Francis and his wife Emily.
1923	*His Religion and Hers: A Study of the Faith of Our Fathers and the Work of Our Mothers* is published.
1929	Completes murder mystery *Unpunished* (published 1997).
1932	Learns that she has inoperable breast cancer.
1934	Houghton dies suddenly of a stroke. Moves to Pasadena to live near her daughter's family.
1935	Writes "The Right to Die" and arranges for its posthumous publication in *Forum*. Secures a publication

contract for *The Living of Charlotte Perkins Gilman: An Autobiography* (April) and completes revisions. August 17: kills herself, having "preferred chloroform to cancer," and is cremated, at her request. Autobiography is published in October and "The Right to Die" in November.

A Note on the Text

Herland originally appeared a chapter at a time over the twelve months of the 1915 volume of Charlotte Perkins Gilman's self-published journal *The Forerunner.* The novel was not republished as a separate volume during Gilman's lifetime. This Broadview edition is based on the original text exactly as it appeared in *The Forerunner.*

Gilman was sole author and editor of *The Forerunner* and thus had complete editorial control. Accordingly, I have attempted to reproduce all of Gilman's spelling, punctuation, italics, paragraph breaks, and so on, even in cases that are inconsistent or "errors." In nearly every case, I have retained the sometimes idiosyncratic usage of the original *Forerunner* text, correcting only the most obvious of errors, such as the misspelling of a word or a character's name that is spelled correctly in all other instances. These instances are marked with square brackets.

In this regard, the present edition differs from previous editions, all of which have "corrected" the text, and all of which have, in some cases intentionally, in others inadvertently, changed spelling, punctuation, and capitalization; altered syntax; and even omitted phrases and entire paragraphs. Of special note, this Broadview edition contains four passages that have not appeared in any edition since the original 1915 publication:

- Page 74 (Chapter 4): "For that matter there were a lot of things Aristotle didn't know."
- Page 89 (Chapter 6): "I'd better try to give a little synopsis of what part of the world knowledge they had developed, and what they had not. The wonder was that they knew so much."
- Page 145 (Chapter 11), the phrase in italics: "They have no capacity for *our higher feelings. Of course they are* faithful and affectionate, and apparently happy—but oh, my dear! my dear!—what can they know of such a love as draws us together?"
- Page 149 (Chapter 11), the phrase in italics: "I fancy at first, when they were together, in her great hope of parentage and his keen joy of conquest—*or what he assumed to be conquest*—that Terry was inconsiderate."

In addition, in keeping with the novel's original serialized form, several of the chapters began with a brief synopsis of preceding events, synopses that have not been reproduced in subsequent editions. I have included these in the footnotes.

HERLAND

Chapter I

A Not Unnatural Enterprise

This is written from memory, unfortunately. If I could have brought with me the material I so carefully prepared, this would be a very different story. Whole books full of notes, carefully copied records, firsthand descriptions and the pictures—that's the worst loss. We had some bird's-eyes of the cities and parks; a lot of lovely views of streets, of buildings, outside and in, and some of those gorgeous gardens, and, most important of all, of the women themselves.

Nobody will ever believe how they looked. Descriptions aren't any good when it comes to women, and I never was good at descriptions anyhow. But it's got to be done somehow; the rest of the world needs to know about that country.

I haven't said where it was for fear some self-appointed missionaries, or traders, or land-greedy expansionists, will take it upon themselves to push in. They will not be wanted, I can tell them that; and will fare worse than we did if they do find it.

It began this way. There were three of us, classmates and friends—Terry O. Nicholson (we used to call him the Old Nick,[1] with good reason), Jeff Margrave, and I, Vandyck Jennings.

We had known each other years and years and in spite of our differences we had a good deal in common. All of us were interested in science.

Terry was rich enough to do as he pleased. His great aim was exploration. He used to make all kinds of a row because there was nothing left to explore now, only patchwork and filling in, he said. He filled in well enough—he had a lot of talents—great on mechanics and electricity. Had all kinds of boats and motor cars, and was one of the best of our airmen.

We never could have done the thing at all without Terry.

Jeff Margrave was born to be a poet, a botanist—or both—but his folks persuaded him to be a doctor instead. He was a good one, for his age, but his real interest was in what he loved to call "the wonders of science."

As for me, Sociology's my major. You have to back that up with a lot of other sciences, of course. I'm interested in them all.

Terry was strong on facts, geography and meteorology and those; Jeff could beat him any time on biology, and I didn't care

---

1 Slang term for Satan.

what it was they talked about, so long as it connected with human life, somehow. There are few things that don't.

We three had a chance to join a big scientific expedition. They needed a doctor, and that gave Jeff an excuse for dropping his just opening practice; they needed Terry's experience, his machine, and his money; and as for me, I got in through Terry's influence.

The expedition was up among the thousand tributaries and enormous hinterland of a great river; up where the maps had to be made, savage dialects studied, and all manner of strange flora and fauna expected.

But this story is not about that expedition. That was only the merest starter for ours.

★　★　★　★　★

My interest was first roused by talk among our guides. I'm quick at languages, know a good many, and pick them up readily. What with that and a really good interpreter we took with us, I made out quite a few legends and folk-myths of these scattered tribes.

And as we got farther and farther upstream, in a dark tangle of rivers, lakes, morasses and dense forests, with here and there an unexpected long spur running out from the big mountains beyond, I noticed that more and more of these savages had a story about a strange and terrible "Woman Land" in the high distance.

"Up yonder," "Over there," "Way up"—was all the direction they could offer, but their legends all agreed in the main point—that there was this strange country where no men lived—only women and girl children.

None of them had ever seen it. It was dangerous, deadly, they said, for any man to go there. But there were tales of long ago, when some brave investigator had seen it—a Big Country, Big Houses, Plenty People—All Women.

Had no one else gone? Yes—a good many—but they never came back. It was no place for men—that they seemed sure of.

I told the boys about these stories, and they laughed at them. Naturally I did myself. I knew the stuff that savage dreams are made of.

But when we had reached our farthest point, just the day before we all had to turn around and start for home again, as the best of expeditions must, in time, we three made a discovery.

The main encampment was on a spit of land running out into the main stream, or what we thought was the main stream. It had the same muddy color we had been seeing for weeks past, the same taste.

I happened to speak of that river to our last guide, a rather superior fellow, with quick, bright eyes.

He told me that there was another river—"over there—short river, sweet water—red and blue."

I was interested in this and anxious to see if I had understood, so I showed him a red and blue pencil I carried, and asked again.

Yes, he pointed to the river, and then to the southwestward. "River—good water—red and blue."

Terry was close by and interested in the fellow's pointing.

"What does he say, Van?"

I told him.

Terry blazed up at once.

"Ask him how far it is."

The man indicated a short journey; I judged about two hours, maybe three.

"Let's go," urged Terry. "Just us three. Maybe we can really find something. May be cinnabar in it."

"May be indigo," Jeff suggested, with his lazy smile.

It was early yet; we had just breakfasted; and leaving word that we'd be back before night, we got away quietly, not wishing to be thought too gullible if we failed, and secretly hoping to have some nice little discovery all to ourselves.

It was a long two hours, nearer three. I fancy the savage could have done it alone much quicker. There was a desperate tangle of wood and water and a swampy patch we never should have found our way across alone. But there was one, and I could see Terry, with compass and notebook, marking directions, and trying to place landmarks.

We came after awhile to a sort of marshy lake, very big, so that the circling forest looked quite low and dim across it. Our guide told us that boats could go from there to our camp—but "long way—all day."

This water was somewhat clearer than we had left, but we could not judge well from the margin. We skirted it for another half hour or so, the ground growing firmer as we advanced, and presently turned the corner of a wooded promontory and saw a quite different country—a sudden view of mountains, steep and bare.

"One of those long easterly spurs," Terry said appraisingly. "May be hundreds of miles from the range. They crop out like that."

Suddenly we left the lake and struck directly toward the cliffs. We heard running water before we reached it, and the guide pointed proudly to his river.

It was short. We could see where it poured down a narrow vertical cataract from an opening in the face of the cliff. It was sweet water. The guide drank eagerly and so did we.

"That's snow water," Terry announced. "Must come from way back in the hills."

But as to being red and blue—it was greenish in tint. The guide seemed not at all surprised. He hunted about a little and showed us a quiet marginal pool where there were smears of red along the border; yes, and of blue.

Terry got out his magnifying glass and squatted down to investigate.

"Chemicals of some sort—I can't tell on the spot. Look to me like dye-stuffs. Let's get nearer," he urged, "up there by the fall."

We scrambled along the steep banks and got close to the pool that foamed and boiled beneath the falling water. Here we searched the border and found traces of color beyond dispute. More—Jeff suddenly held up an unlooked-for trophy.

It was only a rag, a long, ravelled fragment of cloth. But it was a well-woven fabric, with a pattern, and of a clear scarlet that the water had not faded. No savage tribe that we had heard of made such fabrics.

The guide stood serenely on the bank, well pleased with our excitement.

"One day blue—one day red—one day green," he told us, and pulled from his pouch another strip of bright-hued cloth.

"Come down," he said, pointing to the cataract. "Woman Country—up there."

Then we were interested. We had our rest and lunch right there and pumped the man for further information. He could tell us only what the others had—a land of women—no men—babies, but all girls. No place for men—dangerous. Some had gone to see—none had come back.

I could see Terry's jaw set at that. No place for men? Dangerous? He looked as if he might shin up the waterfall on the spot. But the guide would not hear of going up, even if there had been any possible method of scaling that sheer cliff, and we had to get back to our party before night.

"They might stay if we told them," I suggested.

But Terry stopped in his tracks. "Look here, fellows," he said. "This is our find. Let's not tell those cocky old professors. Let's go on home with 'em, and then come back—just us—have a little expedition of our own."

We looked at him, much impressed. There was something attractive to a bunch of unattached young men in finding an undiscovered country of a strictly Amazonian nature.

Of course we didn't believe the story—but yet!

"There is no such cloth made by any of these local tribes," I announced, examining those rags with great care. "Somewhere up yonder they spin and weave and dye—as well as we do."

"That would mean a considerable civilization, Van—there couldn't be such a place—and not known about."

"Oh, well, I don't know; what's that old republic up in the Pyrenees somewhere—Andorra?[1] Precious few people know anything about that, and it's been minding its own business for a thousand years. Then there's Montenegro[2]—splendid little state—you could lose a dozen Montenegroes up and down these great ranges."

We discussed it hotly, all the way back to camp. We discussed it, with care and privacy, on the voyage home. We discussed it after that, still only among ourselves, while Terry was making his arrangements.

He was hot about it. Lucky he had so much money—we might have had to beg and advertise for years to start the thing, and then it would have been a matter of public amusement—just sport for the papers.

But T. O. Nicholson could fix up his big steam yacht, load his specially made big motor-boat aboard, and tuck in a "dissembled" biplane without any more notice than a snip in the society column.

We had provisions and preventives and all manner of supplies. His previous experience stood him in good stead there. It was a very complete little outfit.

We were to leave the yacht at the nearest safe port and go up that endless river in our motor, just the three of us and a pilot; then drop the pilot when we got to that last stopping place of the previous party, and hunt up that clear water stream ourselves.

The motor we were going to leave at anchor in that wide shallow lake. It had a special covering of fitted armor, thin but strong, shut up like a clamshell.

---

1 The smallest country in Europe at 180 square miles, Andorra is located in the Pyrenees Mountains between France and Spain.

2 A small country on the Adriatic Sea, bordering Serbia and Croatia, among other countries. During World War I, when *Herland* was appearing, Montenegro was a kingdom allied with Serbia and the Allied powers against Germany and Austria-Hungary.

"Those natives can't get into it, or hurt it, or move it," Terry explained proudly. "We'll start our flier from the lake and leave the motor as a base to come back to."

"If we come back," I suggested cheerfully.

"'Fraid the ladies will eat you?" he scoffed.

"We're not so sure about those ladies, you know," drawled Jeff. "There may be a contingent of gentlemen with poisoned arrows or something."

"You don't need to go if you don't want to," Terry remarked drily.

"Go? You'll have to get an injunction to stop me!" Both Jeff and I were sure about that.

But we did have differences of opinion, all the long way.

An ocean voyage is an excellent time for discussion. Now we had no eavesdroppers, we could loll and loaf in our deck-chairs and talk and talk—there was nothing else to do. Our absolute lack of facts only made the field of discussion wider.

"We'll leave papers with our consul where the yacht stays," Terry planned. "If we don't come back in—say a month—they can send a relief party after us."

"A punitive expedition," I urged. "If the ladies do eat us we must make reprisals."

"They can locate that last stopping place easy enough, and I've made a sort of chart of that lake and cliff and waterfall."

"Yes, but how will they get up?" asked Jeff.

"Same way we do, of course. If three valuable American citizens are lost up there they will follow somehow—to say nothing of the glittering attractions of that fair land—let's call it 'Feminisia,'" he broke off.

"You're right, Terry. Once the story gets out, the river will crawl with expeditions and the airships rise like a swarm of mosquitoes." I laughed as I thought of it. "We've made a great mistake not to let Mr. Yellow Press in on this. Save us! What headlines!"

"Not much!" said Terry grimly. "This is our party. We're going to find that place alone."

"What are you going to do with it when you do find it—if you do?" Jeff asked mildly.

Jeff was a tender soul. I think he thought that country—if there was one, was just blossoming with roses and babies and canaries and tidies[1]—and all that sort of thing.

---

1 Pieces of fancywork, often crocheted, used to protect the back, arms or headrest of a chair or sofa.

And Terry, in his secret heart, had visions of a sort of sublimated summer resort—just Girls and Girls and Girls—and that he was going to be—well, Terry was popular among women even when there were other men around, and it's not to be wondered at that he had pleasant dreams of what might happen. I could see it in his eye as he lay there, looking at the long blue rollers slipping by, and fingering that impressive mustache of his.

But I thought—then—that I could form a far clearer idea of what was before us than either of them.

"You're all off, boys," I insisted. "If there is such a place—and there does seem some foundation for believing it, you'll find it's built on a sort of matriarchal principle—that's all. The men have a separate cult of their own, less socially developed than the women, and make them an annual visit—a sort of wedding call. This is a condition known to have existed—here's just a survival. They've got some peculiarly isolated valley or tableland up there, and their primeval customs have survived. That's all there is to it."

"How about the boys?" Jeff asked.

"Oh, the men take them away as soon as they are five or six, you see."

"And how about this danger theory all our guides were so sure of?"

"Danger enough, Terry, and we'll have to be mighty careful. Women of that stage of culture are quite able to defend themselves and have no welcome for unseasonable visitors."

We talked and talked.

And with all my airs of sociological superiority I was no nearer than any of them.

It was funny though, in the light of what we did find, those extremely clear ideas of ours as to what a country of women would be like. It was no use to tell ourselves and one another that all this was idle speculation. We were idle and we did speculate, on the ocean voyage and the river voyage, too.

"Admitting the improbability," we'd begin solemnly, and then launch out again.

"They would fight among themselves," Terry insisted. "Women always do. We mustn't look to find any sort of order and organization."

"You're dead wrong," Jeff told him. "It will be like a nunnery under an abbess—a peaceful, harmonious sisterhood."

I snorted derision at this idea.

"Nuns, indeed! Your peaceful sisterhoods were all celibate, Jeff, and under vows of obedience. These are just women, and mothers, and where there's motherhood you don't find sister-hood—not much."

"No, sir—they'll scrap," agreed Terry. "Also we mustn't look for inventions and progress; it'll be awfully primitive."

"How about that cloth mill?" Jeff suggested.

"Oh, cloth! Women have always been spinsters. But there they stop—you'll see."

We joked Terry about his modest impression that he would be warmly received, but he held his ground.

"You'll see," he insisted. "I'll get solid with them all—and play one bunch against another. I'll get myself elected King in no time—whew! Solomon[1] will have to take a back seat!"

"Where do we come in on that deal?" I demanded. "Aren't we Viziers[2] or anything?"

"Couldn't risk it," he asserted solemnly. "You might start a rev-olution—probably would. No, you'll have to be beheaded, or bow-strung—or whatever the popular method of execution is."

"You'd have to do it yourself, remember," grinned Jeff. "No husky black slaves and mamelukes![3] And there'd be two of us and only one of you—eh, Van?"

Jeff's ideas and Terry's were so far apart that sometimes it was all I could do to keep the peace between them. Jeff idealized wom-en in the best Southern style. He was full of chivalry and senti-ment, and all that. And he was a good boy, he lived up to his ideals.

You might say Terry did, too, if you can call his views about women anything so polite as ideals. I always liked Terry. He was a man's man, very much so, generous and brave and clever; but I don't think any of us in college days was quite pleased to have him with our sisters. We weren't very stringent, heavens no! But Terry was "the limit." Later on—why, of course a man's life is his own, we held, and asked no questions.

But barring a possible exception in favor of a not impossible wife, or of his mother, or, of course, the fair relatives of his friends, Terry's idea seemed to be that pretty women were just so much game and homely ones not worth considering.

It was really unpleasant sometimes to see the notions he had.

1　King Solomon in the Bible is said in 1 Kings 11: 1–7 to have had 700 wives and 300 concubines.

2　A vizier is a governor or minister in the Turkish Empire, Persia, and some other Muslim countries.

3　Until 1812, Egypt's ruling military caste; also the curve-bladed swords used by Mameluke warriors.

But I got out of patience with Jeff, too. He had such rose-colored halos on his women folks. I held a middle ground, highly scientific, of course, and used to argue learnedly about the physiological limitations of the sex.

We were not in the least "advanced" on the woman question, any of us, then.

So we joked and disputed and speculated, and after an interminable journey, got to our old camping place at last.

It was not hard to find the river, just poking along that side till we came to it, and it was navigable as far as the lake.

When we reached that and slid out on its broad glistening bosom, with that high gray promontory running out toward us, and the straight white fall clearly visible, it began to be really exciting.

There was some talk, even then, of skirting the rock wall and seeking a possible foot-way up, but the marshy jungle made that method look not only difficult but dangerous.

Terry dismissed the plan sharply.

"Nonsense, fellows! We've decided that. It might take months—we haven't the provisions. No, sir—we've got to take our chances. If we get back safe—all right. If we don't, why, we're not the first explorers to get lost in the shuffle. There are plenty to come after us."

So we got the big biplane together and loaded with our scientifically compressed baggage—the camera, of course; the glasses, a supply of concentrated food. Our pockets were magazines of small necessities, and we had our guns, of course—there was no knowing what might happen.

Up and up and up we sailed, way up at first, to get "the lay of the land," and make note of it.

Out of that dark green sea of crowding forest this high-standing spur rose steeply. It ran back on either side, apparently, to the far off white-crowned peaks in the distance, themselves probably inaccessible.

"Let's make the first trip geographical," I suggested. "Spy out the land, and drop back here for more gasoline. With your tremendous speed we can reach that range and back all right. Then we can leave a sort of map on board—for that relief expedition."

"There's sense in that," Terry agreed. "I'll put off being king of Ladyland for one more day."

So we made a long skirting voyage, turned the point of the cape which was close by, ran up one side of the triangle at our best speed, crossed over the base where it left the higher mountains, and so back to our lake by moonlight.

"That's not a bad little kingdom," we agreed when it was roughly drawn and measured. We could tell the size fairly by our speed. And from what we could see of the sides—and that icy ridge at the back end—"It's a pretty enterprising savage who would manage to get into it," Jeff said.

Of course we had looked at the land itself—eagerly, but we were too high and going too fast to see much. It appeared to be well forested about the edges, but in the interior there were wide plains, and everywhere parklike meadows and open places.

There were cities, too; that I insisted. It looked—well, it looked like any other country—a civilized one, I mean.

We had to sleep after that long sweep through the air, but we turned out early enough next day, and again we rose softly up the height till we could top the crowning trees and see the broad fair land at our pleasure.

"Semi-tropical. Looks like a first-rate climate. It's wonderful what a little height will do for temperature." Terry was studying the forest growth.

"Little height! Is that what you call little?" I asked. Our instruments measured it clearly. We had not realized the long gentle rise from the coast perhaps.

"Mighty lucky piece of land, I call it," Terry pursued. "Now for the folks—I've had enough scenery."

So we sailed low, crossing back and forth, quartering the country as we went, and studying it. We saw—I can't remember now how much of this we noted then and how much was supplemented by our later knowledge, but we could not help seeing this much, even on that excited day—a land in a state of perfect cultivation, where even the forests looked as if they were cared for; a land that looked like an enormous park, only that it was even more evidently an enormous garden.

"I don't see any cattle," I suggested, but Terry was silent. We were approaching a village.

I confess that we paid small attention to the clean, well-built roads, to the attractive architecture, to the ordered beauty of the little town. We had our glasses out, even Terry, setting his machine for a spiral glide, clapped the binoculars to his eyes.

They heard our whirring screw. They ran out of the house[s]— they gathered in from the fields, swift-running light figures, crowds of them. We stared and stared until it was almost too late to catch the levers, sweep off and rise again; and then we held our peace for a long run upward.

"Gosh!" said Terry, after a while.

"Only women there—and children," Jeff urged excitedly.

"But they look—why, this is a *civilized* country!" I protested. "There must be men."

"Of course there are men," said Terry. "Come on, let's find 'em."

He refused to listen to Jeff's suggestion that we examine the country further before we risked leaving our machine.

"There's a fine landing place right there where we came over," he insisted, and it was an excellent one, a wide, flat-topped rock, overlooking the lake, and quite out of sight from the interior.

"They won't find this in a hurry," he asserted, as we scrambled with the utmost difficulty down to safer footing. "Come on, boys—there were some good lookers in that bunch."

Of course it was unwise of us.

It was quite easy to see afterward that our best plan was to have studied the country more fully before we left our swooping airship and trusted ourselves to mere foot service. But we were three young men. We had been talking about this country for over a year, hardly believing that there was such a place, and now—we were in it.

It looked safe and civilized enough, and among those upturned, crowding faces, though some were terrified enough—there was great beauty—that we all agreed.

"Come on!" cried Terry, pushing forward. "Oh, come on! Here goes for Herland!"

Chapter II

Rash Advances[1]

Not more than ten or fifteen miles we judged it from our landing rock to that last village. For all our eagerness we thought it wise to keep to the woods and go carefully.

Even Terry's ardor was held in check by his firm conviction that there were men to be met, and we saw to it that each of us had a good stock of cartridges.

"They may be scarce, and they may be hidden away somewhere,—some kind of a matriarchate, as Jeff tells us; for that matter they may live up in the mountains yonder and keep the women

---

1 Following the chapter title in the original edition appeared the following: (Synopsis) Three young men discover an unknown country in which there are only women.

in this park country—sort of national harem! But there are men somewhere—didn't you see the babies?"

We had all seen babies, children big and little, everywhere that we had come near enough to distinguish the people. And though by dress we could not be sure of all the grown persons, still there had not been one man that we were certain of.

"I always liked that Arab saying, 'First tie your camel and then trust in the Lord,'"[1] Jeff murmured; so we all had our weapons in hand, and stole cautiously through the forest. Terry studied it as we progressed. "Talk of civilization," he cried softly in restrained enthusiasm, "I never saw a forest so petted, even in Germany.[2] Look, there's not a dead bough—the vines are trained—actually! And see here"—he stopped and looked about him, calling Jeff's attention to the kind of trees.

They left me for a landmark and made a limited excursion on either side.

"Food-bearing, practically all of them," they announced returning. "The rest splendid hard-wood. Call this a forest? It's a truck farm!"

"Good thing to have a botanist on hand," I agreed. "Sure there are no medicinal ones? Or any for pure ornament?"

As a matter of fact they were quite right. These towering trees were under as careful cultivation as so many cabbages. In other conditions we should have found those woods full of fair foresters and fruit gatherers; but an airship is a conspicuous object, and by no means quiet—and women are cautious.

All we found moving in those woods, as we started through them, were birds, some gorgeous, some musical, all so tame that it seemed almost to contradict our theory of cultivation; at least until we came upon occasional little glades, where carved stone seats and tables stood in the shade beside clear fountains, with shallow bird baths always added.

"They don't kill birds, and apparently they do kill cats," Terry declared. "*Must* be men here. Hark!"

We had heard something; something not in the least like a bird-song, and very much like a suppressed whisper of laughter—a little happy sound, instantly smothered. We stood like so many pointers, and then used our glasses, swiftly, carefully.

---

1   "Trust in Allah, but first tie your camel." Attributed to the Prophet Mohammed.

2   Schools of forestry founded in Germany in the nineteenth century developed the approach of harvesting trees while maintaining forests for future lumber as well as for wildlife habitat and scenic beauty.

"It couldn't have been far off," said Terry excitedly. "How about this big tree?"

There was a very large and beautiful tree in the glade we had just entered, with thick wide-spreading branches that sloped out in lapping fans like a beech, or pine. It was trimmed underneath some twenty feet up, and stood there like a huge umbrella, with circling seats beneath.

"Look," he pursued. "There are short stumps of branches left to climb on. There's some one up that tree, I believe."

We stole near, cautiously.

"Look out for a poisoned arrow in your eye," I suggested; but Terry pressed forward, sprang up on the seat-back and grasped the trunk. "In my heart, more likely," he answered—"Gee!— Look, boys!"

We rushed close in and looked up. There among the boughs overhead was something—more than one something;—that clung motionless close to the great trunk at first, and then, as one and all we started up the tree, separated into three swift-moving figures and fled upward. As we climbed we could catch glimpses of them scattering above us. By the time we had reached about as far as three men together dared push, they had left the main trunk and moved outwards, each one balanced on a long branch that dipped and swayed beneath the weight.

We paused uncertain. If we pursued further the boughs would break under the double burden. We might shake them off, perhaps, but none of us was so inclined. In the soft dappled light of these high regions, breathless with our rapid climb, we rested awhile, eagerly studying our objects of pursuit; while they in turn, with no more terror than a set of frolicsome children in a game of tag, sat as lightly as so many big bright birds on their precarious perches, and frankly, curiously, stared at us.

"Girls!" whispered Jeff, under breath, as if they might fly if he spoke aloud.

"Peaches!" added Terry, scarcely louder. "Peacherinos—apricot-nectarines! Whew!"

They were girls, of course, no boys could ever have shown that sparkling beauty, and yet none of us was certain at first.

We saw short hair, hatless, loose and shining; a suit of some light firm stuff, the closest of tunics and kneebreeches, met by trim gaiters; as bright and smooth as parrots and as unaware of danger, they swung there before us, wholly at ease, staring as we stared, till first one, and then all of them, burst into peals of delighted laughter.

Then there was a torrent of soft talk, tossed back and forth; no savage sing-song, but clear musical fluent speech.

We met their laughter cordially, and doffed our hats to them, at which they laughed again, delightedly.

Then Terry, wholly in his element, made a polite speech, with explanatory gestures, and proceeded to introduce us, with pointing finger. "Mr. Jeff Margrave," he said clearly; Jeff bowed as gracefully as a man could in the fork of a great limb. "Mr. Vandyck Jennings"—I also tried to make an effective salute and nearly lost my balance.

Then Terry laid his hand upon his chest—a fine chest he had, too, and introduced himself: he was braced carefully for the occasion and achieved an excellent obeisance.

Again they laughed delightedly, and the one nearest me followed his tactics.

"Celis," she said distinctly, pointing to the one in blue; "Alima"—the one in rose; then, with a vivid imitation of Terry's impressive manner, she laid a firm delicate hand on her gold-green jerkin—"Ellador." This was pleasant, but we got no nearer.

"We can't sit here and learn the language," Terry protested. He beckoned to them to come nearer, most winningly—but they gaily shook their heads. He suggested, by signs, that we all go down together; but again they shook their heads, still merrily. Then Ellador clearly indicated that we should go down, pointing to each and all of us, with unmistakable firmness; and further seeming to imply by the sweep of a lithe arm, that we not only go downwards, but go away altogether—at which we shook our heads in turn.

"Have to use bait," grinned Terry. "I don't know about you fellows, but I came prepared." He produced from an inner pocket a little box of purple velvet, that opened with a snap—and out of it he drew a long sparkling thing, a necklace of big vari-colored stones that would have been worth a million if real ones. He held it up, swung it, glittering in the sun, offered it first to one, then to another, holding it out as far as he could reach toward the girl nearest him. He stood braced in the fork, held firmly by one hand—the other, swinging his bright temptation, reached far out along the bough, but not quite to his full stretch.

She was visibly moved I noted, hesitated, spoke to her companion[s]. They chattered softly together, one evidently warning her, the other encouraging. Then, softly and slowly, she drew nearer. This was Alima, a tall long-limbed lass, well-knit and evidently both strong and agile. Her eyes were splendid, wide, fearless, as free from suspicion as a child's who has never been rebuked. Her interest was more that of an intent boy playing a fascinating game than of a girl lured by an ornament.

The others moved a bit farther out, holding firmly, watching. Terry's smile was irreproachable, but I did not like the look in his eyes—it was like a creature about to spring. I could already see it happen—the dropped necklace, the sudden clutching hand—the girl's sharp cry as he seized her and drew her in. But it didn't happen. She made a timid reach with her right hand for the gay swinging thing—he held it a little nearer—then, swift as light, she seized it from him with her left, and dropped on the instant to the bough below.

He made his snatch, quite vainly, almost losing his position as his hand clutched only air; and then, with inconceivable rapidity, the three bright creatures were gone. They dropped from the ends of the big boughs to those below, fairly pouring themselves off the tree, while we climbed downward as swiftly as we could. We heard their vanishing gay laughter, we saw them fleeting away in the wide open reaches of the forest, and gave chase, but we might as well have chased wild antelopes; so we stopped at length somewhat breathless.

"No use," gasped Terry. "They got away with it. My word! The men of this country must be good sprinters!"

"Inhabitants evidently arboreal," I grimly suggested. "Civilized and still arboreal,—peculiar people."

"You shouldn't have tried that way," Jeff protested. "They were perfectly friendly, now we've scared them."

But it was no use grumbling, and Terry refused to admit any mistake. "Nonsense," he said, "They expected it. Women like to be run after. Come on, lets get to that town, maybe we'll find them there. Lets see, it was in this direction and not far from the woods as I remember."

When we reached the edge of the open country we reconnoitered with our field glasses. There it was, about four miles off, the same town we concluded, unless as Jeff ventured, they all had pink houses. The broad green fields and closely cultivated gardens sloped away at our feet, a long easy slant, with good roads winding pleasantly here and there, and narrower paths besides.

"Look at that!" cried Jeff suddenly, "There they go!"

Sure enough, close to the town, across a wide meadow, three bright-hued figures were running swiftly.

"How could they have got that far, in this time? It can't be the same ones," I urged. But through the glasses we could identify our pretty tree-climbers quite plainly, at least by costume.

Terry watched them, we all did for that matter, till they disappeared among the houses. Then he put down his glass and turned to us, drawing a long breath. "Mother of Mike, boys— what Gorgeous Girls! To climb like that! to run like that! and afraid of nothing. This country suits me all right. Let's get ahead."

"Nothing venture, nothing have," I suggested, but Terry preferred "'Faint heart ne'er won fair lady.'"[1]

We set forth in the open, walking briskly. "If there are any men we'd better keep an eye out," I suggested, but Jeff seemed lost in heavenly dreams, and Terry in highly practical plans.

"What a perfect road! What a heavenly country! See the flowers, will you."

This was Jeff, always an enthusiast; but we could agree with him fully.

The road was some sort of hard manufactured stuff, sloped slightly to shed rain, with every curve and grade and gutter as perfect as if it were Europe's best. "No men, eh?" sneered Terry. On either side a double row of trees shaded the footpaths, between the trees bushes or vines, all fruit-bearing, now and then seats and little wayside fountains, everywhere flowers.

"We'd better import some of these ladies and set 'em to parking the United States," I suggested. "Mighty nice place they've got here." We rested a few moments by one of the fountains, tested the fruit that looked ripe, and went on, impressed, for all our gay bravado by the sense of quiet potency which lay about us.

Here was evidently a people highly skilled, efficient, caring for their country as a florist cares for his costliest orchids. Under the soft brilliant blue of that clear sky, in the pleasant shade of those endless rows of trees, we walked unharmed, the placid silence broken only by the birds.

Presently there lay before us at the foot of a long hill the town or village we were aiming for. We stopped and studied it.

---

1   This line comes originally from Miguel de Cervantes' *Don Quixote* 2.3.10, and has been frequently repeated, including in a popular song from Gilbert and Sullivan's *Iolanthe* (1882) and as the title of a movie released in 1914.

Faint heart never won fair lady!
Nothing venture, nothing win—
Blood is thick, but water's thin—
In for a penny, in for a pound—
It's Love that makes the world go round! (*Iolanthe*, Act 2)

Jeff drew a long breath. "I wouldn't have believed a collection of houses could look so lovely," he said.

"They've got architects and landscape gardeners in plenty, that's sure," agreed Terry.

I was astonished myself. You see I come from California, and there's no country lovelier, but when it comes to towns—! I have often groaned at home to see the offensive mess man made in the face of nature, even though I'm no art sharp, like Jeff. But this place—! It was built mostly of a sort of dull rose colored stone, with here and there some clear white houses; and it lay abroad among the green groves and gardens like a broken rosary of pink coral.

"Those big white ones are public buildings evidently," Terry declared. "This is no savage country my friend. But no men? Boys it behooves us to go forward most politely."

The place had an odd look, more impressive as we approached. "It's like an Exposition." "Its too pretty to be true"—"Plenty of palaces but where are the homes?" "Oh there are little ones enough—but—." It certainly was different from any towns we had ever seen.

"There's no dirt," said Jeff suddenly. "There's no smoke," he added after a little.

"There's no noise," I offered; but Terry snubbed me—"That's because they are laying low for us, we'd better be careful how we go in there."

Nothing could induce him to stay out however, so we walked on.

Everything was beauty, order, perfect cleanness and the pleasantest sense of home over it all. As we neared the center of the town the houses stood thicker, ran together as it were, grew into rambling palaces grouped among parks and open squares something as college buildings stand in their quiet greens.

And then, turning a corner, we came into a broad paved space and saw before us a band of women standing close together in even order, evidently waiting for us.

We stopped a moment, and looked back. The street behind was closed by another band, marching steadily, shoulder to shoulder. We went on, there seemed no other way to do; and presently found ourselves quite surrounded by this close-massed multitude; women, all of them, but—.

They were not young. They were not old. They were not, in the girl sense, beautiful, they were not in the least ferocious; and yet, as I looked from face to face, calm, grave, wise, wholly unafraid, evidently assured and determined, I had the funniest feeling—a very early feeling—a feeling that I traced back and back in memory until I caught up with it at last. It was that sense of being hopelessly in the wrong that I had so often felt in early youth when my short legs' utmost effort failed to overcome the fact that I was late to school.

Jeff felt it too, I could see he did. We felt like small boys, very small boys, caught doing mischief in some gracious lady's house. But Terry showed no such consciousness. I saw his quick eyes darting here and there, estimating numbers, measuring distances, judging chances of escape. He examined the close ranks about us, reaching back far on every side, and murmured softly to me "Every one of 'em over forty as I'm a sinner."

Yet they were not old women. Each was in the full bloom of rosy health, erect, serene, standing sure-footed and light as any pugilist. They had no weapons, and we had, but we had no wish to shoot.

"I'd as soon shoot my Aunts," muttered Terry again. "What do they want with us anyhow? They seem to mean business." But in spite of that businesslike aspect, he determined to try his favorite tactics, Terry had come armed on a theory.

He stepped forward, with his brilliant ingratiating smile, and made low obeisance to the women before him. Then he produced another tribute, a broad soft scarf of filmy texture, rich in color and pattern, a lovely thing, even to my eye, and offered it with a deep bow to the tall unsmiling woman who seemed to head the ranks before him. She took it with a gracious nod of acknowledgment, and passed it on to those behind her. He tried again, this time bringing out a circlet of rhine-stones, a glittering crown that should have pleased any woman on earth.

He made a brief address, including Jeff and me as partners in his enterprise, and with another bow presented this.

Again his gift was accepted, and, as before passed out of sight.

"If they were only younger," he muttered between his teeth. "What on earth is a fellow to say to a regiment of old Colonels like this?"

In all our discussions and speculations we had always unconsciously assumed that the women, whatever else they might be, would be young. Most men do think that way, I fancy.

"Woman" in the abstract is young, and, we assume, charming. As they get older they pass off the stage, somehow, into private ownership mostly, or out of it altogether. But these good ladies were very much on the stage, and yet any one of them might have been a grandmother.

We looked for nervousness—there was none.

For terror, perhaps—there was none.

For uneasiness, for curiosity, for excitement,—and all we saw was what might have been a vigilance committee of women doctors, as cool as cucumbers, and evidently meaning to take us to task for being there.

Six of them stepped forward now, one on either side of each of us, and indicated that we were to go with them. We thought best to accede, at first anyway, and marched along, one of these close at each elbow, and the others in close masses before, behind, on both sides.

A large building opened before us, a very heavy thick-walled impressive place, big, and old-looking; of gray stone, not like the rest of the town.

"This won't do!" said Terry to us, quickly, "We mustn't let them get us in this, boys. All together, now"—

We stopped in our tracks. We began to explain, to make signs pointing away toward the big forest—indicating that we would go back to it—at once.

It makes me laugh, knowing all I do now, to think of us three boys—nothing else; three audacious impertinent boys—butting into an unknown country without any sort of a guard or defense. We seemed to think that if there were men we could fight them, and if there were only women—why, they would be no obstacles at all.

Jeff, with his gentle romantic old-fashioned notions of women as a clinging vine; Terry, with his clear decided practical theories that there were two kinds of women—those he wanted and those he didn't; Desirable and Undesirable was his demarcation. The last was a large class, but negligible—he had never thought about them at all.

And now here they were, in great numbers, evidently indifferent to what he might think, evidently determined on some purpose of their own regarding him; and apparently well able to enforce their purpose.

We all of us thought hard just then. It had not seemed wise to object to going with them—even if we could have, our one chance was friendliness—a civilized attitude on both sides.

But once inside that building, there was no knowing what these determined ladies might do to us. Even a peaceful detention was not to our minds, and when we named it imprisonment it looked even worse.

So we made a stand, trying to make clear that we preferred the open country. One of them came forward with a sketch of our flier, asking by signs if we were the aerial visitors they had seen.

This we admitted.

They pointed to it again, and to the outlying country, in different directions—but we pretended we did not know where it was—and in truth we were not quite sure, and gave rather wild an indication of its whereabouts.

Again they motioned us to advance, standing so packed about the door that there remained but the one straight path open. All around us and behind they were massed solidly—there was simply nothing to do but go forward—or fight.

We held a consultation.

"I never fought with women in my life," said Terry, greatly perturbed, "But I'm not going in there. I'm not going to be—herded in—as if we were in a cattle chute."

"We can't fight them, of course," Jeff urged. "They're all women, in spite of their nondescript clothes; nice women, too; good strong sensible faces. I guess we'll have to go in."

"We may never get out, if we do," I told them. "Strong and sensible, yes; but I'm not so sure about the good. Look at those faces!"

They had stood at ease, waiting, while we conferred together; but never relaxing their close attention.

Their attitude was not the rigid discipline of soldiers, there was no sense of compulsion about them. Terry's term of a "vigilance committee" was highly descriptive. They had just the aspect of sturdy burghers, gathered hastily to meet some common need or peril, all moved by precisely the same feelings, to the same end.

Never, anywhere before, had I seen women of precisely this quality. Fishwives and market women might show similar strength, but it was coarse and heavy. These were merely athletic, light and powerful. College professors, teachers, writers,—many women showed similar intelligence but often wore a strained nervous look, while these were as calm as cows, for all their evident intellect.

We observed pretty closely just then, for all of us felt that it was a crucial moment.

The leader gave some word of command and beckoned us on, and the surrounding mass moved a step nearer.

"We've got to decide quick," said Terry, "I vote to go in," Jeff urged. But we were two to one against him and he loyally stood by us. We made one more effort to be let go, urgent, but not imploring. In vain.

"Now for a rush, boys!" Terry said. "And if we can't break 'em I'll shoot in the air."

Then we found ourselves much in the position of the Suffragette trying to get to the Parliament buildings through a triple cordon of London police.[1]

The solidity of those women was something amazing. Terry soon found that it was useless, tore himself loose for a moment, pulled his revolver, and fired upwards. As they caught at it, he fired again—we heard a cry—.

Instantly each of us was seized by five women, each holding arm or leg or head; we were lifted like children, straddling helpless children, and borne onward, wriggling indeed, but most ineffectually.

We were borne inside, struggling manfully, but held secure most womanfully, in spite of our best endeavors.

So carried and so held, we came into a high inner hall, gray and bare, and were brought before a majestic gray-haired woman who seemed to hold a judicial position.

There was some talk, not much, among them, and then suddenly there fell upon each of us at once a firm hand holding a wetted cloth before mouth and nose—an odor of swimming sweetness—anaesthesia.

Chapter III

A Peculiar Imprisonment[2]

From a slumber as deep as death, as refreshing as that of a healthy child, I slowly awakened.

It was like rising up, up, up through a deep warm ocean, nearer and nearer to full light and stirring air. Or like the return to consciousness after concussion of the brain. I was once thrown from a horse while on a visit to a wild mountainous country quite new to me, and I can clearly remember the mental experience of coming back to life, through lifting veils of dream. When I first dimly heard the voices of those about me, and saw the shining

---

1 May refer to any of several marches on the British Parliament in support of votes for women, organized by the Women's Social and Political Union (WSPU) from 1906 to 1913; during some of these marches, demonstrators were arrested and imprisoned.

2 Synopsis from original edition: Three young men discover an unknown country in which there are only women, by whom they are presently captured.

snow-peaks of that mighty range, I assumed that this too would pass, and I should presently find myself in my own home.

That was precisely the experience of this awakening: receding waves of half-caught swirling vision, memories of home, the steamer, the boat, the air-ship, the forest—at last all sinking away one after another, till my eyes were wide open, my brain clear, and I realized what had happened.

The most prominent sensation was of absolute physical comfort. I was lying in a perfect bed, long, broad, smooth; firmly soft and level; with the finest linen, some warm light quilt of blanket, and a counterpane that was a joy to the eye. The sheet turned down some fifteen inches, yet I could stretch my feet at the foot of the bed, free but warmly covered.

I felt as light and clean as a white feather. It took me some time to consciously locate my arms and legs, to feel the vivid sense of life radiate from the wakening center to the extremities.

A big room, high and wide, with many lofty windows whose closed blinds let through soft green-lit air; a beautiful room, in proportion, in color, in smooth simplicity; a scent of blossoming gardens outside.

I lay perfectly still, quite happy, quite conscious, and yet not actively realizing what had happened till I heard Terry.

"Gosh!" was what he said.

I turned my head. There were three beds in this chamber, and plenty of room for them.

Terry was sitting up, looking about him, alert as ever. His remarks, though not loud, roused Jeff also. We all sat up.

Terry swung his legs out of bed, stood up, stretched himself mightily. He was in a long night-robe, a sort of seamless garment, undoubtedly comfortable—we all found ourselves so covered. Shoes were beside each bed, also quite comfortable and good-looking though by no means like our own.

We looked for our clothes—they were not there, nor anything of all the varied contents of our pockets.

A door stood somewhat ajar; it opened into a most attractive bathroom, copiously provided with towels, soap, mirrors, and all such convenient comforts, with indeed our toothbrushes and combs, our notebooks, and, thank goodness, our watches—but no clothes.

Then we made search of the big room again and found a large airy closet, holding plenty of clothing, but not ours.

"A council of war!" demanded Terry. "Come on back to bed— the bed's all right anyhow. Now then, my scientific friend, let us consider our case dispassionately."

He meant me, but Jeff seemed most impressed.

"They haven't hurt us in the least!" he said. "They could have killed us—or—or anything—and I never felt better in my life."

"That argues that they *are* all women," I suggested, "and highly civilized. You know you hit one in the last scrimmage—I heard her sing out—and we kicked awfully."

Terry was grinning at us. "Do you realize what these ladies have done to us?" he pleasantly inquired. "They have taken away *all* our possessions, *all* our clothes—every stitch. We have been stripped and washed and put to bed like so many yearling babies—by these highly civilized women."

Jeff actually blushed. He had a poetic imagination. Terry had imagination enough, of a different kind. So had I, also different. I always flattered myself I had the scientific imagination, which, incidentally, I considered the highest sort. One has a right to a certain amount of egotism if founded on fact—and kept to one's self—*I* think.

"No use kicking, boys," I said. "They've got us, and apparently they're perfectly harmless. It remains for us to cook up some plan of escape like any other bottled heroes. Meanwhile we've got to put on these clothes—Hobson's choice."[1]

The garments were simple in the extreme, and absolutely comfortable, physically, though of course we all felt like supes[2] in the theater. There was a one-piece cotton undergarment, thin and soft, that reached over the knees and shoulders, something like the one-piece pajamas some fellows wear, and a kind of half-hose, that came up to just under the knee and stayed there—had an elastic top of their own, and covered the edges of the first.

Then there was a thicker variety of union suit, a lot of them in the closet, of varying weights and somewhat sturdier material—evidently they would do at a pinch with nothing further. Then there were tunics, knee length, and some long robes. Needless to say we took tunics.

We bathed and dressed quite cheerfully.

"Not half bad," said Terry, surveying himself in a long mirror. His hair was somewhat longer than when we left the last barber, and the hats provided were much like those seen on the Prince in the fairy-tale, lacking the plume.

---

1 An apparent choice that actually offers no alternatives, named after Thomas Hobson (1544–1631), an English liveryman who made customers take the horse closest to the stable door.

2 Supernumerary actors, i.e., extras, actors without speaking parts, such as for crowd scenes.

The costume was similar to that which we had seen on all the women, though some of them, those working in the fields, glimpsed by our glasses when we first flew over, wore only the first two.

I settled my shoulders and stretched my arms, remarking: "They have worked out a mighty sensible dress, I'll say that for them." With which we all agreed.

"Now then," Terry proclaimed, "we've had a fine long sleep— we've had a good bath—we're clothed and in our right minds, though feeling like a lot of neuters. Do you think these highly civilized ladies are going to give us any breakfast?"

"Of course they will," Jeff asserted confidently. "If they had meant to kill us they would have done it before. I believe we are going to be treated as guests."

"Hailed as deliverers, I think," said Terry.

"Studied as curiosities," I told them. "But anyhow, we want food. So now for a sortie!"[1]

A sortie was not so easy.

The bathroom only opened into our chamber, and that had but one outlet, a big heavy door, which was fastened.

We listened.

"There's someone outside," Jeff suggested. "Let's knock."

So we knocked, whereupon the door opened.

Outside was another large room, furnished with a great table at one end, long benches or couches against the wall, some smaller tables and chairs. All these were solid, strong, simple in structure, and comfortable in use, also, incidentally, beautiful.

This room was occupied by a number of women, eighteen to be exact, some of whom we distinctly recalled.

Terry heaved a disappointed sigh. "The Colonels!" I heard him whisper to Jeff.

Jeff, however, advanced and bowed in his best manner; so did we all, and we were saluted civilly by the tall standing women.

We had no need to make pathetic pantomime of hunger; the smaller tables were already laid with food, and we were gravely invited to be seated. The tables were set for two; each of us found ourselves placed vis-a-vis[2] with one of our hosts, and each table had five other stalwarts nearby, unobtrusively watching. We had plenty of time to get tired of those women!

The breakfast was not profuse, but sufficient in amount and excellent in quality. We were all too good travelers to object to

---

1   A sudden issuing of troops from a defensive position against an enemy.
2   Face to face (French).

novelty, and this repast with its new but delicious fruit, its dish of large rich-flavored nuts, and its highly satisfactory little cakes, was most agreeable. There was water to drink, and a hot beverage of a most pleasing quality, some preparation like cocoa.

And then and there, willy-nilly, before we had satisfied our appetites, our education began.

By each of our plates lay a little book, a real printed book, though different from ours both in paper and binding, as well, of course, as in type. We examined them curiously.

"Shades of Sauveur!"[1] muttered Terry. "We're to learn the language!"

We were indeed to learn the language, and not only that, but to teach our own. There were blank books with parallel columns, neatly ruled, evidently prepared for the occasion, and in these, as fast as we learned and wrote down the name of anything we were urged to write our own name for it by its side.

The book we had to study was evidently a school-book, one in which children learned to read, and we judged from this, and from their frequent consultation as to methods, that they had had no previous experience in the art of teaching foreigners their language, or of learning any other.

On the other hand, if they lacked in experience, they made up in genius. Such subtle understanding, such instant recognition of our difficulties, and readiness to meet them, were a constant surprise to us.

Of course, we were willing to meet them half-way. It was wholly to our advantage to be able to understand and speak with them, and as to refusing to teach them—why should we? Later on we did try open rebellion, but only once.

That first meal was pleasant enough, each of us quietly studying his companion, Jeff with sincere admiration, Terry with that highly technical look of his, as of a past master—like a lion-tamer, a serpent charmer, or some such professional. I myself was intensely interested.

It was evident that those sets of five were there to check any outbreak on our part. We had no weapons, and if we did try to do any damage, with a chair, say, why five to one was too many for us, even if they were women; that we had found out to our sorrow. It was not pleasant, having them always around, but we soon got used to it.

---

1 Lambert Sauveur (1827–1907) founded the "direct method" of foreign language instruction, which taught through demonstration, objects, and pictures in an attempt to reproduce the way children learn to speak.

"It's better than being physically restrained ourselves," Jeff philosophically suggested when we were alone. "They've given us a room—with no great possibility of escape—and personal liberty—heavily chaperoned. It's better than we'd have been likely to get in a man-country."

"Man-country! Do you really believe there are no men here, you innocent? Don't you know there must be?" demanded Terry.

"Ye—es," Jeff agreed. "Of course—and yet——"

"And yet—what! Come, you obdurate sentimentalist—what are you thinking about?"

"They may have some peculiar division of labor we've never heard of," I suggested. "The men may live in separate towns, or they may have subdued them—somehow—and keep them shut up. But there must be some."

"That last suggestion of yours is a nice one, Van," Terry protested. "Same as they've got us subdued and shut up! You make me shiver."

"Well, figure it out for yourself, anyway you please. We saw plenty of kids, the first day, and we've seen those girls—"

"Real girls!" Terry agreed, in immense relief. "Glad you mentioned 'em. I declare, if I thought there was nothing in the country but those grenadiers[1] I'd jump out the window."

"Speaking of windows," I suggested, "let's examine ours."

We looked out of all the windows. The blinds opened easily enough, and there were no bars, but the prospect was not reassuring.

This was not the pink-walled town we had so rashly entered the day before. Our chamber was high up, in a projecting wing of a sort of castle, built out on a steep spur of rock. Immediately below us were gardens, fruitful and fragrant, but their high walls followed the edge of the cliff which dropped sheer down, we could not see how far. The distant sound of water suggested a river at the foot.

We could look out east, west and south. To the south-eastward stretched the open country, lying bright and fair in the morning light, but on either side, and evidently behind, rose great mountains.

"This thing is a regular fortress—and no women built it, I can tell you that," said Terry. We nodded agreeingly. "It's right up among the hills—they must have brought us a long way."

"And pretty fast, too," I added.

---

1 A company of the tallest and finest soldiers in a regiment (*OED*).

"We saw some kind of swift moving vehicles the first day," Jeff reminded us. "If they've got motors they *are* civilized."

"Civilized or not, we've got our work cut out for us to get away from here. I don't propose to make a rope of bedclothes and try those walls till I'm sure there is no better way."

We all concurred on this point, and returned to our discussion as to the women.

Jeff continued thoughtful. "All the same, there's something funny about it," he urged. "It isn't just that we don't see any men—but we don't see any signs of them. The—the—reaction of these women is different from any that I've ever met."

"There is something in what you say, Jeff," I agreed. "There is a different—atmosphere."

"They don't seem to notice our being men," he went on. "They treat us—well—just as they do one another. It's as if our being men was a minor incident."

I nodded. I'd noticed it myself. But Terry broke in rudely.

"Fiddlesticks!" he said. "It's because of their advanced age. They're all grandmas, I tell you—or ought to be. Great aunts, anyhow. Those girls were girls all right, weren't they?"

"Yes—" Jeff agreed, still slowly. "But they weren't afraid—they flew up that tree and hid, like school-boys caught out of bounds—not like shy girls."

"And they ran like Marathon winners—you'll admit that, Terry," [he] added.

Terry was moody as the days passed. He seemed to mind our confinement more than Jeff or I did; and he harped on Alima, and how near he'd come to catching her. "If I had—" he would say, rather savagely, "we'd have had a hostage and could have made terms."

But Jeff was getting on excellent terms with his tutor, and even his guards, and so was I. It interested me profoundly, to note and study the subtle difference between these women and other women, and try to account for them. In the matter of personal appearance, there was a great difference. They all wore short hair, some few inches at most; some curly, some not, all light and clean and fresh-looking.

"If their hair was only long," Jeff would complain, "they would look so much more feminine."

I rather liked it myself, after I got used to it. Why we should so admire "a woman's crown of hair,"[1] and not admire a Chinaman's

---

1 Probably alluding to 1 Corinthians 11:15: "But if a woman have long hair, it is a glory to her: for her hair is given her for a covering" (*continued*)

queue[1] is hard to explain, except that we are so convinced that the long hair "belongs" to a woman. Whereas the "mane" in horses, is on both, and in lions, buffalos and such creatures only on the male. But I did miss it—at first.

Our time was quite pleasantly filled. We were free of the garden below our windows, quite long in its irregular rambling shape, bordering the cliff. The walls were perfectly smooth and high, ending in the masonry of the building; and as I studied the great stones I became convinced that the whole structure was extremely old. It was built like the pre-Incan architecture in Peru, of enormous monoliths, fitted as closely as mosaics.

"These folks have a history, that's sure," I told the others. "And *some* time they were fighters—else why a fortress?"

I said we were free of the garden, but not wholly alone in it. There was always a string of those uncomfortably strong women sitting about, always one of them watching us even if the others were reading, playing games, or busy at some kind of handiwork.

"When I see them knit," Terry said, "I can almost call them feminine."

"That don't prove anything," Jeff promptly replied. "Scotch shepherds knit—always knitting."

"When we get out—" Terry stretched himself and looked at the far peaks, "when we get out of this and get to where the real women are—the mothers, and the girls——"

"Well—what'll we do then?" I asked, rather gloomily. "How do you know we'll ever get out?"

This was an unpleasant idea, which we unanimously considered, returning with earnestness to our studies.

"If we are good boys, and learn our lessons well," I suggested. "If we are quiet and respectful and polite and they are not afraid of us—then perhaps they will let us out. And anyway—when we do escape, it is of immense importance that we know the language."

Personally I was tremendously interested in that language, and seeing they had books, was eager to get at them, to dig into their history, if they had one.

Proverbs 16:21: "A gray head is a crown of glory; if it is found in the way of righteousness."

1 Traditionally, Chinese men shaved hair above their temples and wore the rest in a long braid hanging down at the back. The style had once been violently imposed by the Chinese government; the style was being abandoned by the time Gilman wrote *Herland*.

It was not hard to speak, smooth and pleasant to the ear, and so easy to read and write that I marvelled at it. They had an absolutely phonetic system, the whole thing was as scientific as Esparanto,[1] yet bore all the marks of an old and rich civilization.

We were free to study as much as we wished, and were not left merely to wander in the garden for recreation, but introduced to a great gymnasium, partly on the roof and partly in the story below. Here we learned real respect for our tall guards. No change of costume was needed for this work, save to lay off outer clothing. The first one was as perfect a garment for exercise as need be devised, absolutely free to move in, and, I had to admit, much better looking than our usual one.

"Forty—over forty—some of 'em fifty, I bet—and look at 'em!" grumbled Terry in reluctant admiration.

There were no spectacular acrobatics, such as only the young can perform, but for all-round development they had a most excellent system. A good deal of music went with it, with posture dancing, and sometimes, gravely beautiful processional performances.

Jeff was much impressed by it. We did not know then how small a part of their physical culture methods this really was, but found it agreeable to watch, and to take part in.

Oh yes, we took part all right! It wasn't absolutely compulsory, but we thought it better to please.

Terry was the strongest of us, though I was wiry and had good staying power, and Jeff was a great sprinter and hurdler, but I can tell you those old ladies gave us cards and spades. They ran like deer, by which I mean that they ran not as if it was a performance, but as if it was their natural gait. We remembered those fleeting girls of our first bright adventure, and concluded that it was.

They leaped like deer, too, with a quick folding motion of the legs, drawn up and turned to one side with a sidelong twist of the body. I remembered the sprawling spread-eagle way in which some of the fellows used to come over the line—and tried to learn the trick. We did not easily catch up with these experts, however.

"Never thought I'd live to be bossed by a lot of elderly lady acrobats," Terry protested.

---

1   The language of Esperanto was created by Dr. Ludwik Lazarus Zamenhof (1859–1917) and introduced in 1887 with the aim of being an easily learned international second language that would allow people who speak different native languages to communicate, and thus to foster international harmony.

They had games, too, a good many of them, but we found them rather uninteresting at first. It was like two people playing solitaire to see who would get it first; more like a race or a—a competitive examination, than a real game with some fight in it.

I philosophized a bit over this, and told Terry it argued against their having any men about. "There isn't a man-size game in the lot," I said.

"But they are interesting—I like them," Jeff objected, "and I'm sure they are educational."

"I'm sick and tired of being educated," Terry protested. "Fancy going to a dame school[1]—at our age. I want to Get Out!"

But we could not get out, and we were being educated swiftly. Our special tutors rose rapidly in our esteem. They seemed of rather finer quality than the guards, though all were on terms of easy friendliness. Mine was named Somel, Jeff's Zava, and Terry's Moadine. We tried to generalize from the names, those of the guards, and of our three girls, but got nowhere.

"They sound well enough, and they're mostly short, but there's no similarity of termination—and no two alike. However, our acquaintance is limited as yet."

There were many things we meant to ask—as soon as we could talk well enough. Better teaching I never saw. From morning to night there was Somel, always on call except between two and four; always pleasant with a steady friendly kindness that I grew to enjoy very much. Jeff said Miss Zava—he would put on a title, though they apparently had none—was a darling; that she reminded him of his Aunt Esther at home; but Terry refused to be won, and rather jeered at his own companion, when we were alone.

"I'm sick of it!" he protested. "Sick of the whole thing. Here we are cooped up as helpless as a bunch of three-year-old orphans, and being taught what they think is necessary—whether we like it or not. Confound their old-maid impudence!"

Nevertheless we were taught. They brought in a raised map of their country, beautifully made, and increased our knowledge of geographical terms; but when we inquired for information as to the country outside, they smilingly shook their heads.

They brought pictures, not only the engravings in the books, but colored studies of plants and trees and flowers and birds. They brought tools and various small objects—we had plenty of "material" in our school.

---

1 A small school resembling a daycare center for young children, frequently run by a woman in her home.

And, as we made progress, they brought more and more books.

If it had not been for Terry we would have been much more contented, but as the weeks ran into months he grew more and more irritable.

"Don't act like a bear with a sore head," I begged him. "We're getting on finely. Every day we can understand them better, and pretty soon we can make a reasonable plea to be let out——"

"*Let* out!" he stormed. "*Let* out—like children kept after school. I want to Get Out, and I'm going to. I want to find the men of this place and fight!—or the girls——"

"Guess it's the girls you're most interested in," Jeff commented. "What are you going to fight *with*—your fists?"

"Yes—or sticks and stones—I'd just like to!" And Terry squared off and tapped Jeff softly on the jaw—"just for instance," he said.

"Anyhow," he went on, "we could get back to our machine and clear out."

"If it's there——" I cautiously suggested.

"Oh, don't croak, Van! If it isn't there, we'll find our way down somehow—the boat's there, I guess——"

It was hard on Terry, so hard that he finally persuaded us to consider a plan of escape. It was difficult; it was highly dangerous, but he declared that he'd go alone if we wouldn't go with him, and of course we couldn't think of that.

It appeared he had made a pretty careful study of the environment. From our end window that faced the point of the promontory we could get a fair idea of the stretch of wall, and the drop below. Also from the roof we could make out more, and even, in one place, glimpse a sort of path below the wall.

"It's a question of three things," he said. "Ropes, agility, and not being seen."

"That's the hardest part," I urged, still hoping to dissuade him. "One or another pair of eyes is on us every minute except at night."

"Therefore we must do it at night," he answered. "That's easy."

"We've got to think that if they catch us we may not be so well treated afterward," said Jeff.

"That's the business risk we must take. I'm going—if I break my neck." There was no changing him.

The rope problem was not easy. Something strong enough to hold a man and long enough to let us down into the garden, and then down over the wall. There were plenty of strong ropes in the gymnasium—they seemed to love to swing and climb on them—but we were never there by ourselves.

We should have to piece it out from our bedding, rugs, and garments, and moreover, we should have to do it after we were shut in for the night, for every day the place was cleaned to perfection by two of our guardians.

We had no shears, no knives, but Terry was resourceful. "These Jennies have glass and china, you see. We'll break a glass from the bathroom and use that. 'Love will find out a way,'"[1] he hummed. "When we're all out of the window, we'll stand three man high and cut the rope as far up as we can reach, so as to have more for the wall. I know just where I saw that bit of path below, and there's a big tree there, too, or a vine or something—I saw the leaves."

It seemed a crazy risk to take, but this was, in a way, Terry's expedition, and we were all tired of our imprisonment.

So we waited for full moon, retired early, and spent an anxious hour or two in the unskilled manufacture of man-strong ropes.

To retire into the depths of the closet, muffle a glass in thick cloth and break it without noise was not difficult, and broken glass will cut, though not as deftly as a pair of scissors.

The broad moonlight streamed in through four of our windows—we had not dared leave our lights on too long; and we worked hard and fast at our task of destruction.

Hangings, rugs, robes, towels, as well as bed-furniture—even the mattress covers—we left not one stitch upon another, as Jeff put it.

Then at an end window, as less liable to observation, we fastened one end of our cable, strongly, to the firm-set hinge of the inner blind, and dropped our coiled bundle of rope softly over.

"This part's easy enough—I'll come last, so as to cut the rope," said Terry.

So I slipped down first, and stood, well braced against the wall; then Jeff on my shoulders, then Terry, who shook us a little as he sawed through the cord above his head. Then I slowly dropped to the ground, Jeff following, and at last we all three stood safe in the garden, with most of our rope with us.

"Good-bye, Grandma!" whispered Terry, under his breath, and we crept softly toward the wall, taking advantage of the shadow of every bush and tree. He had been foresighted enough to mark the very spot, only a scratch of stone on stone, but we could see

---

1   Ballad, sometimes attributed to Thomas Percy (1729–1811), who included it in his collection *Reliques of Ancient English Poetry* (1765). It includes the lines, "Under floods that are deepest, / Which Neptune obey, / Over rocks that are steepest, / Love will find out the way."

to read in that light. For anchorage there was a tough, fair-sized shrub close to the wall.

"Now I'll climb up on you two again and go over first," said Terry. "That'll hold the rope firm till you both get up on top. Then I'll go down to the end. If I can get off safely you can see me and follow—or, say, I'll twitch it three times. If I find there's absolutely no footing—why I'll climb up again, that's all. I don't think they'll kill us."

From the top he reconnoitered carefully, waved his hand and whispered, "O.K.," then slipped over. Jeff climbed up and I followed, and we rather shivered to see how far down that swaying, wavering figure dropped, hand under hand, till it disappeared in a mass of foliage far below.

Then there were three quick pulls, and Jeff and I, not without a joyous sense of recovered freedom, successfully followed our leader.

Chapter IV

Our Venture

We were standing on a narrow, irregular, all too slanting little ledge, and should doubtless have ignominiously slipped off and broken our rash necks but for the vine. This was a thick-leaved, wide-spreading thing, a little like Amphelopsis.[1]

"It's not *quite* vertical here, you see," said Terry, full of pride and enthusiasm. "This thing never would hold our direct weight, but I think if we sort of slide down on it, one at a time, sticking in with hands and feet, we'll reach that next ledge alive."

"As we do not wish to get up our rope again—and can't comfortably stay here, I approve," said Jeff solemnly.

Terry slid down first—said he'd show us how a Christian meets his death. Luck was with us. We had put on the thickest of those intermediate suits, leaving our tunics behind, and made this scramble quite successfully, though I got a pretty heavy fall just at the end, and was only kept on the second ledge by main force. The next stage was down a sort of "chimney"—a long irregular fissure; and so with scratches many and painful and bruises not a few, we finally reached the stream.

---

1 Ampelopsis, a genus of climbing shrubs in the grape family; Virginia Creeper.

It was darker there, but we felt it highly necessary to put as much distance as possible behind us; so we waded, jumped, and clambered down that rocky river-bed, in the flickering black and white moonlight and leaf shadow, till growing daylight forced a halt.

We found a friendly nut-tree, those large, satisfying, soft-shelled nuts we already knew so well, and filled our pockets.

I see that I have not remarked that these women had pockets in surprising number and variety. They were in all their garments, and the middle one in particular was shingled with them. So we stocked up with nuts till we bulged like a Prussian private in marching order; drank all we could hold, and retired for the day.

It was not a very comfortable place, not at all easy to get at; just a sort of crevice high up along the steep bank; but it was well veiled with foliage and dry. After our exhausting three or four hours' scramble and the good breakfast food, we all lay down along that crack—heads and tails, as it were—and slept till the afternoon sun almost toasted our faces.

Terry poked a tentative foot against my head.

"How are you, Van? Alive yet?"

"Very much so," I told him. And Jeff was equally cheerful.

We had room to stretch, if not to turn around; but we could very carefully roll over, one at a time, behind the sheltering foliage.

It was no use to leave there by daylight. We could not see much of the country, but enough to know that we were now at the beginning of the cultivated area, and no doubt there would be an alarm sent out far and wide.

Terry chuckled softly to himself, lying there on that hot narrow little rim of rock. He dilated on the discomfiture of our guards and tutors, making many discourteous remarks.

I reminded him that we had still a long way to go before getting to the place where we'd left our machine, and no probability of finding it there; but he only kicked me, mildly, for a croaker.

"If you can't boost, don't knock," he protested. "I never said 'twould be a picnic. But I'd run away in the Antarctic ice-fields rather than be a prisoner."

We soon dozed off again.

The long rest and penetrating dry heat were good for us, and that night we covered a considerable distance, keeping always in the rough forested belt of land which we knew bordered the whole country. Sometimes we were near the outer edge, and caught sudden glimpses of the tremendous depths beyond.

"This piece of geography stands up like a basalt column,"[1] Jeff said. "Nice time we'll have getting down if they have confiscated our machine!" For which suggestion he received summary chastisement.

What we could see inland was peaceable enough, but only moonlit glimpses; by daylight we lay very close. As Terry said, we did not wish to kill the old ladies—even if we could; and short of that they were perfectly competent to pick us up bodily and carry us back, if discovered. There was nothing for it but to lie low, and sneak out unseen if we could do it.

There wasn't much talking done. At night we made our Marathon-obstacle-race; we "stayed not for brake and we stopped not for stone,"[2] and swam whatever water was too deep to wade and could not be got around; but that was only necessary twice. By day, sleep, sound and sweet. Mighty lucky it was that we could live off the country as we did. Even that margin of forest seemed rich in food-stuffs.

But Jeff thoughtfully suggested that that very thing showed how careful we should have to be, as we might run into some stalwart group of gardeners or foresters or nut-gatherers any minute. Careful we were, feeling pretty sure that if we did not make good this time we were not likely to have another opportunity; and at last we reached a point from which we could see, far below, the broad stretch of that still lake from which we had made our ascent.

"That looks pretty good to me!" said Terry, gazing down at it. "Now, if we can't find the 'plane, we know where to aim if we have to drop over this wall some other way."

The wall at that point was singularly uninviting. It rose so straight that we had to put our heads over to see the base, and the country below seemed to be a far-off marshy tangle of rank vegetation. We did not have to risk our necks to that extent, however, for at last, stealing along among the rocks and trees like so many creeping savages, we came to that flat space where we had landed; and there, in unbelievable good fortune, we found our machine.

"Covered, too, by jingo! Would you think they had that much sense[?]" cried Terry.

---

1 Vertical formation formed by the rapid cooling of flowing molten lava.
2 The original passage reads, "He stayed not for brake, and he stopped not for stone." From the ballad "Lochinvar," in which a young hero rides to carry away his lady before she is wed to another. From *Marmion* (1808) by Sir Walter Scott (1771–1832).

"If they had that much, they're likely to have more," I warned him, softly. "Bet you the thing's watched."

We reconnoitered as widely as we could in the failing moonlight—moons are of a painfully unreliable nature; but the growing dawn showed us the familiar shape, shrouded in some heavy cloth like canvas, and no slightest sign of any watchman near. We decided to make a quick dash as soon as the light was strong enough for accurate work.

"I don't care if the old thing'll go or not," Terry declared. "We can run her to the edge, get aboard and just plane down—plop!— beside our boat there. Look there—see the boat!"

Sure enough—there was our motor, lying like a gray cocoon on the flat pale sheet of water.

Quietly but swiftly we rushed forward and began to tug at the fastenings of that cover.

"Confound the thing!" Terry cried in desperate impatience. "They've got it sewed up in a bag! And we've not a knife among us!"

Then, as we tugged and pulled at that tough cloth we heard a sound that made Terry lift his head like a war horse,—the sound of an unmistakable giggle; yes—three giggles.

There they were—Celis, Alima, Ellador,—looking just as they did when we first saw them, standing a little way off from us, as interested, as mischievous, as three schoolboys.

"Hold on, Terry—hold on!" I warned. "That's too easy—look out for a trap."

"Let us appeal to their kind hearts," Jeff urged. "I think they will help us. Perhaps they've got knives."

"It's no use rushing them, anyhow." I was absolutely holding on to Terry. "We know they can out-run and out-climb us."

He reluctantly admitted this; and after a brief parley between ourselves, we all advanced slowly toward them, holding out our hands in token of friendliness.

They stood their ground till we had come fairly near, and then indicated that we should stop. To make sure, we advanced a step or two and they promptly and swiftly withdrew. So we stopped at the distance specified. Then we used their language, as far as we were able, to explain our plight; telling how we were imprisoned, how we had escaped—a good deal of pantomime here and vivid interest on their part—how we had traveled by night and hidden by day, living on nuts—and here Terry pretended great hunger.

I know he could not have been hungry; we had found plenty to eat and had not been sparing in helping ourselves. But they seemed somewhat impressed; and after a murmured consultation they produced from their pockets certain little packages, and with the utmost ease and accuracy tossed them into our hands.

Jeff was most appreciative of this; and Terry made extravagant gestures of admiration, which seemed to set them off, boy-fashion, to show their skill. While we ate the excellent biscuit they had thrown us, and while Ellador kept a watchful eye on our movements, Celis ran off to some distance, and set up a sort of "duck-on-a-rock"[1] arrangement, a big yellow nut on top of three balanced sticks; Alima meanwhile, gathering stones.

They urged us to throw at it, and we did, but the thing was a long way off, and it was only after a number of failures, at which those elvish damsels laughed delightedly, that Jeff succeeded in bringing the whole structure to the ground. It took me still longer, and Terry, to his intense annoyance, came third.

Then Celis set up the little tripod again, and looked back at us, knocking it down, pointing at it, and shaking her short curls severely. "No," she said. "Bad—wrong!" We were quite able to follow her.

Then she set it up once more, put the fat nut on top, and returned to the others; and there those aggravating girls sat and took turns throwing little stones at that thing, while one stayed by as a setter-up; and they just popped that nut off, two times out of three, without upsetting the sticks. Pleased as Punch[2] they were too, and we pretended to be, but weren't.

We got very friendly over this game, but I told Terry we'd be sorry if we didn't get off while we could, and then we begged for knives. It was easy to show what we wanted to do, and they each proudly produced a sort of strong clasp-knife from their pockets.

"Yes," we said eagerly, "that's it! Please—" We had learned quite a bit of their language, you see. And we just begged for those knives, but they would not give them to us. If we came a step too near they backed off, standing light and eager for flight.

---

1   A common children's game known by a variety of names, including Duck, Ducks and Drakes, Duckstone, and Ducks-off. A rock (sometimes called a drake) is placed on a larger stone or stump, and other players attempt to hit the smaller off the larger with their own stones, sometimes called ducks, from a throwing line; in some variations the duck on the rock is guarded by a player who tries to tag the others when they attempt to retrieve their stones. A tagged player is then "it."

2   Highly pleased, delighted. From the Punch and Judy puppet show, in which Punch kills his wife, child, a policeman, death, and the devil, etc., each time gleefully squeaking the catchphrase, "That's the way to do it!"

"It's no sort of use," I said. "Come on—let's get a sharp stone or something—we must get this thing off."

So we hunted about and found what edged fragments we could, and hacked away, but it was like trying to cut sailcloth with a clam-shell.

Terry hacked and dug, but said to us under his breath, "Boys— we're in pretty good condition—let's make a life and death dash and get hold of those girls—we've got to."

They had drawn rather nearer, to watch our efforts, and we did take them rather by surprise; also, as Terry said, our recent training had strengthened us in wind and limb, and for a few desperate moments those girls were scared and we almost triumphant.

But just as we stretched out our hands the distance between us widened; they had got their pace apparently, and then, though we ran at our utmost speed, and much farther than I thought wise, they kept just out of reach all the time.

We stopped breathless, at last, at my repeated admonitions.

"This is stark foolishness," I urged. "They are doing it on purpose—come back or you'll be sorry."

We went back, much slower than we came, and in truth we were sorry.

As we reached our swaddled machine, and sought again to tear loose its covering, there rose up from all around the sturdy forms, the quiet determined faces, we knew so well.

"Oh Lord!" groaned Terry. "The Colonels! It's all up—they're forty to one."

It was no use to fight. These women evidently relied on numbers; not so much as a drilled force, but as a multitude actuated by a common impulse. They showed no sign of fear, and since we had no weapons whatever, and there were at least a hundred of them, standing ten deep about us, we gave in as gracefully as we might.

Of course we looked for punishment; a closer imprisonment, solitary confinement maybe; but nothing of the kind happened. They treated us as truants only; and as if they quite understood our truancy.

Back we went; not under an anaesthetic this time, but skimming along in electric motors; enough like ours to be quite recognizable; each of us in a separate vehicle with one able-bodied lady on either side and three facing him.

They were all pleasant enough, and talked with us as much as was possible to our limited powers. And though Terry was keenly mortified, and at first we all rather dreaded harsh treatment, I for one soon began to feel a sort of pleasant confidence, and to enjoy the trip.

Here were my five familiar companions, all good-natured as could be, seeming to have no worse feeling than a mild triumph as of winning some simple game; and even that they politely suppressed.

This was a good opportunity to see the country, too, and the more I saw of it, the better I liked it. We went too swiftly for close observation, but I could appreciate perfect roads, as dustless as a swept floor; the shade of endless lines of trees; the ribbon of flowers that unrolled beneath them, and the rich comfortable country that stretched off and away, full of varied charm.

We rolled through many villages and towns, and I soon saw that the park-like beauty of our first-seen city was no exception. Our swift high-sweeping view from the plane had been most attractive, but lacked detail; and in that first day of struggle and capture, we noticed but little; but now we were swept along at an easy rate of some thirty miles an hour and covered quite a good deal of ground.

We stopped for lunch in quite a sizeable town, and here, rolling slowly through the streets, we saw more of the population. They had come out to look at us everywhere we had passed, but here were more; and when we went in to eat, in a big garden place, with little shaded tables among the trees and flowers, many eyes were upon us. And everywhere, open country, village or city—only women. Old women and young women and a great majority who seemed neither young nor old, but just women; young girls, also, though these, and the children, seeming to be in groups by themselves generally, were less in evidence. We caught many glimpses of girls and children in what seemed to be schools or in playgrounds, and so far as we could judge there were no boys. We all looked, carefully. Everyone gazed at us politely, kindly, and with eager interest. No one was impertinent. We could catch quite a bit of the talk, now; and all they said seemed pleasant enough.

Well—before nightfall we were all safely back in our big room. The damage we had done was quite ignored; the beds as smooth and comfortable as before, new clothing and towels supplied. The only thing those women did was to illuminate the gardens at night, and to set an extra watch. But they called us to account next day. Our three tutors, who had not joined in the recapturing expedition, had been quite busy in preparing for us, and now made explanation.

They knew well we would make for our machine; and also that there was no other way of getting down—alive; so our flight had troubled no one; all they did was to call the inhabitants to keep an eye on our movements all along the edge of the forest between the two points. It appeared that many of those nights we had been seen, by careful ladies sitting snugly in big trees by the river bed, or up among the rocks.

Terry looked immensely disgusted, but it struck me as extremely funny. Here we had been risking our lives, hiding and prowling like outlaws, living on nuts and fruit, getting wet and cold at night, and dry and hot by day, and all the while these estimable women had just been waiting for us to come out.

Now they began to explain, carefully using such words as we could understand. It appeared that we were considered as guests of the country—sort of public wards. Our first violence had made it necessary to keep us safeguarded for a while, but as soon as we learned the language—and would agree to do no harm—they would show us all about the land.

Jeff was eager to reassure them. Of course he did not tell on Terry, but he made it clear that he was ashamed of himself, and that he would now conform. As to the language—we all fell upon it with redoubled energy. They brought us books, in greater numbers, and I began to study them seriously.

"Pretty punk literature," Terry burst forth one day, when we were in the privacy of our own room. "Of course one expects to begin on child-stories, but I would like something more interesting now."

"Can't expect stirring romance and wild adventure without men, can you?" I asked. Nothing irritated Terry more than to have us assume that there were no men; but there were no signs of them in the books they gave us, or the pictures.

"Shut up!" he growled. "What infernal nonsense you talk! I'm going to ask 'em outright—we know enough now."

In truth we had been using our best efforts to master the language, and were able to read fluently, and to discuss what we read with considerable ease.

That afternoon we were all sitting together on the roof; we three and the tutors gathered about a table; no guards about. We had been made to understand some time earlier that if we would agree to do no violence they would withdraw their constant attendance, and we promised most willingly.

So there we sat, at ease; all in similar dress; our hair, by now, as long as theirs, only our beards to distinguish us. We did not want those beards, but had so far been unable to induce them to give us any cutting instruments.

"Ladies," Terry began, out of a clear sky, as it were, "are there no men in this country?"

"Men?" Somel answered. "Like you?"

"Yes, men," Terry indicated his beard, and threw back his broad shoulders. "Men, real men."

"No," she answered quietly. "There are no men in this country. There has not been a man among us for two thousand years."

Her look was clear and truthful, and she did not advance this astonishing statement as if it was astonishing, but quite as a matter of fact.

"But—the people—the children," he protested, not believing her in the least, but not wishing to say so.

"Oh, yes," she smiled. "I do not wonder you are puzzled. We are mothers—all of us; but there are no fathers. We thought you would ask about that long ago—why have you not?" Her look was as frankly kind as always; her tone quite simple.

Terry explained that we had not felt sufficiently used to the language, making rather a mess of it, I thought, but Jeff was franker.

"Will you excuse us all," he said, "if we admit that we find it hard to believe? There is no such—possibility—in the rest of the world."

"Have you no kind of life where it is possible?" asked Zava.

"Why, yes—some low forms, of course."

"How low—or how high, rather?"

"Well—there are some rather high forms of insect life in which it occurs. Parthenogenesis,[1] we call it—that means virgin birth."

She could not follow him.

"*Birth*, we know, of course; but what is *virgin*?"

Terry looked uncomfortable, but Jeff met the question quite calmly. "Among mating animals, the term *virgin* is applied to the female who has not mated," he answered.

"Oh, I see. And does it apply to the male also? Or is there a different term for him?"

He passed this over rather hurriedly, saying that the same term would apply, but was seldom used.

"No?" she said. "But one cannot mate without the other surely. Is not each then—virgin—before mating? And, tell me, have you any forms of life in which there is birth from a father only?"

---

1 Asexual reproduction in which an ovum develops into a new organism without fertilization. Parthenogenesis occurs naturally in some insects, crustaceans, fish, amphibians, and reptiles (Greek).

"I know of none," he answered, and I inquired seriously.

"You ask us to believe that for two thousand years there have been only women here, and only girl babies born?"

"Exactly," answered Somel, nodding gravely. "Of course, we know that among other animals it is not so; that there are fathers as well as mothers; and we see that you are fathers, that you come from a people who are of both kinds. We have been waiting you see, for you to be able to speak freely with us, and teach us about your country, and the rest of the world. You know so much, you see, and we know only our own land."

In the course of our previous studies we had been at some pains to tell them about the big world outside, to draw sketches, maps, to make a globe, even, out of a spherical fruit, and show the size and relation of the countries, and to tell of the numbers of their people. All this had been scant and in outline, but they quite understood.

I find I succeed very poorly in conveying the impression I would like to of these women. So far from being ignorant, they were deeply wise—that we realized more and more; and for clear reasoning, for real brain scope and power, they were A No. 1; but there were a lot of things they did not know.

For that matter there were a lot of things Aristotle[1] didn't know.

They had the evenest tempers, the most perfect patience and good nature—one of the things most impressive about them all was the absence of irritability. So far we had only this group to study, but afterwards I found it a common trait.

We had gradually come to feel that we were in the hands of friends, and very capable ones at that—but we couldn't form any opinion yet of the general level of these women.

"We want you to teach us all you can," Somel went on, her firm shapely hands clasped on the table before her; her clear quiet eyes meeting ours frankly. "And we want to teach you what we have that is novel and useful. You can well imagine that it is a wonderful event to us, to have men among us—after two thousand years. And we want to know about your women."

---

1 The Greek philosopher Aristotle (384–322 BCE). Gilman may have had in mind Aristotle's statement, "the male is by nature superior, and the female inferior; and the one rules, and the other is ruled" (*Politics* 1254 b13); or his explanation in *The Generation of Animals* that only men have the capacity for reproduction, women providing merely the womb in which the man's seed grows; therefore, according to Aristotle, the child inherits only the father's traits.

What she said about our importance gave instant pleasure to Terry. I could see by the way he lifted his head that it pleased him. But when she spoke of our women—someway I had a queer little indescribable feeling; not like any feeling I ever had before when "women" were mentioned.

"Will you tell us how it came about?" Jeff pursued. "You said 'for two thousand years'—did you have men here before that?"

"Yes," answered Zava.

They were all quiet for a little.

"You shall have our full history to read—do not be alarmed—it has been made clear and short—it took us a long time to learn how to write history. Oh, how I should love to read yours!"

She turned with flashing eager eyes, looking from one to the other of us.

"It would be so wonderful—would it not? To compare the history of two thousand years; to see what the differences are—between us, who are only mothers; and you, who are mothers and fathers, too. Of course we see, with our birds, that the father is as useful as the mother, almost; but among insects we find him of less importance, sometimes very little. Is it not so with you?"

"Oh, yes, birds and bugs," Terry said, "but not among animals—have you *no* animals?"

"We have cats," she said. "The father is not very useful."

"Have you no cattle—sheep—horses?" I drew some rough outlines of these beasts and showed them to her.

"We had, in the very old days, these," said Somel, and sketched with swift sure touches a sort of sheep or llama, "and these"—dogs, of two or three kinds, "and that"—pointing to my absurd but recognizable horse.

"What became of them?" asked Jeff.

"We do not want them anymore. They took up too much room—we need all our land to feed our people. It is such a little country, you know."

"Whatever do you do without milk?" Terry demanded incredulously.

"*Milk?* We have milk in abundance—our own."

"But—but—I meant for cooking—for grown people," Terry blundered, while they looked amazed and a shade displeased.

Jeff came to the rescue. "We keep cattle for their milk, as well as for their meat," he explained. "Cow's milk is a staple article of diet—there is a great milk industry—to collect and distribute it."

Still they looked puzzled. I pointed to my outline of a cow. "The farmer milks the cow," I said, and sketched a milk pail, the stool, and in pantomime showed the man milking. "Then it is carried to the city and distributed by milkmen—everybody has it at the door in the morning."

"Has the cow no child?" asked Somel earnestly.

"Oh, yes, of course, a calf, that is."

"Is there milk for the calf and you, too?"

It took some time to make clear to those three sweet-faced women the process which robs the cow of her calf, and the calf of its true food; and the talk led us into a further discussion of the meat business. They heard it out, looking very white, and presently begged to be excused.

Chapter V

A Unique History[1]

It is no use for me to try to piece out this account with adventures. If the people who read it are not interested in these amazing women and their history, they will not be interested at all.

As for us,—three young men to a whole landful of women— what could we do? We did get away, as described, and were peacefully brought back again without, as Terry complained, even the satisfaction of hitting anybody.

There were no adventures because there was nothing to fight. There were no wild beasts in the country and very few tame ones. Of these I might as well stop to describe the one common pet of the country. Cats, of course. But such cats!

What do you suppose these lady Burbanks[2] had done with their cats? By the most prolonged and careful selection and exclusion they had developed a race of cats that did not sing! That's a fact. The most those poor dumb brutes could do was to make a kind of squeak when they were hungry or wanted the door open; and, of course, to purr, and make the various mother-noises to their kittens.

Moreover they had ceased to kill birds. They were rigorously bred to destroy mice and moles and all such enemies of the food supply; but the birds were numerous and safe.

---

1 Synopsis from original edition: Three young men discover an unknown country in which there are only women, by whom they are presently captured. They escape, but are recaptured.

2 Luther Burbank (1849–1926), a California horticulturalist influenced by Charles Darwin, who developed more than 800 improved varieties of fruits, vegetables, and ornamental plants.

While we were discussing birds, Terry asked them if they used feathers for their hats, and they seemed amused at the idea. He made a few sketches of our women's hats, with plumes and quills and those various tickling things that stick out so far; and they were eagerly interested, as at everything about our women.

As for them, they said they only wore hats for shade when working in the sun; and those were big light straw hats, something like those used in China and Japan. In cold weather they wore caps or hoods.

"But for decorative purposes—don't you think they would be becoming?" pursued Terry, making as pretty a picture as he could of a lady with a plumed hat.

They by no means agreed to that, asking quite simply if the men wore the same kind. We hastened to assure her that they did not—and drew for them our kind of headgear.

"And do no men wear feathers in their hats?"

"Only Indians," Jeff explained, "savages, you know." And he sketched a war-bonnet to show them.

"And soldiers," I added, drawing a military hat with plumes.

They never expressed horror or disapproval, nor indeed much surprise—just a keen interest. And the notes they made!—miles of them!

But to return to our pussy-cats. We were a good deal impressed by this achievement in breeding, and when they questioned us—I can tell you we were well pumped for information—we told of what had been done for dogs and horses and cattle, but that there was no effort applied to cats, except for show purposes.

I wish I could represent the kind, quiet, steady, ingenious way they questioned us. It was not just curiosity—they weren't a bit more curious about us than we were about them, if as much. But they were bent on understanding our kind of civilization and their lines of interrogation would gradually surround us and drive us in till we found ourselves up against some admissions we did not want to make.

"Are all these breeds of dogs you have made useful?" they asked.

"Oh—useful! Why, the hunting dogs and watch-dogs and sheep-dogs are useful—and sled-dogs of course!—and ratters, I suppose, but we don't keep dogs for their *usefulness*. The dog is 'the friend of man,' we say—we love them."

That they understood. "We love our cats that way. They surely are our friends, and helpers too. You can see how intelligent and affectionate they are."

It was a fact. I'd never seen such cats, except in a few rare instances. Big, handsome silky things, friendly with everyone and devotedly attached to their special owners.

"You must have a heartbreaking time drowning kittens," we suggested. But they said: "Oh, no! You see we care for them as you do for your valuable cattle. The fathers are few compared to the mothers, just a few very fine ones in each town; they live quite happily in walled gardens and the houses of their friends. But they only have a mating season once a year."

"Rather hard on Thomas, isn't it?" suggested Terry.

"Oh, no—truly! You see it is many centuries that we have been breeding the kind of cats we wanted. They are healthy and happy and friendly, as you see. How do you manage with your dogs? Do you keep them in pairs, or segregate the fathers, or what?"

Then we explained that—well, that it wasn't a question of fathers exactly; that nobody wanted a—a mother dog; that, well, that practically all our dogs were males—there was only a very small percentage of females allowed to live.

Then Zava, observing Terry with her grave sweet smile, quoted back at him: "Rather hard on Thomas, isn't it? Do they enjoy it—living without mates? Are your dogs as uniformly healthy and sweet-tempered as our cats?"

Jeff laughed, eyeing Terry mischievously. As a matter of fact we began to feel Jeff something of a traitor—he so often flopped over and took their side of things; also his medical knowledge gave him a different point of view somehow.

"I'm sorry to admit," he told them, "that the dog, with us, is the most diseased of any animal—next to man. And as to temper—there are always some dogs who bite people—especially children."

That was pure malice. You see, children were the—the *raison d'être*[1] in this country. All our interlocutors sat up straight at once. They were still gentle, still restrained, but there was a note of deep amazement in their voices.

"Do we understand that you keep an animal—an unmated male animal—that bites children? About how many are there of them, please?"

"Thousands—in a large city," said Jeff, "and nearly every family has one in the country."

Terry broke in at this. "You must not imagine they are all dangerous—it's not one in a hundred that ever bites anybody. Why, they are the best friends of the children—a boy doesn't have half a chance that hasn't a dog to play with!"

---

1 Reason or justification for existence (French).

"And the girls?" asked Somel.

"Oh—girls—why they like them too," he said, but his voice flatted a little. They always noticed little things like that, we found later.

Little by little they wrung from us the fact that the friend of man, in the city, was a prisoner; was taken out for his meager exercise on a leash; was liable not only to many diseases, but to the one destroying horror of rabies, and, in many cases, for the safety of the citizens, he had to go muzzled. Jeff maliciously added vivid instances he had known or read of injury and death from mad dogs.

They did not scold or fuss about it. Calm as judges, those women were. But they made notes; Moadine read them to us.

"Please tell me if I have the facts correct," she said. "In your country—and in others too?"

"Yes," we admitted, "in most civilized countries."

"In most civilized countries a kind of animal is kept which is no longer useful—"

"They are a protection," Terry insisted. "They bark if burglars try to get in."

Then she made notes of "burglars" and went on: "because of the love which people bear to this animal."

Zava interrupted here. "Is it the men or the women who love this animal so much?"

"Both!" insisted Terry.

"Equally?" she inquired.

And Jeff said: "Nonsense, Terry—you know men like dogs better than women do—as a whole."

"Because they love it so much—especially men. This animal is kept shut up, or chained."

"Why?" suddenly asked Somel. "We keep our father cats shut up because we do not want too much fathering; but they are not chained—they have large grounds to run in."

"A valuable dog would be stolen if he was let loose," I said. "We put collars on them, with the owner's name, in case they do stray. Besides, they get into fights—a valuable dog might easily be killed by a bigger one."

"I see," she said. "They fight when they meet—is that common?" We admitted that it was.

"They are kept shut up, or chained." She paused again, and asked, "Is not a dog fond of running? Are they not built for speed?" That we admitted too, and Jeff, still malicious, enlightened them farther.

"I've always thought it was a pathetic sight, both ways—to see a man or a woman taking a dog to walk—at the end of a string."

"Have you bred them to be as neat in their habits as cats are?" was the next question. And when Jeff told them of the effect of dogs on sidewalk merchandise and the streets generally, they found it hard to believe.

You see their country was as neat as a Dutch kitchen, and as to sanitation—but I might as well start in now with as much as I can remember of the history of this amazing country before further description.

And I'll summarize here a bit as to our opportunities for learning it. I will not try to repeat the careful, detailed account I lost; I'll just say that we were kept in that fortress a good six months all told; and after that, three in a pleasant enough city where—to Terry's infinite disgust—there were only "Colonels" and little children—no young women whatever. Then we were under surveillance for three more—always with a tutor or a guard or both. But those months were pleasant because we were really getting acquainted with the girls. That was a chapter!—or will be—I will try to do justice to it.

We learned their language pretty thoroughly—had to; and they learned ours much more quickly and used it to hasten our own studies.

Jeff, who was never without reading matter of some sort, had two little books with him, a novel, and a little anthology of verse; and I had one of those pocket encyclopedias—a fat little thing, bursting with facts. These were used in our education—and theirs. Then as soon as we were up to it, they furnished us with plenty of their own books, and I went in for the history part—I wanted to understand the genesis of this miracle of theirs.

And this is what happened, according to their records:

As to geography—at about the time of the Christian era this land had a free passage to the sea. I'm not saying where, for good reasons. But there was a fairly easy pass through that wall of mountains behind us, and there is no doubt in my mind that these people were of Aryan[1] stock, and were once in contact with the

---

1   Originally used to identify groups of historically related languages, the
    term "Aryan" came in the late nineteenth and early twentieth centuries
    to be used as synonym for "Indo-European" or "Caucasian" as an ethnic
    group. Late nineteenth-century anthropologists theorized that the Aryans
    originated in northern Europe and could be identified by their Nordic
    blonde hair and blue eyes; others argued that this group was superior to
    other "races" from an evolutionary perspective.

best civilization of the old world. They were "white," but somewhat darker than our northern races because of their constant exposure to sun and air.

The country was far larger then, including much land beyond the pass, and a strip of coast. They had ships, commerce, an army, a king—for at that time they were what they so calmly called us—a bi-sexual race.

What happened to them first was merely a succession of historic misfortunes such as have befallen other nations often enough. They were decimated by war, driven up from their coast line till finally the reduced population with many of the men killed in battle, occupied this hinterland, and defended it for years, in the mountain passes. Where it was open to any possible attack from below they strengthened the natural defenses so that it became unscalably secure, as we found it.

They were a polygamous people, and a slave-holding people, like all of their time; and during the generation or two of this struggle to defend their mountain home they built the fortresses, such as the one we were held in, and other of their oldest buildings, some still in use. Nothing but earthquakes could destroy such architecture,—huge solid blocks, holding by their own weight. They must have had efficient workmen and enough of them in those days.

They made a brave fight for their existence, but no nation can stand up against what the steamship companies call "an act of God." While the whole fighting force was doing its best to defend their mountain pathway, there occurred a volcanic outburst, with some local tremors, and the result was the complete filling up of the pass,—their only outlet. Instead of a passage, a new ridge, sheer and high, stood between them and the sea; they were walled in, and beneath that wall lay their whole little army. Very few men were left alive, save the slaves; and these now seized their opportunity, rose in revolt, killed their remaining masters even to the youngest boy, killed the old women too, and the mothers, intending to take possession of the country with the remaining young women and girls.

But this succession of misfortunes was too much for those infuriated virgins. There were many of them, and but few of these would-be masters, so the young women, instead of submitting, rose in sheer desperation and slew their brutal conquerors.

This sounds like Titus Andronicus,[1] I know, but that is their account. I suppose they were about crazy—can you blame them?

---

1 *Titus Andronicus* is generally considered William Shakespeare's *(continued)*

There was literally no one left on this beautiful high garden land but a bunch of hysterical girls and some older slave women.

That was about two thousand years ago.

At first there was a period of sheer despair. The mountains towered between them and their old enemies, but also between them and escape. There was no way up or down or out—they simply had to stay there. Some were for suicide, but not the majority. They must have been a plucky lot, as a whole, and they decided to live—as long as they did live. Of course they had hope, as youth must, that something would happen to change their fate.

So they set to work, to bury the dead, to plow and sow, to care for one another.

Speaking of burying the dead, I will set down while I think of it, that they had adopted cremation about the thirteenth century, for the same reason that they had left off raising cattle—they could not spare the room. They were much surprised to learn that we were still burying—asked our reasons for it, and were much dissatisfied with what we gave. We told them of the belief in the resurrection of the body, and they asked if our God was not as well able to resurrect from ashes as from long corruption. We told them of how people thought it repugnant to have their loved ones burn, and they asked if it was less repugnant to have them decay. They were inconveniently reasonable, those women.

Well—that original bunch of girls set to work to clean up the place and make their livings as best they could. Some of the remaining slave women rendered invaluable service, teaching such trades as they knew. They had such records as were then kept, all the tools and implements of the time, and a most fertile land to work in.

There were a handful of the younger matrons who had escaped slaughter, and a few babies were born after the cataclysm—but only two boys and they both died.

For five or ten years they worked together, growing stronger and wiser and more and more mutually attached, and then the miracle happened—one of these young women bore a child. Of course they all thought there must be a man somewhere, but none was found. Then they decided it must be a direct gift from the gods, and placed the proud mother in the Temple of

---

earliest tragedy (c. 1589–92). The revenge plot features abductions, dismemberments, rapes, and murders. The title character is a Roman general.

Maaia[1]—their Goddess of Motherhood—under strict watch. And there, as years passed, this wonder-woman bore child after child, five of them—all girls.

I did my best, keenly interested as I have always been in sociology and social psychology, to reconstruct in my mind the real position of these ancient women. There were some five or six hundred of them, and they were harem-bred; yet for the few preceding generations they had been reared in the atmosphere of such heroic struggle that the stock must have been toughened somewhat. Left alone in that terrific orphanhood, they had clung together, supporting one another and their little sisters, and developing unknown powers in the stress of new necessity. To this pain-hardened and work-strengthened group, who had lost not only the love and care of parents, but the hope of ever having children of their own, there now dawned the new hope.

Here at last was Motherhood, and though it was not for all of them personally, it might—if the Power was inherited—found here a new race.

It may be imagined how those five Daughters of Maaia, Children of the Temple, Mothers of the Future—they had all the titles that love and hope and reverence could give—were reared. The whole little nation of women surrounded them with loving service, and waited, between a boundless hope and an as boundless despair, to see if they too would be Mothers.

And they were! As fast as they reached the age of twenty-five they began bearing. Each of them, like her mother, bore five daughters. Presently there were twenty-five New Women, Mothers in their own right, and the whole spirit of the country changed from mourning and mere courageous resignation, to proud joy. The older women, those who remembered men, died off; the youngest of all the first lot of course died too, after a while, and by that time there were left one hundred and fifty-five parthenogenetic women, founding a new race.

They inherited all that the devoted care of that declining band of original ones could leave them. Their little country was quite safe. Their farms and gardens were all in full production. Such industries as they had were in careful order. The records of their past were all preserved, and for years the older women had spent their

---

1 In Greek mythology, Maia is the mother of Hermes; the playwright Aeschylus conflated Maia with Gaia, Mother Earth, who gave birth to the sky and sea through parthenogenesis. In Roman mythology, Maia is the goddess of spring, after whom the month of May is named.

time in the best teaching they were capable of, that they might leave to the little group of sisters and mothers all they possessed of skill and knowledge.

There you have the start of Herland! One family, all descended from one mother! She lived to be a hundred years old; lived to see her hundred and twenty-five great-granddaughters born; live[d] as Queen-Priestess-Mother of them all; and died with a nobler pride and a fuller joy than perhaps any human soul has ever known—she alone had founded a new race!

The first five daughters had grown up in an atmosphere of holy calm, of awed watchful waiting, of breathless prayer. To them the longed-for Motherhood was not only a personal joy, but a nation's hope. Their twenty-five daughters in turn, with a stronger hope, a richer, wider outlook, with the devoted love and care of all the surviving population, grew up as a holy sisterhood, their whole ardent youth looking forward to their great office. And at last they were left alone; the white-haired First Mother was gone, and this one family, five sisters, twenty-five first cousins, and a hundred and twenty-five second cousins, began a new race.

Here you have human beings, unquestionably, but what we were slow in understanding was how these ultra-women, inheriting only from women, had eliminated not only certain masculine characteristics, which of course we did not look for; but so much of what we had always thought essentially feminine.

The tradition of men as guardians and protectors had quite died out. These stalwart virgins had no men to fear and therefore no need of protection. As to wild beasts—there were none in their sheltered land.

The power of mother-love, that maternal instinct we so highly laud, was theirs of course, raised to its highest power; and a sister-love which, even while recognizing the actual relationship, we found it hard to credit.

Terry, incredulous, even contemptuous, when we were alone, refused to believe the story. "A lot of traditions as old as Herodotus[1]—and about as trustworthy!" he said. "It's likely women—just a pack of women—would have hung together like that! We all know women can't organize—that they scrap like anything—are frightfully jealous."

"But these New Ladies didn't have anyone to be jealous of, remember," drawled Jeff.

---

1   Greek historian (c. 480–c. 425 BCE), often called the "Father of History," but also criticized for bias, exaggeration, and plagiarism. His *Histories* include accounts of the woman warriors called Amazons.

"That's a likely story," Terry sneered.

"Why don't you invent a likelier one?" I asked him. "Here *are* the women—nothing but women, and you admit yourself there's no trace of a man in the country." This was after we had been about a good deal.

"I'll admit that," he growled. "And it's a big miss, too. There's not only no fun without 'em—no real sport—no competition; but these women aren't *womanly*. You know they aren't."

That kind of talk always set Jeff going; and I gradually grew to side with him. "Then you don't call a breed of women whose one concern is Motherhood—womanly?" he asked.

"Indeed I don't," snapped Terry. "What does a man care for motherhood—when he hasn't a ghost of a chance at fatherhood? And besides—what's the good of talking sentiment when we are just men together? What a man wants of women is a good deal more than all this 'motherhood!'"

We were as patient as possible with Terry. He had lived about nine months among the Colonels when he made that outburst; and with no chance at any more strenuous excitement than our gymnastics gave us—save for our escape fiasco. I don't suppose Terry had ever lived so long with neither Love, Combat, or Danger to employ his superabundant energies, and he was irritable. Neither Jeff nor I found it so wearing. I was so much interested intellectually that our confinement did not wear on me; and as for Jeff, bless his heart!—he enjoyed the society of that tutor of his almost as much as if she had been a girl—I don't know but more.

As to Terry's criticism, it was true. These women, whose essential distinction of Motherhood was the dominant note of their whole culture, were strikingly deficient in what we call "femininity." This led me very promptly to the conviction that those "feminine charms" we are so fond of are not feminine at all, but mere reflected masculinity—developed to please us because they had to please us—and in no way essential to the real fulfillment of their great process. But Terry came to no such conclusion.

"Just you wait till I get out!" he muttered.

Then we both cautioned him. "Look here, Terry, my boy! You be careful! They've been mighty good to us—but do you remember the anaesthesia? If you do any mischief in this virgin land, beware of the vengeance of the Maiden Aunts! Come, be a man! It won't be forever."

To return to the history:

They began at once to plan and build for their children, all the strength and intelligence of the whole of them devoted to that one thing. Each girl, of course, was reared in full knowledge of her Crowning Office, and they had, even then, very high ideas of the moulding powers of the mother, as well as those of education.

Such high ideals as they had! Beauty, Health, Strength, Intellect, Goodness—for these they prayed and worked.

They had no enemies; they themselves were all sisters and friends; the land was fair before them,[1] and a great Future began to form itself in their minds.

The religion they had to begin with was much like that of old Greece,—a number of gods and goddesses; but they lost all interest in deities of war and plunder, and gradually centered on their Mother Goddess altogether. Then, as they grew more intelligent, this had turned into a sort of Maternal Pantheism.

Here was Mother Earth, bearing fruit. All that they ate was fruit of motherhood, from seed or egg or their product. By motherhood they were born and by motherhood they lived—life was, to them, just the long cycle of motherhood.

But very early they recognized the need of improvement as well as of mere repetition, and devoted their combined intelligence to that problem—how to make the best kind of people. First this was merely the hope of bearing better ones, and then they recognized that however the children differed at birth, the real growth lay later—through education.

Then things began to hum.

As I learned more and more to appreciate what these women had accomplished, the less proud I was of what we, with all our manhood, had done.

You see, they had had no wars. They had had no kings, and no priests, and no aristocracies. They were sisters, and as they grew, they grew together; not by competition, but by united action.

We tried to put in a good word for competition, and they were keenly interested. Indeed we soon found, from their earnest questions of us, that they were prepared to believe our world must be better than theirs. They were not sure; they wanted to know; but there was no such arrogance about them as might have been expected.

---

1   Compare Milton's description of Adam and Eve's exit from Eden in
    Paradise Lost: "The World was all before them, where to choose / Their
    place of rest, and Providence their guide" (12.646–47).

We rather spread ourselves, telling of the advantages of competition; how it developed fine qualities; that without it there would be "no stimulus to industry." Terry was very strong on that point.

"No stimulus to industry," they repeated, with that puzzled look we had learned to know so well. "*Stimulus? To Industry?* But don't you *like* to work?"

"No man would work unless he had to," Terry declared.

"Oh, no *man!* You mean that is one of your sex distinctions?"

"No, indeed!" he said hastily. "No one, I mean, man or woman, would work without incentive. Competition is the—the motor power, you see."

"It is not with us," they explained gently, "so it is hard for us to understand. Do you mean, for instance, that with you no mother would work for her children without the stimulus of competition?"

No, he admitted that he did not mean that. Mothers, he supposed, would of course work for their children in the home; but the world's work was different—that had to be done by men, and required the competitive element.

All our teachers were eagerly interested.

"We want so much to know—you have the whole world to tell us of, and we have only our little land! And there are two of you—the two sexes—to love and help one another. It must be a rich and wonderful world. Tell us—what is the work of the world, that men do—which we have not here?"

"Oh, everything," Terry said, grandly. "The men do everything, with us." He squared his broad shoulders and lifted his chest. "We do not allow our women to work. Women are loved—idolized—honored—kept in the home to care for the children."

"What is 'the home'?" asked Somel a little wistfully.

But Zava begged: "Tell me first, do *no* women work, really?"

"Why, yes," Terry admitted. "Some have to, of the poorer sort."

"About how many—in your country?"

"About seven or eight million," said Jeff, as mischievous as ever.

Chapter VI

Comparisons Are Odious[1]

I had always been proud of my country, of course. Everyone is. Compared with the other lands and other races I knew, the United States of America had always seemed to me, speaking modestly, as good as the best of them.

But just as a clear-eyed, intelligent, perfectly honest and well-meaning child will frequently jar one's self-esteem by innocent questions, so did these women, without the slightest appearance of malice or satire, continually bring up points of discussion which we spent our best efforts in evading.

Now that we were fairly proficient in their language, had read a lot about their history, and had given them the general outlines of ours, they were able to press their questions closer.

So when Jeff admitted the number of "women wage earners" we had, they instantly asked for the total population, for the proportion of adult women, and found that there were but twenty million or so at the outside.

"Then at least a third of your women are—what is it you call them—wage earners? And they are all *poor*. What is *poor*, exactly?"

"Ours is the best country in the world as to poverty," Terry told them. "We do not have the wretched paupers and beggars of the older countries, I assure you. Why, European visitors tell us we don't know what poverty is."

"Neither do we," answered Zava. "Won't you tell us?"

Terry put it up to me, saying I was the sociologist, and I explained that the laws of nature require a struggle for existence, and that in the struggle the fittest survive, and the unfit perish.[2] In our economic struggle, I continued, there was always plenty of opportunity for the fittest to reach the top, which they did, in great numbers, particularly in our country; that where there was severe economic pressure the lowest classes of course felt it the worst,

---

1 Synopsis from original edition: Three young men discover an unknown country in which there are only women, by whom they are presently captured. Their attempted escape. They learn the history of the country. What happened to the men and how the women became parthenogenetic.

2 A summary of Charles Darwin's theory of evolution in *On the Origin of Species*, using several of Darwin's phrases. The sentences that follow summarize common social Darwinist applications to economics of Darwin's biological theories.

and that among the poorest of all the women were driven into the labor market by necessity.

They listened closely, with the usual note-taking.

"About one-third, then, belong to the poorest class," observed Moadine gravely. "And two-thirds are the ones who are—how was it you so beautifully put it?—'loved, honored, kept in the home to care for the children.' This inferior one-third have no children, I suppose?"

Jeff—he was getting as bad as they were—solemnly replied that, on the contrary, the poorer they were the more children they had. That too, he explained, was a law of nature: "Reproduction is in inverse proportion to individuation."[1]

"These 'laws of nature,'" Zava gently asked, "are they all the laws you have?"

"I should say not!" protested Terry. "We have systems of law that go back thousands and thousands of years—just as you do, no doubt," he finished politely.

"Oh no," Moadine told him. "We have no laws over a hundred years old, and most of them are under twenty. In a few weeks more," she continued, "we are going to have the pleasure of showing you over our little land, and explaining everything you care to know about. We want you to see our people."

"And I assure you," Somel added, "that our people want to see you."

Terry brightened up immensely at this news, and reconciled himself to the renewed demands upon our capacity as teachers. It was lucky that we knew so little, really, and had no books to refer to, else I fancy we might all be there yet, teaching those eager-minded women about the rest of the world.

I'd better try to give a little synopsis of what part of the world knowledge they had developed, and what they had not. The wonder was that they knew so much.

As to geography, they had the tradition of the Great Sea, beyond the mountains; and they could see for themselves the endless thick-forested plains below them—that was all. But from the few records of their ancient condition—not "before the flood" with them, but before that mighty quake which had cut them off so completely—they were aware that there were other peoples and other countries.

In geology they were quite ignorant.

---

1 This idea is argued by social Darwinist Herbert Spencer (1820–1903) in *A Theory of Population* (1852).

As to anthropology, they had those same remnants of information about other peoples, and the knowledge of the savagery of the occupants of those dim forests below. Nevertheless they had inferred (marvelously keen on inference and deduction their minds were!) the existence and development of civilization in other places, much as we infer it on other planets.

When our biplane came whirring over their heads in that first scouting flight of ours, they had instantly accepted it as proof of the high development of Some Where Else, and had prepared to receive us as cautiously and eagerly as we might prepare to welcome visitors who came "by meteor" from Mars.

Of history—outside their own—they knew nothing, of course, save for their ancient traditions.

Of astronomy they had a fair working knowledge—that is a very old science; and with it, a surprising range and facility in mathematics.

Physiology they were quite familiar with. Indeed when it came to the simpler and more concrete sciences, wherein the subject matter was at hand and they had but to exercise their minds upon it, the results were surprising. They had worked out a chemistry, a botany, a physics, with all the blends where a science touches an art, or merges into an industry, to such fullness of knowledge as made us feel like school children.

Also we found this out, as soon as we were free of the country, and by further study and question—that what one knew, all knew, to a very considerable extent.

I talked later with little mountain girls from the fir-dark valleys away up at their highest part, and with sunburned plainswomen, and agile foresters, all over the country, as well as those in the towns, and everywhere there was the same high level of intelligence. Some knew far more than others about one thing— they were specialized of course; but all of them knew more about everything—that is about everything the country was acquainted with—than is the case with us.

We boast a good deal of our "high level of general intelligence" and our "compulsory public education," but in proportion to their opportunities they were far better educated than our people.

With what we told them, from what sketches and models we were able to prepare, they constructed a sort of working outline to fill in as they learned more.

A big globe was made, and our uncertain maps, helped out by those in that precious year-book thing I had, were tentatively indicated upon it.

They sat in eager groups, masses of them who came for the purpose, and listened while Jeff roughly ran over the geologic history of the earth, and showed them their own land in relation to the others. Out of that same pocket reference book of mine came facts and figures which were seized upon and placed in right relation with unerring acumen.

Even Terry grew interested in this work. "If we can keep this up they'll be having us lecture to all the girls' schools and colleges—how about that?" he suggested to us. "Don't know as I'd object to being an Authority to such audiences."

They did, in fact, urge us to give public lectures later, but not to the hearers or with the purpose we expected.

What they were doing with us was like—like—well, say like Napoleon extracting military information from a few illiterate peasants. They knew just what to ask, and just what use to make of it; they had mechanical appliances for disseminating information almost equal to ours at home; and by the time we were led forth to lecture our audiences had thoroughly mastered a well arranged digest of all we had previously given to our teachers, and were prepared with such notes and questions as might have intimidated a University Professor.

They were not audiences of girls either. It was some time before we were allowed to meet the young women.

★ ★ ★ ★ ★

"Do you mind telling what you intend to do with us?" Terry burst forth one day, facing the calm and friendly Moadine with that funny half-blustering air of his. At first he used to storm and flourish quite a good deal, but nothing seemed to amuse them more; they would gather around and watch him as if it was an exhibition, politely, but with evident interest. So he learned to check himself, and was almost reasonable in his bearing—not quite.

She announced smoothly and evenly: "Not in the least. I thought it was quite plain. We are trying to learn of you all we can, and to teach you what you are willing to learn of our country."

"Is that all?" he insisted.

She smiled a quiet enigmatic smile: "That depends."

"Depends on what?"

"Mainly on yourselves," she replied.

"Why do you keep us shut up so closely?"

"Because we do not feel quite safe in allowing you at large where there are so many young women."

Terry was really pleased at that. He had thought as much, inwardly; but he pushed the question. "Why should you be afraid? We are gentlemen."

She smiled that little smile again, and asked: "Are 'gentlemen' always safe?"

"You surely do not think that any of us," he said it with a good deal of emphasis on the "us," "would hurt your young girls?"

"Oh no," she said quickly, in real surprise. "The danger is quite the other way. They might hurt you. If, by any accident, you did harm any one of us, you would have to face a million mothers."

He looked so amazed and outraged that Jeff and I laughed outright, but she went on gently.

"I do not think you quite understand yet. You are but men, three men, in a country where the whole population are mothers—or are going to be. Motherhood means to us something which I cannot yet discover in any of the countries of which you tell us. You have spoken"—she turned to Jeff, "of Human Brotherhood as a great idea among you, but even that I judge is far from a practical expression?"

Jeff nodded rather sadly. "Very far—" he said.

"Here we have Human Motherhood—in full working use," she went on. "Nothing else except the literal sisterhood of our origin, and the far higher and deeper union of our social growth.

"The children in this country are the one center and focus of all our thoughts. Every step of our advance is always considered in its effect on them—on the race. You see we are *Mothers*," she repeated, as if in that she had said it all.

"I don't see how that fact—which is shared by all women—constitutes any risk to us," Terry persisted. "You mean they would defend their children from attack. Of course. Any mothers would. But we are not Savages, my dear Lady; we are not going to hurt any mother's child."

They looked at one another and shook their heads a little, but Zava turned to Jeff and urged him to make us see—said he seemed to understand more fully than we did. And he tried.

I can see it now, or at least much more of it, but it has taken me a long time, and a good deal of honest intellectual effort.

What they call Motherhood was like this:

They began with a really high degree of social development, something like that of Ancient Egypt or Greece. Then they suffered the loss of everything masculine, and supposed at first that all human power and safety had gone too. Then they developed this virgin birth capacity. Then, since the prosperity of their children depended on it, the fullest and subtlest co-ordination began to be practised.

I remember how long Terry baulked at the evident unanimity of these women—the most conspicuous feature of their whole culture. "It's impossible!" he would insist. "Women cannot cooperate—it's against nature."

When we urged the obvious facts he would say: "Fiddlesticks!" or "Hang your facts—I tell you it can't be done!" And we never succeeded in shutting him up till Jeff dragged in the hymenoptera.[1]

"'Go to the ant, thou sluggard'[2]—and learn something," he said triumphantly. "Don't they co-operate pretty well? You can't beat it. This place is just like an enormous ant-hill—you know an ant-hill is nothing but a nursery. And how about bees? Don't they manage to co-operate and love one another?

'As the birds do love the Spring,
Or the bees their careful king,'

as that precious Constable had it.[3] Just show me a combination of male creatures, bird, bug or beast, that works as well, will you? Or one of our masculine countries where the people work together as well as they do here! I tell you, women are the natural co-operators, not men!"

Terry had to learn a good many things he did not want to.

To go back to my little analysis of what happened:—

They developed all this close inter-service in the interests of their children. To do the best work they had to specialize of course; the children needed spinners and weavers, farmers and gardeners, carpenters and masons, as well as mothers.

---

1 Large order of insects that includes bees and ants, as well as wasps and sawflies. Many have evolved complex social systems with division of labor.

2 "Go to the ant, thou sluggard; consider her ways, and be wise." Proverbs 6:6. Compare the story "Bee Wise" in this collection.

3 Henry Constable (1562–1613). The lines are from "Damelus' Song to Diaphenia":

Diaphenia like to all things blessèd,
When all thy praises are expressèd,
Dear joy, how I do love thee!
As the birds do love the spring:
Or the bees their careful king,
Then in requite, sweet virgin, love me!

Then came the filling up of the place. When a population multiplies by five every thirty years it soon reaches the limits of a country, especially a small one like this. They very soon eliminated all the grazing cattle—sheep were the last to go, I believe. Also they worked out a system of intensive agriculture surpassing anything I ever heard of, with the very forests all reset with fruit or nut-bearing trees.

Do what they would, however, there soon came a time when they were confronted with the problem of "the pressure of population"[1] in an acute form. There was really crowding, and with it, unavoidably, a decline in standards.

And how did those women meet it?

Not by a "struggle for existence" which would result in an everlasting writhing mass of underbred people trying to get ahead of one another; some few on top, temporarily; many constantly crushed out underneath, a hopeless substratum of paupers and degenerates, and no serenity or peace for anyone—no possibility for really noble qualities among the people at large.

Neither did they start off in predatory excursions to get more land from somebody else, or to get more food from somebody else, to maintain their struggling mass.

Not at all. They sat down in council together and thought it out. Very clear strong thinkers they were. They said: "With our best endeavors this country will support about so many people, with the standard of peace, comfort, health, beauty and progress we demand. Very well. That is all the people we will make."

★　★　★　★　★

There you have it. You see they were Mothers, not in our sense of helpless involuntary fecundity, forced to fill and overfill the land, every land, and then see their children suffer, sin, and die, fighting horribly with one another; but in the sense of Conscious Makers of People. Mother love with them was not a brute passion, a mere "instinct," a wholly personal feeling; it was—A Religion.

---

1 "The misery and vice arising from the pressure of the population too hard against the limits of subsistence, and the misery and vice arising from promiscuous intercourse, may be considered as the Scylla and Charybdis of human life." Thomas Malthus (1766–1834), *An Essay on the Principle of Population* (1798). In Greek mythology, notably Book 12 of *The Odyssey*, Scylla and Charybdis are a pair of dangerous monsters on either side of a narrow strait. The expression "between Scylla and Charybdis" refers to a choice between two equally bad alternatives.

It included that limitless feeling of sisterhood, that wide unity in service which was so difficult for us to grasp. And it was National, Racial, Human—Oh, I don't know how to say it.

We are used to seeing what we call "a mother" completely wrapped up in her own pink bundle of fascinating babyhood, and taking but the faintest theoretic interest in anybody else's bundle, to say nothing of the common needs of *all* the bundles. But these women were working all together at the grandest of tasks—they were Making People—and they made them well.

There followed a period of "negative Eugenics" which must have been an appalling sacrifice. We are commonly willing to "lay down our lives" for our country, but they had to forego Motherhood for their country—and it was precisely the hardest thing for them to do.

When I got this far in my reading I went to Somel for more light. We were as friendly by that time as I had ever been in my life with any woman. A mighty comfortable soul she was, giving one the nice smooth mother-feeling a man likes in a woman, and yet giving also the clear intelligence and dependableness I used to assume to be masculine qualities. We had talked volumes already.

"See here," said I. "Here was this dreadful period when they got far too thick, and decided to limit the population. We have a lot of talk about that among us but your position is so different that I'd like to know a little more about it.

"I understand that you make Motherhood the highest Social Service—a Sacrament, really; that it is only undertaken once, by the majority of the population; that those held unfit are not allowed even that; and that to be encouraged to bear more than one child is the very highest Reward and Honor in the power of the State."

(She interpolated here that the nearest approach to an aristocracy they had was to come of a line of "Over Mothers"—those who had been so honored.)

"But what I do not understand, naturally, is how you prevent it. I gathered that each woman had five. You have no tyrannical husbands to hold in check—and you surely do not destroy the unborn—"

The look of ghastly horror she gave me I shall never forget. She started from her chair, pale, her eyes blazing.

"Destroy the unborn—!" she said in a hard whisper. "Do men do that in your country?"

"Men!" I began to answer, rather hotly, and then saw the gulf before me. None of us wanted these women to think that *our* women, of whom we boasted so proudly, were in any way inferior to them. I am ashamed to say that I equivocated. I told her about Malthus[1] and his fears. I told her of certain criminal types of women—perverts, or crazy, who had been known to commit infanticide. I told her, truly enough, that there was much in our land which was open to criticism, but that I hated to dwell on our defects until they understood us and our conditions better.

And, making a wide detour, I scrambled back to my question of how they limited the population.

As for Somel, she seemed sorry, a little ashamed even, of her too clearly expressed amazement. As I look back now, knowing them better, I am more and more and more amazed as I appreciate the exquisite courtesy with which they had received over and over again statements and admissions on our part which must have revolted them to the soul.

She explained to me, with sweet seriousness, that as I had supposed, at first each woman bore five children; and that, in their eager desire to build up a nation, they had gone on in that way for a few centuries, till they were confronted with the absolute need of a limit. This fact was equally plain to all—all were equally interested.

They were now as anxious to check their wonderful power as they had been to develop it; and for some generations gave the matter their most earnest thought and study.

"We were living on rations before we worked it out," she said. "But we did work it out. You see, before a child comes to one of us there is a period of utter exaltation—the whole being is uplifted and filled with a concentrated desire for that child. We learned to look forward to that period with the greatest caution. Often our young women, those to whom motherhood had not yet come, would voluntarily defer it. When that deep inner demand for a child began to be felt she would deliberately engage in the most active work, physical and mental; and even more important, would solace her longing by the direct care and service of the babies we already had."

---

1 Thomas R. Malthus argued in *An Essay on the Principle of Population* that because human population grows at a greater rate than the food supply, overpopulation is inevitable; famine, disease, and war are therefore both inevitable and necessary. Attempting to avoid poverty by increasing income or agricultural productivity will only be offset by increased population. In the late nineteenth century, Neo-Malthusians formed organizations to promote contraception.

She paused. Her wise sweet face grew deeply, reverently tender.

"We soon grew to see that mother love has more than one channel of expression. I think the reason our children are so—so fully loved, by all of us, is that we never—any of us—have enough of our own."

This seemed to me infinitely pathetic, and I said so. "We have much that is bitter and hard in our life at home," I told her, "but this seems to me piteous beyond words,—a whole nation of starving mothers!"

But she smiled her deep contented smile, and said I quite misunderstood.

"We each go without a certain range of personal joy," she said, "but remember—we each have a million children to love and serve—*our* children."

It was beyond me. To hear a lot of women talk about "our children"! But I suppose that is the way the ants and bees would talk—do talk, maybe.

That was what they did, anyhow.

When a woman chose to be a mother, she allowed the child-longing to grow within her till it worked its natural miracle. When she did not so choose she put the whole thing out of her mind, and fed her heart with the other babies.

Let me see—with us, children—minors, that is—constitute about three-fifths of the population; with them only about one-third, or less. And precious—! No sole heir to an Empire's throne, no solitary millionaire-baby, no only child of middle-aged parents, could compare as an idol with these Herland Children.

But before I start on that subject I must finish up that little analysis I was trying to make.

They did effectually and permanently limit the population, in numbers, so that the country furnished plenty for the fullest, richest life for all of them; plenty of everything, including room, air, solitude even.

And then they set to work to improve that population in quality—since they were restricted in quantity. This they had been at work on, uninterruptedly, for some fifteen hundred years. Do you wonder they were nice people?

Physiology, hygiene, sanitation, physical culture—all that line of work had been perfected long since. Sickness was almost wholly unknown among them, so much so that a previously high development in what we call the "science of medicine" had become practically a lost art. They were a clean-bred, vigorous lot, having the best of care, the most perfect living conditions always.

When it came to psychology—there was no one thing which left us so dumbfounded, so really awed, as the everyday working knowledge—and practice—they had in this line. As we learned more and more of it, we learned to appreciate the exquisite mastery with which we ourselves, strangers of alien race, of unknown opposite sex, had been understood and provided for from the first.

With this wide, deep, thorough knowledge, they had met and solved the problems of education in ways some of which I hope to make clear later. Those nation-loved children of theirs compared with the average in our country as the most perfectly cultivated richly developed roses compare with—tumbleweeds. Yet they did not *seem* "cultivated" at all—it had all become a natural condition.

And this people, steadily developing in mental capacity, in will-power, in social devotion, had been playing with the arts and sciences—as far as they knew them, for a good many centuries now with inevitable success.

Into this quiet lovely land, among these wise, sweet, strong women, we in our easy assumption of superiority, had suddenly arrived; and now, tamed and trained to a degree they considered safe, we were at last brought out to see the country, to know the people.

Chapter VII[1]

Our Growing Modesty

Being at last considered sufficiently tamed and trained to be trusted with scissors, we barbered ourselves as best we could. A close-trimmed beard is certainly more comfortable than a full one. Razors, naturally, they could not supply.

"With so many old women you'd think there'd be some razors," sneered Terry. Whereat Jeff pointed out that he never before had seen such complete absence of facial hair on women.

"Looks to me as if the absence of men made them more feminine in that regard, anyhow," he suggested.

"Well, it's the only one then," Terry reluctantly agreed. "A less feminine lot I never saw. A child apiece don't seem to be enough to develop what I call motherliness."

---

1 Synopsis from original edition: Three young men discover an unknown country in which there are only women, by whom they are presently captured. Their attempted escape. They learn the history of the country, what happened to the men, how the women became parthenogenetic, and how they limited the population.

Terry's idea of motherliness was the usual one, involving a baby in arms, or "a little flock about her knees," and the complete absorption of the mother in said baby or flock. A motherliness which dominated society, which influenced every art and industry, which absolutely protected all childhood, and gave to it the most perfect care and training, did not seem motherly—to Terry.

We had become well used to the clothes. They were quite as comfortable as our own; in some ways more so; and undeniably better looking. As to pockets they left nothing to be desired. That second garment was fairly quilted with pockets. They were most ingeniously arranged, so as to be convenient to the hand, and not inconvenient to the body, and were so placed as at once to strengthen the garment and add decorative lines of stitching.

In this, as in so many other points we had now to observe, there was shown the action of a practical intelligence, coupled with fine artistic feeling, and, apparently, untrammeled by any injurious influences.

Our first step of comparative freedom was a personally conducted tour of the country. No pentagonal bodyguard now! Only our special tutors, and we got on famously with them. Jeff said he loved Zava like an aunt—"only jollier than any aunt I ever saw"; Somel and I were as chummy as could be—the best of friends; but it was funny to watch Terry and Moadine. She was patient with him, and courteous, but it was like the patience and courtesy of some great man, say a skilled, experienced diplomat, with a schoolgirl. Her grave acquiescence with his most preposterous expression of feeling; her genial laughter, not only with, but I often felt, at him—though impeccably polite; her innocent questions, which almost invariably led him to say more than he intended—Jeff and I found it all amusing to watch.

He never seemed to recognize that quiet background of superiority. When she dropped an argument he always thought he had silenced her; when she laughed he thought it tribute to his wit.

I hated to admit to myself how much Terry had sunk in my esteem. Jeff felt it too, I am sure; but neither of us admitted it to the other. At home we had measured him with other men, and, though we knew his failings, he was by no means an unusual type. We knew his virtues too, and they had always seemed more prominent than the faults. Measured among women—our women at home, I mean—he had always stood high. He was visibly popular. Even where his habits were known there was no discrimination against him; in some cases his reputation for what was felicitously termed "gaiety" seemed a special charm.

But here, against the calm wisdom and quiet restrained humor of these women, with only that blessed Jeff and my inconspicuous self to compare with, Terry did stand out rather strong.

As "a man among men," he didn't; as a man among—I shall have to say, "females," he didn't; his intense masculinity seemed only fit complement to their intense femininity. But here he was all out of drawing.

Moadine was a big woman, with a balanced strength that seldom showed. Her eye was as quietly watchful as a fencer's. She maintained a pleasant relation with her charge, but I doubt if many, even in that country, could have done as well.

He called her "Maud," between ourselves, and said she was "a good old soul, but a little slow"; wherein he was quite wrong. Needless to say he called Jeff's teacher "Java," and sometimes "Mocha," or plain "Coffee"; when specially mischievous, "Chicory," and even "Postum." But Somel rather escaped this form of humor, save for a rather forced "Some 'ell."

"Don't you people have but one name?" he asked one day, after we had been introduced to a whole group of them, all with pleasant, few-syllabled strange names, like the ones we knew.

"Oh yes," Moadine told him. "A good many of us have another, as we get on in life—a descriptive one. That is the name we earn. Sometimes even that is changed, or added to, in an unusually rich life. Such as our present Land-Mother—what you call President or King, I believe. She was called Mera, even as a child; that means 'thinker.' Later there was added Du—Du-Mera—the wise thinker, and now we all know her as O-du-mera—great and wise thinker. You shall meet her."

"No surnames at all then?" pursued Terry, with his somewhat patronizing air. "No family name?"

"Why no," she said. "Why should we? We are all descended from a common source—all one 'family' in reality. You see our comparatively brief and limited history gives us that advantage at least."

"But does not each mother want her own child to bear her name?" I asked.

"No—why should she? The child has its own."

"Why for—for identification—so people will know whose child she is."

"We keep the most careful records," said Somel. "Each one of us has our exact line of descent all the way back to our dear First Mother. There are many reasons for doing that. But as to every one knowing which child belongs to which mother—why should she?"

Here, as in so many other instances, we were led to feel the difference between the purely maternal and the paternal attitude of mind. The element of personal pride seemed strangely lacking.

"How about your other works?" asked Jeff. "Don't you sign your names to them—books and statues and so on?"

"Yes, surely, we are all glad and proud to. Not only books and statues, but all kinds of work. You will find little names on the houses, on the furniture, on the dishes sometimes. Because otherwise one is likely to forget, and we want to know to whom to be grateful."

"You speak as if it were done for the convenience of the consumer—not the pride of the producer," I suggested.

"It's both," said Somel. "We have pride enough in our work."

"Then why not in your children?" urged Jeff.

"But we have! We're magnificently proud of them," she insisted.

"Then why not sign 'em?" said Terry triumphantly.

Moadine turned to him with her slightly quizzical smile. "Because the finished product is not a private one. When they are babies, we do speak of them, at times, as 'Essa's Lato,' or 'Novine's Amel'; but that is merely descriptive and conversational. In the records, of course the child stands in her own line of mothers; but in dealing with it personally it is Lato, or Amel, without dragging in its ancestors."

"But have you names enough to give a new one to each child?"

"Assuredly we have, for each living generation."

Then they asked about our methods, and found first that "we" did so and so, and then that other nations did differently. Upon which they wanted to know which method has been proved best—and we had to admit that so far as we knew there had been no attempt at comparison, each people pursuing its own custom in the fond conviction of superiority, and either despising or quite ignoring the others.

With these women the most salient quality in all their institutions was reasonableness. When I dug into the records to follow out any line of development, that was the most astonishing thing—the conscious effort to make it better.

They had early observed the value of certain improvements; had easily inferred that there was room for more; and took the greatest pains to develop two kinds of minds—the critic and inventor. Those who showed an early tendency to observe, to discriminate, to suggest, were given special training for that function; and some of their highest officials spent their time in the most careful study of one or another branch of work, with a view to its further improvement.

In each generation there was sure to arrive some new mind to detect faults and show need of alterations; and the whole corps of inventors was at hand to apply their special faculty at the point criticized, and offer suggestions.

We had learned by this time not to open a discussion on any of their characteristics without first priming ourselves to answer questions about our own methods; so I kept rather quiet on this matter of conscious improvement. We were not prepared to show our way was better.

There was growing in our minds, at least in Jeff's and mine, a keen appreciation of the advantages of this strange country and its management. Terry remained critical. We laid most of it to his nerves. He certainly was irritable.

The most conspicuous feature of the whole land was the perfection of its food supply. We had begun to notice from that very first walk in the forest, the first partial view from our 'plane. Now we were taken to see this mighty garden, and shown its methods of culture.

The country was about the size of Holland, some ten or twelve thousand square miles. One could lose a good many Hollands along the forest-smothered flanks of those mighty mountains. They had a population of about three million—not a large one, but quality is something. Three million is quite enough to allow for considerable variation, and these people varied more widely than we could at first account for.

Terry had insisted that if they were parthenogenetic they'd be as alike as so many ants or aphids; he urged their visible differences as proof that there must be men—somewhere.

But when we asked them, in our later, more intimate conversations, how they accounted for so much divergence without cross fertilization, they attributed it partly to the careful education, which followed each slight tendency to differ, and partly to the law of mutation. This they had found in their work with plants, and fully proven in their own case.

Physically they were more alike than we, as they lacked all morbid or excessive types. They were tall, strong, healthy, and beautiful as a race, but differed individually in a wide range of feature, coloring and expression.

"But surely the most important growth is in mind—and in the things we make," urged Somel. "Do you find your physical variation accompanied by a proportionate variation in ideas, feelings, and products? Or, among people who look more alike, do you find their internal life and their work as similar?"

We were rather doubtful on this point, and inclined to hold that there was more chance of improvement in greater physical variation.

"It certainly should be," Zava admitted. "We have always thought it a grave initial misfortune to have lost half our little world. Perhaps that is one reason why we have so striven for conscious improvement."

"But acquired traits are not transmissible," Terry declared. "Weissman[1] has proved that."

They never disputed our absolute statements, only made notes of them.

"If that is so, then our improvement must be due either to mutation, or solely to education," she gravely pursued. "We certainly have improved. It may be that all these higher qualities were latent in the original mother; that careful education is bringing them out; and that our personal differences depend on slight variations in prenatal condition."

"I think it is more in your accumulated culture," Jeff suggested. "And in the amazing psychic growth you have made. We know very little about methods of real soul culture—and you seem to know a great deal."

Be that as it might, they certainly presented a higher level of active intelligence, and of behavior, than we had so far really grasped. Having known in our lives several people who showed the same delicate courtesy and were equally pleasant to live with, at least when they wore their "company manners," we had assumed that our companions were a carefully chosen few. Later we were more and more impressed that all this gentle breeding was breeding; that they were born to it, reared in it, that it was as natural and universal with them as the gentleness of doves or the alleged wisdom of serpents.

As for the intelligence, I confess that this was the most impressive and, to me, most mortifying, of any single feature of Herland. We soon ceased to comment on this or other matters which to them were such obvious commonplaces as to call forth embarrassing questions about our own conditions.

---

1   August Weissmann (1834–1914) was a German evolutionary biologist who conducted experiments to disprove the widely held belief that acquired characteristics are passed from parents to offspring.

This was nowhere better shown than in that matter of food supply, which I will now attempt to describe.

Having improved their agriculture to the highest point, and carefully estimated the number of persons who could comfortably live on their square miles; having then limited their population to that number, one would think that was all there was to be done; but they had not thought so. To them the country was a unit— it was Theirs. They themselves were a unit, a conscious group; they thought in terms of the community. As such their time-sense was not limited to the hopes and ambitions of an individual life. Therefore they habitually considered and carried out plans for improvement which might cover centuries.

I had never seen, had scarcely imagined, human beings undertaking such a work as the deliberate replanting of an entire forest area with different kinds of trees. Yet this seemed to them the simplest common-sense, like a man's plowing up an inferior lawn and reseeding it. Now every tree bore fruit—edible fruit, that is. In the case of one tree, in which they took especial pride, it had originally no fruit at all—that is, none humanly edible—yet was so beautiful that they wished to keep it. For nine hundred years they had experimented, and now showed us this particularly lovely graceful tree, with a profuse crop of nutritious seeds.

That trees were the best food plants they had early decided, requiring far less labor in tilling the soil, and bearing a larger amount of food for the same ground space; also doing much to preserve and enrich the soil.

Due regard had been paid to seasonable crops, and their fruit and nuts, grains and berries, kept on almost the year through.

On the higher part of the country, near the backing wall of mountains, they had a real winter with snow. Toward the southeastern point, where there was a large valley with a lake whose outlet was subterranean, the climate was like that of California, and citrus fruits, figs and olives grew abundantly.

What impressed me particularly was their scheme of fertilization. Here was this little shut-in piece of land where one would have thought an ordinary people would have been starved out long ago or reduced to an annual struggle for life. These careful culturists had worked out a perfect scheme of refeeding the soil with all that came out of it. All the scraps and leaving of their food; plant waste from lumber work or textile industry; all the solid matter from the sewage, properly treated and combined; everything which came from the earth went back to it.

The practical result was like that in any healthy forest; an increasingly valuable soil was being built, instead of the progressive impoverishment so often seen in the rest of the world.

When this first burst upon us we made such approving comments that they were surprised that such obvious commonsense should be praised; asked what our methods were; and we had some difficulty in—well, in diverting them, by referring to the extent of our own land, and the—admitted—carelessness with which we had skimmed the cream of it.

At least we thought we had diverted them. Later I found that besides keeping a careful and accurate account of all we told them, they had a sort of skeleton chart, on which the things we said and the things we palpably avoided saying were all set down and studied. It really was child's play for those profound educators to work out a painfully accurate estimate of our conditions—in some lines. When a given line of observation seemed to lead to some very dreadful inference they always gave us the benefit of the doubt, leaving it open to further knowledge. Some of the things we had grown to accept as perfectly natural, or as belonging to our human limitations, they literally could not have believed; and, as I have said, we had all of us joined in a tacit endeavor to conceal much of the social status at home.

"Confound their grandmotherly minds!" Terry said. "Of course they can't understand a Man's World! They aren't human—they're just a pack of Fe-Fe-Females!" This was after he had to admit their parthenogenesis.

"I wish our grandfatherly minds had managed as well," said Jeff. "Do you really think it's to our credit that we have muddled along with all our poverty and disease and the like? They have peace and plenty, wealth and beauty, goodness and intellect. Pretty good people, I think!"

"You'll find they have their faults too," Terry insisted; and partly in self defense, we all three began to look for those faults of theirs. We had been very strong on this subject before we got there—in those baseless speculations of ours.

"Suppose there are," Jeff would put it, over and over, "what'll they be like?"

And we had been cocksure as to the inevitable limitations, the faults and vices, of a lot of women. We had expected them to be given over to what we called "feminine vanity"—"frills and furbelows," and we found they had evolved a costume more perfect than the Chinese dress; richly beautiful when so desired, always useful, of unfailing dignity and good taste.

We had expected a dull submissive monotony, and found a daring social inventiveness far beyond our own, and a mechanical and scientific development fully equal to ours.

We had expected pettiness and found a social consciousness besides which our nations looked like quarreling children—feebleminded ones at that.

We had expected jealousy, and found a broad sisterly affection, a fair-minded intelligence, to which we could produce no parallel.

We had expected hysteria, and found a standard of health and vigor, a calmness of temper, to which the habit of profanity, for instance, was impossible to explain—we tried it.

All these things even Terry had to admit, but he still insisted that we should find out the other side pretty soon.

"It stands to reason, doesn't it?" he argued. "The whole thing's deuced unnatural—I'd say impossible if we weren't in it. And an unnatural condition's sure to have unnatural results. You'll find some awful characteristics—see if you don't! For instance—we don't know yet what they do with their criminals—their defectives—their aged. You notice we haven't seen any! There's got to be something!"

I was inclined to believe that there had to be something, so I took the bull by the horns—the cow, I should say!—and asked Somel.

"I want to find some flaw in all this perfection," I told her flatly. "It simply isn't possible that three million people have no faults. We are trying our best to understand and learn——would you mind helping us by saying what, to your minds, are the worst qualities of this unique civilization of yours?"

We were sitting together in a shaded arbor, in one of those eating-gardens of theirs. The delicious food had been eaten, a plate of fruit still before us. We could look out on one side over a stretch of open country, quietly rich and lovely; on the other the garden, with tables here and there, far apart enough for privacy. Let me say right here that with all their careful "balance of population" there was no crowding in this country. There was room, space, a sunny breezy freedom, everywhere.

Somel set her chin upon her hand; her elbow on the low wall beside her, and looked off over the fair land.

"Of course we have faults—all of us," she said. "In one way you might say that we have more than we used to—that is our standard of perfection seems to get farther and farther away. But we are not discouraged, because our records do show gain—considerable gain.

"When we began—even with the start of one particularly noble mother—we inherited the characteristics of a long race-record behind her. And they cropped out from time to time—alarmingly. But it is—yes, quite six hundred years since we have had what you call a 'criminal.'

"We have, of course, made it our first business to train out, to breed out, when possible, the lowest types."

"Breed out?" I asked. "How could you—with parthenogenesis?"

"If the girl showing the bad qualities had still the power to appreciate social duty, we appealed to her, by that, to renounce motherhood. Some of the few worst types were, fortunately, unable to reproduce. But if the fault was in a disproportionate egotism—then the girl was sure she had the right to have children; even that hers would be better than others."

"I can see that," I said. "And then she would be likely to rear them in the same spirit."

"That we never allowed," answered Somel quietly.

"Allowed?" I queried. "Allowed a mother to rear her own children?"

"Certainly not," said Somel, "unless she was fit for that supreme task."

This was rather a blow to my previous convictions.

"But I thought motherhood was for each of you——"

"Motherhood—yes, that is, maternity, to bear a child. But education is our highest art, only allowed to our highest artists."

"Education?" I was puzzled again. "I don't mean education. I mean by motherhood not only child-bearing, but the care of babies."

"The care of babies involves education, and is entrusted only to the most fit," she repeated.

"Then you separate mother and child!" I cried in cold horror, something of Terry's feeling creeping over me, that there must be something wrong among these many virtues.

"Not usually," she patiently explained. "You see almost every woman values her maternity above everything else. Each girl holds it close and dear, an exquisite joy, a crowning honor, the most intimate, most personal, most precious thing. That is the child-rearing has come to be with us a culture so profoundly studied, practised with such subtlety and skill, that the more we love our children the less we are willing to trust that process to unskilled hands—even our own."

"But a mother's love——" I ventured.

She studied my face, trying to work out a means of clear explanation.

"You told us about your dentists," she said, at length, "those quaintly specialized persons who spend their lives filling little holes in other persons' teeth—even in children's teeth sometimes."

"Yes?" I said, not getting her drift.

"Does mother-love urge mothers—with you—to fill their own children's teeth? Or to wish to?"

"Why no—of course not," I protested. "But that is a highly specialized craft. Surely the care of babies is open to any woman—any mother!"

"We do not think so," she gently replied. "Those of us who are the most highly competent fulfill that office; and a majority of our girls eagerly try for it—I assure you we have the very best."

"But the poor mother—bereaved of her baby——"

"Oh no!" she earnestly assured me. "Not in the least bereaved. It is her baby still—it is with her—she has not lost it. But she is not the only one to care for it. There are others whom she knows to be wiser. She knows it because she has studied as they did, practised as they did, and honors their real superiority. For the child's sake, she is glad to have for it this highest care."

I was unconvinced. Besides, this was only hearsay; I had yet to see the motherhood of Herland.

Chapter VIII

The Girls of Herland

At last Terry's ambition was realized. We were invited, always courteously and with free choice on our part, to address general audiences and classes of girls.

I remember the first time—and how careful we were about our clothes, and our amateur barbering. Terry, in particular, was fussy to a degree about the cut of his beard, and so critical of our combined efforts that we handed him the shears and told him to please himself. We began to rather prize those beards of ours, they were almost our sole distinction among those tall and sturdy women, with their cropped hair and sexless costume. Being offered a wide selection of garments, we had chosen according to our personal taste, and were surprised to find, on meeting large audiences, that we were the most highly decorated, especially Terry.

He was a very impressive figure, his strong features softened by the somewhat longer hair—though he made me trim it as closely as I knew how; and he wore his richly embroidered tunic with its broad, loose girdle, with quite a Henry V[1] air. Jeff looked more like—well, like a Huguenot Lover;[2] and I don't know what I looked like, only that I felt very comfortable. When I got back to our own padded armor and its starched borders I realized with acute regret how comfortable were those Herland clothes.

We scanned that audience, looking for the three bright faces we knew; but they were not to be seen. Just a multitude of girls; quiet, eager, watchful, all eyes and ears to listen and learn.

We had been urged to give, as fully as we cared to, a sort of synopsis of world history, in brief, and to answer questions.

"We are so utterly ignorant, you see," Moadine had explained to us. "We know nothing but such science as we have worked out for ourselves; just the brain work of one small half-country; and you, we gather, have helped one another all over the globe, sharing your discoveries, pooling your progress. How wonderful, how supremely beautiful, your civilization must be!"

Somel gave a further suggestion.

"You do not have to begin all over again, as you did with us. We have made a sort of digest of what we have learned from you, and it has been eagerly absorbed, all over the country. Perhaps you would like to see our outline——?"

We were eager to see it, and deeply impressed. To us, at first, these women, unavoidably ignorant of what to us was the basic commonplace of knowledge, had seemed on the plane of children, or of savages. What we had been forced to admit, with growing acquaintance, was that they were ignorant as Plato and Aristotle were, but with a highly developed mentality quite comparable to that of ancient Greece.

Far be it from me to lumber these pages with an account of what we so imperfectly strove to teach them. The memorable fact is what they taught us, or some faint glimpse of it. And at present, our major interest was not at all in the subject matter of our talk, but in the audience.

Girls—hundreds of them—eager, bright eyed, attentive young faces; crowding questions, and, I regret to say, an increasing inability on our part to answer them effectively.

---

1 King of England 1413–22, famous for leading his army to victory against the French at the Battle of Agincourt in 1415; and title character of a play by Shakespeare.

2 Huguenots were French Protestants of the sixteenth to eighteenth centuries who were driven from Catholic France in a series of persecutions. Possibly a reference to John Everett Millais's painting, *A Huguenot on St. Bartholomew's Day*.

Our special guides, who were on the platform with us, and sometimes aided in clarifying a question; or, oftener, an answer; noticed this effect, and closed the formal lecture part of the evening rather shortly.

"Our young women will be glad to meet you," Somel suggested, "to talk with you more personally, if you are willing?"

Willing! We were impatient and said as much, at which I saw a flickering little smile cross Moadine's face. Even then, with all those eager young things waiting to talk to us, a sudden question crossed my mind: "What was their point of view? What did they think of us?" We learned that later.

Terry plunged in among those young creatures with a sort of rapture; somewhat as a glad swimmer takes to the sea. Jeff, with a rapt look on his high-bred face, approached as to a sacrament. But I was a little chilled by that last thought of mine, and kept my eyes open. I found time to watch Jeff, even while I was surrounded by an eager group of questioners—as we all were—and saw how his worshipping eyes, his grave courtesy, pleased and drew some of them; while others, rather stronger spirits they looked to be, drew away from his group to Terry's or mine.

I watched Terry with special interest, knowing how he had longed for this time, and how irresistible he had always been at home. And I could see, just in snatches, of course, how his suave and masterful approach seemed to irritate them; his too intimate glances were vaguely resented, his compliments puzzled and annoyed. Sometimes a girl would flush, not with drooped eyelids and inviting timidity, but with anger and a quick lift of the head. Girl after girl turned on her heel and left him, till he had but a small ring of questioners, and they, visibly, were the least "girlish" of the lot.

I saw him looking pleased at first, as if he thought he was making a strong impression; but, finally, casting a look at Jeff, or me, he seemed less pleased—and less.

As for me, I was most agreeably surprised. At home I never was "popular." I had my girl friends, good ones, but they were friends—nothing else. Also they were of somewhat the same clan, not "popular" in the sense of swarming admirers. But here, to my astonishment, I found my crowd was the largest.

I have to generalize, of course, rather telescoping many impressions; but that first evening was a good sample of the impression we made. Jeff had a following, if I may call it that, of the more sentimental—though that's not the word I want. The less practical, perhaps; the girls who were artists of some sort, ethicists, teachers—that kind.

Terry was reduced to a rather combative group; keen, logical, inquiring minds; not over sensitive; the very kind he liked least; while, as for me—I became quite cocky over my general popularity.

Terry was furious about it. We could hardly blame him.

"Girls!" he burst forth, when that evening was over, and we were by ourselves once more. "Call those *girls!*"

"Most delightful girls, I call them," said Jeff, his blue eyes dreamily contented.

"What do *you* call them?" I mildly inquired.

"Boys! Nothing but boys, most of 'em. A stand-offish, disagreeable lot at that. Critical, impertinent youngsters. No girls at all."

He was angry and severe, not a little jealous, too, I think. Afterward, when he found out just what it was they did not like, he changed his manner somewhat and got on better. He had to. For, in spite of his criticism, they were girls, and, furthermore, all the girls there were! Always excepting our three!—with whom we presently renewed our acquaintance.

When it came to courtship, which it soon did, I can of course best describe my own—and am least inclined to. But of Jeff I heard somewhat; he was inclined to dwell reverently and admiringly, at some length, on the exalted sentiment and measureless perfection of his Celis; and Terry—Terry made so many false starts and met so many rebuffs, that by the time he really settled down to win Alima, he was considerably wiser. At that, it was not smooth sailing. They broke and quarreled, over and over; he would rush off to console himself with some other fair one—the other fair one would have none of him—and he would drift back to Alima, becoming more and more devoted each time.

She never gave an inch. A big, handsome creature, rather exceptionally strong even in that race of strong women; with a proud head and sweeping level brows that lined across above her dark eager eyes like the wide wings of a soaring hawk.

I was good friends with all three of them, but best of all with Ellador long before that feeling changed, for both of us.

From her, and from Somel, who talked very freely with me, I learned at last something of the viewpoint of Herland toward its visitors.

Here they were, isolated, happy, contented, when the booming buzz of our biplane tore the air above them.

Everybody heard it—saw it—for miles and miles; word flashed all over the country; and a council was held in every town and village.

And this was their rapid determination:

"From another country. Probably men. Evidently highly civilized. Doubtless possessed of much valuable knowledge. May be dangerous. Catch them if possible; tame and train them if necessary. This may be a chance to re-establish a bi-sexual state for our people."

They were not afraid of us—three million highly intelligent women—or two million, counting only grown-ups—were not likely to be afraid of three young men. We thought of them as "Women," and therefore timid; but it was two thousand years since they had had anything to be afraid of, and certainly more than one thousand since they had outgrown the feeling.

We thought—at least Terry did—that we could have our pick of them. They thought—very cautiously and farsightedly—of picking us, if it seemed wise.

All that time we were in training they studied us, analyzed us, prepared reports about us, and this information was widely disseminated all about the land.

Not a girl in that country who had not been learning for months as much as could be gathered about our country, our culture, our personal characters. No wonder their questions were hard to answer. But I am sorry to say, when we were at last brought out and—exhibited (I hate to call it that, but that's what it was), there was no rush of takers. Here was poor old Terry fondly imagining that at last he was free to stray in "a rosebud garden of girls"—and behold! the rosebuds were all with keen appraising eye, studying us.

They were interested, profoundly interested, but it was not the kind of interest we were looking for.

To get an idea of their attitude you have to hold in mind their extremely high sense of solidarity. They were not each choosing a lover, they had no faintest idea of love—sex-love, that is. These girls, to each of whom motherhood was a lode-star, and that motherhood exalted above a mere personal function, looked forward to as the highest social service, as the sacrament of a lifetime; were now confronted with an opportunity to make the great step of changing their whole status, of reverting to their earlier bi-sexual order of nature.

Beside this underlying consideration there was the limitless interest and curiosity in our civilization; purely impersonal; and held by an order of mind beside which we were like—schoolboys.

It was small wonder that our lectures were not a success; and none at all that our, or at least Terry's, advances were so ill received. The reason for my own comparative success was at first far from pleasing to my pride.

"We like you the best," Somel told me, "because you seem more like us."

"More like a lot of women!" I thought to myself disgustedly; and then remembered how little like "women," in our derogatory sense, they were. She was smiling at me, reading my thought.

"We can quite see that we do not seem like—women—to you; of course, in a bi-sexual race the distinctive feature of each sex must be intensified. But surely there are characteristics enough which belong to People, aren't there? That's what I mean about you being more like us—more like People. We feel at ease with you."

Jeff's difficulty was his exalted gallantry. He idealized women, and was always looking for a chance to "protect" or to "serve" them. These needed neither protection nor service. They were living in peace and power and plenty; we were their guests, their prisoners, absolutely dependent.

Of course we could promise whatsoever we might of advantages, if they would come to our country; but the more we knew of theirs, the less we boasted.

Terry's jewels and trinkets they prized as curios; handed them about, asking questions as to workmanship, not in the least as to value; and discussed not ownership, but which museum to put them in.

When a man has nothing to give a woman, is dependent wholly on his personal attraction, his courtship is under limitations.

They were considering these two things: the advisability of making the Great Change; and the degree of personal adaptability which would best serve that end.

Here we had the advantage of our small personal experience with those three fleet forest girls; and that served to draw us together.

As for Ellador: Suppose you come to a strange land and find it pleasant enough; just a little more than ordinarily pleasant; and then you find rich farmland, and then gardens, gorgeous gardens; and then palaces full of rare and curious treasures—incalculable, inexhaustible; and then—mountains—like the Himalayas; and then the sea.

I liked her that day she balanced on the branch before me and named the trio. I thought of her most. Afterward I turned to her like a friend when we met for the third time, and continued the acquaintance. While Jeff's ultra-devotion rather puzzled Celis, really put off their day of happiness; while Terry and Alima quarreled and parted—re-met and re-parted, Ellador and I grew to be close friends.

We talked and talked. We took long walks together. She showed me things, explained them, interpreted much that I had not understood. Through her sympathetic intelligence I became more and more comprehensive of the spirit of the people of Herland; more and more appreciative of its marvelous inner growth as well as outer perfection.

I ceased to feel a stranger, a prisoner. There was a sense of understanding, of identity of purpose. We discussed—everything. And, as I traveled farther and farther, exploring the rich, sweet soul of her, my sense of pleasant friendship became but a broad foundation for such height, such breadth, such interlocked combination of feeling, as left me fairly blinded with the wonder of it.

As I've said, I had never cared very much for women, nor they for me—not Terry-fashion. But this one——

At first I never even thought of her "in that way," as the girls have it. I had not come to the country with any Turkish-harem intentions; and I was no woman-worshipper like Jeff. I just liked that girl "as a friend," as we say. That friendship grew like a tree. She was *such* a good sport! We did all kinds of things together; she taught me games and I taught her games, and we raced and rowed and had all manner of fun, as well as higher comradeship.

Then, as I got on farther, the palace and treasures and snowy mountain ranges opened up. I had never known there could be such a human being. So—great. I don't mean talented. She was a forester—one of the best; but it was not that gift I mean. When I say *great*, I mean great—big, all through. If I had known more of those women, as intimately, I should not have found her so unique; but even among them she was noble. Her mother was an over-mother—and her grandmother, too, I heard later.

So she told me more and more of her beautiful land; and I told her as much, yes, more than I wanted to, about mine; and we became inseparable. Then this deeper recognition came and grew. I felt my own soul rise and lift its wings, as it were. Life got bigger. It seemed as if I understood—as I never had before—as if I could Do things—as if I too could grow—if she would help me. And then It came—to both of us, all at once.

A still day—on the edge of the world, their world. The two of us, gazing out over the far dim forest-land below, talking of heaven and earth and human life, and of my land and other lands and what they needed and what I hoped to do for them——

"If you will help me," I said.

She turned to me, with that high, sweet look of hers, and then, as her eyes rested in mine and her hands too—then suddenly there blazed out between us a farther glory, instant, overwhelming—quite beyond any words of mine to tell.

Celis was a blue-and-gold-and-rose person; Alima black-and-white-and-red, a blazing beauty. Ellador was brown; hair dark and soft, like a seal coat; clear brown skin with a healthy red in it; brown eyes—all the way from topaz to black velvet they seemed to range—splendid girls, all of them.

They had seen us first of all, far down in the lake below; and flashed the tidings across the land even before our first exploring flight. They had watched our landing, flitted through the forest with us, hidden in that tree and—I shrewdly suspect—giggled on purpose.

They had kept watch over our hooded machine, taking turns at it; and when our escape was announced, had followed along-side for a day or two, and been there at the last, as described. They felt a special claim on us—called us "their men"—and when we were at liberty to study the land and people, and be studied by them, their claim was recognized by the wise leaders.

But I felt, we all did, that we should have chosen them among millions, unerringly.

And yet, "the path of true love never did run smooth";[1] this period of courtship was full of the most unsuspected pitfalls.

Writing this as late as I do, after manifold experiences both in Herland and, later, in my own land, I can now understand and philosophize about what was then a continual astonishment and often a temporary tragedy.

The "long suit" in most courtships is sex attraction, of course. Then gradually develops such comradeship as the two temperaments allow. Then, after marriage, there is either the establishment of a slow-growing, widely-based friendship; the deepest, tenderest, sweetest of relations, all lit and warmed by the recurrent flame of love; or else that process is reversed, love cools and fades, no friendship grows, the whole relation turns from beauty to ashes.

Here everything was different. There was no sex-feeling to appeal to, or practically none. Two thousand years' disuse had left very little of the instinct; also we must remember that those who had at times manifested it as atavistic exceptions were often, by that very fact, denied motherhood.

---

1 Slightly misquoted from Shakespeare's *A Midsummer Night's Dream*, 1.1.134: "The course of true love never did run smooth."

Yet while the mother process remains, the inherent ground for sex-distinction remains also; and who shall say what long-forgotten feeling, vague and nameless, was stirred in some of these mother hearts by our arrival?

What left us even more at sea in our approach was the lack of any sex-tradition. There was no accepted standard of what was "manly" and what was "womanly."

When Jeff said, taking the fruit-basket from his adored one, "A woman should not carry anything," Celis said, "Why?" with the frankest amazement. He could not look that fleet-footed, deep-chested young forester in the face and say, "Because she is weaker." She wasn't. One does not call a race-horse weak because it is visibly not a cart horse.

He said, rather lamely, that women were not built for heavy work.

She looked out across the fields to where some women were working, building a new bit of wall, out of large stones; looked back at the nearest town with its woman-built houses; down at the smooth, hard road we were walking on; and then at the little basket he had taken from her.

"I don't understand," she said quite sweetly. "Are the women in your country so weak they could not carry such a thing as that?"

"It is a convention," he said. "We assume that motherhood is a sufficient burden—that men should carry all the others."

"What a beautiful feeling!" she said, her blue eyes shining.

"Does it work?" asked Alima, in her keen, swift way. "Do all men in all countries carry everything? Or is it only in yours?"

"Don't be so literal," Terry begged lazily. "Why aren't you willing to be worshipped and waited on? We like to do it."

"You don't like to have us do it to you," she answered.

"That's different," he said, annoyed; and when she said, "Why is it?" he quite sulked, referring her to me, saying,

"Van's the philosopher."

Ellador and I talked it all out together; so that we had an easier experience of it when the real miracle-time came. Also, between us, we made things clearer to Jeff and Celis. But Terry would not hear to reason.

He was madly in love with Alima. He wanted to take her by storm, and nearly lost her forever.

You see, if a man loves a girl who is in the first place young and inexperienced; who in the second place is educated with a background of cave-man tradition, a middle-ground of poetry and romance, and a foreground of unspoken hope and interest all centering upon the one Event; and who has, furthermore, absolutely no other hope or interest worthy of the name—why, it is a comparatively easy matter to sweep her off her feet by a dashing attack. Terry was a past master in this process. He tried it here, and Alima was so affronted, so repelled, that it was weeks before he got near enough to try again.

The more coldly she denied him, the hotter his determination; he was not used to real refusal. The approach of flattery she dismissed with laughter; gifts and such "attentions" we could not bring to bear; pathos and complaint of cruelty stirred only a reasoning inquiry. It took Terry a long time.

I doubt if she ever accepted her strange lover as fully as did Celis and Ellador theirs; he had hurt and offended her too often; there were reservations.

But I think Alima retained some faint vestige of long descended feeling which made Terry more possible to her than to others; and that she had made up her mind to the experiment and hated to renounce it.

However it came about, we all three at length achieved full understanding, and solemnly faced what was to them a step of measureless importance, a grave question as well as a great happiness; to us a strange, new joy.

Of marriage as a ceremony they knew nothing. Jeff was for bringing them to our country for the religious and the civil ceremony, but neither Celis nor the others would consent.

"We can't expect them to want to go with us—yet," said Terry sagely. "Wait a bit, boys. We've got to take 'em on their own terms—if at all." This, in rueful reminiscence of his repeated failures.

"But our time's coming," he added cheerfully. "These women have never been mastered, you see——" This, as one who had made a discovery.

"You'd better not try to do any mastering if you value your chances," I told him seriously; but he only laughed, and said, "Every man to his trade!"

We couldn't do anything with him. He had to take his own medicine.

If the lack of tradition of courtship, left us much at sea in our wooing, we found ourselves still more bewildered by lack of tradition of matrimony.

And here again, I have to draw on later experience, and as deep an acquaintance with their culture as I could achieve, to explain the gulfs of difference between us.

Two thousand years of one continuous culture with no men. Back of that, only traditions of the harem. They had no exact analogue for our word "home," any more than they had for our Roman-based "family."

They loved one another with a practically universal affection; rising to exquisite and unbroken friendships; and broadening to a devotion to their country and people for which our word "patriotism" is no definition at all.

Patriotism, red hot, is compatible with the existence of a neglect of national interests, a dishonesty, a cold indifference to the suffering of millions. Patriotism is largely pride, and very largely combativeness. Patriotism generally has a chip on its shoulder.

This country had no other country to measure itself by—save the few poor savages far below, with whom they had no contact.

They loved their country because it was their nursery, playground and workshop; theirs and their children's. They were proud of it as a workshop; proud of their record of ever increasing efficiency; they had made a pleasant garden of it, a very practical little heaven; but most of all they valued it—and here it is hard for us to understand them—as a cultural environment for their children.

That, of course, is the keynote of the whole distinction—their children.

From those first breathlessly guarded, half-adored race mothers, all up the ascending line; they had this dominant thought of building up a great race through the children.

All the surrendering devotion our women have put into their private families, these women put into their country and race. All the loyalty and service men expect of wives, they gave, not singly to men, but collectively to one another.

And the mother instinct, with us so painfully intense, so thwarted by conditions, so concentrated in personal devotion to a few; so bitterly hurt by death, disease, or barrenness, and even by the mere growth of the children, leaving the mother alone in her empty nest—all this feeling with them flowed out in a strong, wide current, unbroken through the generations, deepening and widening through the years, including every child in all the land.

With their united power and wisdom, they had studied and overcome the "diseases of childhood"—their children had none.

They had faced the problems of education and so solved them that their children grew up as naturally as young trees; learning through every sense; taught continuously but unconsciously—never knowing they were being educated.

In fact, they did not use the word as we do. Their idea of education was the special training they took, when half grown up, under experts. Then the eager young minds fairly flung themselves on their chosen subjects; and acquired with an ease, a breadth, a grasp, at which I never ceased to wonder.

But the babies and little children never felt the pressure of that "forcible feeding" of the mind that we call education. Of this, more later.

Chapter IX

Our Relations and Theirs

What I'm trying to show here is that with these women the whole relationship of life counted in a glad, eager growing-up to join the ranks of workers in the line best loved; a deep, tender reverence for one's own mother—too deep for them to speak of freely—and beyond that, the whole, free, wide range of sisterhood, the splendid service of the country, and friendships.

To these women we came, filled with the ideas, convictions, traditions, of our culture; and undertook to rouse in them the emotions which—to us—seemed proper.

However much, or little, of true sex-feeling there was between us, it phrased itself in their minds in terms of friendship, the one purely personal love they knew, and of ultimate parentage. Visibly we were not mothers, nor children, nor compatriots; so, if they loved us, we must be friends.

That we should pair off together in our courting days, was natural to them; that we three should remain much together, as they did themselves, was also natural. We had as yet no work, so we hung about them in their forest tasks, that was natural, too.

But when we began to talk about each couple having "homes" of our own, they could not understand it.

"Our work takes us all around the country," explained Celis. "We cannot live in one place all the time."

"We are together now," urged Alima, looking proudly at Terry's stalwart nearness. (This was one of the times when they were "on," though presently "off" again.)

"It's not the same thing at all," he insisted. "A man wants a home of his own, with his wife and family in it."

"Staying in it? All the time?" asked Ellador. "Not imprisoned, surely!"

"Of course not! Living there,—naturally," he answered.

"What does she do there—all the time?" Alima demanded. "What is her work?"

Then Terry patiently explained again that our women did not work,—with reservations.

"But what do they do—if they have no work?" she persisted.

"They take care of the home—and the children."

"At the same time?" asked Ellador.

"Why yes. The children play about, and the mother has charge of it all. There are servants, of course."

It seemed so obvious, so natural to Terry that he always grew impatient; but the girls were honestly anxious to understand.

"How many children do your women have?" Alima had her note-book out now, and a rather firm set of lip. Terry began to dodge.

"There is no set number, my dear," he explained. "Some have more, some have less."

"Some have none at all," I put in mischievously.

They pounced on this admission; and soon wrung from us the general fact that those women who had the most children had the least servants, and those who had the most servants had the least children.

"There!" triumphed Alima. "One or two or no children, and three or four servants. Now what do those women *do*?"

We explained as best we might. We talked of "social duties," disingenuously banking on their not interpreting the words as we did; we talked of hospitality, entertainment, and various "interests." All the time we knew that to these large-minded women, whose whole mental outlook was so collective, the limitations of a wholly personal life were inconceivable.

"We cannot really understand it," Ellador concluded. "We are only half a people. We have our woman-ways and they have their man-ways and their both-ways. We have worked out a system of living which is, of course, limited. They must have a broader, richer, better one. I should like to see it."

"You shall, dearest," I whispered.

★　★　★　★　★

"There's nothing to smoke," complained Terry. He was in the midst of a prolonged quarrel with Alima, and needed a sedative. "There's nothing to drink. These blessed women have no pleasant vices. I wish we could get out of here!"

This wish was vain. We were always under a certain degree of watchfulness. When Terry burst forth to tramp the streets at night he always found a "Colonel" here or there; and when, on an occasion of fierce though temporary despair, he had plunged to the cliff edge with some vague view to escape, he found several of them close by. We were free—but there was a string to it.

"They've no unpleasant ones, either," Jeff reminded him.

"Wish they had!" Terry persisted. "They've neither the vices of men, nor the virtues of women—they're neuters!"

"You know better than that. Don't talk nonsense," said I, severely.

I was thinking of Ellador's eyes, when they gave me a certain look; a look she did not at all realize.

Jeff was equally incensed. "I don't know what 'virtues of women' you miss. Seems to me they have all of them."

"They've no modesty," snapped Terry. "No patience, no submissiveness; none of that natural yielding which is woman's greatest charm."

I shook my head pityingly. "Go and apologize and make friends again, Terry. You've got a grouch, that's all. These women have the virtue of humanity, with less of its faults than any folks I ever saw. As for patience—they'd have pitched us over the cliffs the first day we lit among 'em, if they hadn't that."

"There are no—distractions," he grumbled. "Nowhere a man can go and cut loose a bit. It's an everlasting parlor and nursery."

"And workshop," I added. "And school, and office, and laboratory, and studio, and theatre, and—home."

"*Home!*" he sneered. "There isn't a home in the whole pitiful place."

"There isn't anything else, and you know it," Jeff retorted hotly. "I never saw, I never dreamed of such universal peace and good will and mutual affection."

"Oh, well, of course, if you like a perpetual Sunday-school, it's all very well. But I like Something Doing. Here it's all done."

There was something to this criticism. The years of pioneering lay far behind them. Theirs was a civilization in which the initial difficulties had long since been overcome. The untroubled peace, the unmeasured plenty, the steady health, the large good will and smooth management which ordered everything, left nothing to overcome. It was like a pleasant family in an old established, perfectly-run country place.

I liked it because of my eager and continued interest in the sociological achievements involved. Jeff liked it as he would have liked such a family and such a place anywhere.

Terry did not like it because he found nothing to oppose, to struggle with, to conquer.

"Life is a struggle, has to be," he insisted. "If there is no struggle, there is no life—that's all."

"You're talking nonsense—masculine nonsense," the peaceful Jeff replied. He was certainly a warm defender of Herland. "Ants don't raise their myriads by a struggle, do they? Or the bees?"

"Oh, if you go back to insects—and want to live in an ant-hill—! I tell you the higher grades of life are only reached through struggle—combat. There's no Drama here. Look at their plays! They make me sick."

He rather had us there. The drama of the country was—to our taste—rather flat. You see, they lacked the sex-motive; and with it, jealousy. They had no interplay of warring nations; no aristocracy and its ambitions; no wealth and poverty opposition.

I see I have said little about the economics of the place; it should have come before; but I'll go on about the drama now.

They had their own kind. There was a most impressive array of pageantry, of processions, a sort of grand ritual, with their arts and their religion broadly blended. The very babies joined in it. To see one of their great annual festivals, with the massed and marching stateliness of those great mothers; the young women brave and noble, beautiful and strong; and then the children, taking part as naturally as ours would frolic round a Christmas tree—it was overpowering in the impression of joyous, triumphant life.

They had begun at a period when the drama, the dance, music, religion and education were all very close together; and instead of developing them in detached lines, they had kept the connection. Let me try again to give, if I can, a faint sense of the difference in the life-view—the background and basis on which their culture rested.

Ellador told me a lot about it. She took me to see the children, the growing girls, the special teachers. She picked out books for me to read; she always seemed to understand just what I wanted to know, and how to give it to me.

While Terry and Alima struck sparks and parted,—he always madly drawn to her and she to him—she must have been, or she'd never have stood the way he behaved—Ellador and I had already a deep, restful feeling, as if we'd always had one another. Jeff and Celis were happy; there was no question of that; but it didn't seem to me as if they had the good times we did.

Well, here is the Herland child facing life—as Ellador tried to show it to me. From the first memory, they knew Peace, Beauty,

Order, Safety, Love, Wisdom, Justice, Patience and Plenty. By "plenty" I mean that the babies grew up in an environment which met their needs; just as young fawns might grow up in dewy forest glades and brook-fed meadows. And they enjoyed it as frankly and utterly as the fawns would.

They found themselves in a big bright lovely world, full of the most interesting and enchanting things to learn about and to do. The people everywhere were friendly and polite. No Herland child ever met the overbearing rudeness we so commonly show to children. They were People, too, from the first; the most precious part of the nation.

In each step of the rich experience of living, they found the instance they were studying widen out into contact with an endless range of common interests. The things they learned were *related*, from the first; related to one another, and to the national prosperity.

"It was a butterfly that made me a forester," said Ellador. "I was about eleven years old, and I found a big purple and green butterfly on a low flower. I caught it, very carefully, by the closed wings, as I had been told to do, and carried it to the nearest insect teacher—" (I made a note there to ask her what on earth an insect teacher was) "to ask her its name. She took it from me with a little cry of delight. 'Oh, you blessed child,' she said. 'Do you like obernuts?' Of course I liked obernuts, and said so. It is our best food-nut, you know. 'This is a female of the obernut moth,' she told me, 'they are almost gone. We have been trying to exterminate them for centuries. If you had not caught this one, it might have laid eggs enough to raise worms enough to destroy thousands of our nut trees—thousands of bushels of nuts,—and make years and years of trouble for us.'

"Everybody congratulated me. The children all over the country were told to watch for that moth, if there were any more. I was shown the history of the creature, and account of the damage it used to do, and of how long and hard our foremothers had worked to save that tree for us. I grew a foot, it seemed to me, and determined then and there to be a forester."

This is but an instance; she showed me many. The big difference was that whereas our children grow up in private homes and families, with every effort made to protect and seclude them from a dangerous world; here they grew up in a wide, friendly world, and knew it for theirs, from the first.

Their child literature was a wonderful thing. I could have spent years following the delicate subtleties, the smooth simplicities, with which they had bent that great art to the service of the child mind.

We have two life cycles; the man's and the woman's. To the man there is growth, struggle, conquest, the establishment of his family, and as much further success in gain or ambition, as he can achieve.

To the woman, growth, the securing of a husband, the subordinate activities of family life; and afterward such "social" or charitable interests as her position allows.

Here was but one cycle, and that a large one.

The child entered upon a broad open field of life, in which motherhood was the one great personal contribution to the national life, and all the rest the individual share in their common activities. Every girl I talked to, at any age, above babyhood, had her cheerful determination as to what she was going to be when she grew up.

What Terry meant by saying they had "no modesty," was, that this great life-view had no shady places; they had a high sense of personal decorum, but no shame—no knowledge of anything to be ashamed of.

Even their shortcomings and misdeeds in childhood never were presented to them as sins; merely as errors and misplays—as in a game. Some of them, who were palpably less agreeable than others or who had a real weakness or fault, were treated with cheerful allowance, as a friendly group at whist would treat a poor player.

Their religion, you see, was maternal; and their ethics, based on the full perception of evolution, showed the principle of growth and the beauty of wise culture. They had no theory of the essential opposition of good and evil; life to them was Growth; their pleasure was in growing, and their duty also.

With this background, with their sublimated mother-love, expressed in terms of widest social activity; every phase of their work was modified by its effect on the national growth. The language itself they had deliberately clarified, simplified, made easy and beautiful, for the sake of the children.

This seemed to us a wholly incredible thing; first, that any nation should have the foresight, the strength, and the persistence to plan and fulfill such a task; and second, that women should have had so much initiative. We have assumed, as a matter of course, that women had none; that only the man, with his natural energy and impatience of restriction, would ever invent anything.

Here we found that the pressure of life upon the environment develops in the human mind its inventive reactions, regardless of sex; and further, that a fully awakened motherhood plans and works without limit, for the good of the child.

That the children might be most nobly born, and reared in an environment calculated to allow the richest, freest growth, they had deliberately remodelled and improved the whole state.

I do not mean in the least that they stopped at that; any more than a child stops at childhood. The most impressive part of their whole culture beyond this perfect system of child-rearing, was the range of interests and associations open to them all, for life. But in the field of literature I was most struck, at first, by the child motive.

They had the same gradation of simple repetitive verse and story that we are familiar with, and the most exquisite, imaginative tales; but where, with us, these are the dribbled remnants of ancient folk myths, and primitive lullabies, theirs were the exquisite work of great artists; not only simple and unfailing in appeal to the child mind, but *true*, true to the living world about them.

To sit in one of their nurseries for a day was to change one's views forever as to babyhood. The youngest ones, rosy fatlings in their mothers' arms, or sleeping lightly in the flower-sweet air, seemed natural enough, save that they never cried. I never heard a child cry in Herland, save once or twice at a bad fall; and then people ran to help, as we would at a scream of agony from a grown person.

Each mother had her year of Glory; the time to love and learn, living closely with her child; nursing it proudly, often for two years or more. This perhaps was one reason for their wonderful vigor.

But after the baby-year the mother was not so constantly in attendance, unless, indeed, her work was among the little ones. She was never far off, however, and her attitude toward the co-mothers whose proud child-service was direct and continuous, was lovely to see.

As for the babies—a group of those naked darlings playing on short velvet grass, clean-swept; or rugs as soft; or in shallow pools of bright water; tumbling over with bubbling joyous baby laughter—it was a view of infant happiness such as I had never dreamed.

The babies were reared in the warmer part of the country, and gradually acclimated to the cooler heights as they grew older.

Sturdy children of ten and twelve played in the snow as joyfully as ours do; there were continuous excursions of them, from one part of the land to another, that, to each child, the whole country might be home.

It was all theirs, waiting for them to learn, to love, to use, to serve; as our own little boys plan to be "a big soldier," or "a cowboy," or whatever pleases their fancy; and our little girls plan for the kind of home they mean to have, or how many children; these planned, freely and gaily, with much happy chattering; of what they would do for the country when they were grown.

It was the eager happiness of the children and young people which first made me see the folly of that common notion of ours—that if life was smooth and happy people would not enjoy it. As I studied these youngsters, vigorous, joyous, eager little creatures, and their voracious appetite for life, it shook my previous ideas so thoroughly that they have never been re-established. The steady level of good health gave them all that natural stimulus we used to call "animal spirits"—an odd contradiction in terms. They found themselves in an immediate environment which was agreeable and interesting, and before them stretched the years of learning and discovery, the fascinating, endless process of education.

As I looked into these methods and compared them with our own, my strange uncomfortable sense of race-humility grew apace.

Ellador could not understand my astonishment. She explained things kindly and sweetly, but with some amazement that they needed explaining, and with sudden questions as to how we did it that left me meeker than ever.

I betook myself to Somel one day, carefully not taking Ellador. I did not mind seeming foolish to Somel—she was used to it.

"I want a chapter of explanation," I told her. "You know my stupidities by heart, and I do not want to show them to Ellador—she thinks me so wise!"

She smiled delightedly. "It is beautiful to see," she told me, "this new wonderful love between you. The whole country is interested, you know—how can we help it!"

I had not thought of that. We say: "All the world loves a lover," but to have a couple of million people watching one's courtship—and that a difficult one—was rather embarrassing.

"Tell me about your theory of education," I said. "Make it short and easy. And, to show you what puzzles me, I'll tell you that in our theory great stress is laid on the forced exertion of the child's mind; we think it is good for him to overcome obstacles."

"Of course it is," she unexpectedly agreed. "All our children do that—they love to."

That puzzled me again. If they loved to do it, how could it be educational.

"Our theory is this," she went on carefully. "Here is a young human being. The mind is as natural a thing as the body, a thing that grows, a thing to use and to enjoy. We seek to nourish, to stimulate, to exercise the mind of a child as we do the body. There are the two main divisions in education—you have those of course?—the things it is necessary to know, and things it is necessary to do."

"To do? Mental exercises, you mean?"

"Yes. Our general plan is this: in the matter of feeding the mind, of furnishing information, we use our best powers to meet the natural appetite of a healthy young brain; not to overfeed it, to provide such amount and variety of impressions as seem most welcome to each child. That is the easiest part. The other division is in arranging a properly graduated series of exercises which will best develop each mind; the common faculties we all have, and most carefully, the especial faculties some of us have. You do this also, do you not?"

"In a way," I said rather lamely. "We have not so subtle and highly developed a system as you, not approaching it; but tell me more. As to the information—how do you manage? It appears that all of you know pretty much everything—is that right?"

This she laughingly disclaimed. "By no means. We are, as you soon found out, extremely limited in knowledge. I wish you could realize what a ferment the country is in over the new things you have told us; the passionate eagerness among thousands of us to go to your country and learn—learn—learn! But what we do know is readily divisible into common knowledge and special knowledge. The common knowledge we have long since learned to feed into the minds of our little ones with no waste of time or strength; the special knowledge is open to all, as they desire it. Some of us specialize in one line only; but most take up several; some for their regular work, some to grow with."

"To grow with?"

"Yes; when one settles too close in one kind of work there is a tendency to atrophy in the disused portions of the brain. We like to keep on learning, always."

"What do you study?"

"As much as we know of the different sciences. We have, within our limits, a good deal of knowledge of anatomy, physiology, nutrition—all that pertains to a full and beautiful personal life. We have our botany and chemistry, and so on; very rudimentary, but interesting; our own history, with its accumulating psychology."

"You put psychology with history—not with personal life?"

"Of course. It is ours; it is among and between us, and it changes with the succeeding and improving generations. We are at work, slowly and carefully, developing our whole people along these lines. It is glorious work—splendid! To see the thousands of babies improving, showing stronger clearer minds, sweeter dispositions, higher capacities—don't you find it so in your country?"

This I evaded flatly. I remembered the cheerless claim that the human mind was no better than in its earliest period of savagery, only better informed—a statement I had never believed.

"We try most earnestly for two powers," Somel continued. "The two that seem to us basically necessary for all noble life: a clear, far-reaching judgment, and a strong well-used will. We spend our best efforts, all through childhood and youth, in developing these faculties, individual judgment and will."

"As part of your system of education, you mean?"

"Exactly. As the most valuable part. With the babies, as you may have noticed, we first provide an environment which feeds the mind without tiring it; all manner of simple and interesting things to do, as soon as they are old enough to do them; physical properties of course come first. But as early as possible, going very carefully, not to tax the mind, we provide choices, simple choices, with very obvious causes and consequences. You've noticed the games?"

I had. The children seemed always playing something; or else, sometimes, engaged in peaceful researches of their own. I had wondered at first when they went to school, but soon found that they never did—to their knowledge. It was all education but no schooling.

"We have been working for some sixteen hundred years, devising better and better games for children," continued Somel.

I sat aghast. "Devising games?" I protested. "Making up new ones, you mean?"

"Exactly," she answered. "Don't you?"

Then I remembered the kindergarten,[1] and the "material" devised by Signora Montessori,[2] and guardedly replied: "To some

---

1 The kindergarten (child garden) was developed by Friedrich Froebel (1782–1852) in the 1830s to embody the philosophy that children learn through their play; the first kindergarten in America was opened in 1860.

2 Italian physician Maria Montessori (1870–1952) developed what came to be known as the Montessori Method of education, which includes children learning by manipulating specially designed materials. See Appendix B2.

extent." But most of our games, I told her, were very old—come down from child to child, along the ages, from the remote past.

"And what is their effect?" she asked. "Do they develop the faculties you wish to encourage?"

Again I remembered the claims made by the advocates of "sports," and again replied guardedly that that was, in part, the theory.

"But do the children *like* it?" I asked. "Having things made up and set before them that way? Don't they want the old games?"

"You can see the children," she answered. "Are yours more contented—more interested—happier?"

Then I thought, as in truth I never had thought before, of the dull bored children I had seen, whining: "What can I do now?"; of the little groups and gangs hanging about; of the value of some one strong spirit who possessed initiative and would "start something"; of the children's parties and the onerous duties of the older people set to "amuse the children," also of that troubled ocean of misdirected activity we call "mischief," the foolish, destructive, sometimes evil things done by unoccupied children.

"No," said I grimly. "I don't think they are."

The Herland child was born not only into a world carefully prepared, full of the most fascinating materials and opportunities to learn, but into the society of plentiful numbers of teachers, teachers born and trained, whose business it was to accompany the children along that, to us, impossible thing—the royal road to learning.[1]

There was no mystery in their methods. Being adapted to children it was at least comprehensible to adults. I spent many days with the little ones, sometimes with Ellador, sometimes without, and began to feel a crushing pity for my own childhood, and for all others that I had known.

The houses and gardens planned for babies had in them nothing to hurt—no stairs, no corners, no small loose objects to swallow, no fire—just a babies paradise. They were taught, as rapidly as feasible, to use and control their own bodies, and never did I see such sure-footed, steady-handed, clear-headed little things. It was a joy to watch a row of toddlers learning to walk, not only on a level floor, but, a little later, on a sort of rubber rail raised an inch or two above the soft turf or heavy rugs, and falling off with shrieks of infant joy,

---

1 This saying is attributed first to Euclid as "no royal road to geometry" (c. 300 BCE) and refined by Ralph Waldo Emerson (1803–82) to "no royal road to Learning."

to rush back to the end of the line and try again. Surely we have noticed how children love to get up on something and walk along it! But we have never thought to provide that simple and inexhaustible form of amusement and physical education for the young.

Water they had, of course, and could swim even before they walked. If I feared at first the effects of a too intensive system of culture, that fear was dissipated by seeing the long sunny days of pure physical merriment and natural sleep in which these heavenly babies passed their first years. They never knew they were being educated. They did not dream that in this association of hilarious experiment and achievement they were laying the foundation for that close beautiful group feeling into which they grew so firmly with the years. This was education for citizenship.

Chapter X

Their Religions and Our Marriages

It took me a long time, as a man, a foreigner, and a species of Christian—I was that as much as anything—to get any clear understanding of the religion of Herland.

Its deification of motherhood was obvious enough; but there was far more to it than that; or, at least, than my first interpretation of that.

I think it was only as I grew to love Ellador more than I believed anyone could love anybody, as I grew faintly to appreciate her inner attitude and state of mind, that I began to get some glimpses of this faith of theirs.

When I asked her about it, she tried at first to tell me, and then, seeing me flounder, asked for more information about ours. She soon found that we had many, that they varied widely, but had some points in common. A clear methodical luminous mind had my Ellador, not only reasonable, but swiftly perceptive.

She made a sort of chart, superimposing the different religions as I described them, with a pin run through them all, as it were; their common basis being a Dominant Power or Powers, and some Special Behavior, mostly taboos, to please or placate. There were some common features in certain groups of religions, but the one always present was this Power, and the things which must be done or not done because of it. It was not hard to trace our human imagery of the Divine Force up through successive stages of bloodthirsty, sensual, proud and cruel gods of early times to the conception of a Common Father with its corollary of a Common Brotherhood.

This pleased her very much, and when I expatiated on the Omniscience, Omnipotence, Omnipresence, and so on of our God, and of the loving kindness taught by his Son, she was much impressed.

The story of the Virgin birth naturally did not astonish her, but she was greatly puzzled by the Sacrifice, and still more by the Devil, and the theory of Damnation.

When in an inadvertent moment I said that certain sects had believed in infant damnation—and explained it—she sat very still indeed.

"They believed that God was Love—and Wisdom—and Power?"

"Yes—all of that."

Her eyes grew large, her face ghastly pale.

"And yet that such a God could put little new babies to burn—for eternity?" She fell into a sudden shuddering and left me, running swiftly to the nearest Temple.

Every smallest village had its Temple, and in those gracious retreats sat wise and noble women, quietly busy at some work of their own until they were wanted, always ready to give comfort, light, or help, to any applicant.

Ellador told me afterward how easily this grief of hers was assuaged, and seemed ashamed of not having helped herself out of it.

"You see we are not accustomed to horrible ideas," she said, coming back to me rather apologetically. "We haven't any. And when we get a thing like that into our minds it's like—oh, like red pepper in your eyes. So I just ran to her blinded and almost screaming, and she took it out so quickly—so easily!"

"How?" I asked, very curious.

"'Why, you blessed child,' she said, 'you've got the wrong idea altogether. You do not have to think that there ever was such a God—for there wasn't. Or such a happening—for there wasn't. Nor even that this hideous false idea was believed by anybody. But only this—that people who are utterly ignorant will believe anything—which you certainly knew before.'

"Anyhow," pursued Ellador, "she turned pale for a minute when I first said it."

This was a lesson to me. No wonder this whole nation of women was peaceful and sweet in expression—they had no horrible ideas.

"Surely you had some when you began," I suggested.

"Oh, yes, no doubt. But as soon as our religion grew to any height at all we left them out of course."

From this, as from many other things, I grew to see what I finally put in words.

"Have you no respect for the past? For what was thought and believed by your foremothers?"

"Why, no," she said. "Why should we? They are all gone. They knew less than we do. If we are not beyond them we are unworthy of them—and unworthy of the children who must go beyond us."

This set me thinking in good earnest. I had always imagined—simply from hearing it said, I suppose—that women were by nature conservative. Yet these women, quite unassisted by any masculine spirit of enterprise, had ignored their past and built daringly for the future.

Ellador watched me think. She seemed to know pretty much what was going on in my mind.

"It's because we began in a new way, I suppose. All our folks were swept away at once, and then, after that time of despair, came those wonder children—the first. And then the whole breathless hope of us was for *their* children—if they should have them. And they did! Then there was the period of pride and triumph till we grew too numerous; and after that, when it all came down to one child apiece, we began to really work—to make better ones."

"But how does this account for such a radical difference in your religion?" I persisted.

She said she couldn't talk about the difference very intelligently, not being familiar with other religions, but that theirs seemed simple enough. Their great Mother Spirit was to them what their own motherhood was—only magnified beyond human limits. That meant that they felt beneath and behind them an upholding, unfailing, serviceable love—perhaps it was really the accumulated mother-love of the race they felt—but it was a Power.

"Just what is your theory of worship?" I asked her.

"Worship? What is that?"

I found it singularly difficult to explain. This Divine Love which they felt so strongly did not seem to ask anything of them—"any more than our mothers do," she said.

"But surely your mothers expect honor, reverence, obedience from you. You have to do things for your mothers, surely?"

"Oh, no," she insisted, smiling, shaking her soft brown hair. "We do things *from* our mothers—not *for* them. We don't have to do things *for* them—they don't need it, you know. But we have to live on—splendidly—because of them; and that's the way we feel about God."

I meditated again. I thought of that "God of Battles"[1] o[f] ours, that "Jealous God,"[2] that "Vengeance is mine" God.[3] I thought of our world-nightmare—Hell.

"You have no theory of eternal punishment then, I take it?"

Ellador laughed. Her eyes were as bright as stars, and there were tears in them, too, she was so sorry for me.

"How could we?" she asked, fairly enough. "We have no punishments in life, you see, so we don't imagine them after death."

"Have you *no* punishments. Neither for children or criminals—such mild criminals as you have?" I urged.

"Do you punish a person for a broken leg or a fever? We have preventive measures, and cures; sometimes we have to 'send the patient to bed,' as it were; but that's not a punishment—it's only part of the treatment," she explained.

Then studying my point of view more closely, she added: "You see we recognize, in our human motherhood, a great tender limitless uplifting force—patience and wisdom and all subtlety of delicate method. We credit God—our idea of God—with all that and more. Our mothers are not angry with us—why should God be?"

"Does God mean a person to you?"

This she thought over a little. "Why—in trying to get close to it in our minds we personify the idea, naturally; but we certainly do not assume a Big Woman somewhere, who is God. What we call God is a Pervading Power, you know, an Indwelling Spirit, something inside of us that we want more of. Is your God a Big Man?" she asked innocently.

"Why—yes, to most of us, I think. Of course we call it an Indwelling Spirit just as you do, but we insist that it is Him, a Person, and a Man—with whiskers."

"Whiskers? Oh yes—because you have them! Or do you wear them because He does?"

"On the contrary we shave them off—because it seems cleaner and more comfortable."

---

1   Shakespeare, *Henry V*, 4.1.309.

2   "For I, the Lord your God, am a jealous God, visiting the iniquity of the fathers upon the children" (Exodus 20:5).

3   "Dearly beloved, avenge not yourselves, but rather give place unto wrath: for it is written, Vengeance is mine; I will repay, saith the Lord" (Romans 12:19).

"Does He wear clothes—in your idea, I mean?"

I was thinking over the pictures of God I had seen,—rash advances of the devout mind of man, representing his Omnipotent Deity as an Old Man in a flowing robe, flowing hair, flowing beard, and in the light of her perfectly frank and innocent questions this concept seemed rather unsatisfying.

I explained that the God of the Christian world was really the ancient Hebrew God, and that we had simply taken over the patriarchal idea—that ancient one which quite inevitably clothed its thought of God with the attributes of the patriarchal ruler, the Grandfather.

"I see," she said eagerly, after I had explained the genesis and development of our religious ideals. "They lived in separate groups, with a male head, and he was probably a little—domineering?"

"No doubt of that," I agreed.

"And we live together without any 'head,' in that sense—just our chosen Leaders—that *does* make a difference."

"Your difference is deeper than that," I assured her. "It is in your common motherhood. Your children grow up in a world where everybody loves them. They find life made rich and happy for them by the diffused love and wisdom of all mothers. So it is easy for you to think of God in the terms of a similar diffused and competent love. I think you are far nearer right than we are."

"What I cannot understand," she pursued carefully, "is your preservation of such a very ancient state of mind. This patriarchal idea you tell me is thousands of years old?"

"Oh yes—four, five, six thousand—ever so many."

"And you have made wonderful progress in those years—in other things?"

"We certainly have. But religion is different. You see our religions come from behind us, and are initiated by some great teacher who is dead. He is supposed to have known the whole thing and taught it, finally. All we have to do is Believe—and Obey."

"Who was the great Hebrew teacher?"

"Oh—there it was different. The Hebrew religion is an accumulation of extremely ancient traditions, some far older than their people, and grew by accretion down the ages. We consider it inspired—'the Word of God.'"

"How do you know it is?"

"Because it says so?"

"Does it say so in as many words? Who wrote that in?"

I began to try to recall some text that did say so, and could not bring it to mind.

"Apart from that," she pursued, "what I cannot understand is why you keep these early religious ideas so long. You have changed all your others, haven't you?"

"Pretty generally," I agreed. "But this we call 'revealed religion,' and think it is final. But tell me more about these little Temples of yours," I urged. "And these Temple Mothers you run to."

Then she gave me an extended lesson in applied religion, which I will endeavor to concentrate.

They developed their central theory of a Loving Power, and assumed that its relation to them was motherly—that it desired their welfare and especially their development. Their relation to it, similarly, was filial, a loving appreciation and a glad fulfillment of its high purposes. Then, being nothing if not practical, they set their keen and active minds to discover the kind of conduct expected of them. This worked out in a most admirable system of ethics. The principle of Love was universally recognized—and used.

Patience, gentleness, courtesy, all that we call "good breeding," was part of their code of conduct. But where they went far beyond us was in the special application of religious feeling to every field of life. They had no ritual, no little set of performances called "divine service," save those glorious pageants I have spoken of, and those were as much educational as religion, and as much social as either. But they had a clear established connection between everything they did—and God. Their cleanliness, their health, their exquisite order, the rich peaceful beauty of the whole land, the happiness of the children, and above all the constant progress they made—all this was their religion.

They applied their minds to the thought of God, and worked out the theory that such an Inner Power demanded Outward Expression. They lived as if God was real and at work within them.

As for those little Temples everywhere—some of the women were more skilled, more temperamentally inclined, in this direction, than others. These, whatever their work might be, gave certain hours to the Temple Service which meant being there with all their love and wisdom and trained thought, to smooth out rough places for anyone who needed it. Sometimes it was a real grief, very rarely a quarrel, most often a perplexity; even in Herland the human soul had its hours of darkness. But all through the country their best and wisest were ready to give help.

If the difficulty was unusually profound the applicant was directed to some more specially experienced in that line of thought.

Here was a religion which gave to the searching mind a rational basis in life, the concept of an immense Loving Power working steadily out through them, towards good. It gave to the "soul" that sense of contact with the inmost force, of perception of the uttermost purpose, which we always crave. It gave to the "heart" the blessed feeling of being loved, loved and *understood*. It gave clear, simple, rational directions as to how we should live—and why. And for ritual it gave, first those triumphant group demonstrations when with a union of all the arts, the revivifying combination of great multitudes moved rhythmically with march and dance, song and music, among their own noblest products and the open beauty of their groves and hills. Second, it gave these numerous little centers of wisdom where the least wise could go to the most wise and be helped.

"It is beautiful!" I cried enthusiastically. "It is the most practical, comforting, progressive religion I ever heard of. You *do* love one another—you *do* bear one another's burdens—you *do* realize that a little child is a type of the kingdom of heaven. You are more Christian than any people I ever saw. But—how about Death? And the Life Everlasting? What does your religion teach about Eternity?"

"Nothing," said Ellador. "What is Eternity?"

What indeed? I tried, for the first time in my life, to get a real hold on the idea.

"It is—never stopping."

"Never stopping?" She looked puzzled.

"Yes, life, going on forever."

"Oh—we see that, of course. Life does go on forever, all about us."

"But eternal life goes on *without dying*."

"The same person?"

"Yes, the same person, unending, immortal." I was pleased to think that I had something to teach from our religion, which theirs had never promulgated.

"Here?" asked Ellador. "Never to die—here?" I could see her practical mind heaping up the people, and hurriedly reassured her.

"Oh no, indeed, not here—hereafter. We must die here, of course, but then we 'enter into eternal life.' The soul lives forever."

"How do you know?" she inquired.

"I won't attempt to prove it to you," I hastily continued. "Let us assume it to be so. How does this idea strike you?"

Again she smiled at me, that adorable, dimpling, tender, mischievous, motherly smile of hers. "Shall I be quite, quite honest?"

"You couldn't be anything else," I said, half gladly and half a little sorry. The transparent honesty of these women was a never-ending astonishment to me.

"It seems to me a singularly foolish idea," she said calmly. "And if true, most disagreeable."

Now I had always accepted the doctrine of personal immortality as a thing established. The efforts of inquiring Spiritualists,[1] always seeking to woo their beloved ghosts back again, never seemed to me necessary. I don't say I had ever seriously and courageously discussed the subject with myself even; I had simply assumed it to be a fact. And here was the girl I loved, this creature whose character constantly revealed new heights and ranges far beyond my own, this super-woman of a super-land, saying she thought immortality foolish! She meant it, too.

"What do you *want* it for?" she asked.

"How can you *not* want it!" I protested. "Do you want to go out like a candle? Don't you want to go on and on—growing and—and—being happy, forever?"

"Why, no," she said. "I don't in the least. I want my child—and my child's child—to go on—and they will. Why should *I* want to?"

"But it means Heaven!" I insisted. "Peace and Beauty and Comfort and Love—with God." I had never been so eloquent on the subject of religion. She could be horrified at Damnation, and question the justice of Salvation, but Immortality—that was surely a noble faith.

"Why, Van," she said, holding out her hands to me. "Why Van—darling! How splendid of you to feel it so keenly. That's what we all want, of course—Peace and Beauty, and Comfort and Love—with God! And Progress too, remember; Growth, always and always. That is what our religion teaches us to want and to work for, and we do!"

"But that is *here*," I said, "only for this life on earth."

"Well? And do not you in your country, with your beautiful religion of love and service, have it here, too—for this life—on earth?"

★　★　★　★　★

None of us were willing to tell the women of Herland about the evils of our own beloved land. It was all very well for us to assume them to be necessary and essential, and to criticize—strictly

---

1 Followers of a belief that was particularly popular from the 1840s to the 1920s that spirits of the dead could be contacted and communicated with through "mediums." The adolescent Charlotte Perkins and her mother for a time lived in a spiritualist "cooperative housekeeping" group, in which the residents, led by a woman who identified herself as a psychic, shared domestic duties.

among ourselves—their all-too-perfect civilization, but when it came to telling them about the failures and wastes of our own, we never could bring ourselves to do it.

Moreover we sought to avoid too much discussion, and to press the subject of our approaching marriage.

Jeff was the determined one on this score.

"Of course they haven't any marriage ceremony or service, but we can make it a sort of Quaker Wedding, and have it in the Temple—it is the least we can do for them."

It was. There was so little, after all, that we could do for them. Here we were, penniless guests and strangers, with no chance even to use our strength and courage—nothing to defend them from or protect them against.

"We can at least give them our names," Jeff insisted.

They were very sweet about it, quite willing to do whatever we asked, to please us. As to the names, Alima, frank soul that she was, asked what good it would do.

Terry, always irritating her, said it was a sign of possession. "You are going to be Mrs. Nicholson," he said, "Mrs. T. O. Nicholson. That shows everyone that you are my wife."

"What is a 'wife' exactly?" she demanded, a dangerous gleam in her eyes.

"A wife is the woman who belongs to a man," he began.

But Jeff took it up eagerly: "And a husband is the man who belongs to a woman. It is because we are monogamous, you know. And marriage is the ceremony, civil and religious, that joins the two together—"until death do us part,'" he finished, looking at Celis with unutterable devotion.

"What makes us all feel foolish," I told the girls, "is that here we have nothing to give you—except, of course, our names."

"Do your women have no names before they are married?" Celis suddenly demanded.

"Why, yes," Jeff explained. "They have their maiden names—their father's names, that is."

"And what becomes of them?" asked Alima.

"They change them for their husband's, my dear," Terry answered her.

"Change them? Do the husbands then take the wives' 'maiden names'?"

"Oh, no," he laughed. "The man keeps his own and gives it to her, too."

"Then she just loses hers and takes a new one—how unpleasant! We won't do that!" Alima said decidedly.

Terry was good-humored about it. "I don't care what you do or don't do so long as we have that wedding pretty soon," he said, reaching a strong brown hand after Alima's, quite as brown and nearly as strong.

"As to giving us things—of course we can see that you'd like to, but we are glad you can't," Celis continued. "You see we love you just for yourselves—we wouldn't want you to—to pay anything. Isn't it enough to know that you are loved personally—and just as men?"

Enough or not, that was the way we were married. We had a great triple wedding in the biggest Temple of all, and it looked as if most of the nation were present. It was very solemn and very beautiful. Someone had written a new song for the occasion, nobly beautiful, about the New Hope for their people—the New Tie with other lands—Brotherhood as well as Sisterhood, and, with evident awe, Fatherhood.

Terry was always restive under their talk of fatherhood. "Anybody'd think we were High Priests of—of Philoprogenitiveness!"[1] he protested. "These women think of *nothing* but children, seems to me! We'll teach 'em!"

He was so certain of what he was going to teach, and Alima so uncertain in her moods of reception, that Jeff and I feared the worst. We tried to caution him—much good that did. The big handsome fellow drew himself up to his full height, lifted that great chest of his, and laughed.

"There are three separate marriages," he said. "I won't interfere with yours—nor you with mine."

So the great day came, and the countless crowds of women, and we three bridegrooms without any supporting "best men," or any other men to back us up, felt strangely small as we came forward.

Somel and Zava and Moadine were on hand; we were thankful to have them, too—they seemed almost like relatives.

There was a splendid procession, wreathing dances, the new Anthem I spoke of, and the whole great place pulsed with feeling—the deep awe, the sweet hope, the wondering expectation of a new miracle.

"There has been nothing like this in the country since our Motherhood began!" Somel said softly to me, while we watched the symbolic marches. "You see it is the dawn of a new era. You don't know how much you mean to us. It is not only Fatherhood—that

---

1 Love of offspring or of the young and helpless more generally (Greek).

marvelous dual parentage to which we are strangers—the miracle of union in life-giving—but it is Brotherhood. You are the rest of the world. You join us to our kind—to all the strange lands and peoples we have never seen. We hope to know them—to love and help them—and to learn of them. Ah! You cannot know!"

★　★　★　★　★

Thousands of voices rose in the soaring climax of that great Hymn of The Coming Life. By the great Altar of Motherhood, with its crown of fruit and flowers, stood a new one, crowned as well. Before the Great Over-Mother of the Land and her ring of High Temple Counsellors, before that vast multitude of calm-faced mothers and holy-eyed maidens, came forward our own three chosen ones, and we, three men alone in all that land, joined hands with them and made our marriage vows.

Chapter XI

Our Difficulties

We say, "Marriage is a lottery"; also "Marriages are made in Heaven"—but this is not so widely accepted as the other.

We have a well-founded theory that it is best to marry "in one's class," and certain well-grounded suspicions of international marriages, which seem to persist in the interests of social progress, rather than in those of the contracting parties.

But no combination of alien races, of color, caste, or creed, was ever so basically difficult to establish as that between us, three modern American men and these three women of Herland.

It is all very well to say that we should have been frank about it beforehand. We had been frank. We had discussed—at least Ellador and I had—the conditions of The Great Adventure, and thought the path was clear before us. But there are some things one takes for granted, supposes are mutually understood, and to which both parties may repeatedly refer without ever meaning the same thing.

The differences in the education of the average man and woman are great enough, but the trouble they make is not mostly for the man; he generally carries out his own views of the case. The woman may have imagined the conditions of married life to be different; but what she imagined, was ignorant of, or might have preferred, did not seriously matter.

I can see clearly and speak calmly about this now, writing after a lapse of years, years full of growth and education, but at the time it was rather hard sledding for any of us—especially for Terry. Poor Terry! You see in any other imaginable marriage among the peoples of the earth, whether the woman were black, red, yellow, brown, or white; whether she were ignorant or educated, submissive or rebellious, she would have behind her the marriage tradition of our general history. This tradition relates the woman to the man. He goes on with his business, and she adapts herself to him and to it. Even in citizenship, by some strange hocus-pocus, that fact of birth and geography was waved aside, and the woman automatically acquired the nationality of her husband.

Well—here were we, three aliens in this land of women. It was small in area, and the external differences were not so great as to astound us. We did not yet appreciate the differences between the race-mind of this people and ours.

In the first place, they were a "pure stock" of two thousand uninterrupted years. Where we have some long connected lines of thought and feeling, together with a wide range of differences, often irreconcilable, these people were smoothly and firmly agreed on most of the basic principles of their life; and not only agreed in principle, but accustomed for these sixty odd generations to act on those principles.

This is one thing which we did not understand—had made no allowance for. When in our pre-marital discussions one of those dear girls had said: "We understand it thus and thus," or "We hold such and such to be true," we men, in our own deep-seated convictions of the power of love, and our easy views about beliefs and principles, fondly imagined that we could convince them otherwise. What we imagined, before marriage, did not matter any more than what an average innocent young girl imagines. We found the facts to be different.

It was not that they did not love us; they did, deeply and warmly. But there you are again—what they meant by "love" and what we meant by "love" were so different.

Perhaps it seems rather cold-blooded to say "we" and "they," as if we were not separate couples, with our separate joys and sorrows, but our positions as aliens drove us together constantly. The whole strange experience had made our friendship more close and intimate than it would ever have become in a free and easy lifetime among our own people. Also, as men, with our masculine tradition of far more than two thousand years, we were a unit, small but firm, against this far larger unit of feminine tradition.

I think I can make clear the points of difference without a too painful explicitness. The more external disagreement was in the matter of "the home," and the housekeeping duties and pleasures we, by instinct and long education, supposed to be inherently appropriate to women.

I will give two illustrations, one away up, and the other away down, to show how completely disappointed we were in this regard.

For the lower one, try to imagine a male ant, coming from some state of existence where ants live in pairs, endeavoring to set up housekeeping with a female ant from a highly developed ant-hill. This female ant might regard him with intense personal affection, but her ideas of parentage and economic management would be on a very different scale from his. Now, of course, if she was a stray female in a country of pairing ants, he might have had his way with her; but if he was a stray male in an ant-hill——!

For the higher one, try to imagine a devoted and impassioned man trying to set up housekeeping with a lady Angel, a real wings-and-harp-and-halo Angel, accustomed to fulfilling Divine missions all over interstellar space. This Angel might love the man with an affection quite beyond his power of return or even of appreciation, but her ideas of service and duty would be on a very different scale from his. Of course, if she was a stray Angel in a country of men, he might have had his way with her; but if he was a stray man among Angels——!

Terry, at his worst, in a black fury for which, as a man, I must have some sympathy, preferred the ant simile. More of Terry and his special troubles later. It was hard on Terry.

Jeff—well, Jeff always had a streak that was too good for this world! He's the kind that would have made a saintly priest in earlier times. He accepted the Angel theory, swallowed it whole, tried to force it on us—with varying effect. He so worshipped Celis, and not only Celis, but what she represented; he had become so deeply convinced of the almost supernatural advantages of this country and people, that he took his medicine like a—I cannot say "like a man," but more as if he wasn't one.

Don't misunderstand me for a moment. Dear old Jeff was no milksop or molly-coddle[1] either. He was a strong, brave, efficient man, and an excellent fighter when fighting was necessary. But

---

1 Milksop: a man lacking courage and other qualities deemed manly, a wimp. Mollycoddle: a person, especially a man or a boy, who is pampered and overprotected, an effeminate man.

there was always this angel streak in him. It was rather a wonder, Terry being so different, that he really loved Jeff as he did; but it happens so sometimes, in spite of the difference—perhaps because of it.

As for me, I stood between. I was no such gay Lothario[1] as Terry, and no such Galahad[2] as Jeff. But for all my limitations I think I had the habit of using my brains in regard to behavior rather more frequently than either of them. I had to use brain-power now, I can tell you.

The big point at issue between us and our wives was, as may easily be imagined, in the very nature of the relation.

"Wives! Don't talk to me about wives!" stormed Terry. "They don't know what the word means."

Which is exactly the fact—they didn't. How could they? Back in their prehistoric records of polygamy and slavery there were no ideals of wifehood as we know it, and since then no possibility of forming such.

"The only thing they can think of about a man is *Fatherhood!*" said Terry in high scorn. "*Fatherhood!* As if a man was always wanting to be a *father!*"

This also was correct. They had their long, wide, deep, rich experience of Motherhood, and their only perception of the value of a male creature as such, was for Fatherhood.

Aside from that, of course, was the whole range of personal love; love which as Jeff earnestly phrased it "passeth the love of women!"[3] It did, too. I can give no idea—either now, after long and happy experience of it, or as it seemed then, in the first measureless wonder—of the beauty and power of the love they gave us.

Even Alima—who had a more stormy temperament than either of the others, and who, heaven knows, had far more provocation—even Alima was patience and tenderness and wisdom personified to the man she loved, until he—but I haven't got to that yet.

★ ★ ★ ★ ★

---

1 A man whose chief interest is seducing women, after a character in the play *The Fair Penitent* (1703) by Nicholas Rowe (1674–1718).

2 The purest and noblest knight of King Arthur's Round Table, who succeeds in his quest for the Holy Grail because of his sinless purity.

3 See the story of Jonathan and David in 2 Samuel 1:26: "thy love to me was wonderful, passing the love of women." See also Philippians 4:7: "And the peace of God, which passeth all understanding, shall keep your hearts and minds through Christ Jesus."

These, as Terry put it, "alleged or so-called wives" of ours, went right on with their profession as foresters. We, having no special leanings, had long since qualified as assistants. We had to do something, if only to pass the time, and it had to be work—we couldn't be playing forever.

This kept us out of doors with those dear girls, and more or less together—too much together sometimes.

These people had, it now became clear to us, the highest, keenest, most delicate sense of personal privacy, but not the faintest idea of that "solitude à deux"[1] we are so fond of. They had, everyone of them, the "two rooms and a bath" theory realized. From earliest childhood each had a separate bedroom with toilet conveniences, and one of the marks of coming of age was the addition of an outer room in which to receive friends.

Long since we had been given our own two rooms apiece, and as being of a different sex and race, these were in a separate house. It seemed to be recognized that we should breathe easier if able to free our minds in real seclusion.

For food we either went to any convenient eating-house, ordered a meal brought in, or took it with us to the woods, always and equally good. All this we had become used to and enjoyed—in our courting days.

After marriage there arose in us a somewhat unexpected urge of feeling that called for a separate house; but this feeling found no response in the hearts of those fair ladies.

"We *are* alone, dear," Ellador explained to me with gentle patience. "We are alone in these great forests; we may go and eat in any little summer-house—just we two, or have a separate table anywhere—or even have a separate meal in our own rooms. How could we be aloner?"

This was all very true. We had our pleasant mutual solitude about our work, and our pleasant evening talks in their apartments or ours; we had, as it were, all the pleasures of courtship carried right on; but we had no sense of—perhaps it may be called possession.

"Might as well not be married at all," growled Terry. "They only got up that ceremony to please us—please Jeff, mostly. They've no real idea of being married."

I tried my best to get Ellador's point of view, and naturally I tried to give her mine. Of course what we, as men, wanted to make them see was that there were other, and as we proudly said

1 Solitude for two (French).

"higher" uses in this relation than what Terry called "mere parentage." In the highest terms I knew I tried to explain this to Ellador.

"Anything higher than for mutual love to hope to give life, as we did?" she said. "How is it higher?"

"It develops love," I explained. "All the power of beautiful permanent mated love comes through this higher development."

"Are you sure?" she asked gently. "How do you know that it was so developed? There are some birds who love each other so that they mope and pine if separated, and never pair again if one dies, but they never mate except in the mating season. Among your people do you find high and lasting affection appearing in proportion to this indulgence?"

It is a very awkward thing, sometimes, to have a logical mind.

Of course I knew about those monogamous birds and beasts too, that mate for life and show every sign of mutual affection, without ever having stretched the sex relationship beyond its original range. But what of it?

"Those are lower forms of life!" I protested. "They have no capacity for our higher feelings. Of course they are faithful and affectionate, and apparently happy—but Oh, my dear! my dear!—what can they know of such a love as draws us together? Why, to touch you—to be near you—to come closer and closer—to lose myself in you—surely you feel it too, do you not?"

I came nearer. I seized her hands.

Her eyes were on mine, tender, radiant, but steady and strong. There was something so powerful, so large and changeless, in those eyes that I could not sweep her off her feet by my own emotion as I had unconsciously assumed would be the case.

It made me feel as, one might imagine, a man might feel who loved a goddess—not a Venus,[1] though! She did not resent my attitude, did not repel it, did not in the least fear it, evidently. There was not a shade of that timid withdrawal or pretty resistance which are so—provocative.

"You see, dearest," she said. "You have to be patient with us. We are not like the women of your country. We are Mothers, and we are People, but we have not specialized in this line."

"We" and "we" and "we"—it was so hard to get her to be personal. And, as I thought that, I suddenly remembered how we were always criticizing *our* women for *being* so personal.

---

1 Roman goddess of erotic love and beauty.

Then I did my earnest best to picture to her the sweet intense joy of married lovers, and the result in higher stimulus to all creative work.

"Do you mean," she asked quite calmly, as if I was not holding her cool firm hands in my hot and rather quivering ones, "that with you, when people, marry, they go right on doing this in season and out of season, with no thought of children at all?"

"They do," I said, with some bitterness. "They are not mere parents. They are men and women, and they love each other."

"How long?" asked Ellador, rather unexpectedly.

"How long?" I repeated, a little dashed. "Why as long as they live."

"There is something very beautiful in the idea," she admitted, still as if she were discussing life on Mars. "This climactic expression, which, in all the other life-forms, has but the one purpose, has with you become specialized to higher, purer, nobler uses. It has—I judge from what you tell me—the most ennobling effect on character. People marry, not only for parentage, but for this exquisite interchange—and, as a result, you have a world full of continuous lovers, ardent, happy, mutually devoted, always living on that high tide of supreme emotion which we had supposed to belong only to one season and one use. And you say it has other results, stimulating all high creative work. That must mean floods, oceans of such work, blossoming from this intense happiness of every married pair! It is a beautiful idea!"

She was silent, thinking.

So was I.

She slipped one hand free, and was stroking my hair with it in a gentle motherly way. I bowed my hot head on her shoulder, and felt a dim sense of peace, a restfulness which was very pleasant.

"You must take me there someday, darling," she was saying. "It is not only that I love you so much I want to see your country— your people—your mother—" she paused reverently. "Oh, how I shall love your mother!"

I had not been in love many times—my experience did not compare with Terry's. But such as I had was so different from this that I was perplexed, and full of mixed feelings; partly a growing sense of common ground between us, a pleasant rested calm feeling, which I had imagined could only be attained in one way; and partly a bewildered resentment because what I found was not what I had looked for.

It was their confounded psychology! Here they were with this profound highly developed system of education so bred into them that even if they were not teachers by profession they all had a general proficiency in it—it was second nature to them.

And no child, stormily demanding a cookie "between meals" was ever more subtly diverted into an interest in house-building than was I when I found an apparently imperative demand had disappeared without my noticing it.

And all the time those tender mother eyes, those keen scientific eyes, noting every condition and circumstance, and learning how to "take time by the forelock"[1] and avoid discussion before occasion arose.

I was amazed at the results. I found that much, very much, of what I had honestly supposed to be a physiological necessity was a psychological necessity—or so believed. I found, after my ideas of what was essential had changed, that my feelings changed also. And more than all I found this—a factor of enormous weight—these women were not provocative. That made an immense difference.

The thing that Terry had so complained of when we first came—that they weren't "feminine," they lacked "charm," now became a great comfort. Their vigorous beauty was an aesthetic pleasure, not an irritant. Their dress and ornaments had not a touch of the "come-and-find-me" element.

Even with my own Ellador, my wife, who had for a time unveiled a woman's heart and faced the strange new hope and joy of dual parentage, she afterward withdrew again into the same good comrade she had been at first. They were women, *plus*, and so much plus that when they did not choose to let the womanness appear, you could not find it anywhere.

I don't say it was easy for me; it wasn't. But when I made appeal to her sympathies I came up against another immovable wall. She was sorry, honestly sorry, for my distresses, and made all manner of thoughtful suggestions, often quite useful, as well as the wise foresight I have mentioned above which often saved all difficulty before it arose; but her sympathy did not alter her convictions.

"If I thought it was really right and necessary, I could perhaps bring myself to it, for your sake, dear; but I do not want to—not at all. You would not have a mere submission, would you? That is not the kind of high romantic love you spoke of, surely? It is a pity,

---

1 Act quickly and decisively, taking advantage of the opportunity. "Tell her the joyous time will not be staid, / Unless she do him by the forelock take." Edmund Spenser, *Amoretti*, Sonnet 70 (1595).

of course, that you should have to adjust your highly specialized faculties to our unspecialized ones."

Confound it! I hadn't married the nation, and I told her so. But she only smiled at her own limitations, and explained that she had to "think in we's."

Confound it again! Here I'd have all my energies focused on one wish, and before I knew it she'd have them dissipated in one direction or another, some subject of discussion that began just at the point I was talking about and ended miles away.

It must not be imagined that I was just repelled, ignored, left to cherish a grievance. Not at all. My happiness was in the hands of a larger sweeter womanhood than I had ever imagined. Before our marriage my own ardor had perhaps blinded me to much of this. I was madly in love with, not so much what was there, as with what I supposed to be there. Now I found an endlessly beautiful undiscovered country to explore, and in it the sweetest wisdom and understanding. It was as if I had come to some new place and people, with a desire to eat at all hours, and no other interests in particular; and as if my hosts, instead of merely saying: "You shall not eat," had presently aroused in me a lively desire for music, for pictures, for games, for exercise, for playing in the water, for running some ingenious machine; and, in the multitude of my satisfactions, I forgot the one point which was not satisfied, and got along very well until meal-time.

One of the cleverest and most ingenious of these tricks was only clear to me many years after when we were so wholly at one on this subject that I could laugh at my own predicament then. It was this: You see, with us, women are kept as different as possible and as feminine as possible. We men have our own world, with only men in it; we get tired of our ultra-maleness and turn gladly to the ultra-femaleness. Also, in keeping our women as feminine as possible, we see to it that when we turn to them we find the thing we want always in evidence. Well, the atmosphere of this place was anything but seductive. The very numbers of these human women, always in human relation, made them anything but alluring. When, in spite of this, my hereditary instincts and race-traditions made me long for the feminine response in Ellador, instead of withdrawing so that I should want her more, she deliberately gave me a little too much of her society—always de-feminized, as it were. It was awfully funny, really.

Here was I, with an Ideal in mind, for which I hotly longed, and here was she, deliberately obtruding in the foreground of my consciousness a Fact—a fact which I coolly enjoyed, but which actually interfered with what I wanted. I see now clearly enough why a certain kind of man, like Sir Almroth Wright,[1] resents the professional development of women. It gets in the way of the sex ideal; it temporarily covers and excludes femininity.

Of course, in this case, I was so fond of Ellador my friend, of Ellador my professional companion, that I necessarily enjoyed her society on any terms. Only—when I had had her with me in her de-feminine capacity for a sixteen-hour day, I could go to my own room and sleep without dreaming about her.

The Witch! If ever anybody worked to woo and win and hold a human soul, she did, great Superwoman that she was. I couldn't then half comprehend the skill of it, the wonder. But this I soon began to find; that under all our cultivated attitude of mind toward women there is an older, deeper, more "natural" feeling; the restful reverence which looks up to the Mother Sex.

So we grew together in friendship and happiness, Ellador and I, and so did Jeff and Celis.

When it comes to Terry's part of it, and Alima's, I'm sorry—and I'm ashamed. Of course I blame her somewhat. She wasn't as fine a psychologist as Ellador, and what's more, I think she had a far-descended atavistic trace of more marked femaleness, never apparent till Terry called it out. But when all that is said, it doesn't excuse him. I hadn't realized to the full Terry's character—I couldn't, being a man.

The position was the same as with us, of course, only with these distinctions: Alima a shade more alluring, and several shades less able as a practical psychologist; Terry a hundredfold more demanding—and proportionately less reasonable.

Things grew strained very soon between them. I fancy at first, when they were together, in her great hope of parentage and his keen joy of conquest—or what he assumed to be conquest—that Terry was inconsiderate. In fact, I know it, from things he said.

"You needn't talk to me," he snapped at Jeff one day, just before our weddings. "There never was a woman yet that did not enjoy being *mastered*. All your pretty talk doesn't amount to a hill o'beans—I *know*." And Terry would hum:

"I've taken my fun where I found it,
I've rogued and I've ranged in my time,"

---

1   Sir Almroth Edward Wright (1861–1947), British immunologist and author of *The Unexpurgated Case against Woman Suffrage* (1913). See Appendix B3.

and

> "The things that I learned from the yellow and black,
> They 'ave helped me a 'eap with the white."[1]

★   ★   ★   ★   ★

Jeff turned sharply and left him at the time. I was a bit disquieted myself.

Poor old Terry! The things he'd learned didn't help him a heap in Herland. His idea was To Take—he thought that was the way. He thought, he honestly believed, that women liked it. Not the women of Herland! Not Alima!

I can see her now—one day in the very first week of their marriage, setting forth to her day's work with long determined strides and hard-set mouth, and sticking close to Ellador. She didn't wish to be alone with Terry—you could see that.

But the more she kept away from him, the more he wanted her—naturally.

He made a tremendous row about their separate establishments; tried to keep her in his rooms, tried to stay in hers. But there she drew the line sharply.

He came away one night, and stamped up and down the moonlight road, swearing under his breath. I was taking a walk that night too, but I wasn't in his state of mind. To hear him rage you'd not have believed that he loved Alima at all—you'd have thought that she was some quarry he was pursuing, something to catch and conquer.

I think that owing to all those differences I spoke of they soon lost the common ground they had at first, and were unable to meet sanely and dispassionately. I fancy too—this is pure conjecture—that he had succeeded in driving Alima beyond her best judgment, her real conscience, and that after that her own sense of shame, the reaction of the thing, made her bitter perhaps.

They quarreled, really quarreled, and after making it up once or twice, they seemed to come to a real break—she would not be alone with him at all. And perhaps she was a bit nervous, I don't know, but she got Moadine to come and stay next door to her. Also she had a sturdy assistant detailed to accompany her in her work.

---

1 From "The Ladies" (1892), by Rudyard Kipling (1865–1936).

Terry had his own ideas, as I've tried to show. I daresay he thought he had a right to do as he did. Perhaps he even convinced himself that it would be better for her. Anyhow he hid himself in her bedroom one night....

The women of Herland have no fear of men. Why should they have? They are not timid in any sense. They are not weak; and they all have strong trained athletic bodies. Othello could not have extinguished Alima with a pillow, as if she were a mouse.[1]

Terry put in practice his pet conviction that a woman loves to be mastered, and by sheer brute force, in all the pride and passion of his intense masculinity, he tried to master this woman.

It did not work. I got a pretty clear account of it later from Ellador, but what we heard at the time was the noise of a tremendous struggle, and Alima calling to Moadine. Moadine was close by and came at once; one or two more strong grave women followed.

Terry dashed about like a madman; he would cheerfully have killed them—he told me that, himself—but he couldn't. When he swung a chair over his head one sprang in the air and caught it, two threw themselves bodily upon him and forced him to the floor; it was only the work of a few moments to have him tied hand and foot, and then, in sheer pity for his futile rage, to anaesthetize him.

★ ★ ★ ★ ★

Alima was in a cold fury. She wanted him killed—actually.

There was a trial before the local Over-Mother, and this woman, who did not enjoy being mastered, stated her case.

In a court in our country he would have been held quite "within his rights," of course. But this was not our country, it was theirs. They seemed to measure the enormity of the offense by its effect upon a possible fatherhood, and he scorned even to reply to this way of putting it.

He did let himself go once, and explained in definite terms that they were incapable of understanding a man's needs, a man's desires, a man's point of view. He called them neuters, epicenes, bloodless, sexless creatures. He said they could of course kill him—as so many insects could—but that he despised them none the less.

---

1 Reference to the smothering by Othello of his wife Desdemona in Shakespeare's tragedy *Othello*.

And all those stern grave mothers did not seem to mind his despising them, not in the least.

It was a long trial, and many interesting points were brought out, as to their views of our habits, and after awhile Terry had his sentence. He waited, grim and defiant. The sentence was: "You must go home!"

Chapter XII

Expelled

We had all meant to go home again. Indeed we had *not* meant—not by any means—to stay as long as we had. But when it came to being turned out, dismissed, sent away for bad conduct, we none of us really liked it.

Terry said he did. He professed great scorn of the penalty and the trial, as well as all the other characteristics of "this miserable half-country." But he knew, and we knew, that in any "whole" country we should never have been as forgivingly treated as we had been here.

"If the people had come after us according to the directions we left, there'd have been quite a different story!" said Terry. We found out later why no reserve party had arrived. All our careful directions had been destroyed in a fire. We might have all died there and no one at home have ever known our whereabouts.

Terry was under guard now, all the time; known as unsafe, convicted of what was to them an unpardonable sin.

He laughed at their chill horror. "Parcel of old maids!" he called them. "They're all old maids—children or not. They don't know the first thing about Sex."

When Terry said *Sex*, *sex* with a very large *S*, he meant the male sex, naturally; its special values, its profound conviction of being "the life force," its cheerful ignoring of the true life process, and its interpretation of the other sex solely from its own point of view.

I had learned to see these things very differently since living with Ellador; and as for Jeff, he was so thoroughly Herlandized that he wasn't fair to Terry, who fretted sharply in his new restraint.

Moadine, grave and strong, as sadly patient as a mother with a degenerate[1] child, kept steady watch on him, with enough other

---

1 In the sense of "degeneration," or having been born with traits that are counter to evolutionary progress, such as a developmental disability.

women close at hand to prevent an outbreak. He had no weapons, and well knew that all his strength was of small avail against those grim, quiet women.

We were allowed to visit him freely, but he had only his room, and a small high-walled garden to walk in, while the preparations for our departure were under way.

Three of us were to go; Terry, because he must; I, because two were safer for our flyer, and the long boat trip to the coast; Ellador, because she would not let me go without her.

If Jeff had elected to return, Celis would have gone too—they were the most absorbed of lovers; but Jeff had no desire that way.

"Why should I want to go back to all our noise and dirt, our vice and crime, our disease and degeneracy?" he demanded of me privately. We never spoke like that before the women. "I wouldn't take Celis there for anything on earth!" he protested. "She'd die! She'd die of horror and shame to see our slums and hospitals. How can you risk it with Ellador? You'd better break it to her gently before she really makes up her mind."

Jeff was right. I ought to have told her more fully than I did, of all the things we had to be ashamed of. But it is very hard to bridge the gulf of as deep a difference as existed between our life and theirs. I tried to.

"Look here, my dear," I said to her. "If you are really going to my country with me you've got to be prepared for a good many shocks. It's not as beautiful as this—the cities, I mean, the civilized parts—of course the wild country is."

"I shall enjoy it all," she said, her eyes starry with hope. "I understand it's not like ours. I can see how monotonous our quiet life must seem to you, how much more stirring yours must be. It must be like the biological change you told me about when the second sex was introduced—a far greater movement, constant change, with new possibilities of growth."

I had told her of the later biological theories of sex, and she was deeply convinced of the superior advantages of having two, the superiority of a world with men in it.

"We have done what we could alone; perhaps we have some things better in a quiet way, but you have the whole world—all the people of the different nations—all the long rich history behind you—all the wonderful new knowledge—Oh, I just can't wait to see it!"

What could I do? I told her in so many words that we had our unsolved problems, that we had dishonesty and corruption, vice and crime, disease and insanity, prisons and hospitals; and it made no more impression on her than it would to tell a South Sea Islander about the temperature of the Arctic Circle. She could intellectually see that it was bad to have those things; but she could not *feel* it.

We had quite easily come to accept the Herland life as normal, because it was normal—none of us make any outcry over mere health and peace and happy industry. And the abnormal, to which we are all so sadly well acclimated, she had never seen.

The two things she cared most to hear about, and wanted most to see, were these: the beautiful relation of marriage and the lovely women who were mothers and nothing else; beyond these her keen, active mind hungered eagerly for the world life.

"I'm almost as anxious to go as you are yourself," she insisted, "and you must be desperately homesick."

I assured her that no one could be homesick in such a paradise as theirs, but she would none of it.

"Oh, yes—I know. It's like those little tropical islands you've told me about, shining like jewels in the big blue sea—I can't wait to see the sea! The little island may be as perfect as a garden, but you always want to get back to your own big country, don't you? Even if it is bad in some ways?"

Ellador was more than willing. But the nearer it came to our really going, and to my having to take her back to our "civilization," after the clean peace and beauty of theirs, the more I began to dread it, and the more I tried to explain.

Of course I had been homesick at first, while we were prisoners, before I had Ellador. And of course I had, at first, rather idealized my country and its ways, in describing it. Also I had always accepted certain evils as integral parts of our civilization and never dwelt on them at all. Even when I tried to tell her the worst, I never remembered some things—which, when she came to see them, impressed her at once, as they had never impressed me. Now, in my efforts at explanation, I began to see both ways more keenly than I had before; to see the painful defects of my own land, the marvelous gains of this.

In missing men we three visitors had naturally missed the larger part of life, and had unconsciously assumed that they must miss it too. It took me a long time to realize—Terry never did realize—how little it meant to them. When we say *men, man, manly, manhood,* and all the other masculine derivatives, we have in the background of our minds a huge vague crowded picture of the world and all its activities. To grow up and "be a man," to act "like a man"—the meaning and connotation is wide indeed. That vast background is full of marching columns of men, of changing lines of men, of long processions of men; of men steering their ships into new seas, exploring unknown mountains, breaking horses, herding cattle, ploughing and sowing and reaping, toiling at the forge and furnace, digging in the mine, building roads and bridges and high cathedrals, managing great businesses, teaching in all the colleges, preaching in all the churches; men everywhere, doing everything—The World.

And when we say *Women*, we think *Female*—the sex.

But to these women, in the unbroken sweep of this two-thousand-year-old feminine civilization, the word *woman* called up all that big background, so far as they had gone in social development; and the word *man* meant to them only *male*—the sex.

Of course we could *tell* them that in our world men did everything; but that did not alter the background of their minds. That man, "the male," did all these things was to them a statement, making no more change in the point of view than was made in ours when we first faced the astounding fact—to us—that in Herland women were "the world."

We had been living there more than a year. We had learned their limited history, with its straight, smooth, upreaching lines, reaching higher and going faster up to the smooth comfort of their present life. We had learned a little of their psychology, a much wider field than the history, but here we could not follow so readily. We were now well used to seeing women not as females, but as people; people of all sorts, doing every kind of work.

This outbreak of Terry's and the strong reaction against it, gave us a new light on their genuine femininity. This was given me with great clearness, by both Ellador and Somel. The feeling was the same, sick revulsion and horror, such as would be felt at some climactic blasphemy.

They had no faintest approach to such a thing in their minds, knowing nothing of the custom of marital indulgence among us. To them the one high purpose of Motherhood had been for so long the governing law of life, and the contribution of the father, though known to them, so distinctly another method to the same end, that they could not, with all their effort, get the point of view of the male creature whose desires quite ignore parentage and seek only for what we euphoniously term "the joys of love."

When I tried to tell Ellador that women too felt so, with us, she drew away from me, and tried hard to grasp intellectually what she could in no way sympathize with.

"You mean—that with you—love between man and woman expresses itself in that way—without regard to motherhood? To parentage, I mean," she added carefully.

"Yes, surely. It is Love we think of—the deep sweet love between two. Of course we want children, and children come—but that is not what we think about."

"But—but—it seems so against nature!" she said. "None of the creatures we know do that. Do other animals—in your country?"

"We are not animals!" I replied with some sharpness. "At least we are something more—something higher. This is a far nobler and more beautiful relation, as I have explained before. Your view seems to us rather—shall I say, practical? Prosaic? Merely a means to an end! With us—Oh, my dear girl—cannot you see? Cannot you feel? It is the last sweetest, highest consummation of mutual love."

She was impressed visibly. She trembled in my arms, as I held her close, kissing her hungrily. But there rose in her eyes that look I knew so well, that remote clear look as if she had gone far away even though I held her beautiful body so close, and was now on some snowy mountain regarding me from a distance.

"I feel it quite clearly," she said to me. "It gives me a deep sympathy with what you feel, no doubt more strongly still. But what I feel, even what you feel, dearest, does not convince me that it is right. Until I am sure of that, of course I cannot do as you wish."

Ellador, at times like this, always reminded me of Epictetus.[1] "I will put you in prison!" said his master. "My body, you mean," replied Epictetus calmly. "I will cut your head off," said his master. "Have I said that my head could not be cut off?" A difficult person, Epictetus.

What is this miracle by which a woman, even in your arms, may withdraw herself, utterly disappear till what you hold is as inaccessible as the face of a cliff?

"Be patient with me, dear," she urged sweetly. "I know it is hard for you. And I begin to see—a little—how Terry was so driven to crime."

"Oh, come, that's a pretty hard word for it. After all, Alima was his wife, you know," I urged, feeling at the moment a sudden burst of sympathy for poor Terry. For a man of his temperament,—and habits—it must have been an unbearable situation.

---

1 Greek Stoic philosopher (55–135 CE), who was born a slave. He taught that philosophy is a way of life and that happiness derives from calmly accepting that we cannot control most events in our lives. The passage quoted is from *The Discourses*, Book I, chap. 29.

But Ellador, for all her wide intellectual grasp, and the broad sympathy in which their religion trained them, could not make allowance for such—to her—sacrilegious brutality.

It was the more difficult to explain to her, because we three, in our constant talks and lectures about the rest of the world, had naturally avoided the seamy side; not so much from a desire to deceive, but from wishing to put the best foot foremost for our civilization, in the face of the beauty and comfort of theirs. Also we really thought some things were right, or at least unavoidable, which we could readily see would be repugnant to them, and therefore did not discuss. Again there was much of our world's life which we, being used to it, had not noticed as anything worth describing. And still further, there was about these women a colossal innocence upon which many of the things we did say had made no impression whatever.

I am thus explicit about it because it shows how unexpectedly strong was the impression made upon Ellador when she at last entered our civilization.

She urged me to be patient, and I was patient. You see I loved her so much that even the restrictions she so firmly established left me much happiness. We were lovers, and there is surely delight enough in that.

Do not imagine that these young women utterly refused "the Great New Hope," as they called it, that of dual parentage. For that they had agreed to marry us, though the marrying part of it was a concession to our prejudices rather than theirs. To them the process was the holy thing—and they meant to keep it holy.

But so far only Celis, her blue eyes swimming in happy tears, her heart lifted with that tide of race motherhood which was their supreme passion, could with ineffable joy and pride announce that she was to be a mother. "The New Motherhood" they called it, and the whole country knew. There was no pleasure, no service, no honor in all the land that Celis might not have had. Almost like the breathless reverence with which, two thousand years ago, that dwindling band of women had watched the miracle of virgin birth, was the deep awe and warm expectancy with which they greeted this new miracle of union.

All mothers in that land were holy. To them, for long ages, the approach to motherhood has been by the most intense and exquisite love and longing, by the Supreme Desire, the overmastering demand for a Child. Every thought they held in connection with the processes of maternity was open to the day, simple, yet sacred.

Every woman of them placed Motherhood not only higher than other duties, but so far higher that there were no other duties, one might almost say. All their wide mutual love, all the subtle interplay of mutual friendship and service, the urge of progressive thought and invention, the deepest religious emotion, every feeling and every act was related to this great central Power, to the River of Life pouring through them, which made them the bearers of the very Spirit of God.

Of all this I learned more and more; from their books, from talk, especially from Ellador. She was at first, for a brief moment, envious of her friend—a thought she put away from her at once and forever.

"It is better," she said to me. "It is much better that it has not come to me yet—to us, that is. For if I am to go with you to your country, we may have 'adventures by sea and land,'[1] as you say (and as in truth we did), and it might not be at all safe for a baby. So we won't try again, dear, till it is safe—will we?"

This was a hard saying for a very loving husband.

"Unless," she went on, "if one is coming, you will leave me behind. You can come back, you know—and I shall have the Child."

Then that deep ancient chill of male jealousy of even his own progeny touched my heart.

"I'd rather have you, Ellador, than all the children in the world. I'd rather have you with me—on your own terms—than not to have you."

This was a very stupid saying. Of course I would! For if she wasn't there I should want all of her and have none of her. But if she went along as a sort of sublimated sister—only much closer and warmer than that, really—why I should have all of her but that one thing. And I was beginning to find that Ellador's friendship, Ellador's comradeship, Ellador's sisterly affection, Ellador's perfectly sincere love—none the less deep that she held it back on a definite line of reserve—were enough to live on very happily.

I find it quite beyond me to describe what this woman was to me. We talk fine things about women, but in our hearts we know that they are very limited beings—most of them. We honor them for their functional powers, even while we dishonor them by our use of it; we honor them for their carefully enforced virtue, even

---

1 This phrase appears in the title of several nineteenth-century books about travel and exploration, any or all of which Gilman might have been consciously parodying at times in *Herland*.

while we show by our own conduct how little we think of that virtue; we value them, sincerely, for the perverted maternal activities which make our wives the most comfortable of servants, bound to us for life with the wages wholly at our own decision, their whole business, outside of the temporary duties of such motherhood as they may achieve, to meet our needs in every way. Oh, we value them, all right, "in their place;" which place is the home, where they perform that mixture of duties so ably described by Mrs. Josephine Dodge Daskam Bacon,[1] in which the services of "a mistress" are carefully specified. She is a very clear writer, Mrs. J.D.D. Bacon, and understands her subject—from her own point of view. But—that combination of industries, while convenient, and in a way economical, does not arouse the kind of emotion commanded by the woman of Herland. These were women one had to love "up," very high up, instead of down. They were not pets. They were not servants. They were not timid, inexperienced, weak.

After I got over the jar to my pride (which Jeff, I truly think, never felt—he was a born worshipper, and which Terry never got over—he was quite clear in his ideas of "the position of women") I found that loving "up" was a very good sensation after all. It gave me a queer feeling, way down deep, as of the stirring of some ancient dim prehistoric consciousness, a feeling that they were right somehow—that this was the way to feel. It was like—coming home to mother. I don't mean the underflannels-and-doughnuts mother, the fussy person that waits on you and spoils you and doesn't really know you. I mean the feeling that a very little child would have, who had been lost—for ever so long. It was a sense of getting home; of being clean and rested; of safety and yet freedom; of love that was always there, warm like sunshine in May, not hot like a stove or a feather-bed—a love that didn't irritate and didn't smother.

I looked at Ellador as if I hadn't seen her before. "If you won't go," I said, "I'll get Terry to the coast and come back alone. You can let me down a rope. And if you will go—why you blessed Wonder-Woman—I would rather live with you all my life—like this—than to have any other woman I ever saw, or any number of them, to do as I liked with. Will you come?"

---

1 American author (1876–1961) of more than forty books of poetry and fiction, frequently with female protagonists or concerned with "women's issues."

She was keen for coming. So the plans went on. She'd have liked to wait for that Marvel of Celis's, but Terry had no such desire. He was crazy to be out of it all. It made him sick, he said, *sick*; this everlasting mother-mother-mothering. I don't think Terry had what the phrenologists call "the lump of philoprogenitiveness"[1] at all well developed.

"Morbid one-sided cripples," he called them, even when from his window he could see their splendid vigor and beauty; even while Moadine, as patient and friendly as if she had never helped Alima to hold and bind him, sat there in the room, the picture of wisdom and serene strength. "Sexless, epicene, undeveloped neuters!" he went on bitterly. He sounded like Sir Almwroth Wright.[2]

Well—it was hard. He was madly in love with Alima, really; more so than he had ever been before, and their tempestuous courtship, quarrels and reconciliations, had fanned the flame. And then when he sought by that supreme conquest which seems so natural a thing to that type of man, to force her to love him as her master—to have the sturdy athletic furious woman rise up and master him—she and her friends—it was no wonder he raged.

Come to think of it, I do not recall a similar case in all history or fiction. Women have killed themselves rather than submit to outrage; they have killed the outrager; they have escaped, or they have submitted—sometimes seeming to get on very well with the victor afterward. There was that adventure of "false Sextus," for instance, who "found Lucrese combing the fleece, under the midnight lamp."[3] He threatened, as I remember, that if she did not submit he would slay her, slay a slave and place him beside her and say he found him there. A poor device, it always seemed to me. If Mr. Lucretius had asked him how he came to be in his

---

1 See p. 139, note 1. In the pseudo-science of phrenology, developed by Franz Joseph Gall in the late eighteenth century, character was "read" by examining the shape of the head; the lump of progenitiveness is located at the very back of the head.

2 See p. 149, note 1 and Appendix B3.

3 In the accounts by the Roman historian Livy and Roman poet Ovid, Sextus Tarquinius, impressed by the virtue of the chaste Lucretia, broke into her bedroom and made her choose between having sex with him or being killed, along with a slave, so that it would look like she had been caught having sex with the slave; afterwards she reported the rape to her father and husband and then stabbed herself. The best-known retelling is Shakespeare's *The Rape of Lucrece*, but Gilman's quotation is from "Virginia," by Thomas Babington Macauley (1800–59).

wife's bedroom overlooking her morals, what could he have said? But the point is Lucrese submitted, and Alima didn't.

"She kicked me," confided the embittered prisoner—he had to talk to someone. "I was doubled up with the pain, of course, and she jumped on me and yelled for this old Harpy (Moadine couldn't hear him) and they had me trussed up in no time. I believe Alima could have done it alone," he added with reluctant admiration. "She's as strong as a horse. And of course a man's helpless when you hit him like that. No woman with a shade of decency—"

I had to grin at that, and even Terry did, sourly. He wasn't given to reasoning, but it did strike him that an assault like his rather waived considerations of decency.

"I'd give a year of my life to have her alone again," he said slowly, his hands clenched till the knuckles were white.

But he never did. She left our end of the country entirely; went up into the fir-forest on the highest slopes, and stayed there. Before we left he quite desperately longed to see her, but she would not come and he could not go. They watched him like lynxes. (Do lynxes watch any better than mousing cats, I wonder!)

Well—we had to get the flyer in order, and be sure there was enough fuel left, though Terry said we could glide all right, down to that lake, once we got started. We'd have gone gladly in a week's time, of course, but there was a great to-do all over the country about Ellador's leaving them. She had interviews with some of the leading ethicists—wise women with still eyes, and with the best of the teachers. There was a stir, a thrill, a deep excitement everywhere.

Our teaching about the rest of the world has given them all a sense of isolation, of remoteness, of being a little outlying sample of a country, overlooked and forgotten among the family of nations. We had called it "the family of nations," and they liked the phrase immensely.

They were deeply aroused on the subject of evolution; indeed, the whole field of natural science drew them irresistibly. Any number of them would have risked everything to go to the strange unknown lands and study; but we could take only one, and it had to be Ellador, naturally.

We planned greatly about coming back, about establishing a connecting route by water; about penetrating those vast forests and civilizing—or exterminating—the dangerous savages. That is, we men talked of that last—not with the women. They had a definite aversion to killing things.

But meanwhile there was high council being held among the wisest of them all. The students and thinkers who had been gathering facts from us all this time, collating and relating them, and making inferences, laid the result of their labors before the council.

Little had we thought that our careful efforts at concealment had been so easily seen through, with never a word to show us that they saw. They had followed up words of ours on the science of optics, asked innocent questions about glasses and the like, and were aware of the defective eyesight so common among us.

With the lightest touch, different women asking different questions at different times, and putting all our answers together like a picture puzzle, they had figured out a sort of skeleton chart as to the prevalence of disease among us. Even more subtly with no show of horror or condemnation, they had gathered something— far from the truth, but something pretty clear, about poverty, vice and crime. They even had a goodly number of our dangers all itemized, from asking us about insurance and innocent things like that.

They were well posted as to the different races, beginning with their poison-arrow natives down below and widening out to the broad racial divisions we had told them about. Never a shocked expression of the face, or exclamation of revolt had warned us; they had been extracting the evidence without our knowing it all this time, and now were studying with the most devout earnestness the matter they had prepared.

The result was rather distressing to us. They first explained the matter fully to Ellador, as she was the one who purposed visiting the Rest of the World. To Celis they said nothing. She must not be in any way distressed, while the whole nation waited on her Great Work.

Finally Jeff and I were called in. Somel and Zava were there, and Ellador, with many others that we knew.

They had a great globe, quite fairly mapped out from the small section maps in that compendium of ours. They had the different peoples of the earth roughly outlined, and their status in civilization indicated. They had charts and figures and estimates, based on the facts in that traitorous little book and what they had learned from us.

Somel explained: "We find that in all your historic period, so much longer than ours, that with all the interplay of services, the exchange of inventions and discoveries, and the wonderful progress we so admire, that in this widespread Other World of yours, there is still much disease, often contagious."

We admitted this at once.

"Also there is still, in varying degree, ignorance, with prejudice and unbridled emotion."

This too was admitted.

"We find also that in spite of the advance of democracy and the increase of wealth, that there is still unrest and sometimes combat."

Yes, yes, we admitted it all. We were used to these things and saw no reason for so much seriousness.

"All things considered," they said, and they did not say a hundredth part of the things they were considering, "we are unwilling to expose our country to free communication with the rest of the world—as yet. If Ellador comes back, and we approve her report, it may be done later—but not yet.

"So we have this to ask of you Gentlemen (they knew that word was held a title of honor with us), that you promise not in any way to betray the location of this country until permission—after Ellador's return."

Jeff was perfectly satisfied. He thought they were quite right. He always did. I never saw an alien become naturalized more quickly than that man in Herland.

I studied it awhile, thinking of the time they'd have if some of our contagions got loose there, and concluded they were right. So I agreed.

Terry was the obstacle. "Indeed I won't!" he protested. "The first thing I'll do is to get an expedition fixed up to force an entrance into Ma-land."

"Then," they said quite calmly, "he must remain an absolute prisoner, always."

"Anesthesia would be kinder,"[1] urged Moadine.

"And safer," added Zava.

"He will promise, I think," said Ellador.

And he did. With which agreement we at last left Herland.

---

1 See "Imprisonment for Life" in this collection. Gilman, who had experimented with the anesthetic chloroform as early as age seventeen, ended her own life by inhaling chloroform after she was debilitated by inoperable breast cancer.

RELATED WRITINGS

Fiction

"Five Girls"
The Impress (1 December 1894): 4–5

[This story appeared in the first journal Gilman edited, *The Impress*, as part of a series called "Story Studies." Gilman wrote each story in the style of a different author, and readers were to try to identify the story's style. "Five Girls," written in imitation of Louisa May Alcott's *Little Women* (1868–69) but radically revising Alcott's ideas about the domestic, offers an early, small-scale example of women designing a model community.]

"There won't be many more such good times as these for us," said Olive Sargent, mournfully hugging her knees as she sat on the floor under the big Victory; "we've got to go out into the cold world presently and earn our livings."

"I don't mind earning the living a bit," pretty Molly Edgerton asserted; "I like to, and I shall never give it up; but I do hate to be separated the way we shall be. I wish we needn't." And Molly dusted the crumbs of her luncheon from her spotless gingham apron.

The other girls always had charcoal on their aprons, or water colors, or oil, or dabs of clay; even sometimes all of these; but Molly's was always clean. To be sure, her work was mostly pencil drawing, the making of delicately beautiful designs for jewelry, for fans, for wood carving, for lace even—she was a born designer, and made the other girls green with envy.

Then Serena Woods opened her mouth and spoke. Serena was going to be an architect; indeed she was one already in a modest way, having planned the school-house in her native town, and also the dwelling of her married sister. To be sure, the sister did sometimes complain to intimate friends of certain minor deficiencies in the edifice, but what is that to a rising architect whose brain glows with enthusiasm and lives in a luminous cloud of architraves, pediments, and facades. She spoke slowly, looking down from her perch on a high stool. "Girls, let's not separate. Let's go and live together in a house of our own. I'll build it."

"O do!" said Julia Morse, "I'll decorate it! We shall each have a room in our favorite color, with most appropriate designs, and the rooms down stairs shall be a real sermon and poem in one!" And Julia gushed on with fervid descriptions of her proposed scheme of mural decoration, while the others joined in rapturous applause.

Then Maud Annersley joined in. Maud was a tall, pale, slender girl, with dark, thoughtful, blue eyes and a quiet voice. She was a painter, and had had a picture in the last exhibition which had won approval from the best critics. "Do you know," she said earnestly, "that we really might do this thing? We are all good friends and used to rooming together for these two years. We know all we mean to each other and when to stop—when to let each other alone. We've all got to earn our living, as Olive says, and it would be cheaper to earn it together than it would apart." And Maud rinsed her biggest brush in the turpentine cup with severe decision.

Olive rose to her feet tempestuously.

"I do believe we could!" she said, her blue eyes lighting with sudden fervor. "What is to hinder our joining forces and working on together, having the sweetest, grandest, most useful life in the world! We could club our funds, go to some nice place where land is cheap, and Serena could really plan for us one of those splendid compound houses that are so beautiful and convenient. We could arrange it with studios, all as they should be, and other artists could rent them of us to help on. You know I shall have some money as soon as I'm twenty-one; and I'd rather invest it so than any way I know." Olive stopped for breath, flushed and triumphant; and the others looked at each other with new earnestness.

"We're talking of an awfully serious thing," said Maud. "It would mean living, you know, really living right along;" and she scraped her palette softly as she talked, making a beautiful mixed tint of the spotty little dabs of burnt sienna, cadmium and terre vert. "There is no reason we should not do it though. But it ought to mean for life, and we're not all going to be single, I hope."

Beautiful Maud, with her pale, sweet, oval face and wealth of soft, glistening, chestnut hair, had seen her lover buried, and turned to her chosen art as a life-long companion. But, she could speak all the more earnestly to her heart free friends; though there was a tell-tale blush on pretty Mollie's cheek, and Julia looked a little conscious as she spoke.

"Well anyway," said the last named damsel, with rather a defiant tone; "if we do marry we don't mean to give up our work I hope. I mean to marry some time, perhaps—but I don't mean to cook! I mean to decorate always, and make lots of money and hire a housekeeper."

"I don't see," said Mollie dimpling softly, "why that should be an obstacle. Couldn't we have a house so big and beautiful and live so happily and get to be so famous that—that—if any one wanted to marry us they could come there too?"

"What sort of compound fractions do you think we are?" demanded Serena. "Any one marry us indeed! It would take five to marry us, Mollie!"

"Now stop joking, girls," said Olive. "We are all grown and trained. We all want to always work—indeed, some of us have got to. Now, honestly, why shouldn't we build a sort of apartment home you know, a beautiful "model tenement" affair, artistic and hygienic and esthetic and everything else; with central kitchens and all those things; and studios and rooms for ourselves, and a hall to exhibit in and so on. Then we could have suites of apartments for families and let them; and bye and bye, if we are families, we can occupy those ourselves and let the others!"

And Olive hugged the headless Victory in her enthusiasm while the girls applauded rapturously.

Then what a happy year they had before their course at the Institute was finished! Such innumerable plans and elevations; such glowing schemes of color, such torrents of design for carving and painting and modelling, such wild visions of decoration, where races and epochs and styles waltzed madly together in interminable procession.

The class work went on, of course, and Maud's great picture won the first prize at the exhibition, though no one guessed that the lovely walls in the background were from one of Serena's least practicable elevations, and that the group of girls in front were the future owners thereof. There was a troubadour in it also, but he was purely imaginary; though Maud did tell Mollie that he was the fortunate youth that was going to marry them.

It was but a year or two before the lovely plan came true, for after all there was nothing impossible in it. Between them all there was money enough to buy the lot and build the house, and the "families" consented to hire apartments therein to such an extent as to furnish all the funds for running expenses.

Julia Morse's redoubtable Aunt Susan came down from her New Hampshire home to keep house in the new mansion, and declared that she never had had half a chance to show what was in her before.

Olive's widowed mother made the dearest of chaperones for the girls, and their long parlor rang with music and merriment on the pleasant winter evenings.

The studios were easy to let also, and the velveteen coat and loose blouse became as frequent in the long halls as the paint-daubed gingham apron. Also the troubadour materialized in the shape of a most angelic-voiced singing master; who occupied a room on the top floor; and who, though he did not marry them all, as was aforetime suggested, did marry Olive in due season and stayed in the same pleasant quarters thereafter. Only a "family" was evicted, so to speak, for their convenience, and Olive's room was let to an aspiring little sister of the troubadour.

Pretty Mollie followed suit in a few months more—it took some time to convince her devoted but conservative lover that they could just as well have a suite in this beautiful great home cluster as in a flat near the park. Every girl of them married, as years passed on; even Maud, who forgot her early sorrow in a newer, deeper joy.

But live together they did, and work together always, with various breaks and lapses, as the sweet home cares sometimes interfered with working hours, and the charming little kindergarten in the south wing grew fuller and fuller.

"There's nothing like planning things for life," said Olive one still June evening in after years, as the same five girls sat together on the rose shadowed porch; older, but no less earnest in their work and their love for each other.

"That's so," said Serena heartily—"especially when you do the things you plan."

"The Unnatural Mother"
The Forerunner 7.11 (November 1916): 281–85. Previously published as "An Unnatural Mother" in *The Impress* (16 February 1895): 4–5; and in abridged form in *The Forerunner* 4.6 (June 1913): 141–43

[Written shortly after Gilman herself was called an "unnatural mother" because she had sent her daughter to live with her ex-husband and his new wife, this story both comments on specific child-rearing techniques and argues for a larger definition of effective motherhood, much like that in *Herland*. Gilman's repeated republication of the story indicates its importance to her.]

"Don't tell me!" said old Mis' Briggs, with a forbidding shake of the head; "no mother that was a mother would desert her own child for anything on earth!"

"And leaving it a care on the town, too!" put in Susannah Jacobs, "as if we hadn't enough to do to take care of our own!"

Miss Jacobs was a well-to-do old maid, owning a comfortable farm and homestead, and living alone with an impoverished cousin acting as general servant, companion and protégée. Mis' Briggs, on the contrary, had had thirteen children, five of whom remained to bless her, so that what maternal feeling Miss Jacobs might lack, Mis' Briggs could certainly supply.

"I should think," piped little Martha Ann Simmons, the village dressmaker, "that she might a saved her young one first and then tried what she could do for the town."

Martha had been married, had lost her husband, and had one sickly boy to care for.

The youngest Briggs girl, still unmarried at thirty-six, and in her mother's eyes a most tender infant, now ventured to make a remark.

"You don't any of you seem to think what she did for all of us— if she hadn't left hers we should all have lost ours, sure."

"You ain't no call to judge, Maria Melia," her mother hastened to reply; "you've no children of your own, and you can't judge of a mother's duty. No mother ought to leave her child, whatever happens. The Lord gave it to her to take care of—he never gave her other people's. You needn't tell me!"

"She was an unnatural mother!" repeated Miss Jacobs harshly, "as I said to begin with."

"What is the story?" asked the City Boarder. The City Boarder was interested in stories from a business point of view, but they did not know that. "What did this woman do?" she asked.

There was no difficulty in eliciting particulars. The difficulty was rather in discriminating amidst their profusion and contradictoriness. But when the City Boarder got it clear in her mind it was somewhat as follows:

The name of the much condemned heroine was Esther Greenwood, and she lived and died here in Toddsville.

Toddsville was a mill village. The Todds lived on a beautiful eminence overlooking the little town, as the castles of robber barons on the Rhine used to overlook their little towns. The mills and the mill hands' houses were built close along the bed of the river. They had to be pretty close, because the valley was a narrow one, and the bordering hills were too steep for travel, but the water power was fine. Above the village was the reservoir, filling the entire valley save for a narrow road beside it, a fair blue smiling lake, edged with lilies and blue flag, rich in pickerel and perch. This lake gave them fish, it gave them ice, it gave the power that ran the mills that gave the town its bread. Blue Lake was both useful and ornamental.

In this pretty and industrious village Esther had grown up, the somewhat neglected child of a heart-broken widower. He had lost a young wife, and three fair babies before her—this one was left him, and he said he meant that she should have all the chance there was.

"That was what ailed her in the first place!" they all eagerly explained to the City Boarder. "She never knew what 'twas to have a mother, and she grew up a regular tomboy! Why she used to roam the country for miles around, in all weather like an Injun! And her father wouldn't take no advice!"

This topic lent itself to eager discussion. The recreant father, it appeared, was a doctor, not their accepted standby, the resident physician of the neighborhood, but an alien doctor, possessed of "views."

"You never heard such things as he advocated," Miss Jacobs explained. "He wouldn't give no medicines, hardly; said 'nature' did the curing—he couldn't."

"And he couldn't either—that was clear," Mrs. Briggs agreed. "Look at his wife and children dying on his hands, as it were! 'Physician heal thyself,' I say."

"But, mother," Maria Amelia put in, "she was an invalid when he married her, they say; and those children died of polly—polly—what's that thing that nobody can help?"

"That may all be so," Miss Jacobs admitted, "but all the same it's a doctor's business to give medicine. If 'nature' was all that was wanted, we needn't have any doctor at all!"

"I believe in medicine and plenty of it. I always gave my children a good clearance,[1] spring and fall, whether anything ailed 'em or not, just to be on the safe side. And if there was anything the matter with 'em they had plenty more. I never had anything to reproach myself with on that score," stated Mrs. Briggs, firmly. Then as a sort of concession to the family graveyard, she added piously, "The Lord giveth and the Lord taketh away."

"You should have seen the way he dressed that child!" pursued Miss Jacobs. "It was a reproach to the town. Why, you couldn't tell at a distance whether it was a boy or a girl. And barefoot! He let that child go barefoot till she was so big we was actually mortified to see her."

It appeared that a wild, healthy childhood had made Esther very different in her early womanhood from the meek, well-behaved damsels of the little place. She was well enough liked by those who knew her at all, and the children of the place adored her, but the worthy matrons shook their heads and prophesied no good of a girl who was "queer."

---

1 Purging with a laxative.

She was described with rich detail in reminiscence, how she wore her hair short till she was fifteen—"just shingled like a boy's—it did seem a shame that girl had no mother to look after her—and her clo'se was almost a scandal, even when she did put on shoes and stockings." "Just gingham—brown gingham—and *short!*"

"I think she was a real nice girl," said Maria Amelia. "I can remember her just as well! She was *so* nice to us children. She was five or six years older than I was, and most girls that age won't have anything to do with little ones. But she was as kind and pleasant. She'd take us berrying and on all sorts of walks, and teach us new games and tell us things. I don't remember any one that ever did us the good she did!"

Maria Amelia's thin chest heaved with emotion; and there were tears in her eyes; but her mother took her up somewhat sharply.

"That sounds well I must say—right before your own mother that's toiled and slaved for you! It's all very well for a young thing that's got nothing on earth to do to make herself agreeable to young ones. That poor blinded father of hers never taught her to do the work a girl should—naturally he couldn't."

"At least he might have married again and given her another mother," said Susannah Jacobs, with decision, with so much decision in fact that the City Boarder studied her expression for a moment and concluded that if this recreant father had not married again it was not for lack of opportunity.

Mrs. Simmons cast an understanding glance upon Miss Jacobs, and nodded wisely.

"Yes, he ought to have done that, of course. A man's not fit to bring up children, anyhow—How can they? Mothers have the instinct—that is, all natural mothers have. But, dear me! There's some as don't seem to *be* mothers—even when they have a child!"

"You're quite right, Mis' Simmons," agreed the mother of thirteen. "It's a divine instinct, I say. I'm sorry for the child that lacks it. Now this Esther. We always knew she wan't like other girls—she never seemed to care for dress and company and things girls naturally do, but was always philandering over the hills with a parcel of young ones. There wan't a child in town but would run after her. She made more trouble 'n a little in families, the young ones quotin' what Aunt Esther said, and tellin' what Aunt Esther did to their own mothers, and she only a young girl. Why she actually seemed to care more for them children than she did for beaux or anything—it wasn't natural!"

"But she did marry?" pursued the City Boarder.

"Marry! Yes, she married finally. We all thought she never would, but she did. After the things her father taught her it did seem as if he'd ruined *all* her chances. It's simply terrible the way that girl was trained."

"Him being a doctor," put in Mrs. Simmons, "made it different, I suppose."

"Doctor or no doctor," Miss Jacobs rigidly interposed, "it was a crying shame to have a young girl so instructed."

"Maria Melia," said her mother, "I want you should get me my smelling salts. They're up in the spare chamber, I believe—When your Aunt Marcia was here she had one of her spells—don't you remember?—and she asked for salts. Look in the top bureau drawer—they must be there."

Maria Amelia, thirty-six, but unmarried, withdrew dutifully, and the other ladies drew closer to the City Boarder.

"It's the most shocking thing I ever heard of," murmured Mrs. Briggs. "Do you know he—a father—actually taught his daughter how babies come!"

There was a breathless hush.

"He did," eagerly chimed in the little dressmaker, "all the particulars. It was perfectly awful!"

"He said," continued Mrs. Briggs, "that he expected her to be a mother and that she ought to understand what was before her!"

"He was waited on by a committee of ladies from the church, married ladies, all older than he was," explained Miss Jacobs severely. "They told him it was creating a scandal in the town—and what do you think he said?"

There was another breathless silence.

Above, the steps of Maria Amelia were heard, approaching the stairs.

"It ain't there, Ma!"

"Well, you look in the high boy[1] and in the top drawer; they're somewhere up there," her mother replied.

Then, in a sepulchral whisper:

"He told us—yes, ma'am, I was on that committee—he told us that until young women knew what was before them as mothers they would not do their duty in choosing a father for their children! That was his expression—'choosing a father!' A nice thing for a young girl to be thinking of—a father for her children!"

"Yes, and more than that," inserted Miss Jacobs, who, though not on the committee, seemed familiar with its workings. "He

---

1 A tall chest of drawers supported on four legs.

told them——" But Mrs. Briggs waved her aside and continued swiftly——

"He taught that innocent girl about—the Bad Disease![1] Actually!"

"He did!" said the dressmaker. "It got out, too, all over town. There wasn't a man here would have married her after that."

Miss Jacobs insisted on taking up the tale. "I understand that he said it was 'to protect her!' Protect her, indeed! Against matrimony! As if any man alive would want to marry a young girl who knew all the evil of life! I was brought up differently, I assure you!"

"Young girls should be kept innocent!" Mrs. Briggs solemnly proclaimed. "Why, when I was married I knew no more what was before me than a babe unborn and my girls were all brought up so, too!"

Then, as Maria Amelia returned with the salts, she continued more loudly, "but she did marry after all. And a mighty queer husband she got, too. He was an artist or something, made pictures for the magazines and such as that, and they do say she met him first out in the hills. That's the first 'twas known of it here, anyhow—them two trapesing about all over; him with his painting things! They married and just settled down to live with her father, for she vowed she wouldn't leave him, and he said it didn't make no difference where he lived, he took his business with him."

"They seemed very happy together," said Maria Amelia.

"Happy! Well, they might have been, I suppose. It was a pretty queer family, I think." And her mother shook her head in retrospection. "They got on all right for a while; but the old man died, and those two—well, I don't call it housekeeping—the way they lived!"

"No," said Miss Jacobs. "They spent more time out of doors than they did in the house. She followed him around everywhere. And for open love making——"

They all showed deep disapproval at this memory. All but the City Boarder and Maria Amelia.

"She had one child, a girl," continued Mrs. Briggs, "and it was just shocking to see how she neglected that child from the beginnin'. She never seemed to have no maternal feelin' at all!"

"But I thought you said she was very fond of children," remonstrated the City Boarder.

---

1 Syphilis.

"Oh, *children*, yes. She'd take up with any dirty faced brat in town, even to them Kanucks.[1] I've seen her again and again with a whole swarm of the mill hands' young ones round her, goin' on some picnic or other—'open air school,' she used to call it—*Such* notions as she had. But when it come to her own child! Why——"
Here the speaker's voice sank to a horrified hush.

"She never had no baby clo'se for it! Not a single sock!"

The City Boarder was interested. "Why, what did she do with the little thing?"

"The Lord knows!" answered old Mis' Briggs. "She never would let us hardly see it when 'twas little. 'Shamed too, I don't doubt. But that's strange feelin's for a mother. Why, I was so proud of my babies! And I kept 'em lookin' so pretty! I'd a-sat up all night and sewed and washed, but I'd a had my children look well!" And the poor old eyes filled with tears as she thought of the eight little graves in the churchyard, which she never failed to keep looking pretty, even now. "She just let that young one roll round in the grass like a puppy with hardly nothin' on! Why, a squaw does better. She does keep 'em done up for a spell! That child was treated worse'n an Injun! We all done what we could, of course. We felt it no more'n right. But she was real hateful about it, and we had to let her be."

"The child died?" asked the City Boarder.

"Died! Dear no! That's it you saw going by; a great strappin' girl she is, too, and promisin' to grow up well, thanks to Mrs. Stone's taking her. Mrs. Stone always thought a heap of Esther. It's a mercy to the child that she lost her mother, I do believe! How she ever survived that kind of treatment beats all! Why that woman never seemed to have the first spark of maternal feeling to the end! She seemed just as fond of the other young ones after she had her own as she was before, and that's against nature. The way it happened was this. You see they lived up the valley nearer to the lake than the village. He was away, and was coming home that night, it seems, driving from Drayton along the lake road. And she set out to meet him. She must a walked up to the dam to look for him; and we think maybe she saw the team clear across the lake. Maybe she thought he could get to the house and save little Esther in time—that's the only explanation we ever could put on it. But this is what she did; and you can judge for yourselves if any mother in her senses *could* ha' done such a thing! You see 'twas the

---

1 Canuck; slang term for a Canadian, especially a French Canadian. Often considered derogatory.

time of that awful disaster, you've read of it, likely, that destroyed three villages. Well, she got to the dam and see that 'twas givin' way—she was always great for knowin' all such things. And she just turned and ran. Jake Elder was up on the hill after a stray cow, and he seen her go. He was too far off to imagine what ailed her, but he said he never saw a woman run so in his life.

"And, if you'll believe it, she run right by her own house—never stopped—never looked at it. Just run for the village. Of course, she may have lost her head with the fright, but that wasn't like her. No, I think she had made up her mind to leave that innocent baby to die! She just ran down here and give warnin', and, of course, we sent word down valley on horseback, and there was no lives lost in all three villages. She started to run back as soon as we was 'roused, but 'twas too late then.

"Jake saw it all, though he was too far off to do a thing. He said he couldn't stir a foot, it was so awful. He seen the wagon drivin' along as nice as you please till it got close to the dam, and then Greenwood seemed to see the danger and whipped up like mad. He was the father, you know. But he wasn't quite in time—the dam give way and the water went over him like a tidal wave. She was almost to the gate when it struck the house and her—and we never found her body nor his for days and days. They was washed clear down river.

"Their house was strong and it stood a little high, and had some big trees between it and the lake too. It was moved off the place and brought up against the side of the stone church down yonder, but 'twant wholly in pieces. And that child was found swimmin' round in its bed, most drowned, but not quite. The wonder is, it didn't die of a cold, but it's here yet—must have a strong constitution. Their folks never did nothing for it—so we had to keep it here."

"Well, now, mother," said Maria Amelia Briggs. "It does seem to me that she did her duty. You know yourself that if she hadn't give warnin' all three of the villages would a' been cleaned out—a matter of fifteen hundred people. And if she'd stopped to lug that child, she couldn't have got here in time. Don't you believe she was thinkin' of those mill-hands' children?"

"Maria 'Melia, I'm ashamed of you!" said old Mis' Briggs. "But you ain't married and ain't a mother. A mother's duty is to her own child! She neglected her own to look after other folks—the Lord never gave her them other children to care for!"

"Yes," said Miss Jacobs, "and here's her child, a burden on the town! She was an unnatural mother!"

"When I Was a Witch"
The Forerunner 1.7 (May 1910): 1–6

[This humorous fantasy imagines magic as a means to instant social change, taking on many of the same targets as *Herland*, but
with a bit more venom.]

If I had understood the terms of that one-sided contract with Satan, the Time of Witching would have lasted longer—you may be
sure of that. But how was I to tell? It just happened, and has never
happened again, though I've tried the same preliminaries as far as
I could control them.

The thing began all of a sudden, one October midnight—the
30th, to be exact. It had been hot, really hot, all day, and was sul-
try and thunderous in the evening—no air stirring, and the whole
house stewing with that ill-advised activity which always seems to
move the steam radiator when it isn't wanted.

I was in a state of simmering rage—hot enough, even without
the weather and the furnace—and I went up on the roof to cool
off. A top-floor apartment has that advantage, among others—you
can take a walk without the mediation of an elevator boy!

There are things enough in New York to lose one's temper over
at the best of times, and on this particular day they seemed to all
happen at once, and some fresh ones. The night before, cats and
dogs had broken my rest, of course. My morning paper was more
than usually mendacious; and my neighbor's morning paper—
more visible than my own as I went downtown—was more than
usually salacious. My cream wasn't cream—my egg was a relic of
the past. My "new" napkins were giving out.

Being a woman, I'm supposed not to swear; but when the motorman disregarded my plain signal, and grinned as he rushed
by; when the subway guard waited till I was just about to step on
board, and then slammed the door in my face—standing behind
it calmly for some minutes before the bell rang to warrant his
closing—I desired to swear like a mule-driver.

At night it was worse. The way people paw one's back in the
crowd! The cow-puncher who packs the people in or jerks them
out—the men who smoke and spit, law or no law—the women
whose saw-edged cartwheel hats, swashing feathers, and deadly
pins add so to one's comfort inside.

Well, as I said, I was in a particularly bad temper, and went up
on the roof to cool off. Heavy black clouds hung low overhead,
and lightning flickered threateningly here and there.

A starved black cat stole from behind a chimney and mewed dolefully. Poor thing! She had been scalded.

The street was quiet for New York. I leaned over a little and looked up and down the long parallels of twinkling lights. A belated cab drew near, the horse so tired he could hardly hold his head up.

Then the driver, with a skill born of plenteous practice, flung out his long-lashed whip and curled it under the poor beast's belly with a stinging cut that made me shudder. The horse shuddered too, poor wretch, and jingled his harness with an effort at a trot.

I leaned over the parapet and watched that man with a spirit of unmitigated ill-will.

"I wish," said I, slowly—and I did wish it with all my heart— "that every person who strikes or otherwise hurts a horse unnecessarily shall feel the pain intended—and the horse not feel it!"

It did me good to say it, anyhow, but I never expected any result. I saw the man swing his great whip again, and lay on heartily. I saw him throw up his hands—heard him scream—but I never thought what the matter was, even then.

The lean black cat, timid but trustful, rubbed against my skirt and mewed.

"Poor Kitty!" I said. "Poor Kitty! It is a shame!" And I thought tenderly of all the thousands of hungry, hunted cats who slink and suffer in a great city.

Later, when I tried to sleep, and up across the stillness rose the raucous shrieks of some of these same sufferers, my pity turned cold. "Any fool that will try to keep a cat in a city!" I muttered, angrily.

Another yell—a pause—an ear-torturing, continuous cry. "I wish," I burst forth, "that every cat in the city was comfortably dead!"

A sudden silence fell, and in the course of time I got to sleep.

Things went fairly well next morning, till I tried another egg. They were expensive eggs, too.

"I can't help it!" said my sister, who keeps house.

"I know you can't," I admitted. "But somebody could help it. I wish the people who are responsible had to eat their old eggs, and never got a good one till they sold good ones!"

"They'd stop eating eggs, that's all," said my sister, "and eat meat."

"Let 'em eat meat!" I said, recklessly. "The meat is as bad as the eggs! It's so long since we've had a clean, fresh chicken that I've forgotten how they taste!"

"It's cold storage," said my sister. She is a peaceable sort; I'm not.

"Yes, cold storage!" I snapped. "It ought to be a blessing—to tide over shortages, equalize supplies, and lower prices. What does it do? Corner the market, raise prices the year round, and make all the food bad!"

My anger rose. "If there was any way of getting at them!" I cried. "The law doesn't touch 'em. They need to be cursed somehow! I'd like to do it! I wish the whole crowd that profit by this vicious business might taste their bad meat, their old fish, their stale milk—whatever they ate. Yes, and feel the prices as we do!"

"They couldn't, you know; they're rich," said my sister.

"I know that, "I admitted, sulkily. "There's no way of getting at 'em. But I wish they could. And I wish they knew how people hated 'em, and felt that too—till they mended their ways!"

When I left for my office I saw a funny thing. A man who drove a garbage cart took his horse by the bits and jerked and wrenched brutally. I was amazed to see him clap his hands to his own jaws with a moan, while the horse philosophically licked his chops and looked at him.

The man seemed to resent his expression, and struck him on the head, only to rub his own poll and swear amazedly, looking around to see who had hit him. The horse advanced a step, stretching a hungry nose toward a garbage pail crowned with cabbage leaves, and the man, recovering his sense of proprietorship, swore at him and kicked him in the ribs. That time he had to sit down, turning pale and weak. I watched with growing wonder and delight.

A market wagon came clattering down the street, the hard-faced young ruffian fresh for his morning task. He gathered the ends of the reins and brought them down on the horse's back with a resounding thwack. The horse did not notice this at all, but the boy did. He yelled!

I came to a place where many teamsters were at work hauling dirt and crushed stone. A strange silence and peace hung over the scene where usually the sound of the lash and sight of brutal blows made me hurry by. The men were talking together a little, and seemed to be exchanging notes. It was too good to be true. I gazed and marvelled, waiting for my car.

It came, merrily running along. It was not full. There was one not far ahead, which I had missed in watching the horses; there was no other near it in the rear.

Yet the coarse-faced person in authority who ran it went gaily by without stopping, though I stood on the track almost, and waved my umbrella.

A hot flush of rage surged to my face. "I wish you felt the blow you deserve," said I, viciously, looking after the car. "I wish you'd have to stop, and back to here, and open the door and apologize. I wish that would happen to all of you, every time you play that trick."

To my infinite amazement, that car stopped and backed up till the front door was before me. The motorman opened it, holding his hand to his cheek. "Beg your pardon, madam!" he said.

I passed in, dazed, overwhelmed. Could it be? Could it possibly be that—that what I wished came true? The idea sobered me, but I dismissed it with a scornful smile. "No such luck!" said I.

Opposite me sat a person in petticoats. She was of a sort I particularly detest. No real body of bones and muscles, but the contours of grouped sausages. Complacent, gaudily dressed, heavily wigged and ratted, with powder and perfume and flowers and jewels—and a dog.

A poor, wretched, little, artificial dog—alive, but only so by virtue of man's insolence; not a real creature that God made. And the dog had clothes on—and a bracelet! His fitted jacket had a pocket—and a pocket-handkerchief! He looked sick and unhappy.

I meditated on his pitiful position, and that of all the other poor chained prisoners, leading unnatural lives of enforced celibacy, cut off from sunlight, fresh air, the use of their limbs; led forth at stated intervals by unwilling servants, to defile our streets; over-fed, under-exercised, nervous, and unhealthy.

"And we say we love them!" said I, bitterly to myself. "No wonder they bark and howl and go mad. No wonder they have almost as many diseases as we do! I wish—" Here the thought I had dismissed struck me again. "I wish that all the unhappy dogs in cities would die at once!"

I watched the sad-eyed little invalid across the car. He dropped his head and died. She never noticed it till she got off; then she made fuss enough.

The evening papers were full of it. Some sudden pestilence had struck both dogs and cats, it would appear. Red headlines struck the eye, big letters, and columns were filled out of the complaints of those who had lost their "pets," of the sudden labors of the board of health, and of interviews with doctors.

All day, as I went through the office routine, the strange sense of this new power struggled with reason and common knowledge.

I even tried a few furtive test "wishes"—wished that the waste-basket would fall over, that the inkstand would fill itself; but they didn't.

I dismissed the idea as pure foolishness, till I saw those news-papers and heard people telling worse stories.

One thing I decided at once—not to tell a soul. "Nobody'd believe me if I did," said I to myself. "And I won't give 'em the chance. I've scored on cats and dogs, anyhow—and horses."

As I watched the horses at work that afternoon, and thought of all their unknown sufferings from crowded city stables, bad air and insufficient food, and from the wearing strain of asphalt pave-ments in wet and icy weather, I decided to have another try on horses.

"I wish," said I, slowly and carefully, but with a fixed inten-sity of purpose, "that every horse owner, keeper, hirer, and driver or rider, might feel what the horse feels, when he suffers at our hands. Feel it keenly and constantly till the case is mended."

I wasn't able to verify this attempt for some time; but the effect was so general that it got widely talked about soon; and this "new wave of humane feeling" soon raised the status of horses in our city. Also it diminished their numbers. People began to prefer mo-tor drays—which was a mighty good thing.

Now I felt pretty well assured in my own mind, and kept my assurance to myself. Also I began to make a list of my cherished grudges, with a fine sense of power and pleasure.

"I must be careful," I said to myself, "very careful; and, above all things, 'make the punishment fit the crime.'"

The subway crowding came to my mind next—both the people who crowd because they have to, and the people who make them. "I musn't punish anybody for what they can't help," I mused. "But when it's pure meanness!" Then I bethought me of the remote stockholders, of the more immediate directors, of the painfully prominent officials and insolent employees—and got to work.

"I might as well make a good job of it while this lasts," said I to myself. "It's quite a responsibility, but lots of fun." And I wished that every person responsible for the condition of our subways might be mysteriously compelled to ride up and down in them continuously during rush hours.

This experiment I watched with keen interest, but for the life of me I could see little difference. There were a few more well-dressed persons in the crowds, that was all. So I came to the con-clusion that the general public was mostly to blame, and carried their daily punishment without knowing it.

For the insolent guards and cheating ticket-sellers who give you short change, very slowly, when you are dancing on one foot and your train is there, I merely wished that they might feel the pain their victims would like to give them, short of real injury. They did, I guess.

Then I wished similar things for all manner of corporations and officials. It worked. It worked amazingly. There was a sudden conscientious revival all over the country. The dry bones rattled and sat up. Boards of directors, having troubles enough of their own, were aggravated by innumerable communications from suddenly sensitive stockholders.

In mills and mines and railroads, things began to mend. The country buzzed. The papers fattened. The churches sat up and took the credit for themselves. I was incensed at this; and, after brief consideration, wished that every minister would preach to his congregation exactly what he believed and what he thought of them.

I went to six services the next Sunday—about ten minutes each, for two sessions. It was most amusing. A thousand pulpits were emptied forthwith, refilled, reemptied, and so on, from week to week. People began to go to church—men largely; women didn't like it as well. They had always supposed the ministers thought more highly of them than now appeared to be the case.

One of my oldest grudges was against the sleeping-car people; and I now began to consider them. How often I had grinned and borne it—with other thousands—submitting helplessly.

Here is a railroad—a common carrier—and you have to use it. You pay for your transportation, a good round sum.

Then if you wish to stay in the sleeping car during the day, they charge you another two dollars and a half for the privilege of sitting there, whereas you have paid for a seat when you bought your ticket. That seat is now sold to another person—twice sold. Five dollars for twenty-four hours in a space six feet by three by three at night, and one seat by day; twenty-four of these privileges to a car—$120 a day for the rent of the car—and the passengers to pay the porter besides. That makes $44,800 a year.

Sleeping cars are expensive to build, they say. So are hotels; but they do not charge at such a rate. Now, what could I do to get even? Nothing could ever put back the dollars into the millions of pockets; but it might be stopped now, this beautiful process.

So I wished that all persons who profited by this performance might feel a shame so keen that they would make public avowal and apology, and, as partial restitution, offer their wealth to promote the cause of free railroads!

Then I remembered parrots. This was lucky, for my wrath flamed again. It was really cooking, as I tried to work out responsibility and adjust penalties. But parrots! Any person who wants to keep a parrot should go and live on an island alone with their preferred conversationalist!

There was a huge, squawky parrot right across the street from me, adding its senseless, rasping cries to the more necessary evils of other noises.

I had also an aunt with a parrot. She was a wealthy, ostentatious person, who had been an only child and inherited her money.

Uncle Joseph hated the yelling bird, but that didn't make any difference to Aunt Mathilda.

I didn't like this aunt, and wouldn't visit her, lest she think I was truckling for the sake of her money; but after I had wished this time, I called at the time set for my curse to work; and it did work with a vengeance. There sat poor Uncle Joe, looking thinner and meeker than ever; and my aunt, like an over-ripe plum, complacent enough.

"Let me out!" said Polly, suddenly. "Let me out to take a walk!"

"The clever thing!" said Aunt Mathilda. "He never said that before."

She let him out. Then he flapped up on the chandelier and sat among the prisms, quite safe.

"What an old pig you are, Mathilda!" said the parrot.

She started to her feet—naturally.

"Born a pig—trained a pig—a pig by nature and education!" said the parrot. "Nobody'd put up with you, except for your money, unless it's this long-suffering husband of yours. He wouldn't, if he hadn't the patience of Job!"

"Hold your tongue!" screamed Aunt Mathilda. "Come down from there! Come here!"

Polly cocked his head and jingled the prisms. "Sit down, Mathilda!" he said, cheerfully. "You've got to listen. You are fat and homely and selfish. You are a nuisance to everybody about you. You have got to feed me and take care of me better than ever—and you've got to listen to me when I talk. Pig!"

I visited another person with a parrot the next day. She put a cloth over his cage when I came in.

"Take it off!" said Polly. She took it off.

"Won't you come into the other room?" she asked me, nervously.

"Better stay here!" said her pet. "Sit still—sit still!"

She sat still.

"Your hair is mostly false," said pretty Poll. "And your teeth—and your outlines. You eat too much. You are lazy. You ought to exercise, and don't know enough. Better apologize to this lady for backbiting! You've got to listen."

The trade in parrots fell off from that day; they say there is no call for them. But the people who kept parrots keep them yet—parrots live a long time.

Bores were a class of offenders against whom I had long borne undying enmity. Now I rubbed my hands and began on them, with this simple wish: that every person whom they bored should tell them the plain truth.

There is one man whom I have specially in mind. He was blackballed at a pleasant club, but continues to go there. He isn't a member—he just goes; and no one does anything to him.

It was very funny after this. He appeared that very night at a meeting, and almost every person present asked him how he came there. "You're not a member, you know," they said. "Why do you butt in? Nobody likes you."

Some were more lenient with him. "Why don't you learn to be more considerate of others, and make some real friends?" they said. "To have a few friends who do enjoy your visits ought to be pleasanter than being a public nuisance."

He disappeared from that club, anyway.

I began to feel very cocky indeed.

In the food business there was already a marked improvement, and in transportation. The hubbub of reformation waxed louder daily, urged on by the unknown sufferings of all the profiters by iniquity.

The papers thrived on all this; and as I watched the loud-voiced protestations of my pet abomination in journalism, I had a brilliant idea, literally.

Next morning I was downtown early, watching the men open their papers. My abomination was shamefully popular, and never more so than this morning. Across the top was printed in gold letters:

All intentional lies, in adv., editorial, news, or any other column	Scarlet
All malicious matter	Crimson
All careless or ignorant mistakes	Pink
All for direct self-interest of owner	Dark green
All mere bait to sell the paper	Bright green

All advertising, primary or secondary	Brown
All sensational and salacious matter	Yellow
All hired hypocrisy	Purple
Good fun, instruction, and entertainment	Blue
True and necessary news and honest editorials	Ordinary print

You never saw such a crazy quilt of a paper. They were bought like hot cakes for some days; but the real business fell off very soon. They'd have stopped it all if they could; but the papers looked all right when they came off the press. The color scheme flamed out only to the bona-fide reader.

I let this work for about a week, to the immense joy of all the other papers, and then turned it on to them, all at once. Newspaper reading became very exciting for a little, but the trade fell off. Even newspaper editors could not keep on feeding a market like that. The blue printed and ordinary printed matter grew from column to column and page to page. Some papers—small, to be sure, but refreshing—began to appear in blue and black alone.

This kept me interested and happy for quite a while, so much so that I quite forgot to be angry at other things. There was *such* a change in all kinds of business, following the mere printing of truth in the newspapers. It began to appear as if we had lived in a sort of delirium—not really knowing the facts about anything. As soon as we really knew the facts, we began to behave very differently, of course.

What really brought all my enjoyment to an end was women. Being a woman, I was naturally interested in them, and could see some things more clearly than men could. I saw their real power, their real dignity, their real responsibility in the world; and then the way they dress and behave used to make me fairly frantic. 'Twas like seeing archangels playing jackstraws—or real horses used only as rocking-horses. So I determined to get after them.

How to manage it! What to hit first! Their hats, their ugly, inane, outrageous hats—that is what one thinks of first. Their silly, expensive clothes—their diddling beads and jewelry—their greedy childishness—mostly of the women provided for by rich men.

Then I thought of all the other women, the real ones, the vast majority, patiently doing the work of servants without even a servant's pay—and neglecting the noblest duties of motherhood in favor of house-service; the greatest power on earth, blind, chained, untaught, in a treadmill. I thought of what they might do, compared to what they did do, and my heart swelled with something that was far from anger.

Then I wished—with all my strength—that women, all women, might realize Womanhood at last; its power and pride and place in life; that they might see their duty as mothers of the world—to love and care for everyone alive; that they might see their duty to men—to choose only the best, and then to bear and rear better ones; that they might see their duty as human beings, and come right out into full life and work and happiness!

I stopped, breathless, with shining eyes. I waited, trembling, for things to happen.

Nothing happened.

You see, this magic which had fallen on me was black magic—and I had wished white.

It didn't work at all, and, what was worse, it stopped all the other things that were working so nicely.

Oh, if I had only thought to wish permanence for those lovely punishments! If only I had done more while I could do it, had half appreciated my privileges when I was a Witch!

"Bee Wise"
The Forerunner 4.7 (July 1913): 169–73

[Published a year and a half before *Herland*, this utopian short story anticipates the novella in its portrayal of a self-supporting, ideal community, a "little Eden," planned and maintained by women.]

"It's a queer name," said the man reporter.

"No queerer than the other," said the woman reporter. "There are two of them, you know—Beewise and Herways."

"It reminds me of something," he said, "some quotation—do you get it?"

"I think I do," she said. "But I won't tell. You have to consider for yourself." And she laughed quietly. But his education did not supply the phrase.

They were sent down, both of them, from different papers, to write up a pair of growing towns in California which had been built up so swiftly and yet so quietly that it was only now after they were well established and prosperous that the world had discovered something strange about them.

This seems improbable enough in the land of most unbridled and well-spurred reporters, but so it was.

One town was a little seaport, a tiny sheltered nook, rather cut off by the coast hills from previous adoption. The other lay up beyond those hills, in a delightful valley all its own with two most precious streams in it that used to tumble in roaring white during the rainy season down their steep little canyons to the sea, and trickled there, unseen, the rest of the year.

The man reporter wrote up the story in his best descriptive vein, adding embellishments where they seemed desirable, withholding such facts as appeared to contradict his treatment, and doing his best to cast over the whole a strong sex-interest and the glamor of vague suspicions.

The remarkable thing about the two towns was that their population consisted very largely of women and more largely of children, but there were men also, who seemed happy enough, and answered the questions of the reporters with good-will. They disclaimed, these men residents, anything peculiar or ultra-feminine in the settlements, and one hearty young Englishman assured them that the disproportion was no greater than in England. "Or in some of our New England towns," said another citizen, "where the men have all gone west or to the big cities, and there's a whole township of withering women-folks with a few ministers and hired men."

The woman reporter questioned more deeply perhaps, perhaps less offensively; at any rate she learned more than the other of the true nature of the sudden civic growth. After both of them had turned in their reports, after all the other papers had sent down representatives, and later magazine articles had been written with impressive pictures, after the accounts of permitted visitors and tourists had been given, there came to be a fuller knowledge than was possible at first, naturally, but no one got a clearer vision of it all than was given to the woman reporter that first day, when she discovered that the Mayor of Herways was an old college mate of hers.

The story was far better than the one she sent in, but she was a lady as well as a reporter, and respected confidence.

It appeared that the whole thing started in that college class, the year after the reporter had left it, being suddenly forced to drop education and take to earning a living. In the senior class was a group of girls of markedly different types, and yet so similar in their basic beliefs and ultimate purposes that they had grown through the four years of college life into a little "sorority" of their own. They called it "The Morning Club," which sounded innocent enough, and kept it secret among themselves. They were girls of strong character, all of them, each with a definite purpose as to her life work.

There was the one they all called "Mother," because her whole heart and brain were dominated by the love of children, the thought of children, the wish to care for children; and very close to her was the "Teacher," with a third, the "Nurse," forming a group within a group. These three had endless discussions among themselves, with big vague plans for future usefulness.

Then there was the "Minister," the "Doctor," and the far-seeing one they called the "Statesman." One sturdy, squarebrowed little girl was dubbed "Manager" for reasons frankly prominent, as with the "Artist" and the "Engineer." There were some dozen or twenty of them, all choosing various professions, but all alike in their determination to practice those professions, married or single, and in their vivid hope for better methods of living. "Advanced" in their ideas they were, even in an age of advancement, and held together in especial by the earnest words of the Minister, who was always urging upon them the power of solidarity.

Just before their graduation something happened. It happened to the Manager, and she called a special meeting to lay it before the club.

The Manager was a plain girl, strong and quiet. She was the one who always overflowed with plans and possessed the unusual faculty of carrying out the plans she made, a girl who had always looked forward to working hard for her own living of choice as well as necessity, and enjoyed the prospect.

"Girls!" said she, when they were all grouped and quiet. "I've news for you—splendid news! I wouldn't spring it on you like this, but we shall be all broken and scattered in a little while—it's just in time!" She looked around at their eager faces, enjoying the sensation created.

"Say—look here!" she suddenly interjected. "You aren't any of you engaged, are you?"

One hand was lifted, modestly.

"What does he *do*?" pursued the speaker. "I don't care who he is, and I know he's all right or you wouldn't look at him—but what does he *do*?"

"He isn't sure yet," meekly answered the Minister, "but he's to be a manufacturer, I think."

"No objection to your preaching, of course." This was hardly a question.

"He says he'll hear me every Sunday—if I'll let him off at home on week-days," the Minister replied with a little giggle.

They all smiled approval.

"He's all right," the Manager emphatically agreed. "Now then girls—to put you out of your misery at once—what has happened to me is ten million dollars."

There was a pause, and then a joyous clapping of hands.

"Bully for you!"

"Hurrah for Margery!"

"You deserve it!"

"Say, you'll treat, won't you?"

They were as pleased as if the huge and sudden fortune were common property.

"Long lost uncle—or what, Marge?"

"Great uncle—my grandmother's brother. Went to California with the 'forty-niners'[1]—got lost, for reasons of his own, I suspect. Found some prodigious gold mine—solid veins and nuggets, and spent quiet years in piling it up and investing it."

"When did he die?" asked the Nurse softly.

"He's not dead—but I'm afraid he soon will be," answered the Manager slowly. "It appears he's hired people to look up the family and see what they were like—said he didn't propose to ruin any feeble-minded people with all that money. He was pleased to like my record. Said—" she chuckled, "said I was a man after his own heart! And he's come on here to get acquainted and to make this over before he's gone. He says no dead man's bequest would be as safe as a live man's gift."

"And he's *given* you all that!"

"Solid and safe as can be. Says he's quite enough left to end his days in peace. He's pretty old.... Now then, girls—" She was all animation. "Here's my plan. Part of this property is land, land and water, in California. An upland valley, a little port on the coast—an economic base, you see—and capital to develop it. I propose that we form a combination, go out there, settle, build, manage—make a sample town—set a new example to the world—a place of woman's work and world-work too.... What do you say?"

They said nothing for the moment. This was a large proposition.

The Manager went on eagerly: "I'm not binding you to anything; this is a plain business offer. What I propose to do is to develop that little port, open a few industries and so on, build a reservoir up above and regulate the water supply—use it for power—have great gardens and vineyards. Oh, girls—it's California!

---

1 Participants in the 1849 California gold rush.

We can make a little Eden! And as to Motherhood—" she looked around with a slow, tender smile, "there's no place better for babies!"

The Mother, the Nurse, and the Teacher all agreed to this.

"I've only got it roughly sketched out in my mind," pursued the speaker eagerly. "It will take time and care to work it all out right. But there's capital enough to tide us over first difficulties, and then it shall be just as solid and simple as any other place, a practical paying proposition, a perfectly natural little town, planned, built, and managed—" her voice grew solemn, "by women—for women—and *children*! A place that will be of real help to humanity.—Oh girls, it's such a chance!"

That was the beginning.

* * * * *

The woman reporter was profoundly interested. "I wish I could have stayed that year," she said soberly.

"I wish you had, Jean! But never mind—you can stay now. We need the right kind of work on our little local paper—not just reporting—you can do more than that, can't you?"

"I should hope so!" Jean answered heartily. "I spent six months on a little country paper—ran the whole thing nearly, except editorials and setting up. If there's room here for me I can tell you I'm coming—day before yesterday!" So the Woman Reporter came to Herways to work, and went up, o'nights, to Beewise to live, whereby she gradually learned in completeness what this bunch of women had done, and was able to prepare vivid little pamphlets of detailed explanations which paved the way for so many other regenerated towns.

And this is what they did:

The economic base was a large tract of land from the sea-coast hills back to the high rich valley beyond. Two spring-fed brooks ran from the opposite ends of the valley and fell steeply to the beach below through narrow canyons.

The first cash outlay of the Manager, after starting the cable line from beach to hill which made the whole growth possible, was to build a reservoir at either end, one of which furnished drinking water and irrigation in the long summer, the other a swimming pool and steady stream of power. The powerhouse in the canyon was supplemented by wind-mills on the heights and tide-mill on the beach, and among them they furnished light, heat, and power—clean, economical electric energy. Later they set up a solar engine which furnished additional force, to minimize labor and add to their producing capacity.

For supporting industries, to link them with the world, they had these: First a modest export of preserved fruits, exquisitely prepared, packed in the new fibre cartons which are more sanitary than tin and lighter than glass. In the hills they raised Angora goats, and from their wool supplied a little mill with high-grade down-soft yarn, and sent out fluffy blankets, flannels and knitted garments. Cotton too they raised, magnificent cotton, and silk of the best, and their own mill supplied their principal needs. Small mills, pretty and healthful, with bright-clad women singing at their looms for the short working hours. From these materials the designers and craftswomen, helped by the Artist, made garments, beautiful, comfortable, easy and lasting, and from year to year the demand for "Beewise" gowns and coats increased.

In a windy corner, far from their homes, they set up a tannery, and from the well-prepared hides of their goats they made various leather goods, gloves and shoes,—"Beewise" shoes, that came to be known at last through the length and breadth of the land—a shoe that fitted the human foot, allowed for free action, and was pleasant to the eye. Many of the townspeople wore sandals and they were also made for merchandise.

Their wooded heights they treasured carefully. A forestry service was started, the whole area studied, and the best rate of planting and cutting established. Their gardens were rich and beautiful; they sold honey, and distilled perfumes.

"This place is to grow in value, not deteriorate," said the Manager, and she planted for the future.

At first they made a tent city, the tents dyed with rich colors, dry-floored and warm. Later, the Artist and the Architect and the Engineer to the fore, they built houses of stone and wood and heavy sheathing paper, making their concrete of the dead palm leaves and the loose bark of swift-growing eucalyptus, which was planted everywhere and rose over night almost, like the Beanstalk—houses beautiful, comfortable, sea-shell clean.

Steadily the Manager held forth to her associates on what she called "the business end" of their enterprise. "The whole thing must pay," she said, "else it cannot stand—it will not be imitated. We want to show what a bunch of women can do successfully. Men can help, but this time we will manage."

Among their first enterprises was a guest house, planned and arranged mainly for women and children. In connection with this was a pleasure garden for all manner of games, gymnastics and dancing, with wide courts and fields and roofed places for use in the rainy season.

There was a sanitarium, where the Doctor and the Nurse gathered helpers about them, attended to casual illness, to the needs of child-birth, and to such visitors who came to them as needed care.

Further there was a baby-garden that grew to a kindergarten, and that to a school, and in time the fame of their educational work spread far and wide, and there was a constantly increasing list of applicants, for "Beewise" was a Residence club; no one could live there without being admitted by the others.

The beach town, Herways, teemed with industry. At the little pier their small coast steamer landed, bringing such supplies as they did not make, leaving and taking passengers. Where the beach was level and safe they bathed and swam, having a water-pavilion for shelter and refreshment. From beach to hill-top ran a shuttle service of light cars; "Jacob's Ladder,"[1] they called it.

The broad plan of the Manager was this: with her initial capital to develop a working plant that would then run itself at a profit, and she was surprised to find how soon that profit appeared, and how considerable it was.

Then came in sufficient numbers, friends, relatives, curious strangers. These women had no objection to marrying on their own terms. And when a man is sufficiently in love he sees no serious objection to living in an earthly paradise and doing his share in building up a new community. But the men were carefully selected. They must prove clean health—for a high grade of motherhood was the continuing ideal of the group.

Visitors came, increasing in numbers as accommodations increased. But as the accommodations, even to land for tenting, must be applied for beforehand, there was no horde of gaping tourists to vulgarize the place.

As for working people—there were no other. Everyone in Herways and Beewise worked, especially the women—that was the prime condition of admission; every citizen must be clean physically and morally as far as could be ascertained, but no amount of negative virtues availed them if they were not valuable in social service. So they had eager applications from professional women as fast as the place was known, and some they made room for—in proportion. Of doctors they could maintain but a few; a dentist or two, a handful of nurses, more teachers, several artists of the more practical sort who made beauty for the use of their neighbors, and

---

1 Ladder to Heaven, seen by Jacob in a dream (Genesis 28:11–19).

a few far-reaching world servants, who might live here, at least part of the time, and send their work broadcast, such as poets, writers and composers.

But most of the people were the more immediately necessary workers, the men who built and dug and ran the engines, the women who spun and wove and worked among the flowers, or vice versa if they chose, and those who attended to the daily wants of the community.

There were no servants in the old sense. The dainty houses had no kitchens, only the small electric outfit where those who would might prepare coffee and the like. Food was prepared in clean wide laboratories, attended by a few skilled experts, highly paid, who knew their business, and great progress was made in the study of nutrition, and in the keeping of all the people well. Nevertheless the food cost less than if prepared by many unskilled, ill-paid cooks in imperfect kitchens.

The great art of child-culture grew apace among them with the best methods now known. Froebelian[1] and Montessorian[2] ideas and systems were honored and well used, and with the growing knowledge accumulated by years of observation and experience the right development of childhood at last became not merely an ideal, but a commonplace. Well-born children grew there like the roses they played among, raced and swam and swung, and knew only health, happiness and the joy of unconscious learning.

The two towns filled to their normal limits.

"Here we must stop," said the Manager in twenty years' time. "If we have more people here we shall develop the diseases of cities. But look at our financial standing—every cent laid out is now returned, the place is absolutely self-supporting and will grow richer as years pass. Now we'll swarm like the bees and start another—what do you say?"

And they did, beginning another rational paradise in another beautiful valley, safer and surer for the experience behind them.

But far wider than their own immediate increase was the spread of their ideas, of the proven truth of their idea, that a group of human beings could live together in such wise as to decrease the

---

1 Friedrich Froebel (1782–1852), the inventor of the kindergarten ("child garden"), based his educational theories on the idea that children learn from games and play.

2 Educational approach devised by the Italian physician Maria Montessori (1870–1952), a self-directed approach in which children learn by manipulating specially designed materials. See Appendix B2.

hours of labor, increase the value of the product, ensure health, peace and prosperity, and multiply human happiness beyond measure.

In every part of the world the thing was possible; wherever people could live at all they could live to better advantage. The economic base might vary widely, but wherever there were a few hundred women banded together their combined labor could produce wealth, and their combined motherhood ensure order, comfort, happiness, and the improvement of humanity.

"Go to the ant, thou sluggard, consider her ways and be wise."[1]

---

1 Proverbs 6:6. See *Herland*, Chapter 6.

Verse

"She Walketh Veiled and Sleeping"
Woman's Journal (12 October 1889): 326

[One of Gilman's earliest publications, this poem reflects both her personal situation in the unhappy marriage she had left and her belief in the potential of women in general.]

SHE WALKETH VEILED AND SLEEPING

She walketh veiled and sleeping,
For she knoweth not her power;
She obeyeth but the pleading
Of her heart, and the high leading
Of her soul, unto this hour.
Slow advancing, halting, creeping,
Comes the Woman to the hour!—
She walketh veiled and sleeping,
For she knoweth not her power.

"Females"
Woman's Journal (18 June 1892): 200

[This poem anticipates Gilman's evolutionary arguments in *Women and Economics* and *Herland*: that women are naturally equal to men—and should behave accordingly.]

FEMALES

The female fox she is a fox;
    The female whale a whale;
The female eagle holds her place
As representative of race
    As truly as the male.

The mother hen doth scratch for her chicks,
    And scratch for herself beside;
The mother cow doth nurse her calf,
Yet fares as well as her other half
    In the pasture free and wide.

The female bird doth soar in air;
    The female fish doth swim;
The fleet-foot mare upon the course
Doth hold her own with the flying horse—
    Yea, and she beateth him!

One female in the world we find
    Telling a different tale.
It is the female of our race,
Who holds a parasitic place
    Dependent on the male.

Not so, saith she, ye slander me!
    No parasite am I!
I earn my living as a wife;
My children take my very life.
Why should I share in human strife.
    To plant and build and buy?

The human race holds highest place
    In all the world so wide,
Yet these inferior females wive,
And raise their little ones alive,
    And feed themselves beside.

The race is higher than the sex,
    Though sex be fair and good;
A Human Creature is your state,
And to be human is more great
    Than even womanhood!

The female fox she is a fox;
    The female whale a whale;
The female eagle holds her place
As representative of race
    As truly as the male.

Nonfiction

From *Women and Economics: A Study of the Economic Relation between Men and Women as a Factor in Social Evolution.* Boston: Small, Maynard & Company, 1898

[Widely reprinted and translated into several languages, *Women and Economics* is generally considered Gilman's most influential publication. The sections excerpted here exemplify theories about gender and evolution that she would later embody in *Herland*.]

From Chapter 1

[A]ttention is now called to a certain marked and peculiar economic condition affecting the human race, and unparalleled in the organic world. We are the only animal species in which the female depends on the male for food, the only animal species in which the sex-relation is also an economic relation. With us an entire sex lives in a relation of economic dependence upon the other sex, and the economic relation is combined with the sex-relation. The economic status of the human female is relative to the sex-relation.
[...]

From Chapter 2

Where both sexes obtain their food through the same exertions, from the same sources, under the same conditions, both sexes are acted upon alike, and developed alike by their environment. Where the two sexes obtain their food under different conditions, and where that difference consists in one of them being fed by the other, then the feeding sex becomes the environment of the fed. Man, in supporting woman, has become her economic environment. Under natural selection, every creature is modified to its environment, developing perforce the qualities needed to obtain its livelihood under that environment. Man, as the feeder of woman, becomes the strongest modifying force in her economic condition. Under sexual selection the human creature is of course modified to its mate, as with all creatures. When the mate becomes also the master, when economic necessity is added to sex-attraction, we have the two great evolutionary forces acting together to the same end; namely, to develop sex-distinction in the human female. For, in her position of economic dependence in the sex-relation, sex-distinction is with her not only a means of attracting a mate, as with all creatures, but a means of getting her livelihood, as is the case with no other creature under heaven. Because of the economic dependence of the human female on her mate, she is modified to sex to an excessive degree. This excessive modification she transmits to her children; and so is steadily implanted in the human constitution the morbid tendency to excess in this relation, which has acted so universally upon us in all ages, in spite of our best efforts to restrain it. It is not the normal sex-tendency, common to all creatures, but an abnormal sex-tendency, produced and maintained by the abnormal economic relation which makes one sex get its living from the other by the exercise of sex-functions. This is the immediate effect upon individuals of the peculiar sexuo-economic relation which obtains among us.

From Chapter 3

Physically, woman belongs to a tall, vigorous, beautiful animal species, capable of great and varied exertion. In every race and time when she has opportunity for racial activity, she develops accordingly, and is no less a woman for being a healthy human creature. In every race and time where she is denied this opportunity,—and few, indeed, have been her years of freedom,—she has developed in the lines of action to which she was confined; and those were always lines of sex-activity. In consequence the body of woman, speaking in the largest generalization, manifests sex-distinction predominantly.

Woman's femininity—and "the eternal feminine" means simply the eternal sexual—is more apparent in proportion to her humanity than the femininity of other animals in proportion to their caninity or felinity or equinity. "A feminine hand" or "a feminine foot" is distinguishable anywhere. We do not hear of "a feminine paw" or "a feminine hoof." A hand is an organ of prehension, a foot an organ of locomotion: they are not secondary sexual characteristics. The comparative smallness and feebleness of woman is a sex-distinction. We have carried it to such an excess that women are commonly known as "the weaker sex." There is no such glaring difference between male and female in other advanced species. [...]

The degree of feebleness and clumsiness common to women, the comparative inability to stand, walk, run, jump, climb, and perform other race-functions common to both sexes, is an excessive sex-distinction; and the ensuing transmission of this relative feebleness to their children, boys and girls alike, retards human development. Strong, free, active women, the sturdy, field-working peasant, the burden-bearing savage, are no less good mothers for their human strength. But our civilized "feminine delicacy," which appears somewhat less delicate when recognized as an expression of sexuality in excess,—makes us no better mothers, but worse. The relative weakness of women is a sex-distinction. It is apparent in her to a degree that injures motherhood, that injures wifehood, that injures the individual. The sex-usefulness and the human usefulness of women, their general duty to their kind, are greatly injured by this degree of distinction. In every way the over-sexed condition of the human female reacts unfavorably upon herself, her husband, her children, and the race. [...]

From Chapter 7

Maternal energy is the force through which have come into the world both love and industry. It is through the tireless activity of this desire, the mother's wish to serve the young, that she began the first of the arts and crafts whereby we live. While the male savage was still a mere hunter and fighter, expressing masculine energy, the katabolic force, along its essential line, expanding, scattering, the female savage worked out in equally natural ways the conserving force of female energy. She gathered together and saved nutrition for the child, as the germ-cell gathers and saves nutrition in the unconscious silences of nature. She wrapped it in garments and built a shelter for its head as naturally as the same maternal function had loved, clothed, and sheltered the unborn. Maternal energy, working externally through our elaborate organism, is the source of productive industry, the main current of social life.
[...]
　　The time has come when we are open to deeper and wider impulses than the sex-instinct; the social instincts are strong enough to come into full use at last. This is shown by the twin struggle that convulses the world to-day,—in sex and economics,—the "woman's movement" and the "labor movement." Neither name is wholly correct. Both make a class issue of what is in truth a social issue, a question involving every human interest. But the women naturally feel most the growing healthful pain of their position. They personally revolt, and think it is they who are most to

be benefited. Similarly, since the "laboring classes" feel most the growing healthful pain of their position, they as naturally revolt under the same conviction. Sociologically, these conditions, which some find so painful and alarming, mean but one thing—the increase of social consciousness. The progress of social organization has produced a corresponding degree of individualization, which has reached at last even to women,—even to the lowest grade of unskilled labor. This higher degree of individualization means a sharp personal consciousness of the evils of a situation hitherto little felt. With this higher growth of individual consciousness, and forming a part of it, comes the commensurate growth of social consciousness. We have grown to care for one another.

The woman's movement rests not alone on her larger personality, with its tingling sense of revolt against injustice, but on the wide, deep sympathy of women for one another. It is a concerted movement, based on the recognition of a common evil and seeking a common good. So with the labor movement. It is not alone that the individual laborer is a better educated, more highly developed man than the stolid peasant of earlier days, but also that with this keener personal consciousness has come the wider social consciousness, without which no class can better its conditions. The traits incident to our sexuo-economic relation have developed till they forbid the continuance of that relation. In the economic world, excessive masculinity, in its fierce competition and primitive individualism; and excessive femininity, in its inordinate consumption and hindering conservatism; have reached a stage where they work more evil than good. [...]

Democracy means, requires, is, individual liberty. While the sexuo-economic relation makes the family the centre of industrial activity, no higher collectivity than we have to-day is possible. But, as women become free, economic, social factors, so becomes possible the full social combination of individuals in collective industry. With such freedom, such independence, such wider union, becomes possible also a union between man and woman such as the world has long dreamed of in vain.

From *A Woman's Utopia*, Introduction (1907)

[*A Woman's Utopia* was Gilman's first sustained foray into utopian fiction. Chapters 1–4 were published serially in *The Times Magazine*, January through March of 1907; Chapters 1–5 are collected in *Daring to Dream: Utopian Fiction by United States Women before 1950*, edited by Carol Farley Kessler. The book was never completed. Like *Herland, A Woman's Utopia* argues that mother-hood is the basis for envisioning social improvements.]

There is an instinctive demand for happiness in the human heart which has been so far most ignorantly misunderstood.

When it was plain animal happiness that we wanted; good and sufficient food, warmth, rest, the companionship of one's kind, with mate and young—all these natural impulses were at best at-tributed to "our lower nature," and at worst to "temptations of the devil."

So also in our steadily enlarging desire for human things, for the rich product of man's skill and social energy; all these wishes were called "worldly," "material," proofs of our mortal weakness.

Now, when we felt the still higher longing, that deep, strong in-stinct of a social creature for the love and peace and power of wide union, of manifold organization, and for the scarce imaginable delight of the multiplied sensation and expression of such full hu-man relationship—all this was ascribed to "another world"—sup-posed impossible in this one.

Yet these are all natural instincts, the first kind natural to all an-imals, the last equally natural to social animals of our grade; and their presence in us is sure indication of their possible fulfilment.

Nature does not develop in fish a longing for foot-races; nor in pigs a passion for swimming. What a species is born desiring, is good for it.

We, being human, and having reached a high degree of sociali-zation, are capable even now of methods of living which would guarantee in us a minimum of happiness far beyond our present average, and a maximum which we can scarce imagine.

But the longing is in us, the instinct, the demand for heaven, not after death, but here. This hope has found expression since we wrote books, in the numerous "Utopias" which earnest men have written; and it is to be noticed as time passes that the changes portrayed in these pictures of a better life are less and less distant from immediate conditions.

When Plato planned his "New Republic,"[1] the world was still mainly savage. When More's "Utopia"[2] appeared, the world's av-erage was higher; not to More's level, but nearer than in Plato's time. Our "Looking Backward"[3] has scarce a feature beyond the

---

1 Plato (429–347 BCE) *The Republic* (c. 360 BCE).

2 Sir Thomas More (1478–1535), *Utopia* (1516).

3 Edward Bellamy (1850–98), *Looking Backward: 2000–1887* (1888).

grasp of the average citizen—as the traveling man remarked when he read it: "That's what we want!—and that's what we're going to have! The best of it is there's none of your damned socialism in it!"

The "Modern Utopia" of Mr. Wells[1] is more subtle in analysis, and may not appeal so quickly to the general mind, but it is a very human world he makes, leaving a percentage of criminals and defectives to run their island communities to suit themselves.

We are beginning to see that Utopian dreams are to life what an architect's plans are to a house—we may build it—if we can. Of course if he has planned wrongly—if the thing won't stand, or does not suit our purpose, then we lay it aside and choose another.

But it is perfectly practical to make plans before you build; much more so than to build without a plan. So far society has grown like a coral island, each individual polyp contributing his calcareous mite, and the thing getting indisputably bigger. But society is not a mere aggregate of polyps—it is an organization of persons; and mere size is not enough. As the social organization becomes conscious it keenly appreciates its various discomforts and limitations, and seeks to remove them. In this work there is necessary clear and careful planning, lest our conscious steps lead us more astray than our unconscious ones.

Of one thing we may be certain—that the plan cannot be found behind us. It is not reversion which is needed—there is no going back to an earlier and "simpler" condition—we must go on to a later and better one.

Our previous Utopias have been of a large and glittering generality. They always assume extreme differences, another age, another country—another world. Even Mr. Wells, with his comet, must have another atmosphere, a complete and sudden change.

Now, if we are really coming to Utopia, there is a road to it. That road ends in a glorious future, but it begins here and now.

We need not only general Utopias, world schemes, necessarily laid far in the future, and involving so many preliminary stages undescribed; but we need particular Utopias, plans of betterment so plainly desirable that a majority will want them, and as workable and profitable as the other new inventions with which we are continually advancing our condition.

We have only to look back one century, before matches were invented, or steam locomotion introduced, to see how insanely visionary to the people of that time would have appeared the daily necessities of this. Also, we can see in the years behind us how our

---

1   H.G. Wells (1866–1946), *A Modern Utopia* (1905).

progress was needlessly impeded by the density, the inertia, the prejudice and cowardice and sodden ignorance of the multitude. A century of science has helped the common mind. Our socialized schools and libraries, our freedom of thought and speech, and our undeniable achievements, all make us better able to take further steps.

Now that a living man may mark the world's progress in his own lifetime, he can no longer deny it. We know we can move, we are willing enough, but we wish to be sure of the way.

Now is the time for practical Utopias. Heretofore all these visions of better living have been given us by men. Never a voice from a woman to say how she would like the world. The main stream of life, the Mother, has been silent. But she is vocal enough today. She speaks and writes, lectures and preaches, teaches in school and college, spreads steadily out into all human industries. And so far her voice is the voice of complaining.

Small wonder! She has cause enough, and centuries of dumb endurance to make up for. But even if one has cause for complaining, it is a poor business.

One feels like saying, "Well, well, admitting it is as you say— what do you want done about it?"

Suppose the Mother makes up her mind as to what she wants, and speaks.

From "Effect of Literature upon the Mind," *Our Brains and What Ails Them. The Forerunner* **3.5 (May 1912): 137–39**

[In this excerpt, Gilman outlines her views of the positive effects the best literature can have on its readers. In doing so, she suggests her goals for her own writing.]

We are a race of animals developing into Humanity. Humanity consists in its mind, of a group of emotions, a mass of knowledge, a flow of power; in its body, of the whole manufactured world about us. The social spirit; complex, highly intelligent, accumulating vast knowledge, is lodged in a social body of buildings, clothing, tools and implements of all sorts. The inter-action of these gives the conduct of Society, the current of action which constitutes social life. That conduct is most modified by the brain, its character and contents; and that brain, in humanity, is mainly on paper.

Now conduct is modified not only by what we know, but by how we feel. One must have power in order to act, and that power varies not only in quantity, but in its habitual lines of discharge. A given mind, for instance, may show endless power in patient repetition, and no power of initiative; bursts of tender emotion over the killing of animals, and none over the working of children. How we feel, how much, how often, in what lines, is as important as what we think. This mind, having special ability for thinking, makes scientific discoveries and is giving them to the world—a great gift. Another mind, having special ability for feeling—makes a song like the Marseillaise[1]—and millions march in courage. One may write a book of fact like "Helper"[2] on slavery, and stir a nation to think more wisely. Another may write a book of fiction like "Uncle Tom's Cabin"[3] and rouse the nation to act.

The power of the artist to enlarge our world of feeling; to lift and carry less favored souls into a richer life; to put his feeling into immortal form, and leave it pouring light and strength, peace, patience or courage, beauty or terror, down the ages, is as noble work as the world knows. To see—where others are blind; to hear—when they are deaf; to speak—when they are dumb; to be a special sensorium for the world, and to build up and tenderly develop its capacity for higher perception and emotion—that is the business of the artist.

As that great work is fulfilled the world's heart softens, its range of sensibility widens, its power of feeling deepens, as it becomes more able to grow and to do; to enjoy and to achieve. Wordsworth,[4] for instance, expressed a new appreciation of a side of nature as yet voiceless; and, in his frame of words, thousands may see again as he did, feel again as he did, find their own vaguer sentiments brought into consciousness through him.

[...]

The novel is more fluent, less tradition-bound than poetry. It has responded more healthfully to the needs of its age. It is to-day by far the most powerful department in this kind of literature. Its

---

1 The French national anthem, written in 1792 during the French Revolution by Claude Joseph Rouget de Lisle.

2 Hinton Rowan Helper (1829–1909) published *The Impending Crisis of the South* (1857), which argued that slavery was not in the self-interest of whites; Helper explicitly rejected emotional appeals like those in *Uncle Tom's Cabin*.

3 Best-selling and highly influential 1852 anti-slavery novel by Harriet Beecher Stowe, Gilman's great aunt.

4 Poet William Wordsworth (1770–1850), who pioneered the idea that poetry is "the spontaneous overflow of powerful feelings," wrote about the natural world, peasants, and children.

service is enormous; and its special need to-day is being met with splendid vigor by those socially evolved for the purpose.

We misunderstood it for long years, because of the dragging influence of earlier periods. The minstrel, singing praises of the warriors who fed and protected him, and making love-songs to gratify both master and mistress, meant to please people who did little besides fight, hunt and make love. He was not a noble functionary. So long as fiction imitated this work, it was not noble either. But when the mind, specially sensitized to see and understand some part of life, began to use this fluent power to revisualize and interpret that life to others, a great art was born.

To feel and see some vital phase of human life; to throw that feeling, that perception, into such forms as to be easily assimilable to others—that is the art of fiction. It explains life. It translates the general into the particular and presents it to other minds; which, impressed by the particular instance, can re-generalize again in its own brain.

Dickens felt strongly about many boys' schools. He wrote Nicholas Nickleby[1]—about one. Then England was touched—stirred—it saw, through the form of fiction, what it had not seen in glaring fact; and the work of improving schools rushed forward.

We have in our fiction to-day the lingering remnants of the oldest kind, tale-telling pure and simple, the same old burden of love and war and huntsmanship; we have the variations due to the development of the individual artist; following his nose as it were, wherever it leads him; the variation due to those who make of fiction moral textbooks outright; and that of the widening social sense, seeing far more in life than those ancient tale-tellers could see, and developing splendid power to throw their mighty visions upon paper, to be seen and felt and acted on by the world.

All these fields of fiction are hampered from within and roundabout by the dragging weight of literary tradition; and cramped by economic pressure as in earlier times by power of church and king.

But in its splendid vision and clear force; and in its trivial weakness, its mere flat useless repetition of old themes; does fiction fill

---

1 Novel by Charles Dickens (1812–70), serialized in 1838–39, features a cruel schoolmaster, Wackford Squeers, who pockets the tuition of unwanted students sent to his boarding school, Dotheboys Hall, then starves and beats the boys.

and modify the social mind. As it rises, the mind rises; as it sinks, the mind sinks; as it is narrow, morbid, monotonous, confused, ineffectual, so is that Social Brain of which this world of books is so literally the outer form.

"Imprisonment for Life." *The Forerunner* 3.9 (September 1912): 237

[Gilman's 1912 meditation on the death penalty illuminates the legal proceedings in the final chapter of *Herland*, written three years later.]

In Italy they have sentenced a murderer to imprisonment for life. He is to pass the first seven years in a cell some 6x6x4—a sort of tall coffin. He is to see no one, speak to no one, save his parents *once a year*. He is to have no air, no exercise, save a walk for an hour in the prison yard, once a month. After that seven years the pressure is relieved a little, and quite safely so, as none ever come out of that coffin sane.

To keep the body alive in unbroken misery, long enough to torture the brain into insanity, is more "humane" than execution—is it?

What a testimony it is to our general disuse of the thinking power that such a punishment as this, with all its permanent mechanism of stone prisons and their warders—warders who are injured as surely as are the prisoners, by their de-humanizing work, should be considered a step up from the practice of killing convicted criminals.

If a member of society is so harmful as to need to be removed, excision clean and swift is better than this encysting process, which involves the prolonged agony and destruction of the diseased part and an injury also to the surrounding tissues. If we are sensitive to pain, let the offending member be chloroformed, while asleep; then he would be utterly removed, with no suffering. But if he is worth keeping, keep him *alive*.

"As to Parthenogenesis and Humanity." *Forerunner* 7.3 (March 1916): 83

[This brief note appeared in *The Forerunner*'s Comment and Review section, in the year following *Herland*'s serialization and in conjunction with the third chapter of *Herland*'s sequel, *With Her in Ourland*.]

Several subscribers have asked if there is any foundation in biology for the condition of parthenogenesis—virgin birth—alleged in *Herland*.

For human beings, no; nor would it be desirable. Fertilization is a higher process, a superior process; the highest types in nature do not revert to lower ones.

But the reproduction of the species by the female alone is common enough among low orders of life, and is found, to some extent in creatures as high as the bees, where the female can bring forth alone, but only of one sex; or as with the aphis, which has both faculties, reproducing parthenogenetically for a long time, and then laying eggs which hatch males, and taking up the bisexual method.

The idea in *Herland* is purely arbitrary, and used only to bring out as clearly as possible the essential qualities of a purely feminine culture. Our bisexual culture should be nobler yet, and will be, some day, when the female has her full share in it.

From *His Religion and Hers: A Study of the Faith of Our Fathers and the Work of Our Mothers*. New York: Century, 1923

[Gilman's last published book expands on the ideas about religion explored in *Herland*, especially Chapter 10.]

Chapter III: Suggested Causes

[...] What would have been the effect upon religion if it had come to us through the minds of women?

If we are to trace our engrossing interest in death to the constant fighting and killing of early man, to the fact that death was the crisis in his activities, the significant event, rousing him to thought, what other interest are we to look for in the life of woman? What crisis set her mind at work, and what would have been its influence on religion?

The business of primitive woman was to work and to bear children. Her work was regular and repetitive; save for the gradual budding of invention and blossoming of decoration, it had no climax. There was small excitement in this, no thrilling event.

Yet her life held one crisis more impressive, more arousing, far, than man's; her glory was in giving life, not taking it. To her the miracle, the stimulus to thought, was birth.

Had the religions of the world developed through her mind, they would have shown one deep, essential difference, the difference between birth and death. The man was interested in one end of life, she in the other. He was moved to faith, fear, and hope for the future; she to love and labor in the present.

To the death-based religion the main question is, "What is going to happen to me after I am dead?"—a posthumous egotism.

To the birth-based religion the main question is, "What must be done for the child who is born?"—an immediate altruism.

Woman was not given to bootless speculation as to where the new soul came from, because of the instant exigencies of its presence. It had come, indeed, but in a small and feeble state, utterly dependent on her love and service. With birth as the major crisis of life, awakening thought leads inevitably to that love and service, to defense and care and teaching, to all the labors that maintain and improve life.

The death-based religions have led to a limitless individualism, a demand for the eternal extension of personality. Such good conduct as they required was to placate the deity or to benefit one's self—to "acquire merit," as the Buddhist frankly puts it. The birth-based religion is necessarily and essentially altruistic, a forgetting of oneself for the good of the child, and tends to develop naturally into love and labor for the widening range of family, state, and world. The first leads our thoughts away from this world about which we know something, into another world about which we know nothing. The first is something to be believed. The second is something to be done.

Before we attempt to indicate the natural consequences of birth-based religion, it should be repeated that here is no denial of personal immortality, against which there is no proof. Neither is there any condemnation of the male sex as such—only of its excessive development and disproportionate influence upon social evolution. Nor are women, such as we see about us, overrated or held capable of suddenly producing a flood of new truth and wise direction.

The position is that the tendencies of motherhood are in line with social progress, while the tendencies of the male sex, though quite legitimate in the propagation of the species, are often inimical to its social progress. Even had man and woman grown and worked together, her influence would have been more toward peaceful industrial development, and his more toward competitive methods; and, during the long period of her suppression and his expansion, an ultra-masculinity has interfered with normal social evolution. [...]

Birth-based religion would steadily hold before our eyes the vision of a splendid race, the duty of upbuilding it. It would tell no story of old sins, of anguish and despair, of passionate pleading for forgiveness for the mischief we have made, but would offer always the sunrise of a fresh hope: "Here is a new baby. Begin again!"

To the mother comes the apprehension of God as something coming; she sees his work, the newborn child, as visibly unfinished and calling for continuous service. The first festival of her religion would be the Birth Day, with gifts and rejoicings, with glad thanksgiving for life. In the man's religion, the demand for ever-watching love and care, is that of the child, always turning to its mother—

> An infant crying in the night,
> An infant crying for the light,
> And with no language but a cry.[1]

The mother, feeling in herself that love and that care, pours them forth on man, her child. Such recognition and expression of divine power are better than "worship." You cannot worship a force within you; the desire of the mother soul is to give benefit rather than to receive it.

As the thought of God slowly unfolded in the mind of woman, that great Power would have been apprehended as the Life-giver, the Teacher, the Provider, the Protector—not the proud, angry, jealous, vengeful deity men have imagined. She would have seen a God of Service, not a God of Battles. It is no wonder that Christianity was so eagerly adopted by woman. Here was a religion which made no degrading discrimination against her, and the fulfilment of which called for the essentially motherly attributes of love and service.

From *The Living of Charlotte Perkins Gilman: An Autobiography.* Appleton, 1935

[This is Gilman's account of the history and reception of *The Forerunner*, the wholly self-produced magazine in which *Herland* appeared.]

As years passed and continuous writing and speaking developed the various lines of thought I was following, my work grew in importance but lost in market value. Social philosophy, however

---

1 From section 54, lines 18–20, of *In Memoriam, A.H.H.*, by Alfred, Lord Tennyson (1809–92), which focuses on the speaker's response to the death of his friend.

ingeniously presented, does not command wide popular interest. I wrote more and sold less.

Theodore Dreiser,[1] then on the *Delineator*, as I remember, looked gloomily at me over his desk, and said, "You should consider more what the editors want." Of course I should have, if I had been a competent professional writer. There are those who write as artists, real ones; they often find it difficult to consider what the editor wants. There are those who write to earn a living, they, if they succeed, *must* please the editor. The editor, having his living to earn, must please his purchasers, the public, so we have this great trade of literary catering. But if one writes to express important truths, needed yet unpopular, the market is necessarily limited.

As all my principal topics were in direct contravention of established views, beliefs and emotions, it is a wonder that so many editors took so much of my work for so long.

But as time passed there was less and less market for what I had to say, more and more of my stuff was declined. Think I must and write I must, the manuscripts accumulated far faster than I could sell them, some of the best, almost all—and finally I announced: "If the editors and publishers will not bring out my work, I will!" And I did. In November, 1909, I started the *Forerunner*.

This was a small monthly magazine, written entirely by myself. There have been other one-man magazines, but smaller and confined to one kind of writing as a rule. Mine was not very big, but its ten-by-seven pages, twenty-eight of them, seven hundred and fifty words to a page, made some twenty-one thousand to the issue. It equaled four books a year, books of thirty-six thousand words.[2]

Each issue included one installment of a novel, also of a book published serially; a short story, articles of various length; poems, verses, allegories, humor and nonsense, with book reviews and comment on current events. For a time it carried some advertisements, which I wrote myself, honestly recommending things I knew from experience to be good. One friend offered some advertising, I told him I did not know his stuff. He sent me some samples, I did not like it, and therefore declined it. This attitude did not make for business success.

---

1 Journalist and controversial American novelist—author of *Sister Carrie, An American Tragedy*, and other novels—Dreiser (1871–1945) edited *The Delineator, A Journal of Fashion, Culture, and the Fine Arts*, from 1907 to 1910.

2 Gilman has transposed her numbers: 21,000 words a month or 252,000 words a year is the equivalent of four books at 63,000 words, not 36,000 words.

The cost of publishing this work was $3,000 a year; its price, a dollar. If I could have achieved three thousand subscribers then I would cheerfully have done the work for nothing, but I never had sense enough—business sense, that is, to get them. About fifteen hundred was our income, and the rest of the expense I met by doing extra work in writing—outside of the "four book" demands of the magazine, and as usual, lecturing.

It was an undertaking, especially on long trips, as when abroad, or on the Pacific Coast, to keep up with the manuscript, and see that it reached the printer. We had a most sympathetic printer, a good German, Rudolph Rochow, who was very patient with my efforts at proof-reading. He liked the magazine so well that he subscribed to it! Which reminds me of an early compliment on *Women and Economics*—that the very type-setters read it and enjoyed it.

The range of circulation was all over this country, quite widely in Europe, and as far afield as India and Australia, but scanty in numbers. What I had banked on in starting was my really wide reputation, the advertising possibilities of continued lecturing, and the low price. But I found to my amusement that among women ten dollars for a hat is cheap while one dollar for a magazine is an unwarranted expense. One woman in a town would take it, and then proudly tell me how she circulated it among all her friends—thus saving them the cost of subscribing!

It seemed to me that out of, say thirty states, there would be a hundred women in each who cared enough for my teachings to pay a dollar a year for them, and I think so still. What was lacking was enough capacity on my part to manage the business properly. However, one cannot have everything. Production is easier than distribution, to some kinds of people at least.

As to engaging a business manager, there was not enough money in the thing at its best to pay a capable man for pushing it. I had a good advertising man for a little while, but he explained to me that for less effort he could sell a page of *Scribner's Magazine* for several hundreds than a page of the *Forerunner* for $25.00, and left.

Similarly, I have never had a good lecture agent or manager for any length of time. Such a person, to succeed, must have a strong conviction of the value of my work, *and* business ability. These do not coexist. There have been many who were profoundly impressed with the importance of the work, but they were not good press-agents, and good press-agents do not care to promote small, unpopular undertakings. Also, can a press-agent be imagined who would work for a woman who would not allow the least exaggeration or misstatement?

However, regardless of difficulties, I wrote and published the *Forerunner* for seven years. This meant seven novels (by which I definitely proved that I am not a novelist)! and seven other books, of considerable value, as *The Man-made World* (widely translated in Europe), *Our Brains and What Ails Them, Social Ethics, The Dress of Women*, and others; enough verse for another volume, and all the rest of the varied material.

It was an immense task to get the work done, to write more than I could ever have done without some such definite compulsion, and to say exactly what I had to say, fully and freely. If possible I hope to see a "library edition," some day, with the best of the *Forerunner* and all my other books, this autobiography trailing along at the end.

[...]

It has always seemed to me something of a joke on the American critics of this period that not one of them, save one woman who was already a friend, should have recognized this literary *tour de force* by an established author as worth mentioning. Without any question as to its artistic merit, it was certainly a unique piece of work, worth recording. But that is not the first joke on critics, by any means.

In regard to the general attitude of hearers, readers and editors, toward my work, I have met a far wider and warmer welcome than I ever expected. Not aiming in the least at literary virtuosity, still less at financial success, I have been most agreeably surprised by the acceptance of so much of what I had to offer. One cannot undertake to alter the ideas, feelings and habits of the people and expect them to like it.

Consider the theses this one woman was advancing against the previous convictions of the world: in religion a practical, impersonal Deism, seeing God as a working power which asks no worship, only fulfilment:

God is a force to give way to—
God is a thing you have to Do!

With no concern for immortality or salvation, merely a carrying out of the divine will. In ethics its presentation as a wholly social science, applicable to every act in life, the measure of merit being the effect on social advancement. In economics, a change in the basis of that science, as with ethics, from the individual to the group, involving a complete reversal of most of our previous economic theories; and in what is of far more interest to most of us, our domestic and sex relationships, the claim that we as a race of animals are oversexed—abnormally developed in that function from long centuries of excessive indulgence, and that it is disadvantageous to social progress to have the feeding of humanity and the care of young children carried on by amateurs.

This last is the view which has been most violently opposed. The food habits of a people are extremely difficult to change, and as to the care of young children, the obvious need and value of the mother have blinded us to her as obvious deficiencies. The position as to sex is most amusingly in contradiction of our present theory of its dominant importance, a theory which claims as "natural" an indulgence absolutely without parallel in nature.

Being so universal a heretic it is much to the credit of our advance in liberal thought that my work has been for the most part well received. The slowness and indifference of the public mind was of course to be expected, and its very general misunderstanding; the only thing I have to complain of in the way of ill-treatment has been from newspapers, and even among them there has been much, very much, of fair and helpful recognition.

So general an attack upon what we have long held incontrovertible must needs have met misunderstanding and opposition. If the world had been able to easily receive it then it would not have been necessary. The clear logic of the position, the reasoning which supported it, made small impression on the average mind. Reason is the least used of our faculties, the most difficult—even painful. That is why successful orators do not need it.

This is also why my little *Forerunner* had so few subscribers, at least one reason why. There were some who were with me on one point and some on two, but when it came to five or more distinct heresies, to a magazine which even ridiculed Fashion, and held blazing before its readers a heaven on earth which they did not in the least want—it narrowed the subscription list.

The magazine came to an end with 1916. For a while I did little writing—I had said all I had to say. Then presently I undertook a new game, writing short bits of daily stuff for a newspaper syndicate. "Could I keep it up?" anxiously inquired the gentleman who engaged me. I told him what I had been keeping up for seven years, and he was satisfied. But alas! though I tried my best to reach and hold the popular taste, I couldn't do it, so after a year that effort came to an end. It was the only time in my life when I had a "pay-envelope," and that was most enjoyable.

Volume 6 No. 3   MARCH, 1915

THE FORERUNNER

BY

Charlotte Perkins Gilman.

CONTENTS

1.00 A YEAR   67 WALL ST.   NEW YORK   .10 A COPY

Cover of the March 1915 issue of *The Forerunner*, in which the third chapter of *Herland* appeared. The illustration, portraying a man and woman supporting a child standing on a globe, was designed by Gilman's daughter Katharine Stetson Chamberlin and appeared on every issue. The image reflects Gilman's focus on children and cooperation.

Materials That Appeared in The Forerunner *in 1915, alongside* Herland

"Standardizing Towns"
The Forerunner **6.**2 (February 1915): 53–55

[In this essay, published in the same issue of *The Forerunner* in which readers first glimpse the towns of Herland, Gilman lists ways to measure the quality of American towns and suggests that women can lead the way to improving them.]

Time was when every baby was a "gold child"—to its fond parents. "Every crow," says the proverb, "thinks its own young ones the blackest."

That vigorous young movement, spreading so fast over our country, called "The Better Babies' Contest," is teaching us something. The mother, taking her heart's idol to compare with the idols of other hearts, was surprised to learn even idols have "points," and that a "Blue Ribbon" baby was a better base for parental pride than some puny infant which no amount of idolatry could make a prizewinner.

No mother loved her baby less because it was not up to standard. Perhaps she loved it more. But at any rate she learned what a child of a given age should be; she had her "score card," her list of measurements, her new knowledge, new pride, new shame; and next year, when the Contest was open again she brought back the same baby—and took a prize.

Local pride is a strong feeling, a healthy and natural feeling, and one that should be used to better advantage. At present we are proud of our towns, cities, states, countries, just because they are ours, like the mother of the weazened indigestive infant.

What we need is a Better Towns Contest, a standardized scale of measurements, a score-card—and Blue Ribbons.

We race our horses, we race our yachts, we match our dogs and cats and pigeons. Why not start a new competition race—the highest open to us, which has no limit till the whole earth is well ordered, and ready to enter in the great choral contest of the moving stars!

To begin this we must first have some idea of what a Town should be. We have measured them, so far, by their natural beauty, by their rate of growth, by their wealth and commercial standing. Yet beauty of natural surroundings did not make Carthage[1] a type of noble cityhood, nor does wealth make us respect Monaco.[2] Commercial growth has given us some of the blackest, ugliest, sickest and wickedest of our cities, for which we should wear the sackcloth and ashes of shame. And as to size and "population"—that cheap boast of mere numbers, linear space—these may be but cases of civic acromegaly, the lumbering, brainless, giant cities, swollen but feeble—no ground for pride.

How then, shall we measure our cities? How prepare a score-card by which to register progress? How standardize civic "points" for a Better Towns Contest?

Here is a suggested outline, a faint beginning, trusted to wiser heads, to more capable hands for full development.

A brief list of ten "Points" is offered:

1. Health
2. Beauty
3. Virtue
4. Public Spirit
5. Educational Facilities
6. Social Facilities
7. Minimum of Prosperity
8. Administrative Efficiency
9. Administrative Honesty
10. Progressiveness

These call for careful subdivision. Under Health comes first the all important matter of vital statistics, that reliable record of births, deaths and diseases, on which knowledge of a city's physical well-being must rest. If there are no such records, the first effort of the delinquent town should be to begin them, and to see that they are properly kept.

All matters of civic hygiene come in here, as the water supply, disposal of sewage and garbage, extinction of flies and other vermin, proper building laws, registration of quarantine, contagious diseases, and such active measures as may be taken to secure and improve the physical health of the citizens.

---

1 Powerful ancient commercial and military city near modern Tunis.
2 Small Mediterranean city-state neighboring France, known since the mid-nineteenth century as a tourist site for gambling.

Civic Beauty does not refer to chances of location, but to what the city itself has done to build and lay out loveliness for its people. We in America will rank low here, but we can grow—we are growing—in this line. Since the World's Fair at Chicago in 1893 we have had our Dream Cities. Soon we can have them real.

It seems a pity to make a study of vice and crime to promote virtue, but we must do it as we record diseases in the interests of health.

All citizens should know how their town stands as compared with others of its size:—in gambling, in drunkenness, in prostitution, in theft, arson and murder, of course, and further, in the subtler, larger vices, such as adulteration of food or drugs, manufacture of shoddy, and other sins against the public.

Against this we should have the Honor Record of "Public Spirit," not of the individual virtues such as are possessed by many a burglar or crooked politician but the civic virtues shown in works of true public service. All the obvious "good works" of charity, correction and reform come in here, and those bequests to the advantage of the community; but we should add to our list of the vicious the names of men who have robbed or cheated the community.

Already we are proud of our Educational Facilities, and already they are widening and improving year by year. But towns vary; there is room for improvement in all; and, in some, for a great deal.

Social Facilities are as necessary, and to this too we are beginning to waken, here and there. The school extension movement, using the school buildings as social centers, is all in the right direction. Every smallest village should have some place where men and women may gather freely, for amusement and social intercourse, as well as for instruction.

The Minimum of Prosperity is a new thing to put forward. We "point with pride" to our "residence quarter," our "magnates," and millionaires. We must learn to see that the prosperity of a town means that of all its people, and to be proud only when we have no poverty.

Administrative Efficiency and Honesty can be measured, and we should add to them an honor record, worth our boasting,

Progressiveness should be measured, too; the town that is most courageous, most willing to advance, being most honored.

All these need to be arranged in clear simple form, with an illustrative model to measure by, and blanks to fill in with local records.

Town after town should enter the contest, learning its own "points," and its own standing.

Here is work for our Women's Clubs!

"War-Maids and War-Widows"
The Forerunner 6.3 (March 1915): 63–65

[The Great War (World War I) had begun in Europe in July of 1914, and Gilman actively opposed the "masculism" of it and all wars (though by the time the US declared war on Germany in 1917 she supported defeat of Germany's "ultra-masculine culture"). This essay recommends that women organize themselves not only to end war but to transform the whole culture in a manner similar to the Herlanders' woman-made world.]

We have to consider a much larger question than any hasty war measure of assisted marriages; namely, the duty of women now and after this war, as to making it the last one.

Here there is no confusion, no perplexity. If women object so heartily to war—and they do—it is their duty to stop it—and they can.

Not by killing themselves and incidentally their unborn children; not by the mere dumb protest of remaining childless—the peace won by national extinction is neither useful or noble; it merely begs the question, taking refuge in the grave.

No, we need action from women. This war, like all wars, must leave behind vast numbers of the unmarried and the widowed. Let them accept the glorious opportunity made possible by their bereavement. Facing fairly the plain fact that they cannot be "housewives"; that the private family with its close circle of love, care and duty, is hopelessly out of reach; let them consecrate their lives to such organized activity as will indeed end war.

Large numbers of unmarried women are as valuable to society as large numbers of worker-bees are to the hive. Social heredity is more potent than physical.

It should be the duty of these women to get together, and to work for two things; for such political power as shall give them their full share in public action; and, equally, if not more important, for such industrial organization as shall give them their full share in economic power.

The one thing women need more than any other is the *sense of collectivity*. This men have gained by working together, even by fighting together, and women have been prevented from gaining by being forced to work alone.

Now here we have a huge accession to the ranks of unmarried women, coming all at once, open-eyed, to frank recognition of their permanent singleness. They will have no men to stand by and take care of them. Let them stand by and take care of one another.

In every town there should be formed an association with some simple name, such as Woman's Mutual Service League, and these all federated nationally; the purposes of the organization to be the improvement of the condition of women, Economic, Educational, Social and Political.

In beginning, some member could furnish some room to meet in, perhaps a club-house. Those who had work could pay dues, and those who had not could work for the association. In each small town the League could constitute itself:

a. A reliable employment agency for members;
b. A training school to fit members for employment;
c. An industrial enterprise to increase the funds and develop the work of the League.

Women of all classes should unite in such work, helping one another by virtue of their differences; sinking their petty social prejudices and their religious prejudices, too, in this recognition of the need of a united womanhood; self-supporting, intelligent, strong to work against war.

There should be, as soon as possible, a good club-house, where an income could be raised by letting rooms to other societies, to boys' and girls' clubs, and for entertainments. In connection with this should be an admirable restaurant, making a specialty of scientifically prepared foods, excellent and inexpensive; and this restaurant combine the advantages of a training-school for some members, and the furnishing of meals to the clubhouse.

A dairy farm, a market garden, an orchard, could be used in this connection to supply the restaurant; and saleable foods, nurse's supplies, pure confections, and the general products of a "woman's exchange," made part of the work.

The Woman's League House ought to prove an invaluable economic clearing house for numbers of women; and an intellectual one also. Its reading room, its library, its evening classes, its lecture hall, should steadily serve to raise the mental average of the membership, and that of the town as well. When strong enough it could constitute itself a local Lyceum; employ lecturers, and again add to its funds.

Year by year with increase of power it could extend its functions; working out improved apartment houses in cities; service of hot cooked food to detached homes; day nurseries and kindergartens; dressmaking establishments; as well as all the other lines of work open to its members.

We have already in Europe *The Lyceum Club*,[1] extending many social advantages to professional women. Such a Mutual Service League ought to furnish a convenient club-house in every town: and have at least a Rest-Room, with books and papers, even in the smallest hamlet.

With careful and gradual extension of industry it ought to give a substantial dividend to its members; and to lay up a fund for steady enlargement.

There is nothing unreasonable in this proposal. It involves in the beginning a simple mutual aid society, in which women suffering a common bereavement could join hands and learn to help one another. It should grow slowly and cautiously, using the gifts and powers of its members to the best advantage, and becoming yearly more useful.

Its service to society would be enormous. In establishing comfortable dwelling houses for women, not "Homes," full of ignominious restrictions, but attractive group-houses, where single women could enjoy both privacy and companionship, the League would serve not only its own members, but all other women the world over.

We must establish clearly that mere human comfort, with many of the pleasures of life, is not dependent upon marriage. The man or woman who does not marry loses much, but that is no reason for losing all.

To establish the power of women to stand by one another, to co-operate in mutual service, to find joy in friendship, in mental and physical exercise, and in social service—this alone is a great work.

The most perfect instances of successful group life are those among the hymenoptera, the sterile females of the bees and ants. We, with our higher social instincts, our far wider range of activity, growth, and enjoyment, ought to be able to show an infinitely nobler and happier group, with a far higher range of achievement.

---

1   A women's educational organization founded in 1904 in London; by 1915 it had spread to several European countries, including Germany, Sweden, and the Netherlands.

When so established; not lonely, not a burden on anyone, not crushed by personal loss; these women could then constitute centers of outpouring social love and service of immense value. The mother-power, forbidden exercise in private care of the separate family, would become available in caring for the community, thus helping society and satisfying the mother-instinct as well.

Moreover these Leagues would not be the timid helpless flocking together of the weak, as might have been the case a century ago. Women today are different. They have some education. They have some experience in industry, in economic freedom. The "surplus women" of England, for instance, have not lived in vain, for they have shown, perforce, that women can support themselves and more.

Now let us suppose this earnest, determined coming together of women bereaved by the present war. Surely most of them are convinced that our civilization as it exists will not do. It is not safe. It cannot be depended on. We must have a better world.

Christianity—as previously taught and used—has not saved us from this Fall of Man—this colossal Failure of Male Civilization.

We need a new kind of social structure, composed of women and men, equal. They cannot be equal until the women support themselves. Women cannot support themselves while they face life alone, each, if married, working for her own family; if single, for her own self.

The single women, being freer, younger—this last great flood of them—and stronger now because of better education, can lead the way to economic organization among women.

Such an organization, when members do marry, should have its maternity fund, whereby the mother should be able to take a six-months' vacation, or a year, if necessary, when a child was born.

Such an organization, as a high social duty, should be able to work out the problems of furnishing good food at a minimum price, house service by the hour, and expert child-care; those practical problems which the married woman, alone, is unable to solve.

And year by year, such a knitting together of womanhood, such a spread of necessary information, such an improvement, in local conditions, such growth in the collective spirit, would raise the level of citizenship in all these women; in the men they met and married, if they did marry; and in the children of the whole community.

Such a new citizenship will have no more war.

From *The Dress of Women*, On Clothing and Sexual Attraction, from Chapter 5, "Beauty vs. Sex Distinction"
***The Forerunner* 6.5 (May 1915)**

[Serialized monthly in the 1915 volume of *The Forerunner*, alongside *Herland*, *The Dress of Women* is a sociological analysis of ideas about beauty and clothing that are touched on more briefly in the novel. In this excerpt, which anticipates the explorers' concerns about clothing in Chapter 8 of *Herland*, Gilman argues that women's concern with fashion derives from the economic necessity of attracting a husband.]

Men are not averse to studying their own fashions, especially when young and "in love," but in a given number of men and women not young and not in love, a much greater proportion of the latter will be found studying the "fashion page."

This our easy androcentric view has casually set down as "woman's weakness"; whereas we need to learn how this bit of man's weakness has been so completely transferred to the other sex. If we study it for the moment, in him, as among the unblushing gorgeousness of savage "bucks" and the discriminating splendor of a Beau Brummel,[1] or a "Sir Piercie Shafton,"[2] we may begin to trace the line of evolution.

The primitive male exhibits his natural sex tendency in decoration as innocently as any peacock; and so do more sophisticated males under conditions which allow it. Blazing masculine splendor, with velvet, embroidery, jewels and lace, was found among men who did not "have to work"—knights and nobles and "gentlemen." The gradual development of our present economic era, where work and manhood are almost coterminous; and where, as with us, it is a point of masculine pride to maintain women in idleness, or at least in domestic industry without pay, shows us the original characteristics completely changed. The man now, instead of laboriously developing crest and wattle, mane and tail-feathers on himself, or their equivalent in gorgeous raiment, now exhibits them on his woman.

It is pathetically amusing to see the struggle between a man's human common sense, expressed in his opinions about women's clothes, and his masculine instinct, expressed in his actions. His

---

1   British Dandy (1778–1840) who was known for setting men's fashions, including the modern suit and tie.
2   Courtier in Sir Walter Scott's novel, *The Monastery* (1820).

critical human judgment loudly complains of the vanity of women, the extravagance of women, the women's silly submission to fashion, but his male instinct leads him straight to the most vain, extravagant and fashionable of them all. Women are not fools, nor are they so vain as is supposed. Vanity, from prancing stag to strutting cock is inherently male. Never a female creature do you find that can be called "vain" till you come to woman, and her so-called "feminine vanity" is by no means inherent, but acquired under the pressure of economic necessity.

Let a man try to put himself in the place of a young woman, with every chance of "fun," all his good times, all his opportunities to go anywhere, to see anything, to dance, to ride, to walk even—in some cases, depending on some girl's asking him! Suppose the girl was the one who "had the price." He would have then to please the girl—naturally. He would have not only his natural impulse in that direction, but this new and heavy necessity. This is what has happened to women for thousands of years. There was no liberty for woman. It was a man's world, and not safe for her to go about in. She was liable to be attacked at any time, by one of her "natural protectors." Except under his escort she was housebound, a prisoner.

All this is as a mere aside from that still more vital necessity of securing a permanent livelihood by marrying, and the natural desire to please the one you love.

The way to a man's heart, we are told, is through his stomach, and we sagely add: "Every woman should know how to cook." But the shortest route to a man's heart is through his eyes. We have no record of the culinary skill of Cleopatra, or Ninon de l'Enclos, or Madame Recamier.[1] There have been millions of assiduous female cooks—but the record heart-breakers, from Aphrodite[2] down, did it by good looks.

We are not all born beautiful; neither do we all have by nature that capricious charm which holds the vacillating fancy of the male. One of our amiable androcentric proverbs is that women are eternally changeable—"varium et mutabile."[3] Yes? Are *other* females? In other races the male, the naturally variable factor,

---

1 Cleopatra: Notoriously beautiful Egyptian queen (69–30 BCE); Ninon de l'Enclos: French author and courtesan (1620–1705); Madame Récamier: society hostess (1777–1849) considered the most beautiful woman of her day.

2 Greek goddess of beauty and erotic love.

3 *Varium et mutabile semper femina* (Latin): Woman is always a changeable and fickle thing. From Vergil's *Aeneid.*

changes and fluctuates as he may, so offering choice to the female; she, the natural selector, thus by discrimination, improving the race. But with us we find him doing the choosing, and we find the woman, depending on his favor not only for mating, but for bread, caters to his taste by this admired capriciousness.

Let it be clearly understood that it is *not* a pleasure to all women to spend their lives in an endless and hopeless pursuit of new fashions—like a cat chasing her tail. It adds heavily to the care, the labor, the expense, of living. It is a pitiful, senseless, degrading business, and they know it. But let one of them be misled by man's loud contempt for "the folly of women"; let her show originality in design, daring in execution; let her appear in public in a sensible, comfortable, hygienic, beautiful, but *unfashionable* costume—! Do the admiring men flock to her side? Do they say: "*Here* is a woman not silly and sheep-like, not extravagant and running after constant charge!"? They do not. If they are near enough to feel responsible, they murmur softly: "My dear—I hate to have you so conspicuous. A woman must never be conspicuous." If very honest, they may add: "It reflects on me. It looks as if I couldn't afford to dress my wife properly." As for the others—they simply stay away. With lip-service they praise the "common-sense" costume, but with full dance-cards and crowding invitations they pursue the highest-heeled, scantest-skirted, biggest-hatted, "very latest" lady. (At this date, April, 1915, "skirts are fuller," hats very small, and we hear "the small waist is coming in again"!)

Women are foolish, beyond doubt, but they are not nearly so foolish as they look. Those "looks" of theirs, especially in the matter of ever-changing dress, are most valuable assets. Now let no woman take this as a charge of deliberate calculation. It is nothing of the sort. It is an "acquired characteristic" of the female of genus homo, quite unconscious. But it is by no means a "feminine distinction." When women have freed themselves from their false and ignominious position of economic dependence on men, then they can develop in themselves and their clothing, true beauty. They will then recognize that since the human body does not change in its proportions and activities from day to day, neither should its clothing; that if the eye of the observer craves variety, or the mood of the wearer, this may be found legitimately in color and decoration, without the silly variations which make of that noble instrument, the body, a mere dummy, for exhibition purposes.

"Birth Control"
The Forerunner 6.7 (July 1915): 177–80

[Gilman here argues systematically a position explored in the final chapters of *Herland*: that under natural conditions couples would have sex infrequently and only for reproduction.]

The time will come when every nation must face the question, "How many people can live comfortably, healthfully, happily, upon this land?" That is the ultimate reason why we must learn that "the pressure of population"[1] is not an unavoidable fate, but a result of our own irresponsible indulgence.

This time is still a long way off. At present the main reasons advanced in advocacy of the conscious limitation of offspring are these: the economic pressure which often makes it difficult, if not impossible, to rear large families without degradation of the stock from injurious conditions; the injury to women of a continuous repetition of maternity, especially when combined with hard work and lack of comfort; and back of these, less freely stated, a desire for "safe" and free indulgence of the sex instinct without this natural consequence.

Of the first reason it may be said that the economic pressure is of our own making and may be removed when we choose. That a race of our intelligence should sink into conditions so miserable that it is difficult to raise healthy children; and then, instead of changing those miserable conditions, should weakly renounce parentage, is not creditable to that intelligence. While we have not come within centuries of "the limit of subsistence"; while there is land enough and water enough to feed a vast population as yet unapproached; it is contemptible for us to accept mere local and temporary injustice as if it were a natural condition. That the more ignorant masses should do this would not be strange; but they are not the main culprits. So far they have faced the evils around them with nature's process—the less chance of a living, the more young ones.

Wiser people, more far-seeing, with a higher standard of living to keep up, have accepted their restrictions as final, and sought so to limit their own numbers as to maintain that standard for the few.

---

1   Thomas Malthus's theory in *An Essay on the Principle of Population*
(1798), that human population increases faster than the food supply,
until it reaches the "limit of subsistence"—the point at which no more
lives can be supported—and will be kept at that level by famine, disease,
or war. The only controls to over-population besides misery, according to
Malthus, are "self-restraint" and "vice" (birth control).

If we would apply our reasoning power and united force to secure a fair standard of living for all of us, we could go on enjoying our families for many centuries.

In the meantime, accepting our present limitations, we do have to face the very practical and personal problem—how many children ought a woman to have whose husband's wages average $600 a year. That is the average for millions, even in our country.

Face this fairly: $2.00 a day for all but the fifty-two Sundays, say three holidays, and a most modest allowance of ten days' unemployment—less than $12.00 a week the year around, with rent and food prices what they are now. How many children *ought* a woman to have under these circumstances?

Then, either for this woman, overworked and underfed; or for the professor's wife, also overworked in the demands of her environment; and, though having enough to eat, also underfed in the rest and relaxation she needs; we must face the limitations of physical strength.

Here again, in a large sense, our position is pusillanimous. Maternity is a natural process. It should benefit and not injure the mother. That women have allowed themselves to sink into a condition where they are unfit to perform the very functions for which their bodies are specially constructed, is no credit to their intelligence. Instead of accepting the limitations and saying: "We are not strong enough to bear children," the wise and noble thing to do is to say: "Our condition of health is shameful. We must become strong and clean again that we may function naturally as mothers."

In spite of this, the practical and personal problem confronts the individual mother: "I have had three children in three years. I am a wreck already. If I have another I may die or become a hopeless invalid. Is it not my duty for the sake of those I have, to refuse to have more?"

The third reason, by no means so outspoken, but far more universal than the others, is at once the strongest force urging us toward birth control, and the strongest ground of opposition to it.

The prejudice against the prevention of conception and the publication of knowledge as to the proper methods, is based partly on religious conviction, and partly on an objection to the third reason above given. The religious objection is neither more nor less difficult to meet than others of the same class. A wider enlightenment steadily tends to disabuse our minds of unthinking credulity as to ancient traditions. We are beginning at last to have a higher opinion of God than we used to entertain. The modern mind will not credit an Infinite Wisdom, an Infinite Love, with motives and commands unworthy the love and wisdom of a mere earthly father. Still, for those who hold this objection, and upon whom it is enforced by their Church, it is a very serious one.

The other is still more serious; so much so that no one can rightly judge the question without squarely facing this, its biological base—what is sex union for. No one can deny its original purpose, its sole purpose through all the millions of years of prehuman life on earth. But when human life is under consideration there are two opinions.

The first holds that the human species is sui generis[1] in this regard; that we differ from all other animals in this process; that it has, for us, both a biological use quite aside from reproduction, and a psychological use entirely beyond that.

The second is to the effect that for our race, as for others, this is a biological process for the perpetuation of the species, and that its continuous indulgence with no regard to reproduction or in direct exclusion of reproduction indicates an abnormal development peculiar to our species.

The first opinion is held by practically everyone; the second by a mere handful. To those who have watched the growth of ideas in the human mind this disproportion proves nothing whatever. Of course a few people are as likely to be wrong as a great many people. Of course a small minority of people have held views as absurd as those of large majorities. Nevertheless it remains true that every advance in all human history has been begun by the ideas of a few, even of one perhaps, and opposed with cheerful unanimity by all the rest of the world.

An idea must be discussed on its merits, not measured by the numbers of people who "believe" this, or "think" that, or "feel" so and so. Especially as to feeling. The emotional responses of the mass of people are invariably reactionary. "Feelings" which belong to a more advanced state are always hard to find. Even in one's own mind, the intellectual perception comes first, the settled conviction later, and the appropriate emotional response later still.

One may be fairly forced by sheer reason and logic to admit the justice and expedience of equal suffrage for men and women; one may accept this as a strong belief and act accordingly. Yet the swift warm sense of approval for what is still called a "womanly woman," the cold aversion to what we have for long assumed to be "unwomanly," remain.

---

1 Constituting a separate class; unique (Latin).

Because of these simple and common phenomena we must not be swayed too much in our judgment on this question as to the true use and purpose and the legitimate limits of the sex function, by the overwhelming mass of sentiment on the side of continuous indulgence.

For clear discussion it will be well to state definitely the thesis here advanced, which is:

That with the human species as with others the normal purpose of sex-union is reproduction;

That its continuous repetition, wholly disassociated with this use, results in a disproportionate development of the preliminary sex emotions and functional capacities, to the detriment of the parental emotions and functional capacities, and to the grave injury of the higher processes of human development;

That our present standard of "normal indulgence" is abnormal; this by no means in the sense of any individual abnormity, but in the sense of a whole race thus developed by thousands of generations of over-indulgence;

That, when the human species, gradually modifying its conduct by the adoption of changed ideas, becomes normal in this regard, it will show a very different scale of emotional and functional demand; the element of sex-desire greatly reduced in proportion to the higher development of parental activities worthy of our race; and of a whole range of social emotions and functions now impossible because of the proportionate predominance of this one process and its emotions;

That this change will necessarily be a slow one; and involves, not the pious struggles of a convicted sinner against a sin, but the wise gradual efforts of a conscious race to so change its habits, to so modify itself, as to breed out the tendency to excessive indulgence, and allow the re-assumption of normal habits;

That the resultant status is not of an emasculate or effeminate race; or of one violently repressing its desires; but rather that of a race whose entire standard has changed; in physical inclination, in emotion, and in idea; so that the impulse to that form of sex-expression comes only in a yearly season, as with other species of the same gestative period.

The opposing thesis is so universally held as hardly to need statement, but may be fairly put in this way:

That it is "natural" for the human species to continually indulge sex-emotion and its physical expression, with no regard whatever to reproduction.

That this indulgence has "a higher function" in no way associated with so crude a purpose as bringing forth children, but is

(a) an expression of pure and lofty affection; (b) a concomitant of all noble creative work; (c) a physical necessity to maintain the health of men—some say also of women.

This position is reinforced not only by the originally strong sex instinct in all animals, and by the excessive force of that instinct in the human race; but by the world's accumulated psychology on the subject—its pictures, statues, stories, poems, music, drama, even its religions, all of which have been elaborated by the sex which has the most to gain and the least to lose by upholding such a standard.

Without expecting to make much impression upon such a measureless mass of instinct, sentiment, habit, and tradition, we may offer this much consideration of the above position.

First as to the use of the word "natural." The forces of nature tend to preserve life—under any conditions. Up to the last limits of possibility, the form, size, and structure, habits and feelings of a living species, will change and change and change again in order that it may live.

Anything will be sacrificed—so that the one main necessity is maintained—that the creature be not extinct. "Nature," in the sense of creatures below mankind, often failed in this effort, and many species did become extinct. Our human conditions, which are natural too, but not in this special sense, are so favorable that human life is maintained where less able creatures would die.

It is quite possible for a part of society to so conduct itself as would inevitably cause its own destruction if it were not meanwhile fed and clothed and sheltered by another part. It is possible for quite a small fraction of society to promote ideas, theories and habits which would corrupt and degrade the whole if they were not offset by other tendencies. In the specific matter in question the one absolute condition of life was merely this: that enough women reached the bearing age and produced enough children to maintain the race in existence.

The condition of said race might be as low as that of the fella-heen[1] of Egypt, of the Australian savage, of the Bushman of Africa. No matter—if they still live, "Nature" seems to be satisfied.

Moreover, we may say that so universal a habit as the use of alcohol is "natural," meaning that it is easily adopted by all races and classes of men. To call a thing "natural" in that sense does not show it to be advantageous.

---

1 Agricultural workers who live off the land, as opposed to nomads; stereotyped as wretchedly poor (Arabic).

As to "the higher function," we should be clear in our minds about the relation between the "height" of the function and its frequence. It may be advanced, similarly, that eating with us, has a "higher function," being used as a form of hospitality, a medium of entertainment, of aesthetic as well as gustatory pleasure. All that may be true of the preparation, service, and consumption of food which is perfectly suited to the needs of the body, and for which one has a genuine appetite. One would hardly seek to justify a ceaseless gluttony, or even an erratic consumption of unnecessary food, on those grounds.

It remains further to be discussed in detail whether noble and lofty affection may not be otherwise expressed; whether it is true that the highest creative work, or the most, or even any great part, is associated with our present degree of indulgence on this line; and whether that claim of "physical necessity" really holds good for either sex.

It may be shown that a person, today, is in better health if free to gratify his present degree of desire; but that is not the real point at issue, which is—is it normal for the human race to have this degree of desire?

Against the visible sum of our noble achievements, which may be urged as justification of our peculiarities, may be set the as visible sum of our shameful diseases, sufferings, poverty, crime, degeneracy. As a race we do not show such an exceptionally high average of health and happiness in the sex relation as to indicate a "higher" method. Rather, on the contrary, the morbid phenomena with which this area of life is associated, plainly show some wrong condition.

Upon which general basis, returning to the subject of birth control, it is advanced:

That the normal sex relation is a periodic one, related to the reproductive process;

That the resultant "natural" product of a child a year is being gradually reduced by the action of that biological law— "reproduction is in inverse proportion to individualization";

That when we are all reared in suitable conditions for the highest individual development, we shall only crave this indulgence for a brief annual period, and that, with no efforts at "prevention," our average birth rate will be but two or three to a family;

That, in the meantime, under specially hard conditions, it is right for a woman to refuse to bear more than that, or possibly to bear any;

That for reputable physicians or other competent persons to teach proper methods of such restriction, is quite right.

As for needing a "safe," free and unlimited indulgence in the exercises of this function, I hold that to be an abnormal condition.

"Full Motherhood"
The Forerunner 6.10 (October 1915): 272

[This poem, published in the same issue as *Herland*'s Chapter 10, "Their Religions and Our Marriages," echoes Herland's religion based on motherly concern for the welfare of all children.]

FULL MOTHERHOOD
(*A Villanelle*)[1]

> There are children many—this child is mine;
>   Shall I love them all or only one?
> What motherhood is the world's design?
>
> Born of a known and honored line,
>   Blossom of love, an only son—
> There are children many, this child is mine;
>
> But what of the others who starve and pine,
>   Where no wise mother tasks are done?
> What motherhood is the world's design?
>
> Unless my baby is fair and fine
>   The game is lost and the race not run;
> There are children many, this child is mine.
>
> Unless we love both mine and thine,
>   Heaven on earth can come for none—
> What motherhood is the world's design?
>
> We must care for all with a love divine;
>   Only so may the game be won;
> There are children many—this child is mine—
>   Full motherhood is the world's design.

---

1 A villanelle is a nineteen-line poem made up of five tercets and a final quatrain (three- and four-line stanzas). It has only two rhyme sounds; the first and third lines of the first stanza are rhyming refrains that alternate as the third line of later stanzas and form the final couplet.

"Having Faith in Evolution"
The Forerunner 6.11 (November 1915): 299–300

[Gilman argues in this article that evolution—progress—is in the nature of things, but we need to "provide right conditions" to assist with evolution. This position is partly acknowledging the importance of "nurture," but it also reflects Gilman's belief that acquired characteristics are inherited, so improved conditions for the current generation will improve the next generation.]

A great many people nowadays have lost their faith in what we used to call "The Finger of Providence." We no longer believe that the whole world was arranged for our service and pleasure, and discuss the merits of each bird, beast, fish and plant according to its "use" to us.

"No doubt made for some wise purpose," we used to piously remark, gazing at some slimy sea-beast we never saw before. Now we see the creature as a step up, or a step down, or a step aside, in the great evolutionary process. His "purpose" is far beyond him. Perhaps we are his purpose; perhaps the making of a horse or cow or dog is what he was tending toward, or what he diverged from, or from which he sank away, a disappearing rudiment.

If we find on Norwegian mountains, away upon the edge of the snow line, a tiny little plant, less than inch high, with only three leaves, and some convenient botanist tells us it is a birch tree, we no longer imagine that an all-wise Providence made birch trees in assorted sizes "for some wise purpose." We merely recognize that what we call a birch tree is the result of certain hereditary tendencies, acting under certain conditions; and that the shape, size, and quality of the tree vary with the conditions. If the changes come too fast, or go too far—that ends the birch tree. But as long as it can live, on any terms, it does; and, give it the right conditions, it becomes a tall, strong, beautiful tree.

This is an instance of the force called Evolution that is always pushing, pushing, upward and onward, through a world of changing conditions. You can count on it. It is always there. It is "the will to live," and behind that is "the will to improve."

We know this, in a general way, but we haven't enough faith in it. We ought to take that idea and expatiate on it as widely and subtly as we used to on the methods of that Finger.

This is a force, dominant in nature. If you see deep enough you may as well call it the Will of God as call it Evolution; but by any name, it is *there*, and it works.

Relying on that, knowing that it will furnish the push, and all we have to do is to arrange the conditions, we have already done wonders in the way of developing peaches, strawberries, dogs and prize cattle. We must provide right conditions; that great pushing life-force of Evolution does the rest.

Why don't we realize this in regard to people? Here are People,—tall, strong, healthy, clever, beautiful, well mannered, and high-moraled,—creditable specimens of humanity. And here are other People, as inferior to these as that stubbed little birch, which the Norwegian mountaineers call "Dog's Ear," is to the tall birch tree of the fjords. That tree has plenty of water, enough warm weather, a suitable soil, and it grows accordingly.

Well? Can't we apply that to people? Have we not seen even a sodden tramp respond to a bath, a shave, and a new outfit of clothes? Even a hardened criminal reacts to some justice and kindness in treatment.

It has been shown that children of the poorest stock, from the worst slums, when placed in good ordinary families and given mere ordinary kindness and education, turn out as well as other average children.

It has been shown, too, in careful study by the Royal Commission to Investigate the Physical Deterioration of the English Poor that the babies, at birth, were good average specimens (unless they were cursed with some special disease), but that their rapid downfall came from the abominable conditions in which they were reared.

Conditions can be changed; we can do that. Evolution, a force to be definitely counted on, will do the rest. Let us have faith in Evolution.

"Looking Across"
Forerunner 6.12 (December 1915): 315

[Appearing in the same issue as the final chapter of *Herland*, this poem optimistically suggests that a "motherliness which dominated society," as in Herland, can eventually turn around the culture that led to the Great War in Europe.]

Looking Across

How can one write of love
    When all the world is hating?
How can one write of peace
    When all the world's at war?

How can one write of wisdom
　　When folly unabating
Shows that mankind has no idea
　　Of what our life is for?

How can one write of life
　　When all the world is killing?
How can one write of work
　　When all the world destroys?
When under human hands
　　Our human blood is spilling,
And the human brain that keeps us,
　　Goes mad in fire and noise?

Only by seeing far
　　Across this red destruction,
Back on the long dark path,
　　Where this was done before;
On to the shining way
　　Of joyous ripe production;
When willing work rebuilds the world
　　With all we had, and more.

To see new people born
　　From wiser stronger mothers;
Upreared in new ideals,
　　With the New Great Flag unfurled;
Taught in new ways to love
　　And understand the others;
Giving glad lives to serve
　　A New United World.

From With Her in Ourland *(1916)*, the *Sequel to* Herland

Chapter 6, "The Diagnosis"
The Forerunner 7.6 (June 1917)

[*With Her in Ourland* (1916), the sequel to *Herland*, finds Van and his Herland companion traveling the world beyond Herland, where she evaluates contemporary human civilization and its flaws. In this passage, she explains from a Herland perspective why the American experiment, though noble, has not yet fulfilled its potential. The explanation reflects Gilman's own growing xenophobia.]

"I've been reading a lot, had to, to get background and perspective, and I feel as if I understood a good deal better. Still———. You helped me ever so much by saying that you were not new people, just mixed Europeans. But the new country and the new conditions began to make you all into a new people. Only——— [...] Only you have done it too fast and too much in the dark. You weren't conscious you see."

"Not conscious—America not conscious?"

"Not self-conscious, I mean, Van."

This I scouted entirely, till she added patiently: "Perhaps I should say nationally conscious, or socially conscious. You were plunged into an enormous social enterprise, a huge swift, violent experiment; the current of social evolution burst forth over here like a subterranean river finding an outlet. Things that the stratified crust of Asia could not let through, and the heavy shell of European culture could not either, just burst forth over here and swept you along. Democracy had been—accumulating, through all the centuries. The other nations forced it back, held it down. It boiled over in France, but the lid was clapped on again for awhile. Here it could pour forward—and it poured. Then all the people of the same period of social development wanted to come too, and did,—lots of them. That was inevitable. All that 'America' means in this sense is a new phase of social development, and anyone can be an American who belongs to it."

"Guess you are right so far, Mrs. Doctor. Go ahead!"

"But while this was happening to you, you were doing things yourselves, some of them in line with your real position and movement, some dead against it. For instance, your religion."

"Religion against what? Expound further."

"Against Democracy."

"You don't mean the Christian religion, do you?" I urged, rather shocked.

"Oh, no, indeed. That would have been a great help to the world if they had ever taken it up."

I was always entertained and somewhat startled by Ellador's detached view. She knew the same facts so familiar to us, but they had not the same connotations.

"I think Jesus was simply wonderful," she went on. "What a pity it was he did not live longer!"

This was a new suggestion to me. Of course I no longer accepted that pitiful old idea of his being a pre-arranged sacrifice to his own father, but I never deliberately thought of his having continued alive, and its possible effects.

"He is supposed to have been executed at about the age of thirty-three, was he not?" she went on. "Think of it—hardly a grown man! He should have had thirty or forty more years of teaching. It would all have become clearer, more consistent. He would have worked things out, explained them, made people understand. He would have made clear to them what they were to *do*. It was an awful loss."

I said nothing at all, but watched the sweet earnest face, the wise far-seeing eyes, and really agreed with her, though in my mind rose a confused dim throng of horrified objections belonging not to my own mind, but to those of other people.

"Tell me how you mean that our religion was against democracy," I persisted.

"It was so personal," she said, "and so unjust. There must have crept into it, in early times, a lot of the Buddhist philosophy, either direct or filtered, the 'acquiring merit' idea, and asceticism. The worst part of all was the idea of sacrifice—that is so ancient. Of course what Jesus meant was social unity, that your neighbor *was* yourself—that we were all one humanity—'many gifts, but the same spirit.' He must have meant that—for that is So.

"What I mean by 'your religion' is the grade of Calvinism[1] which dominated young America, with the still older branches, and the various small newer ones. It was all so personal. *My* soul—*my* salvation. *My* conscience—*my* sins. And here was the great

---

1 Christian belief system derived from the ideas of John Calvin (1509–64), best known for the idea of predestination. The Puritans who settled Massachusetts were Calvinists, as were many other early American settlers.

living working truth of democracy carrying you on in spite of yourselves—*E Pluribus Unum*.[1]

"Your economic philosophy was dead against it too—that foolish *laissez-faire*[2] idea And your politics, though what was new in it started pretty well, has never been able to make much headway against the highest religious sanction, the increasing economic pressure, and the general drag of custom and tradition—inertia."

"You are somewhat puzzling, my fair Marco Polo,"[3] I urged. "So you mean to extol our politics, American politics?"

"Why of course!" she said, her eyes shining. "The principles of democracy are wholly right. The law of federation, the method of rotation in office, the stark necessity for general education that the people may understand clearly, the establishment of liberty—that they may act freely—it is splendidly, gloriously right! But why do I say this to an American!"

"I wish you could say it to every American man, woman, and child," I answered soberly. "Of course we used to feel that way about it, but things have changed somehow."

"Yes, yes," she went on eagerly. "That's what I mean. You started right, for the most part, but those high-minded brave old ancestors of yours did not understand sociology—how should they? it wasn't even born. They did not know how society worked, or what would hurt it the most. So the preachers went on exhorting the people to save their own souls, or get it done for them by imputed virtues of someone else—and no one understood the needs of the country.

"Why, Van! Vandyke Jennings! As I understand more and more how noble and courageous and high-minded was this Splendid Child, and then see it now, bloated and weak, with unnatural growth, preyed on by all manner of parasites inside and out, attacked by diseases of all kinds, sneered at, criticized, condemned by the older nations, and yet bravely stumbling on, making progress in spite of it all—I'm getting to just *love* America!"

That pleased me, naturally, but I didn't like her picture of my country as bloated and verminous. I demanded explanation.

"Do you think we're too big?" I asked. "Too much country to be handled properly?"

---

1 Out of many, one (Latin). Motto on the Great Seal of the United States, which appears on most US currency.

2 In economics, the idea that government should not interfere with business affairs. Literally "leave it alone" (French).

3 Venetian merchant (c. 1254–1324) whose account of travels through Asia inspired many later explorers.

"Oh, *no!*" she answered promptly. "Not too big in land. That would have been like the long lean lines of youth, the far-reaching bones of a country gradually rounding out and filling in as you grow. But you couldn't wait to grow, you just—swelled."

. "What on earth do you mean, Ellador?"

"You have stuffed yourself with the most ill-assorted and unassimilable mass of human material that ever was held together by artificial means," she answered remorselessly. "You go to England, and the people are English. Only three per cent of aliens even in London, I understand. And in France the people are French—bless them! And in Italy, Italian. But here—it's no wonder I was discouraged at first. It has taken a lot of study and hard thinking, to see a way out at all. But I do see it. It was simply awful when I began.

"Just look! Here you were, a little band of really promising people, of different nations, yet of the same general stock, and *like-minded*—that was the main thing. The real union is the union of idea; without that—no nation. You made settlements, you grew strong and bold, you shook off the old government, you set up a new flag, and then————!"

"Then," said I proudly, "we opened our arms to all the world, if that is what you are finding fault with. We welcomed other people to our big new country—'the poor and oppressed of all nations!'"[1] I quoted solemnly.

"That's what I mean by saying you were ignorant of sociology," was her cheerful reply. "It never occurred to you that the poor and oppressed were not necessarily good stuff for a democracy."

I looked at her rather rebelliously.

"Why, just study them," she went on, in that large sweeping way of hers. "Hadn't there been poor and oppressed enough in the past? In Chaldaea and Assyria and Egypt and Rome—in all Europe—everywhere? Why, Van, it is the poor and oppressed who make monarchy and despotism—don't you see that?"

"Hold on, my dear—hold on! This is too much. Are you *blaming* the poor helpless things for their tyrannical oppression?"

---

1   "Happy, thrice happy shall they be pronounced hereafter, who have contributed any thing, who have performed the meanest office in erecting this stupendous fabrick of Freedom and Empire on the broad basis of Independency; who have assisted in protecting the rights of humane nature and establishing an Asylum for the poor and oppressed of all nations and religions," George Washington, General Orders, 18 April 1783.

"No more than I blame an apple-tree for bearing apples," she answered. "You don't seriously advance the idea that the oppressor began it, do you? Just one oppressor jumping on the necks of a thousand free men? Surely you see that the general status and character of a people creates and maintains its own kind of government?"

"Y-e-es," I agreed. "But all the same, they are *human*, and if you give them proper conditions they can all rise—surely we have proved that."

"Give them proper conditions, and give them time—yes."

"Time! They do it in one generation. We have citizens, good citizens, of all races, who were born in despotic countries, all equal in our democracy."

"How many Chinese and Japanese citizens have you?" she asked quietly. "How are your African citizens treated in this 'equal' democracy!"

This was rather a facer.

"About the first awful mistake you made was in loading yourself up with those reluctant Africans," Ellador went on. "If it wasn't so horrible, it would be funny, awfully funny. A beautiful healthy young country, saddling itself with an antique sin every other civilized nation had repudiated. And here they are, by millions and millions, flatly denied citizenship, socially excluded, an enormous alien element in your democracy."

"They are not aliens," I persisted stoutly. "They are Americans, loyal Americans; they make admirable soldiers————"

"Yes, and servants. You will let them serve you and fight for you—but that's all, apparently. Nearly a tenth of the population, and not part of the democracy. And they never asked to come!"

"Well," I said, rather sullenly. "I admit it—everyone does. It was an enormous costly national mistake, and we paid for it heavily. Also it's there yet, an unsolved question. I admit it all. Go on please. We were dead wrong on the blacks, and pretty hard on the reds; we may be wrong on the yellows. I guess this is a white man's country, isn't it? You're not objecting to the white immigrants, are you?"

"To legitimate immigrants, able and willing to be American citizens, there can be no objection, unless even they come too fast. But to millions of deliberately imported people, not immigrants at all, but victims, poor ignorant people scraped up by paid agents, deceived by lying advertisements, brought over here by greedy American ship owners and employers of labor—there are objections many and strong."

"But Ellador—even granting it is as you say, they too can be made into American citizens, surely?"

"They can be, but are they? I suppose you all tacitly assume that they are; but an outsider does not see it. We have been all over the country now, pretty thoroughly. I have met and talked with people of all classes and all races, both men and women. Remember I'm new to 'the world,' and I've just come here from studying Europe, and Asia, and Africa. I have the hinterland of history pretty clearly summarized, though of course I can't pretend to be thorough, and I tell you, Van, there are millions of people in your country who do not belong to it at all."

She saw that I was about to defend our foreign born, and went on: "I do not mean the immigrants solely. There are Bostonians of Beacon Hill who belong in London; there are New Yorkers of five generations who belong in Paris; there are vast multitudes who belong in Berlin, in Dublin, in Jerusalem; and there are plenty of native Sons and Daughters of the Revolution who are aristocrats, plutocrats, anything but democrats."

"Why of course there are! We believe in having all kinds—there's room for everybody—this is the 'melting-pot,' you know."

"And do you think that you can put a little of everything into a melting-pot and produce a good metal? Well fused and flawless? Gold, silver, copper and iron, lead, radium, pipe clay, coal dust, and plain dirt?"

A simile is an untrustworthy animal if you ride it too hard. I grinned and admitted that there were limits to the powers of fusion.

"Please understand," she urged gently. "I am not looking down on one kind of people because they are different from others. I like them all. I think your prejudice against the black is silly, wicked, and—hypocritical. You have no idea how ridiculous it looks, to an outsider, to hear your Southern enthusiasts raving about the horrors of 'miscegenation' and then to count the mulattos, quadroons, octoroons and all the successive shades by which the black race becomes white before their eyes. Or to see them shudder at 'social equality' while the babies are nourished at black breasts, and cared for in their most impressionable years by black nurses—their *children*!"

She stopped at that, turned away from me and walked to the opposite window, where she stood for some time with her hands clenched and her shoulders heaving.

"Where was I?" she asked presently, definitely dropping the question of children. "Black—yes, and how about the yellow? Do they 'melt'? Do you want them to melt? Isn't your exclusion of them an admission that you think some kinds of people unassimilable? That democracy must pick and choose a little?"

"What would you have us do?" I asked rather sullenly. "Exclude everybody? Think we are superior to the whole world?"

Ellador laughed, and kissed me. "I think *you* are," she whispered tenderly. "No—I don't mean that at all. It would be too great a strain on the imagination! If you want a prescription—far too late—it is this: Democracy is a psychic relation. It requires the intelligent conscious co-operation of a great many persons all 'equal' in the characteristics required to play that kind of a game. You could have safely welcomed to your great undertaking people of every race and nation who were individually fitted to assist. Not by any means because they were 'poor and oppressed,' nor because of that glittering generality that 'all men are born free and equal,' but because the human race is in different stages of development, and only some of the races—or some individuals in a given race—have reached the democratic stage."

"But how could we discriminate?"

"You mustn't ask me too much, Van. I'm a stranger; I don't know all I ought to, and, of course I'm all the time measuring by my background of experience in my own country. I find you people talk a good bit about the Brotherhood of Man, but you haven't seemed to think about the possibilities of a sisterhood of women."

I looked up alertly, but she gave a mischievous smile and shook her head. "You do not want to hear about the women, I remember. But seriously, dear, this is one of the most dangerous mistakes you have made; it complicates everything. It makes your efforts to establish democracy like trying to make a ship go by steam and at the same time admitting banks of oars, masses of sails and cordage, and mere paddles and outriggers."

"You can certainly make some prescription for this particularly dreadful state, can't you?" I urged. "Sometimes 'an outsider' can see better than those who are—being melted."

She pondered awhile, then began slowly: "Legitimate immigration is like the coming of children to you,—new blood for the nation, citizens made, not born. And they should be met like children, with loving welcome, with adequate preparation, with the fullest and wisest education for their new place. Where you have that crowded little filter on Ellis Island, you ought to have Immigration Bureaus on either coast, at ports so specified, with a great additional department to definitely Americanize the newcomers, to teach them the language, spirit, traditions and customs of the country. Talk about offering hospitality to all the world! What kind of hospitality is it to let your guests crowd and pack into the front hall, and to offer them neither bed, bread nor association? That's what I mean by saying that you are not conscious. You haven't taken your immigration seriously enough. The consequence is that you are only partially America, an America clogged and confused, weakened and mismanaged, for lack of political compatibility."

"Is this all?" I asked after a little. "You make me feel as if my country was a cross between a patchwork quilt and a pudding stone."[1]

"Oh, dear, no!" she cheerfully assured me. "That's only a beginning of my diagnosis. The patient's worst disease was that disgraceful out-of-date attack of slavery, only escaped by a surgical operation, painful, costly, and not by any means wholly successful. The second is this chronic distension from absorbing too much and too varied material, just pumping it in at wild speed. The third is the most conspicuously foolish of all—to a Herlander."

"Oh—leaving the women out?"

"Yes. It's so—so—well, I can't express to you how *ridiculous* it looks."

---

1   Rock made up of a mixture of different, irregular grains and pebbles.

Appendix A: Travel and Nature Writing

1. From George Alsop, *Character of the Province of Mary-Land* (London: 1666). From Chapter 1, "Of the Situation and Plenty of the Province of Mary-Land"

[The early chapters of *Herland* parody exploration narratives like this one from early colonial America. Its author, George Alsop (c. 1636–c. 1673), emigrated from London to Maryland in 1658 as an indentured servant. Like the explorers of Herland, Alsop implicitly compares the landscape to a woman's body, to be scrutinized and conquered.]

Mary-Land is a Province situated upon the large extending bowels of America, under the government of the Lord Baltimore, adjacent north-wardly upon the confines of New-England, and neighbouring south-wardly upon Virginia, dwelling pleasantly upon the Bay of Chesapeake between the Degrees of 36 and 38, in the Zone temperate, and by Mathematical computation is eleven hundred and odd Leagues in Longitude from England, being within her own embraces extraordinary pleasant and fertile. Pleasant, in respect of the multitude of navigable rivers and creeks that conveniently and most profitably lodge within the arms of her green, spreading, and delightful woods; whose natural womb (by her plenty) maintains and preserves the several diversities of animals that rangingly inhabit her woods; as she doth otherwise gener-ously fructify this piece of Earth with almost all sorts of vegetables, as well flowers with their varieties of colours and smells, as herbs and roots with their several effects and operative virtues, that offer their benefits daily to supply the want of the inhabitant whene'er their necessities shall *subpoena* them to wait on their commands. So that he, who out of curiosity desires to see the Landskip[1] of the Creation drawn to the life, or to read Nature's universal Herbal without book, may with the Opticks of a discreet discerning, view Mary-Land dressed in her green and fragrant mantle of the Spring. Neither do I think there is any place under the Heavenly altitude, or that has footing or room upon the cir-cular globe of this world, that can parallel this fertile and pleasant piece of ground in its multiplicity, or rather Nature's extravagancy of a super-abounding plenty. For so much doth this country increase in a swelling spring-tide of rich variety and diversities of all things, not only common provisions that supply the reaching stomach of man with a satisfactory plenty, but also extends with its liberality and free convenient benefits

---

1 Landscape.

to each sensitive faculty, according to their several desiring appetites. So that had Nature made it her business, on purpose to have found out a situation for the soul of profitable ingenuity, she could not have fitted herself better in the traverse of the whole Universe, nor in convenienter terms have told man, *Dwell here, live plentifully and be rich.*

The trees, plants, fruits, flowers, and roots that grow here in Mary-Land, are the only emblems or hieroglyphics of our Adamitical or primitive situation, as well for their variety as odoriferous smells, together with their virtues, according to their several effects, kinds and properties, which still bear the effigies of innocency according to their original grafts; which by their dumb vegetable oratory, each hour speaks to the inhabitant in silent acts, that they need not look for any other terrestrial paradise, to suspend or tire their curiosity upon, while she is extant. For within her doth dwell so much of variety, so much of natural plenty, that there is not any thing that is or may be rare, but it inhabits within this plenteous soil: so that those parts of the Creation that have borne the bell away (for many ages) for a vegetable plenteousness, must now in silence strike and veil all, and whisper softly in the auditual parts of Mary-Land, that *None but she in this dwells singular;* and that as well for that she doth exceed in those fruits, plants, trees and roots, that dwell and grow in their several climes or habitable parts of the Earth besides, as the rareness and superexcellency of her own glory, which she flourishly abounds in, by the abundancy of reserved rarities, such as the remainder of the world (with all its speculative art) never bore any occular testimony of as yet.

2. From John Muir, *The Yosemite* (New York: Century, 1912)

[John Muir (1838–1914) was an American naturalist and early environmentalist. The founder of the Sierra Club, his activism helped to preserve the Yosemite Valley and Sequoia National Park. In *With Her in Ourland*, the sequel to *Herland*, a visitor from Herland visits Yosemite and "read John Muir with rapture. 'How I should have loved him!' she said." Both *Herland* and *With Her in Ourland* are written as travel books in Muir's tradition and echo his environmentalism, though Gilman celebrates Herland's cultivation rather than its wildness.]

It appears, therefore, that Hetch Hetchy Valley, far from being a plain, common, rock-bound meadow, as many who have not seen it seem to suppose, is a grand landscape garden, one of Nature's rarest and most precious mountain temples. As in Yosemite, the sublime rocks of its walls seem to glow with life, whether leaning back in repose or standing erect in thoughtful attitudes, giving welcome to storms and calms alike, their brows in the sky, their feet set in the groves and gay flowery meadows, while birds, bees, and butterflies help the river and waterfalls to stir all the air into music—things frail and fleeting and types of permanence meeting here and blending, just as they do in Yosemite, to draw her lovers into close and confiding communion with her.

Sad to say, this most precious and sublime feature of the Yosemite National Park, one of the greatest of all our natural resources for the uplifting joy and peace and health of the people, is in danger of being dammed and made into a reservoir to help supply San Francisco with water and light, thus flooding it from wall to wall and burying its gardens and groves one or two hundred feet deep. This grossly destructive commercial scheme has long been planned and urged (though water as pure and abundant can be got from sources outside of the people's park, in a dozen different places), because of the comparative cheapness of the dam and of the territory which it is sought to divert from the great uses to which it was dedicated in the Act of 1890 establishing the Yosemite National Park.

The making of gardens and parks goes on with civilization all over the world, and they increase both in size and number as their value is recognized. Everybody needs beauty as well as bread, places to play in and pray in, where Nature may heal and cheer and give strength to body and soul alike. This natural beauty-hunger is made manifest in the little window-sill gardens of the poor, though perhaps only a geranium slip in a broken cup, as well as in the carefully tended rose and lily gardens of the rich, the thousands of spacious city parks and botanical gardens, and in our magnificent National parks—the Yellowstone, Yosemite, Sequoia, etc.—Nature's sublime wonderlands, the admiration and joy of the world. Nevertheless, like anything else worth while, from the very beginning, however well guarded, they have always been subject to attack by despoiling gain-seekers and mischief-makers of every degree from Satan to Senators, eagerly trying to make everything immediately and selfishly commercial, with schemes disguised in smug-smiling philanthropy, industriously, sham-piously crying, "Conservation, conservation, panutilization," that man and beast may be fed and the dear Nation made great. Thus long ago a few enterprising merchants utilized the Jerusalem temple as a place of business instead of a place of prayer, changing money, buying and selling cattle and sheep and doves; and earlier still, the first forest reservation, including only one tree, was likewise despoiled.[1] Ever since the establishment of the Yosemite National Park, strife has been going on around its borders and I suppose this will go on as part of the universal battle between right and wrong, however much its boundaries may be shorn, or its wild beauty destroyed.

---

1 Allusions to the story of Jesus and the moneylenders in the temple (Matthew 21:12; John 2: 13–16) and the Garden of Eden (Genesis 1:1–3).

Appendix B: Social Theories Addressed *in* Herland

1. Edward Bellamy, "Socialism and Nationalism." *The New Nation* (27 January 1894): 38

[Gilman was an enthusiastic proponent of the "nationalism" described by Edward Bellamy in his 1888 Utopian novel *Looking Backward: 2000–1887.* In this article, Bellamy provides a brief explanation of nationalism by explaining its similarities and differences from socialism.]

Our esteemed local contemporary, the *Dawn*,[1] the January number, has an instructive article on the proper meaning of the word socialism. It says:

> He then, is not a socialist who believes in this or that scheme but he who accepts and works for the definite principle of organizing trade and industry collectively, by having land and industrial capital owned by the community (in some form), and operated co-operatively for the equitable (not necessarily the equal) good of all. Such, we believe, in sharp contradistinction to many popular conceptions, to be by an overwhelming consensus of the best authorities, the correct use of the word.

This we think is an accurate statement of the case, and brings out clearly the reason why a socialist is not necessarily a nationalist, and why nationalists must needs have a distinctive name for their doctrine, in order to prevent confusion.

In the first place, socialism, as stated in the above definition, while demanding an organization of capital and labor which shall be collective "in some form," does not require that the form shall be nationalization or municipalization, or any other form that shall be identical with the political corporation. Any plan of co-operative or "associated" industrial organization is socialistic, and the socialistic ideal has been conceived of by some eminent socialist writers as a sort of developed and perfected trades-unionism, each trade ruling as its exclusive domain some branch of industry.

Nationalists, on the other hand, as the word implies, advocate not merely collective industrial organization "in some form," but in a particular form, namely, nationalization, which term includes

---

1 *The Dawn, A Journal of Christian Socialism,* was the journal of the Christian Socialist Society in the United States and appeared monthly from 1889 to 1896.

municipalization, it being of course assumed that the form of national government is already democratic.

Socialism, moreover, as stated in the above definition does not necessarily imply economic equality as the ultimate and ideal social condition. As to the principle on which the product of the collective industrial organization is to be shared, socialism is not precise, but admits of various methods, and makes no objection to inequalities, requiring only that the method of sharing should be "just" or "equitable," which of course are words that settle nothing, but leave the way open to indefinite metaphysical arguments as to what is "just" and "equitable."

Nationalism, on the other hand, instead of leaving in uncertainty the very vital question on what basis the people are to share the benefits of the collective organization, declares that the basis must be and can only be that of an invariable and indefeasible equality. This proposition is held by nationalists not as an arbitrary dogma but as an obvious corollary of the democratic principle applied to economic condition. Political equality so soon as popular government is applied to economics must lead to and bring about economic equality. Equals must and will be equals. The permanent preservation of political equality requires indeed the establishment of economic equality, without which the former will soon be undermined and lost.

That is to say, nationalism, while containing all the meaning of socialism, goes further and defines two vital points which socialism leaves in the fog, namely, the process and form of the proposed collective organization of industry, and the basis on which the people are to share its products. The definition of these two points is carried by the term nationalism itself. The word implies, of course, that the collective organization is to be national and the process and form nationalization, that is to say, that the industrial and political state are to be identical. This again implies that the principle on which the duties and results of the collective industrial organization are to be shared must be one of equality without respect of persons, for all national or public undertakings in a popular state are and must be for the common and equal benefit of all citizens.

Socialism is a useful and necessary generic term for grouping together all who agree in believing that private capitalism should be set aside in favor of some sort of collective administration of industry. In that sense probably most of the readers of this paper are socialists, but the word ceases to be an adequate description of social reformers whose creed goes further than the general proposition above stated. Socialism is in fact a broad blanket under which very ill-assorted bedfellows find place. It is well for us to bear in mind that nationalism means a great deal more than socialism does and something quite different from what some socialists mean.

2. From Josephine Tozier, "The Montessori Schools in Rome: The Revolutionary Educational Work of Maria Montessori as Carried Out in Her Own Schools." *McClure's Magazine* 38.2 (December 1911): 123–37

[Gilman directly compares the education system of Herland to the Montessori system. There is evidence that Gilman read this article, one of a series of articles about the Montessori system published in *McClure's*.]

The Montessori system of education is more than a mere method of teaching young children: it is a branch of applied modern science—directed toward the development of a new race of men. "The external world," says Madame Montessori, "transformed by the tremendous development of experimental science in the last century, must have as its master a transformed man. If the progress of the human individual does not keep pace with the progress of science, civilization will find itself checked." Madame Montessori, who is an anthropologist of European reputation as well as a teacher, has adopted the inductive methods of experimental science to insure the development of the individual, under freedom, to his highest capacity.

"The conception of freedom which must inspire pedagogy," she says, "is that which the biological sciences of the nineteenth century have shown us in their methods of studying life. The old-time pedagogy was incompetent and vague, because it did not understand the principles of studying the pupil before educating him, and of leaving him free for spontaneous manifestations. Such an attitude has been rendered possible and practical only through the contribution of the experimental sciences of the last century."

The methods of this new system of pedagogy are exactly the same as are adopted by all modern investigators in the field of biology.

Deftness and Bodily Poise a Result of the Montessori Sense Training

In the first place, Madame Montessori tries to give the child an environment that liberates his personality; she places him in an atmosphere where there are no restraints, where there is no opposition, nothing to make him perverse or self-conscious, or to put him on the defensive. His personality is thus liberated into free action, and the thing he is expresses itself.

Secondly, by her system of sense training she develops in the child a sense of his relation to his material surroundings and a facility in accommodating himself to them. As a result of the sense training, he learns to manage his body deftly, to walk without stumbling, to carry without dropping, to touch objects delicately and surely—in short, to move among the material things that surround him, whatever they may be, with ease and freedom, and with the least possible fret and wear to his spirit and to his body. Every element of embarrassment and self-consciousness is overcome, and he inevitably prefers harmonious action to the discord by which the untrained and awkward child so often tries to hide his inadeptness.

Thirdly, Madame Montessori tries, through her sense education, to reach and to stimulate the intellect itself. Through the child's interest in the materials with which he works, she leads him to purely intellectual concepts of form and the relation of numbers.

The Modern Baby No Longer the Plaything of Its Parents

Madame Montessori starts all her system of primary training from the premise of independence and self-reliance which underlies the modern practice of infant hygiene—a comparatively new branch of medical science which, she says, has sprung out of the experimental methods of modern biology. A new-born baby is no longer allowed to be wrapped in folds of woolen or cotton cloth, to be shaken or patted into sleep, to be talked to and constantly handled. Its clothing is arranged to give its body as much freedom as possible. It is kept free from excitement, and is no longer made the plaything of its parents. The nurse has now become an observer rather than an arbitrary personage imposing her authority upon a helpless charge. The nurse's first duty is to watch the little animal grow; her second duty is to prevent the expenditure of energy by useless effort on the part of the child.

And these, Madame Montessori believes, are the first duties of the teachers of young children. The whole movement of society to-day is toward the protection of a child's individuality. Formerly, in hospitals, orphan asylums, and children's homes, the effort was to protect the child's life merely—to prevent infant mortality and to conserve so many living human organisms to society. But society is beginning to realize that it may have succeeded in preserving the living human organism and still have lost something that might have been infinitely valuable to the world. In other words, we have begun to give protection to the potential individual which is in every child's body—to keep it away from those things that would distort and destroy it, or force it into any given mold. We are trying to insure this individuality a chance to reveal itself, rare or commonplace, whatever it may be.

The protection of this individuality, then, is the foremost duty of the nurse in the first instance, and of the teacher in the second.

The most thoughtful modern teachers in America will find in the Montessori system all their best ideas reduced to scientific simplicity and precision. Dr. Montessori's chapter on discipline, one of the most important in her, book, may be given briefly as follows:

Montessori Methods of Discipline

"Discipline through liberty. Here is a principle difficult for the followers of the common-school methods to understand. How shall one attain discipline in a class of free children? Certainly, in our system, we have a different conception of what discipline is. If the discipline be founded upon liberty, it (the discipline) must be *active*. We do not call an individual disciplined only when he is rendered artificially silent as a mute and immovable as a paralytic. Such an individual is *annihilated*, not *disciplined*.[1]

"We call an individual disciplined when he is master of himself, and can, therefore, regulate his own conduct when it shall be necessary to follow some rule of life.

"Such a concept of *active discipline* is not easy either to comprehend or to attain; but certainly it contains a great educational principle, and is very different from the absolute coercion to immobility.

"A special technique is necessary to the teacher if she is to lead the child along such a road of discipline, if she is to make it possible for him to continue in this way all his life, advancing always toward perfect self-mastery. Since the child now learns to move rather than to sit still, he prepares himself, not for the school, but for life; for he becomes able, through habit and through practice, to perform easily and correctly the simple acts of social or community life. The discipline to which the child habituates himself here is, in its character, not limited to the school environment, but extends to society." [...]

3. Sir Almroth E. Wright, "Suffrage Fallacies: Sir Almroth Wright on Militant Hysteria." Letter to the Editor of the London *Times* (28 March 1912): 7–8

[Wright (1861–1947) was a medical doctor and immunologist. One of the most notorious antifeminist documents of the period, his letter to *The Times* is referred to in Chapters 11 and 12 of *Herland*.]

SIR,—For man the physiology and psychology of woman is full of difficulties. He is not a little mystified when he encounters in her periodically recurring phases of hypersensitiveness, unreasonableness, and loss of the sense of proportion. He is frankly perplexed when confronted with a complete alteration of character in a woman who is child-bearing.

---

1   The italics are Madame Montessori's own. [Tozier's note]

When he is a witness of the "tendency of woman to morally warp when nervously ill," and of the terrible physical havoc which the pangs of a disappointed love may work, he is appalled. And it leaves on his mind an eerie feeling when he sees serious and long-continued mental disorders developing in connexion with the approaching extinction of a woman's reproductive faculty. No man can close his eyes to these things; but he does not feel at liberty to speak of them.

For the woman that God gave him is not his to give away.[1]

As for woman herself, she makes very light of any of these mental upsettings. She perhaps smiles a little at them. The woman of the world will even gaily assure you that "of course half the women in London have to be shut up when they come to the change of life." None the less, these upsettings of her mental equilibrium are the things that a woman has most cause to fear; and no doctor can ever lose sight of the fact that the mind of woman is always threatened with danger from the rever-berations of her physiological emergencies. It is with such thoughts that the doctor lets his eyes rest upon the militant suffragist. He cannot shut them to the fact that there is mixed up with the woman's movement much mental disorder; and he cannot conceal from himself the physi-ological emergencies which lie behind.

The recruiting field for the militant suffragists is the half million of our excess female population—that half million which had better long ago have gone out to mate with its complement of men beyond the sea. Among them there are the following different types of women:

First—let us put them first—come a class of women who hold, with minds otherwise unwarped, that they may, whenever it is to their ad-vantage, lawfully resort to physical violence. The programme, as distin-guished from the methods, of these women is not very different from that of the ordinary suffragist woman. There file past next a class of women who have all their life-long been strangers to joy, women in whom instincts long suppressed have in the end broken into flame. These are the sexually embittered women in whom everything has turned into gall and bitterness of heart, and hatred of men. Their legis-lative programme is license for themselves or else restrictions for man.

Next there file past the incomplete. One side of their nature has undergone atrophy, with the result that they have lost touch with their

---

1 From "The Female of the Species" by Rudyard Kipling (English writer of poetry and fiction, 1865-1936):

   Man's timid heart is bursting with the things he must not say,
   For the Woman that God gave him isn't his to give away;
   But when hunter meets with husbands, each confirms the other's tale—
   The female of the species is more deadly than the male. (13-16)

living fellow men and women. Their programme is to convert the whole world into an epicene institution—an epicene institution in which man and woman shall everywhere work side by side at the self-same tasks and for the self-same pay. These wishes can never by any possibility be realised. Even in animals—I say *even*, because in these at least one of the sexes has periods of complete quiescence—male and female cannot be safely worked side by side, except when they are incomplete. While in the human species safety can be obtained, it can be obtained only at the price of continual constraint. And even then woman, though she protests that she does not require it, and that she does not receive it, practically always does receive differential treatment at the hands of man. It would be well, I often think, that every woman should be clearly told—and the woman of the world will immediately understand—that when man sets his face against the proposal to bring in an epicene world, he does so because he can do his best work only in surroundings where he is perfectly free from suggestion and from restraint, and from the onus which all differential treatment imposes.

[...]

Inextricably mixed up with the types which we have been discussing is the type of woman whom Dr. Leonard Williams's recent letter brought so distinctly before our eyes—the woman who is poisoned by her misplaced self-esteem; and who flies out at every man who does not pay homage to her intellect. She is the woman who is affronted when a man avers that *for him* the glory of woman lies in her power of attraction, in her capacity for motherhood, and in unswerving allegiance to the ethics which are special to her sex. I have heard such an intellectually embittered woman say, though a man had taken her to wife, that "never in the whole course of her life had a man ever as much as done her a kindness."

The programme of this type of woman is, as a preliminary, to compel man to admit her claim to be his intellectual equal; and, that done, to compel him to divide up everything with her to the last farthing, and so make her also his financial equal. And her journals exhibit to us the kind of parliamentary representative she desiderates. He humbly, hat in hand, asks for his orders from a knot of washerwomen standing arms a-kimbo. Following in the wake of these embittered human beings come troops of girls just grown up. All these will assure you, these young girls—and what is seething in their minds is stirring also in the minds in the girls in the colleges and schools which are staffed by unmarried suffragists—that woman has suffered all manner of indignity and injustice at the hands of man. And these young girls have been told about the intellectual and moral and financial value of woman—such tales as it never entered into the heart of man to conceive. The programme of these young women is to be married upon their own terms. Man shall—so runs their scheme—work for their support—to that end giving up his freedom, and putting himself under orders, for many hours of the day; but they themselves must not be asked to give up any of their liberty to him, or to subordinate themselves to his interests, or to obey him in anything. To obey *a man* would be to commit the unpardonable sin.

It is not necessary, in connexion with a movement which proceeds on the lines set out above, any further to labour the point that there is in it an element of mental disorder. It is plain that it is there.

There is also a quite fatuous element in the programmes of the militant suffragist. We have this element, for instance, in the doctrine that, notwithstanding the fact that the conditions of the labour market deny it to her, woman ought to receive the same wage as a man for the same work. This doctrine is fatuous, because it leaves out of sight that, even if woman succeeds in doing the same work as man, he has behind him a much larger reserve of physical strength. As soon as a time of strain comes, a reserve of strength and freedom from periodic indisposition is worth paying extra for. Fatuous also is the dogma that woman ought to have the same pay for the same work—fatuous because it leaves out of sight that woman's commercial value in many of the best fields of work is subject to a very heavy discount by reason of the fact that she cannot, like a male employee, work cheek by jowl with a male employer; nor work among men as a man with his fellow employees. So much for the woman suffragist's protest that she can conceive of no reason for a differential rate of pay for man.

Quite as fatuous are the marriage projects of the militant suffragist. Every woman of the world could tell her—whispering it into her private ear—that if a sufficient number of men should come to the conclusion that it was not worth their while to marry except on the terms of fair give-and-take, the suffragist woman's demands would have to come down. It is not at all certain that the institution of matrimony—which, after all, is the great instrument in the levelling up of the financial situation of woman—can endure apart from some willing subordination on the part of the wife.

[...]

Peace will come again. It will come when woman ceases to believe and to teach all manner of evil of man despitefully. It will come when she ceases to impute to him as a crime her own natural disabilities, when she ceases to resent the fact that man cannot and does not wish to work side by side with her. And peace will return when every woman for whom there is no room in England seeks "rest" beyond the sea, "each one in the house of her husband," and when the woman who remains in England comes to recognise that she can, without sacrifice of dignity, give a willing subordination to the husband or father, who, when all is said and done, earns and lays up money for her.

Appendix C: Scientific and Eugenic Theories Addressed in Herland

1. From Herbert Spencer, *Social Statics* (London: John Chapman, 1851)

[Herbert Spencer (1820–1903), a British biologist, philosopher, and political theorist, coined the phrase "survival of the fittest" to apply Charles Darwin's arguments in *On the Origin of Species* to sociology and ethics. Spencer's ideas, which became known as "Social Darwinism," are cited by the visitors to Herland, before they learn about Herland's alternative ideas about evolution.]

Pervading all nature we may see at work a stern discipline, which is a little cruel that it may be very kind. That state of universal warfare maintained throughout the lower creation, to the great perplexity of many worthy people, is at bottom the most merciful provision which the circumstances admit of. It is much better that the ruminant animal, when deprived by age of the vigour which made its existence a pleasure, should be killed by some beast of prey, than that it should linger out a life made painful by infirmities, and eventually die of starvation. By the destruction of all such, not only is existence ended before it becomes burdensome, but room is made for a younger generation capable of the fullest enjoyment; and, moreover, out of the very act of substitution happiness is derived for a tribe of predatory creatures. Note further, that their carnivorous enemies not only remove from herbivorous herds individuals past their prime, but also weed out the sickly, the malformed, and the least fleet or powerful. By the aid of which purifying process, as well as by the fighting, so universal in the pairing season, all vitiation of the race through the multiplication of its inferior samples is prevented; and the maintenance of a constitution completely adapted to surrounding conditions, and therefore most productive of happiness, is ensured.

The development of the higher creation is a progress towards a form of being capable of a happiness undiminished by these drawbacks. It is in the human race that the consummation is to be accomplished. Civilization is the last stage of its accomplishment. And the ideal man is the man in whom all the conditions of that accomplishment are fulfilled. Meanwhile the well-being of existing humanity, and the unfolding of it into this ultimate perfection, are both secured by that same beneficent, though severe discipline, to which the animate creation at large is subject: a discipline which is pitiless in the working out of good: a felicity-pursuing law which never swerves for the avoidance of partial and temporary suffering. The poverty of the incapable, the distresses that come upon the imprudent, the starvation of the idle, and those shoulderings aside of the weak by the strong, which leave so many "in shallows and in miseries,"[1] are the decrees of a large, far-seeing benevolence. It seems hard that an unskilfulness which with all his efforts he cannot overcome, should entail hunger upon the artizan. It seems hard that a labourer incapacitated by sickness from competing with his stronger fellows, should have to bear the resulting privations. It seems hard that widows and orphans should be left to struggle for life or death. Nevertheless, when regarded not separately, but in connection with the interests of universal humanity, these harsh fatalities are seen to be full of the highest beneficence—the same beneficence which brings to early graves the children of diseased parents, and singles out the low-spirited, the intemperate, and the debilitated as the victims of an epidemic.

There are many very amiable people—people over whom in so far as their feelings are concerned we may fitly rejoice—who have not the nerve to look this matter fairly in the face. Disabled as they are by their sympathies with present suffering, from duly regarding ultimate consequences, they pursue a course which is very injudicious, and in the end even cruel. We do not consider it true kindness in a mother to gratify her child with sweetmeats that are certain to make it ill. We should think it a very foolish sort of benevolence which led a surgeon to let his patient's disease progress to a fatal issue, rather than inflict pain by an operation. Similarly, we must call those spurious philanthropists, who, to prevent present misery, would entail greater misery upon future generations. All defenders of a poor-law must, however, be classed amongst such. That rigorous necessity which, when allowed to act on them, becomes so sharp a spur to the lazy, and so strong a bridle to the random, these paupers' friends would repeal, because of the wailings it here and there produces. Blind to the fact, that under the natural order of things society is constantly excreting its unhealthy, imbecile, slow, vacillating, faithless members, these unthinking, though

---

1   From Shakespeare, *Julius Caesar*, Act 4, Sc. 3:
    Brutus: There is a tide in the affairs of men
    Which, taken at the flood, leads on to fortune;
    Omitted, all the voyage of their life
    Is bound in shallows and in miseries.
    On such a full sea are we now afloat;
    And we must take the current when it serves,
    Or lose the ventures before us.

well-meaning, men advocate an interference which not only stops the purifying process, but even increases the vitiation—absolutely encourages the multiplication of the reckless and incompetent by offering them an unfailing provision, and *dis*courages the multiplication of the competent and provident by heightening the prospective difficulty of maintaining a family. And thus, in their eagerness to prevent the really salutary sufferings that surround us, these sigh-wise and groan-foolish people bequeath to posterity a continually increasing curse.

2. Francis Galton, "Eugenics: Its Definition, Scope, and Aims." *The American Journal of Sociology* 10.1 (July 1904)

[Francis Galton (1822–1911), Charles Darwin's cousin, coined the term "eugenics" and the phrase "nature *versus* nurture." After studying eminent men and their families, he concluded that genius was hereditary and advocated encouraging marriage and reproduction by talented couples.]

Eugenics is the science which deals with all influences that improve the inborn qualities of a race; also with those that develop them to the utmost advantage. The improvement of the inborn qualities, or stock, of some one human population will alone be discussed here.

What is meant by improvement? What by the syllable *eu* in "eugenics," whose English equivalent is "good"? There is considerable difference between goodness in the several qualities and in that of the character as a whole. The character depends largely on the *proportion* between qualities, whose balance may be much influenced by education. We must therefore leave morals as far as possible out of the discussion, not entangling ourselves with the almost hopeless difficulties they raise as to whether a character as a whole is good or bad. Moreover, the goodness or badness of character is not absolute, but relative to the current form of civilization. A fable will best explain what is meant. Let the scene be the zoological gardens in the quiet hours of the night, and suppose that, as in old fables, the animals are able to converse, and that some very wise creature who had easy access to all the cages, say a philosophic sparrow or rat, was engaged in collecting the opinions of all sorts of animals with a view of elaborating a system of absolute morality. It is needless to enlarge on the contrariety of ideals between the beasts that prey and those they prey upon, between those of the animals that have to work hard for their food and the sedentary parasites that cling to their bodies and suck their blood, and so forth. A large number of suffrages in favor of maternal affection would be obtained, but most species of fish would repudiate it, while among the voices of birds would be heard the musical protest of the cuckoo. Though no agreement could be reached as to absolute morality, the essentials of eugenics may be easily defined. All creatures would agree that it was better to be healthy than sick, vigorous than weak, well-fitted than ill-fitted for their part in life; in short, that it was better to be good rather than bad specimens of their kind, whatever that kind might be. So with men. There are a vast number of conflicting ideals, of alternative characters, of incompatible civilizations; but they are wanted to give fullness and interest to life. Society would be very dull if every man resembled the highly estimable Marcus Aurelius[1] or Adam Bede.[2] The aim of eugenics is to represent each class or sect by its best specimens; that done, to leave them to work out their common civilization in their own way.

A considerable list of qualities can easily be compiled that nearly everyone except "cranks" would take into account when picking out the best specimens of his class. It would include health, energy, ability, manliness, and courteous disposition. Recollect that the natural differences between dogs are highly marked in all these respects, and that men are quite as variable by nature as other animals of like species. Special aptitudes would be assessed highly by those who possessed them, as the artistic faculties by artists, fearlessness of inquiry and veracity by scientists, religious absorption by mystics, and so on. There would be self-sacrificers, self-tormentors, and other exceptional idealists; but the representatives of these would be better members of a community than the body of their electors. They would have more of those qualities that are needed in a state—more vigor, more ability, and more consistency of purpose. The community might be trusted to refuse representatives of criminals, and of others whom it rates as undesirable.

Let us for a moment suppose that the practice of eugenics should hereafter raise the average quality of our nation to that of its better moiety at the present day, and consider the gain. The general tone of domestic, social, and political life would be higher. The race as a whole would be less foolish, less frivolous, less excitable, and politically more provident than now. Its demagogues who "played to the gallery" would play to a more sensible gallery than at present. We should be better fitted to fulfil our vast imperial opportunities. Lastly, men of an order of ability which is now very rare would become more frequent, because the level out of which they rose would itself have risen.

The aim of eugenics is to bring as many influences as can be reasonably employed, to cause the useful classes in the community to contribute *more* than their proportion to the next generation.

---

1 Roman Emperor (161–180 CE) and author of *Meditations*, a book of Stoic philosophy.

2 Virtuous hero of an 1859 novel of the same name, by George Eliot (Mary Ann Evans).

The course of procedure that lies within the functions of a learned and active society, such as the sociological may become, would be somewhat as follows:

1. Dissemination of a knowledge of the laws of heredity, so far as they are surely known, and promotion of their further study. Few seem to be aware how greatly the knowledge of what may be termed the *actuarial* side of heredity has advanced in recent years. The *average* closeness of kinship in each degree now admits of exact definition and of being treated mathematically, like birth- and death-rates, and the other topics with which actuaries are concerned.

2. Historical inquiry into the rates with which the various classes of society (classified according to civic usefulness) have contributed to the population at various times, in ancient and modern nations. There is strong reason for believing that national rise and decline is closely connected with this influence. It seems to be the tendency of high civilization to check fertility in the upper classes, through numerous causes, some of which are well known, others are inferred, and others again are wholly obscure. The latter class are apparently analogous to those which bar the fertility of most species of wild animals in zoological gardens. Out of the hundreds and thousands of species that have been tamed, very few indeed are fertile when their liberty is restricted and their struggles for livelihood are abolished; those which are so, and are otherwise useful to man, becoming domesticated. There is perhaps some connection between this obscure action and the disappearance of most savage races when brought into contact with high civilization, though there are other and well-known concomitant causes. But while most barbarous races disappear, some, like the negro, do not. It may therefore be expected that types of our race will be found to exist which can be highly civilized without losing fertility; nay, they may become more fertile under artificial conditions, as is the case with many domestic animals.

3. Systematic collection of facts showing the circumstances under which large and thriving families have most frequently originated; in other words, the *conditions* of eugenics. The definition of a thriving family, that will pass muster for the moment at least, is one in which the children have gained distinctly superior positions to those who were their classmates in early life. Families may be considered "large" that contain not less than three adult male children. It would be no great burden to a society including many members who had eugenics at heart, to initiate and to preserve a large collection of such records for the use of statistical students. The committee charged with the task would have to consider very carefully the form of their circular and the persons intrusted to distribute it. They should ask only for as much useful information as could be easily, and would be readily, supplied

by any member of the family appealed to. The point to be ascertained is the *status* of the two parents at the time of their marriage, whence its more or less eugenic character might have been predicted, if the larger knowledge that we now hope to obtain had then existed. Some account would be wanted of their race, profession, and residence; also of their own respective parentages, and of their brothers and sisters. Finally the reasons would be required why the children deserved to be entitled a "thriving" family. This manuscript collection might hereafter develop into a "golden book" of thriving families. The Chinese, whose customs have often much sound sense, make their honors retrospective. We might learn from them to show that respect to the parents of noteworthy children which the contributors of such valuable assets to the national wealth richly deserve. The act of systematically collecting records of thriving families would have the further advantage of familiarizing the public with the fact that eugenics had at length become a subject of serious scientific study by an energetic society.

4. Influences affecting marriage. The remarks of Lord Bacon[1] in his essay on *Death* may appropriately be quoted here. He says with the view of minimizing its terrors: "There is no passion in the mind of men so weak but it mates and masters the fear of death.... Revenge triumphs over death; love slights it; honour aspireth to it; grief flyeth to it; fear pre-occupateth it." Exactly the same kind of considerations apply to marriage. The passion of love seems so overpowering that it may be thought folly to try to direct its course. But plain facts do not confirm this view. Social influences of all kinds have immense power in the end, and they are very various. If unsuitable marriages from the eugenic point of view were banned socially, or even regarded with the unreasonable disfavor which some attach to cousin-marriages, very few would be made. The multitude of marriage restrictions that have proved prohibitive among uncivilized people would require a volume to describe.

5. Persistence in setting forth the national importance of eugenics. There are three stages to be passed through: (1) It must be made familiar as an academic question, until its exact importance has been understood and accepted as a fact. (2) It must be recognized as a subject whose practical development deserves serious consideration. (3) It must be introduced into the national conscience, like a new religion. It has, indeed, strong claims to become an orthodox religious tenet of the future, for eugenics co-operate with the workings of nature by securing that humanity shall be represented by the fittest races. What nature does blindly, slowly, and ruthlessly, man may do providently, quickly, and kindly. As it lies within his power, so it becomes his duty to work

---

1 Francis Bacon (1561–1626). Credited with developing the scientific method, his collection of *Essays*, which includes "Death," was published in 1597.

in that direction. The improvement of our stock seems to me one of the highest objects that we can reasonably attempt. We are ignorant of the ultimate destinies of humanity, but feel perfectly sure that it is as noble a work to raise its level, in the sense already explained, as it would be disgraceful to abase it. I see no impossibility in eugenics becoming a religious dogma among mankind, but its details must first be worked out sedulously in the study. Overzeal leading to hasty action would do harm, by holding out expectations of a near golden age, which will certainly be falsified and cause the science to be discredited. The first and main point is to secure the general intellectual acceptance of eugenics as a hopeful and most important study. Then let its principles work into the heart of the nation, which will gradually give practical effect to them in ways that we may not wholly foresee.

3. From Lester Frank Ward, "Our Better Halves." *Forum* (November 1888)

[Gilman frequently acknowledged the influence of Lester Frank Ward's gynæcocentric theory of evolution, and "Our Better Halves" in particular, on her own thinking and writing. Ward (1841–1913) was a sociologist and a leading figure among American reform Social Darwinists.]

But let us now inquire what grounds there are for accepting this mental and physical inferiority of women as something inherent in the nature of things. Is it really true that the larger part taken by the female in the work of reproduction necessarily impairs her strength, dwarfs her proportions, and renders her a physically inferior and dependent being? In most human races it may be admitted that women are less stalwart than men, although all the stories of Amazonian tribes are not mere fictions. It is also true, as has been insisted upon, that the males of most mammals and birds exceed the females in size and strength, and often differ from them greatly in appearance. But this is by no means always the case. The fable of the hedgehog that won the race with the hare by cunningly stationing Mrs. Hedgehog at the other end of the course, instructed to claim the stakes, is founded upon an exception which has many parallels. Among birds there are cases in which the rule is reversed. There are some entire families, as for example the hawks, in which the females exceed the males. If we go further down the scale, however, we find this attribute of male superiority to disappear almost entirely throughout the reptiles and amphibians, with a decided leaning toward female supremacy; and in the fishes, where male rivalry does not exist, the female, as every fisherman knows, is almost invariably the heavier game.

But it is not until we go below the vertebrate series and contemplate the invertebrate and vegetable worlds that we really begin to find the data for a philosophical study of the meaning of sex. It has been frequently remarked that the laws governing the higher forms of life can be rightly comprehended only by an acquaintance with the lower and more formative types of being. In no problem is this more true than in that of sex.

In studying this problem it is found that there is a great world of life that wholly antedates the appearance of sex—the world of asexual life—nor is the passage from the sexless to the distinctly male and female definite and abrupt. Between them occur parthenogenesis or virgin reproduction, hermaphroditism, in which the male being consists simply of an organ, and parasitic males, of which we shall presently speak, while the other devices of nature for perpetuating life are innumerable and infinitely varied. But so far as sex can be predicated of these beings, they must all be regarded as female. The asexual parent must be contemplated as, to all intents and purposes, maternal. The parthenogenetic aphis or shrimp is in all essential respects a mother. The hermaphrodite creature, whatever else it may be, is also necessarily a female. Following these states come the numberless cases in which the female form continues to constitute the type of life, the insignificant male appearing to be a mere afterthought.

The vegetable kingdom, except in its very lowest stages, affords comparatively few pointed illustrations of this truth. The strange behavior of the hemp plant, in which, as has long been known, the female plants crowd out the male plants by overshadowing them as soon as they have been fertilized by the latter, used to be frequently commented upon as a perverse anomaly in nature. Now it is correctly interpreted as an expression of the general law that the primary purpose of the male sex is to enable the female, or type form, to reproduce, after performing which function the male form is useless and a mere cumberer of the ground. But the hemp plant is by no means alone in possessing this peculiarity. I could enumerate several pretty well known species that have a somewhat similar habit. I will mention only one, the common cud-weed, or everlasting (*Antennaria plantaginifolia*), which, unlike the hemp, has colonies of males separate from the females, and these male plants are small and short-lived. Long after their flowering stalks have disappeared the female plants continue to grow, and they become large and thrifty herbs lasting until frost.

In the animal kingdom below the vertebrates female superiority is well-nigh universal. In the few cases where it does not occur it is generally found that the males combat each other, after the manner of the higher animals, for the possession of the females. The cases that I shall name are such as all are familiar with. The only new thing in their presentation is their application to the point at issue.

The superiority of the queen bee over the drone is only a well-known illustration of a condition which, with the usual variations and exceptions, is common to a great natural order of insects. The only mosquito that the unscientific world knows is the female mosquito. The male mosquito is a frail and harmless little creature that swarms with the females in the early season and passes away when his work is done. There are many insects of which the males possess no organs of nutrition in the imago state, their duties during their ephemeral existence being confined to what the Germans call the *Minnedienst*.[1] Such is the life of many male moths and butterflies. But much greater inequalities are often found. I should, perhaps, apologize for citing the familiar case of spiders, in some species of which the miniature lover is often seized and devoured during his courtship by the gigantic object of his affections. Something similar, I learn, sometimes occurs with the mantis or "praying insect."

Merely mentioning the extreme case of Sphaerularia, in which the female is several thousand times as large as the male, I may surely be permitted to introduce the barnacle, since it is one of the creatures upon which Prof. Brooks lays considerable stress in the article to which I have referred. Not being myself a zoologist, I am only too happy to quote him. He says:

Among the barnacles there are a few species the males and females of which differ remarkably. The female is an ordinary barnacle, with all the peculiarities of the group fully developed, while the male is a small parasite upon the body of the female, and is so different from the female of its own species, and from all ordinary barnacles, that no one would ever recognize in the adult male any affinity whatever to its closest allies.

The barnacle, or cirripede, is the creature which Mr. Darwin so long studied, and from which he learned so many lessons leading up to his grand generalizations. In a letter to Sir Charles Lyell, dated September 14, 1849, he recounts some of his discoveries while engaged in this study. Having learned that most cirripedes, but not all, were hermaphrodite, he remarks:

The other day I got a curious case of a unisexual instead of hermaphrodite cirripede, in which the female had the common cirripedial character, and in two valves of her shell had two little pockets in each of which she kept a little husband. I do not know of any other case where a female invariably has two husbands. I have one

---

1 Service of love.

still odder fact, common to several species, namely, that though they are hermaphrodite, they have small additional, or, as I call them, complemental males. One specimen, itself hermaphrodite, had no less than seven of these complemental males attached to it.

Prof. Brooks brings forward facts of this class to demonstrate that the male is the variable sex, while the female is comparatively stable. However much we may doubt his further conclusion that variability rather than supplementary procreative power was the primary purpose of the separate male principle, we must, it would seem, concede that variability and adaptability are the distinguishing characteristics of the male sex everywhere, as the transmitting power and permanence of type are those of the female. But this is a very different thing from saying that the female sex is incapable of progress, or that man is destined to develop indefinitely, leaving woman constantly farther and farther in the rear. Does the class of philosophers to which reference has been made look forward to a time when woman shall become as insignificant an object compared to man as the male spider is compared to the female? This would be the logical outcome of their argument if based upon the relative variability of the male sex.

We have now seen that, whether we contemplate the higher animals, among which male superiority prevails, or the lower forms, among which female superiority prevails, the argument from biology that the existing relations between the sexes in the human race are precisely what nature intended them to be, that they ought not to be disturbed and cannot be improved, leads, when carried to its logical conclusion, to a palpable absurdity. But have we, then, profited nothing by the thoughtful contemplation of the subject from these two points of view? Those who rightly interpret the facts cannot avoid learning a most important lesson from each of these lines of inquiry. From the first the truth comes clearly forth that the relations of the sexes among the higher animals are widely abnormal, warped, and strained by a long line of curious influences, chiefly psychic, which are incident to the development of animal organisms under the competitive principle that prevails throughout nature. From the second comes now into full view the still more important truth with which we first set out, that the female sex is primary in point both of origin and of importance in the history and economy of organic life. And as life is the highest product of nature and human life the highest type of life, it follows that the grandest fact in nature is woman.

But we have learned even more than this, that which is certainly of more practical value. We have learned how to carry forward the progress of development so far advanced by the unconscious agencies of nature. Accepting evolution as we must, recognizing heredity as the distinctive attribute of the female sex, it becomes clear that it must be from the steady advance of woman rather than from the uncertain fluctuations of man that the sure and solid progress of the future is to come. The attempt to move the whole race forward by elevating only the sex that represents the principle of instability, has long enough been tried. The many cases of superior men the sons of superior mothers, coupled with the many more cases of degenerate sons of superior sires, have taught us over and over again that the way to civilize the race is to civilize woman. And now, thanks to science, we see why this is so. Woman is the unchanging trunk of the great genealogic tree; while man, with all his vaunted superiority, is but a branch, a grafted scion, as it were, whose acquired qualities die with the individual, while those of woman are handed on to futurity. Woman *is* the race, and the race can be raised up only as she is raised up. There is no fixed rule by which Nature has intended that one sex should excel the other, any more than there is any fixed point beyond which either cannot further develop. Nature has no intentions, and evolution has no limits. True science teaches that the elevation of woman is the only sure road to the evolution of man.

Select Bibliography

Allen, Judith. *The Feminism of Charlotte Perkins Gilman: Sexualities, Histories, Progressivism.* Chicago: U of Chicago P, 2009.

Ceplair, Larry, ed. *Charlotte Perkins Gilman: A Nonfiction Reader.* New York: Columbia UP, 1991.

Davis, Cynthia J. *Charlotte Perkins Gilman: A Biography.* Stanford, CA: Stanford UP, 2010.

—— and Denise D. Knight, eds. *Charlotte Perkins Gilman and Her Contemporaries: Literary and Intellectual Contexts.* Tuscaloosa: U of Alabama P, 2004.

Deegan, Mary Jo. "Introduction." *With Her in Ourland: Sequel to Herland.* Ed. Mary Jo Deegan and Michael R. Hill. Westport, CT: Praeger, 1997. 1–57.

Doskow, Minna. "Charlotte Perkins Gilman: The Female Face of Social Darwinism." *Weber Studies* 14.3 (Fall 1997): 9–22.

Gilman, Charlotte Perkins. *The Living of Charlotte Perkins Gilman: An Autobiography.* New York: Appleton, 1935. Rpt. New York: Harper, 1975.

Golden, Catherine J. and Joanna Schneider Zangrando, eds. *The Mixed Legacy of Charlotte Perkins Gilman.* Newark: U of Delaware P, 2000.

Gough, Val and Jill Rudd, eds. *A Very Different Story: Studies on the Fiction of Charlotte Perkins Gilman.* Liverpool: Liverpool UP, 1998.

Gubar, Susan. "She in Herland." *Coordinates: Placing Science Fiction and Fantasy.* Ed. George E. Slusser, Eric S. Rabkin and Robert Scholes. Carbondale: Southern Illinois UP, 1983.

Karpinski, Joanne B., ed. *Critical Essays on Charlotte Perkins Gilman.* New York: Hall, 1992.

Kessler, Carol Farley. *Charlotte Perkins Gilman: Her Progress toward Utopia with Selected Writings.* Syracuse, NY: Syracuse UP, 1995.

Knight, Denise D. *Charlotte Perkins Gilman: A Study of the Short Fiction.* Twayne Studies in Short Fiction, Twayne Publishers, 1997.

—— and Cynthia J. Davis., eds. *Approaches to Teaching Gilman's "The Yellow Wall-Paper" and Herland.* New York: Modern Language Association, 2003.

Knittel, Janna. "Environmental History and Charlotte Perkins Gilman's *Herland.*" *Foundation: The International Review of Science Fiction* 35.96 (Spring 2006): 49–67.

Lane, Ann J. "Introduction." *Herland: A Lost Feminist Utopian Novel,* Charlotte Perkins Gilman. New York: Pantheon, 1979.

——. "The Fictional World of Charlotte Perkins Gilman." *The Charlotte Perkins Gilman Reader.* Ed. Ann J. Lane. New York: Pantheon, 1980.

Meyering, Sheryl L., ed. *Charlotte Perkins Gilman: The Woman and Her Work*. Ann Arbor: UMI Research Press, 1989.

Rudd, Jill and Val Gough, eds. *Charlotte Perkins Gilman: Optimist Reformer*. Iowa City: U of Iowa P, 1999.

Scharnhorst, Gary. *Charlotte Perkins Gilman*. Boston: Twayne, 1985.

———. *Charlotte Perkins Gilman: A Bibliography*. Metuchen, NJ: Scarecrow, 1985.

Stetson, Charles Walter. *Endure: The Diaries of Charles Walter Stetson*. Ed. Mary A. Hill. Philadelphia: Temple UP, 1985.

Weinbaum, Alys Eve. "Writing Feminist Genealogy: Charlotte Perkins Gilman, Racial Nationalism, and the Reproduction of Maternalist Feminism." *Feminist Studies* 27 (Summer 2001): 271–30.